By Dean Murray

Lost

Dean Murray

Published by Fir'shan Publishing

ISBN 978-1-9393633-7-4

www.FirshanPublishing.com

First Edition

For Sara

Thank you for helping show Katie and me the way this year

Chapter 1

Isaac Nazir
Right-Size Burger and Gas
Outside of Dallas, Texas

Things had been...strained between Ash and I since the attack on the estate. I guess that's the right word, the right English word. I know a few other languages and there are some other words that are a better fit, but they aren't *that* much better of a fit. No word really captures the true level of tension you get when you lock two shape shifters who don't like each other inside of a car for more than a day.

Under other circumstances I could have probably gotten along just fine with Ash. He was competent and deadly, which are two of the characteristics that most shape shifters think are the most important in any individual. Competent means that you won't have to worry about cleaning up after them. Deadly means that they can protect themselves and maybe even watch your back if you end up against some kind of external threat.

That's good—there are a lot of external threats out there when you're a shape shifter. Vampires, werewolves, even other shape shifter packs, and that's just the more common stuff. The problem is that the external threats have only ever banded us together for a short time. Sooner or later we always ended up turning on each other. Which is exactly what happened again outside of Dallas less than twenty-four hours after we split off from the rest of Alec's people.

"Turn the cell phone off, Isaac."

Kristin had disappeared a minute before having mumbled something about needing a bathroom break while Ash and I ordered food from the cheerily-painted burger joint that was attached to the gas station.

"Back off, Ash. Alec said his guys have things under control. I need to check in and make sure I haven't missed a call from anyone."

"Look, I get it. You're worried about Andrew, Jess, and the rest. Trust me, it can wait until we make it to the safe house that I've got lined up for us. Until then we'd be stupid to rely on Alec's hackers to protect us. We're safer just leaving the phones off."

"He's right. Besides, I can basically guarantee that Jessica isn't going to be calling you anytime soon."

I'd heard Kristin leave the restroom; I should have known that she wouldn't be able to keep her mouth shut.

"This doesn't involve you."

Ash shut her up with a look before she could launch into whatever scathing retort she had on the end of her tongue. Once he was confident she was going to stay silent for at least the next three seconds he turned back to me.

"Actually, it does. I know that you're good with this kind of stuff, but you don't want to go head to head with the best hackers on the Coun'hij payroll, not like this—working off of a shoestring with everything at stake for the three of us as well as Alec, Jess and the others."

"Stop saying Jess' name. There is zero reason for the two of you to keep bringing her up. Alec said that he wanted everyone to stay on comms. If you had a problem with that, you should have brought it up with him before we left."

"Are you mental? We keep mentioning Jess because she's still all you think about. We aren't idiots, this is *all* about Jess."

Ash didn't look particularly happy at Kristin's decision to jump back in the conversation.

"I did talk to Alec before we left, Isaac. I explained my concerns to him and he agreed that it would be a good idea to have a couple of the groups stay silent for a while in case his hackers couldn't keep a lid on things."

"Why wasn't I informed? I've been with him for longer than the two of you, and this is my area of expertise."

"You were too busy trying to get Jess to give you one more chance before she left with Wyatt."

I spun around and took a step towards Kristin. I was moving fast—not as fast as I could have, not in public, I wasn't that far gone—but I still only made it a single step before I heard a click as Ash pulled the hammer back on the big .45 semi-auto that he always had somewhere close at hand. It wasn't a loud sound, but given just how distinctive that particular sound is—and the sensitivity of my hearing—it froze me in my tracks.

"You wouldn't dare, not in a public place like this."

My words were something less than a whisper. Kristin wouldn't be able to hear them, but she apparently didn't need to know what was being said to know that things had just gotten serious. I could tell by the way that she was standing against the wall that she already had her pistol out, screened behind her body, but ready to go at a second's notice.

"Isaac, don't push me. You'd be surprised what I'd be willing to do right now. The police response time out here is at least three minutes. Kristin and I can easily lose ourselves downtown before the police can tighten a noose around us. Turn the phone off—now—or you'll force my hand. You can possibly beat one of us, but you can't take both of us, not in human form, not when we are standing so far apart."

I tried to stay loose, but my body tensed up as I calculated odds. My beast wanted a piece of Ash and Kristin both. Neither of them was a match for us, and we were tired of being pushed around.

The temptation to shift forms and lunge towards Ash was nearly overpowering. I'd had a harder time keeping my cool lately, but this was more than that. Dominance was important. It wasn't just about establishing a pecking order inside of a pack, it was about figuring out who the go-to guys and gals were for when things got dicey. It was about figuring out who called the shots when lives were on the line.

In a bad pack, one that was unhealthy, dominance fights ended up with someone dead more often than not, but it didn't have to be like that. In a good pack, dominance fights were a way of blowing off steam before things heated up to the point that people felt like the only choice left for them was to try and kill someone. It was more about knowing where you fit in. Once you knew that, it was a lot easier to deal with everyone, and if someone started pushing too hard then the two of you beat the tar out of each other until someone came out on top.

That was how it was supposed to work, and if you had a decent alpha who made sure that nobody got too carried away it was a good system, only Ash threw everything off. He didn't have a prayer of standing up to me without his weapons so he didn't even try. There weren't any shades of gray with Ash, everything was binary for him.

Something was either worth fighting over or it wasn't. If it wasn't then you could push him around with an almost reckless abandon, but if it was important, then he'd pull a weapon on you so fast that your head would spin. For Ash, if it was worth fighting over then it was worth dying over.

I'd thought that things were pretty rough when we'd been up against Brandon's pack, but even then there had usually been a kind of underlying honor code to the war. Ash had been trained by people who didn't let *anything* get in the way of their objective.

"You're out of time, Isaac. Your phone just finished booting up. If someone is looking for you they'll be able to ping it within the next few seconds. I won't ask again."

I looked over at my right hand and realized that I hadn't ever put my phone back in my pocket. Ash was right, it was decision time. If I was right, then he was getting really worked up over nothing, but even if I was right, he'd backed me into a corner. Killing Ash and Kristin wouldn't actually accomplish anything. Best-case scenario I ended up by myself and on the run from the cops, worst-case scenario I'd be dead. Neither option put me in a position to help Jess or anyone else.

I reached over and powered down my phone. "One of these days you're going to push me too far, Ash."

"Yeah, I know. Believe me when I say that I don't look forward to that day any more than you do."

The cute brunette behind the counter put the last of our order on the two trays she'd been assembling and gave the three of us a cheery smile.

"Here you go, have a nice day."

She'd never even suspected that the restaurant had been a hair's breadth from turning into a war zone. I mustered up what I hoped was a convincing smile of my own, and picked up the second tray.

Ash and I sat at separate booths. It wasn't something that either of us had ever discussed; it was just one of those things. You don't chain two pit bulls inside the same cage unless you want them to fight. Keeping a buffer of space between us usually kept things from boiling over as frequently.

Kristin moved like a professional herself these days. She'd always been dangerous, at least she'd been that way for as long as I'd known her, but

Ash had honed her to a fine edge during the last few months. She stayed clear of Ash's right hand at all times and she kept hers free too.

"It's days like today that make me wonder how many times back home I was completely oblivious to the fact that people were just about to kill each other. I used to work in a place like this, you know."

I unwrapped my first burger as I considered Kristin's comment. "That must have been nice, a normal life. Do you miss it?"

She looked at me like I was crazy. "Are you kidding? I spent every waking minute trying to find a way out of that place. The last thing I ever wanted to be was *ordinary*. This isn't quite the way I originally planned on trying to make my mark on the world, but it's a ton better than the life most of the kids from my school will be looking at once they graduate."

Ash didn't seem particularly interested in joining in the conversation. He was paying attention, I'd never seen Ash be anything other than *on*, but he simply grabbed another handful of fries.

"You can't really mean that, Kristin. The three of us are living on borrowed time. We're probably not going to make it through the year. Even if Alec's war against the Coun'hij ends up going our way, we'll still have targets on our back. There will always be another set of bad guys who need taken down. The vampires or the jaguars will practically be lining up for a shot at toppling Alec from the throne. Anyone in their right mind would choose a normal, safe life in a heartbeat."

That earned me a frown. Kristin took in all of the empty tables and booths around us in one sweeping gesture.

"Safety is an illusion. It's all relative. Someone could walk through those doors tomorrow and gun down a dozen 'normal' people who just happen to be in the wrong place at the wrong time. People think that they're safe, but they're just a bunch of sheep. I'd rather know what is going on around me, and die having done the best I could to save myself, than just wander around in a daze hoping that my number hasn't come up on any given day.

"You can romanticize about the joys of a normal life all you want, but the truth is that a normal life is mostly just a lot of drudgery—the soul-crushing monthly mortgage payment kind of drudgery—and ninety-nine out of a hundred people wish that they could be different, that they could be special somehow. You fantasize about normal life because it's something you've never had. It's the most compelling argument you could have made as to the fact that you've always been special."

My beast wanted to lash out at her—verbally would do despite not being as satisfying—but I knew that wasn't the right response. Kristin wasn't trying to be in my face, she just felt strongly about this subject. I brought my beast under control with a shadow of the smoothness that had been my trademark for so many years, but I got it under control.

I'd thought James was just undisciplined, but now I wasn't so sure of that. Maybe I'd just been taking credit all of that time for something that had nothing to do with me. I'd thought it was my will and self-control that made me who I was, but those things don't just evaporate between one day and the next.

I'd spent a lot of time recently trying to convince myself that I was still in control, but the truth was that I wasn't, not fully. Everything had changed when Jess had lost her memories. I'd never realized how much Jess and Andrew had grounded me.

I'd thought I was something unique, but once Jess had lost her memories she'd become a different person and I'd lost the cornerstone of my world. Andrew had tried to still be there for me, but we both knew that things couldn't be the same. Maybe they could have been if I hadn't kept pushing Jess, but I had. Andrew had been forced to make a choice between the daughter who'd lost her memory and me.

He'd made the right choice and I respected him for it, but it didn't make things any easier. I was drifting in the middle of a black ocean with no land in sight.

I closed my eyes for a couple of seconds, and when I looked back over at Kristin I felt at least a little bit like my old self.

"Maybe you're right, but since I've never had the benefit of a normal, safe life, you'll just have to pardon me if I continue to long for something different."

I'd meant it as a peace offering. It wasn't perfect, but considering how much friction there had been between the three of us lately, it wasn't a bad attempt. I'd thought I'd get an eye roll, or maybe a smile. I hadn't expected Kristin to go completely white and stop breathing.

"Guys, we need to get out of here right now! I've dreamed this before and what happens next isn't pretty."

Chapter 2

Isaac Nazir
Right-Size Burger and Gas
Outside of Dallas, Texas

Ash started moving while I was still scanning the burger joint for threats. He grabbed all of the food he could hold in his left hand and started towards the door without looking back. Kristin was half a step behind him with a big fountain drink in her free hand, but I caught up with the two of them before they made it outside.

We were almost back to Ash's car when the first bruiser stepped around the corner of the building. That was apparently the signal because other guys started appearing from behind trees and cars.

Ash was in the lead and he never even broke stride. The first guy, a heavily-tattooed Latino, tried to hit him, but Ash checked the blow, stepping into his opponent and driving an elbow into the guy's throat. It was a killing blow against a human, but Ash didn't take any chances. He followed his elbow up by spinning the first guy around and throwing him headfirst into the side of the building.

"Get into the car!"

Kristin didn't look like she was happy about Ash's order, but she already had her keys out and was only two steps from the car. I paced her, half a step behind as my mind finished processing the situation.

Three more guys had almost reached us, but none of them were giving off the characteristic energy surge I would have expected from shape shifters. Ash stepped forward to deal with the guy on his side of the car as Kristin threw herself across the passenger seat, and then it was my turn.

The taller of my two opponents, a skinny white guy with a mohawk, threw a jab at me, but everything about the attack was human-slow. I didn't try to block it. I could have probably absorbed the blow without going down if it had come to that. Being a shape shifter made me strong and let me take a lot more damage than a human, even in this form, but there wasn't any need to take the hit.

I lashed out with my fist, connecting with his strike and shattering his hand and wrist in a move that no trained fighter would have used, but that was okay, I'd never trained to fight as a human. There wasn't any reason to waste time learning to fight in this form, not when there was still so much to learn about fighting as a hybrid.

A flicker of motion brought me around just in time to intercept an elbow strike from the next guy. I hit his arm with an open palm a split second before he would have connected with my throat and then stepped in and hit him in the ribs with the other hand.

He went down to one knee from the sheer shock of having the entire right side of his chest caved in, and then I spun back around and punched the taller guy in the throat with a blow that was carefully measured so that I wouldn't break his neck.

My side of the exchange had taken less than two seconds. Ash's car roared to life as I looked up just in time to see a new guy step up behind Ash and hit him in the kidney hard enough to shatter Ash's floating ribs.

A normal human would have probably collapsed on the spot, but Ash was a shape shifter. He wasn't particularly strong or fast as a wolf, and he'd never manifested a hybrid form, but he was still one of us. Ash blocked the next blow with his elbow, and then he stuck a knife in the new guy.

It wasn't a very big knife, but Ash knew how to use a knife with the best of them. I expected the new guy to fall to the ground in a spray of blood, but he just backhanded Ash across the parking lot. It was the kind of thing you sometimes saw in a movie, but it was next to impossible for a normal human to hit someone that hard.

The pieces clicked into place. This last guy wasn't just local muscle like the rest—he was a shape shifter, and based off of his tattoos and piercings, he was a Coun'hij enforcer. I'd already started forward to back Ash up. For all I knew getting thrown across the parking lot had been part of Ash's plan all along. It got him far enough away to get his handgun into play, which was his best chance against a hybrid, but it was still a plan born of desperation.

Ash was on the ground, off balance and disoriented from the force of the blow he'd taken. He was fast, but a hybrid was faster. Luckily Ash wasn't by himself, he had me.

Shifting forms in public went against everything I'd been taught since I'd first found out that I wasn't like other kids, but I didn't even think twice about it. My beast cut loose with a hammer blow of power and between one step and the next my human body exploded out into the hulking form of my hybrid shape.

The wash of power was unmistakable for one of our kind, and the other shape shifter spun back towards me to honor the greater threat that I represented. He shifted as he moved, and then I crashed into him.

In this form I was nearly six feet seven inches tall and I was several hundred pounds heavier than I'd been just a few seconds before, but I still gave up more than fifty pounds and nearly a full inch to the new guy.

I'd hoped to bowl him over with my initial rush, but he dug in and dropped his shoulder. We stumbled back away from each other, rocked by the force of the impact, and then he slashed at me with seven inches of razor-sharp semi-retractable claws that were harder than steel.

I moved forward, trying to get inside the arc of his attack, but he ducked under my arm and tore a long gash in my side. I reversed direction and checked his next attack, grabbing his left arm a split second before he could sink it into my back.

I didn't try to hold onto him as he tore his wrist free, he was stronger than me, but I managed to nick a couple of the smaller veins in his arm in exchange. He darted toward me and I slapped his claws away, but he was even faster than I'd realized.

His other hand came out of nowhere and buried itself in my stomach. Even my hybrid body couldn't continue to take that level of damage for much longer. Every nerve I had lit up in agony, but I ignored that and threw myself backward.

The Coun'hij guy didn't want to let me go, he tightened his grip and tried to pull me closer, but that just provided me with the leverage that I'd been looking for. I walked up the side of his body, sinking the talons on my feet into his legs and chest as I extended his arm all of the way out.

His claws pulled free of my gut and then I heaved against his shoulder with every ounce of strength I had. I'd seen Carson do something similar in a sparring session back at the estate before everything had fallen apart. Done right, it dislocated the other guy's shoulder, but either I hadn't managed to execute the technique correctly, or the other hybrid was just too strong for it to work.

For one long second I thought I had him, but then he started reeling me back in. I would have said that nobody was strong enough to lift me by one arm like that, but this guy didn't just lift me, he whipped me through the air and slammed me into the side of the gas station.

I initially thought that the popping noise I was hearing was my vertebrae, but as I stumbled away from the wall I realized that the other hybrid hadn't stayed around to finish me off.

Kristin had screamed to a stop a couple of feet from where Ash had landed and they both had their guns out. The Coun'hij enforcer had disappeared behind the detached car wash in an effort to avoid the hail of bullets that they'd sent his way, but there was too much blood on the pavement for it all to be mine.

I started after the other hybrid, but Ash yelled at me before I could make it more than a step or two.

"Get to the car, they wouldn't have been waiting if they didn't have more people coming, and the cops are on their way!"

Part of me wanted to argue with him, but he was right. I turned and sprinted towards the car, huge hybrid legs devouring the distance. Ash climbed inside the vehicle as soon as I started moving, but Kristin sped up her rate of fire to compensate. It only took her about a second to shoot herself dry, but that was all that Ash needed to get into position behind her and he picked up firing with hardly any break at all.

Kristin was on the move now, the car was already doing twenty, but Ash managed to space his shots out just enough to keep the enforcer pinned down for the extra second it took me to catch up with the car.

I managed to shift back to human form on the run without stumbling, and then threw myself into the car just before Kristin cranked it up to forty.

"How did they find us? My phone wasn't on for long enough to track."

Kristin didn't look away from the road. "Are you sure of that? It's the logical explanation."

Ash shook his head as he scanned our surroundings for somewhere we could lose the cops. "No, Isaac is right. Those guys had to be moving into position even before Isaac turned his phone on. One hybrid and a car full of hired muscle—they'd been tracking us before we even stopped for gas, it's the only explanation. It was an opportunistic hit; they knew where we were and happened to have one guy and some contacts in the area where we stopped."

"That means that they have something other than cell phone tracking in play then. Alec needs to know that, every single one of his people could be walking into traps as we speak."

Ash didn't look happy, but this time he couldn't argue with me. "Fine. Get your phone powered on. You have one minute before it needs to go back off and this time just pull the battery. It's going to be anyone's guess as to whether or not we're going to be able to lose the police."

I fished my phone back out of the compartment inside my ha'bit where I stored it and pushed the power button. It was going to take forty-five seconds to boot up, so I reached back into the back seat for the first-aid kit next to Ash. If we ended up on foot at some point over the next hour or two then I needed to not look like I'd just finished fighting for my life.

I slapped a big square of white gauze over the hole in my stomach and then used half of a roll of tape to hold it in place. I finished right as my phone finished booting up. Alec picked up on the first ring.

"Isaac, I thought you guys were going to stay dark for the next few days."

"Yeah, not that anyone bothered to tell me that before we left." I wanted to say more, but I knew it wasn't the time or place for recriminations. "We just got jumped. One hybrid, who was probably hoping not to have to get involved, and a bunch of local thugs. It looked like they had someone else on the way."

There was a second of silence as Alec digested the news. "So they were tracking you. You're positive that you all had your phones off the entire time?"

"Yeah, I had mine on for about fifteen seconds, but that isn't long enough to run any kind of trace on it."

He cut me off before I could finish explaining. "Then we don't have proof. Are you guys going to be able to help if another team in the area runs into the same kind of problems?"

Ash responded before I could. "No, we have to go to ground in the next five minutes or we're going to end up in a jail somewhere. Is there anything you can do to take some heat off of us?"

"No. The Chicago pack just went silent, and I suspect that all of the rest of our people are in hot water up to their necks. I'll let you know as soon as I can shake someone loose to help out, but for now you guys are on your own."

Chapter 3

Isaac Nazir
I-30
Eastern Texas

I pulled on a fresh set of clothes and then we ditched Ash's car inside what I was pretty sure was the oldest, most decrepit parking garage in the city of Dallas. Ash had a lot of history with that particular car, but he walked away from it without looking back.

From there we headed on foot to a shopping mall. We spent the next four hours ducking in and out of places as we made abrupt changes to our appearances.

Kristin had a good eye for spotting security cameras, but Ash was even better. It was like he had a sixth sense when it came to anticipating where we were most likely to find blind spots. We moved quickly. We kept it down to a walk whenever there were people around, but it was a

DEAN MURRAY

deceptively fast walk and we covered a lot of
ground.

I was in so much pain by the end that it was all
I could do to keep walking normally. My bandages
were starting to soak through by the time that we
finally ducked into another parking garage. Ash
found a black SUV with a 'for sale' sign in it, and
then convinced an early twentysomething to let
him borrow her phone for a couple of minutes so
that he could dial the number on the sign.

Twenty minutes after that we pulled out of
the parking garage fifteen thousand dollars
poorer, but driving the SUV.

Ash shook his head when I offered to drive.

"You need to replace your bandages and get
some sleep. Kristin too, that's part of the reason I
picked this set of wheels. We need space so we
can spread out and rest without having to sleep
on top of each other."

Kristin didn't argue, she just reclined the
passenger seat back as she closed her eyes.

"You took some damage too, you can't be
much better off than me."

Ash shrugged. "Yeah, I've got some broken
ribs and a ton of internal bruising, but that isn't
anything compared to the amount of blood loss
that you've experienced. You're tougher than me,
there isn't any disputing that, but you took some
nasty blows in that fight."

My beast bristled a little bit at the
implication that I couldn't continue to function

despite everything I'd just been through, but Ash *had* pointed out that I had more staying power than him.

"Okay, I'll catch some sleep. Can we pull through a drive-through on our way out of town though? We never finished up lunch and I'm going to burn through a lot of reserves healing back from what that enforcer did to me."

"Sure. Let me keep an eye on our back trail for another five or ten minutes and then if it looks like we made a clean getaway I'll stop somewhere and we can pick up dinner for both of us."

"What about Kristin?"

Ash's smile was part proud teacher and part worried boyfriend. "She's out already and she won't be waking up for at least four or five hours. We can stop for something later if she's hungry."

I started to nod before I realized what was bothering me about the situation. Kristin had fallen asleep far too quickly. Any good soldier deployed to the front lines for an extended period of time learned to get sleep wherever they could find it.

By that yardstick, it was entirely reasonable for Kristin to have dropped off quickly, but Kristin hadn't spent months in that kind of danger recently. She'd spent a few days on the run with Ash, but the last little while had been spent at the estate with the rest of the pack. It was hard to get much safer than that.

"How long has she been dropping off instantly like that?"

"A week or two maybe. I first noticed when I stayed late in her room to watch a movie with her. She fell asleep before the opening credits had even finished rolling."

He wasn't telling me everything, that went without saying, but this was potentially even more serious than I'd realized. Now that she was asleep, Kristin smelled *wrong* somehow.

I didn't figure it out until Ash exited the interstate and pulled up to the drive-through window. Kristin had been stressed out while we'd been running from the cops, but she'd kept it under control. If I hadn't been able to smell the adrenaline coming out of her pores I probably wouldn't have been able to tell that she was rattled at all.

She was more freaked out now than she'd been then. I'd never seen anything like that; I would have said that it wasn't possible for someone to remain asleep with that much adrenaline in their system. She'd fallen asleep without ever calming down.

My suspicions were confirmed when she started thrashing around and screaming as we pulled back onto the main road.

"She's being attacked by Dream Stealer."

For a second I thought Ash was going to pretend that he hadn't heard me.

"Yeah. He's got his hooks pretty deep into her. She's not getting any real sleep most nights. She tried to go without sleep, but eventually she got to the point where the exhaustion was stronger than even the terror of what he'd do next."

"She needs to be locked up! It's only a matter of time before he breaks her, and when that happens there isn't anything that she won't do."

"No. We aren't locking her up. We'll keep her in the dark so she can't pass anything important on; she's already started cutting herself out of the loop when it comes to operational stuff."

"That isn't good enough, Ash, and you know it. Even if we can keep her in the dark when it comes to Alec and the others, that won't protect the three of us. It's for her safety as much as it is for ours. For all you know she was the reason that we got jumped earlier today."

"She wasn't. I've been careful not to tell her where we are headed on any given day."

"That explains why you've been so evasive lately, but you did tell me and I might have told her."

"When? The three of us have hardly been out of sight of each other since we left Nevada."

My beast should have been ready to rip Ash's head off, but I couldn't seem to muster the energy for real anger. Maybe it was all of the blood that I'd lost, that or maybe I was just tired.

I wasn't mad, I just wanted to go somewhere I wouldn't have to deal with the inherent messiness of pack life. My life had turned into some kind of federal disaster area and I was ready to be done with it.

"I don't know, Ash. Maybe you're right and I never had a chance to tell her where we were headed, but I can't guarantee that, which means that we may have just broken radio silence for no reason. I can't believe that you've kept this to yourself. You're not usually this reckless."

"I didn't keep it to myself, at least not completely. Alec knows. That's why he wanted you to come along with Kristin and me. My plan was to just take her away somewhere safe, somewhere she couldn't do any harm if he manages to break her, but Alec ordered me to bring you along."

"I wish he would have told me the score for a change, but it makes sense. By yourself it would just be a matter of time before you ended up dead. Once Dream Stealer turned her, she'd just have to wait until you fell asleep and then you'd be a sitting duck. This way we can watch each other's backs at least."

I would have been happy to just leave things there, but Ash was apparently made of sterner stuff even than I'd realized.

"That isn't the only reason Alec wanted you to come with us."

"I know, Ash. He's hoping that I'll be able to put her down if she becomes too dangerous to allow for any other option."

"I'm not just going to stand by and let you kill her, Isaac. I'll fight you if it comes to that."

Ash had both of his hands on the steering wheel, there wasn't ever going to be a better time to deal with him than right now. The temptation was overwhelming. If I waited, then I was eventually going to have to fight him on his terms, and that was a fight I might not be able to win.

I sighed and leaned back in my tan leather seat. "Why did you even agree to have me come along then, Ash? I get not wanting to see Kristin get hurt, I would have done almost anything to protect Jess, but you could have just saved both of us a lot of headache and gone off by yourself like you were planning."

"I wanted you along because I'll need your help if I'm going to have any chance of hunting Dream Stealer down."

It was too fantastical to believe. A guy like Alec could talk about hunting down and killing someone like Dream Stealer or Puppeteer, but that was because he was in the same league as them. Alec could mow down normal hybrids like pawns on a chessboard simply by unleashing his ability on them and draining them dry.

These days the only hybrid who could hope to consistently beat Alec was Puppeteer, and even that wasn't guaranteed. Ash and I didn't have those kinds of advantages. Even if we could find Dream Stealer he'd be surrounded by enforcers like the one who had just wiped the floor with me. There was no way that the two of us could hope to bring down a member of the Coun'hij by ourselves. It was something worse than a suicide mission—we would die without any hope of succeeding.

"That's never going to happen, Ash, and you know it. Maybe if we could find Dream Stealer then Alec could put together a strike force capable of bringing him down, but there is literally zero chance of the two of us finding him. He's got more than two hundred years of practice at staying hidden."

"I have a plan. It's a long shot, but I think it could work. The only question is whether you're in."

I rubbed my forehead, trying to buy myself time to think. "Tell me again why you picked me instead of someone else? There were a lot of hybrids back at the estate you could have asked Alec to send in my place."

"I picked you because you were the best option. You're no enforcer, but you've got more combat experience than most hybrids four or five times your age. You know your way around the technology side of things, so you can help run a stable of hackers if it comes to that."

"That kind of talent doesn't come cheap."

"I know, but money isn't an issue. I made off with plenty when I left home. I can fund any conceivable spend for at least a few months. I just need someone who can talk the talk well enough to keep whatever talent I bring onboard honest. Besides, Alec trusts you, probably even more than you realize. He's not going to be willing to send a strike force of his best and brightest into danger on the word of just anyone."

"He trusts you too, Ash."

"Yeah, but I don't know if he trusts me that much. If he sends a force that size into a trap it will be the end of the rebellion. It's a big ask. With the two of us to confirm each other's story he'll be more likely to believe that it's a real opportunity. Alec knows that you aren't particularly fond of Kristin or me. You won't buy off on an attack op unless you believe it's the real deal—not just to save Kristin."

I couldn't help myself. I laughed, loud enough that it should have woken Kristin up, but she didn't even stir.

"So I got signed up for a suicide mission because I don't like you. That's karma if I've ever heard of it."

"That's not the only reason, Isaac. I wanted you because I knew you would understand what I was going through. You may not like us, but you'd do the same thing for Jess if our positions were reversed. More than any of the others, you understand me."

"Yeah, I guess you're right there. I know what it feels like to worry that you've lost the single most important person in your life."

Chapter 4

Isaac Nazir
I-30
Western Arkansas

We made it through the night without any problems. I got a full three hours of sleep, and then once Ash was satisfied that I wasn't going to pass out at the drop of a hat he finally resigned the wheel and let me drive until almost dawn while he slept.

Kristin slept the entire time without waking up, but it wasn't a peaceful slumber by any stretch of the imagination. She thrashed around almost constantly while Ash was asleep in the back of the SUV, and a few times she yelled loud enough that she woke up Ash.

It was one of the more disturbing experiences that I'd had to endure. It felt like I was sitting next to a bomb. Dream Stealer had a long history of driving people insane, he just usually worked with a finer touch than this. Most of the time his victims didn't even realize what was going on until it was too late.

From the outside, most people never even saw it coming. You woke up one morning and met a friend for breakfast. Maybe it was your girlfriend, maybe it was a buddy you'd known since before you could walk.

Sometimes you knew that they'd been struggling with insomnia, sometimes you didn't. Maybe they weren't there when you arrived at the restaurant, maybe they arrived late, maybe they never arrived at all and you didn't know what had happened until you saw the special report on the news later that day.

Sometimes they snapped and drove a fuel truck into an elementary school. Other times they walked up to you and stabbed you in the chest before you could get out of your seat. There was no telling how one of Dream Stealer's victims would go off of the rails, but they all went off of the deep end eventually and they usually took someone else with them when it happened.

Ash seemed confident that Kristin still had things under control, but I wasn't so sure. Dream Stealer had turned two-hundred-year-old shape shifters. A teenage girl who occasionally had visions of the future didn't stand a chance against him no matter how spunky she was.

I spent the entire time I was driving worried Kristin was going to wake up and try to stick a knife in the side of my neck. It wasn't exactly conducive to recovering from nearly being disemboweled, so I protested a lot less than normal when Ash offered to relieve me behind the wheel.

We made the switch at the next gas station and then hit another drive-through for a fatty breakfast of sausage and biscuits that had plenty of calories to stoke bodies that had all been pushed to their limits in one way or another.

The smell of the food was enough to finally wake Kristin, but she was so groggy that I was done with my food before she'd done much more than start picking at hers. I made a mental note to ask Ash if the lethargy was a new development as I pulled out my tablet and plugged it into the keyboard that turned it into the equivalent of a laptop.

"Is that safe given what happened the last time you fired up one of your gadgets?"

I was pretty sure Kristin was trying to get a rise out of me. Knowing that made it easier to avoid rising to the bait.

"My tablet doesn't have any kind of cellular connection on it and I've even got the wi-fi turned off. There is zero chance of anyone using this to track us down. Besides, you're one to talk."

Ash shot me a look and then reached over with his free hand and intertwined his fingers with Kristin's.

"Isaac knows. He figured it out last night."

Kristin almost seemed to come apart before my very eyes. The facade of the strong, independent, devil-may-care woman crumbled into pieces and for the first time I could remember I saw real fear in Kristin's eyes.

"What are you going to do now that you know?"

Ash interrupted before I could respond. "He's not going to hurt you. Even if he wanted to I wouldn't let anything happen to you."

Kristin gave Ash a sad smile before she turned back to me. "Isaac is a big boy, he can answer the question for himself."

I held her gaze for a dozen seconds before I spoke. "What would you do in my place?"

"I'd put you down and never look back. It's the only smart answer, the only way to guarantee that you wouldn't eventually rip my heart out of my chest. You wouldn't even need to get the drop on me because I have zero chance of beating you unless I have surprise on my side."

I nodded. "You're not wrong. What about if it was Ash who was under attack by Dream Stealer, what would you do then?"

I'd only thought that I was seeing the real Kristin a few seconds before. She'd let me see *some* of what was going on inside of her, but the look in her eyes now was like the thinnest layer of sanity imaginable stretched over a hungry pit.

"I'd do exactly what he's doing. I'd try to help him fight it, but I'd get him off where he couldn't do any damage when he finally snapped, and I'd bring along someone who could put him down quick and painlessly if it came to that."

Kristin was good, maybe in another year or two she'd be able to lie with her body as well as she already lied with her face and voice, but she wasn't there yet. Ash and I both knew that she wouldn't have been able to stand by while someone tried to kill Ash.

Kristin had one of the strongest survival instincts I'd ever seen. Plenty of wolves and hybrids would have just given up in the face of someone like Anton. He'd been a relentless, nearly unstoppable killing machine, but Ash and Kristin had just kept fighting until they managed to beat him. They'd had help, but even that almost hadn't been enough. If either of them had blinked at any point in that last fight we all would have died.

It was almost inconceivable for someone like Kristin to choose a path she knew would get her killed when there was another option out there, but that was exactly what she was trying so hard not to tell us.

She really would execute me without a second thought if I was the one who was a living time-bomb, but she wouldn't kill Ash, not in a million years, not even knowing that failing to do so would mean he would eventually snap and kill her.

"Is that why you've been extra unpleasant lately? Are you trying to make it easier on me when the time comes to put you down?"

I got a single, short nod in response. "Yeah, I guess so."

"Okay then, it sounds like we all understand each other. Ash will do whatever he has to in order to keep you alive, right up to and possibly including killing me. I will kill both of you before I let you hurt Alec and the rest of my friends, and you'll hold out for as long as you possibly can because you know that once Dream Stealer turns you, Ash is a dead man. He might be able to beat me, but he won't be able to beat you."

"Yeah, I guess that about sums it up."

I wanted to close my eyes and pretend none of this was happening. This was exactly the kind of impossible situation that Alec had faced the first time that we'd crossed paths with Agony. I didn't have any good options. If—no, when—Kristin buckled under the pressure of Dream Stealer's nightly attacks, nothing I did would be right. The best I could do at that point was try to pick a bad choice that would still leave me able to look at myself in the mirror once it was all said and done.

I'd spent months hating Alec for his choices the night Jess' memories had been torn away from her, and now I was about to walk a mile in his shoes.

"Fine. I'm willing to give the two of you some time before we do anything final. I'll even help when it comes to trying to track down Dream Stealer, not that I think we have a chance in hell of actually finding him, but I'll do my best. The secrets and the lying stop now though. We keep detailed logs of how you are doing each day, and you tell us the moment that something changes.

"Assuming that there is a lock out there that Ash hasn't already taught you to pick, I'll even buy off on the idea of locking you up if it becomes obvious that you are at the end of your rope, but I'm not going to leave anything to chance. From here on out you know as little about what's going on as possible.

"The best way to make sure that you don't do any damage to the cause is to keep you completely in the dark about what's going on with everyone else. We don't tell you where we are headed, and when you fall asleep we change directions so that even if you break we still can't be tracked down."

Ash shook his head. "That's going too far, Isaac. That's no way to live, she's still got control of things, there's no reason to make her a prisoner this soon."

I didn't look at Ash, choosing instead to hold Kristin's gaze. "Is it too much, Kristin?"

She gave me a thin, bitter smile. "I rather suspect that you're just getting started, aren't you, Isaac?"

"Answer the question before Ash decides he needs to try to draw down on me."

Kristin turned in her seat so she could look at Ash and then she turned back to me. "That's fine. I'll put up with a lot worse if that's what it takes to keep from cutting Ash's throat while he sleeps."

"Like you said, I'm just getting started."

That earned me another smile. "That's okay, Isaac. If nothing else, all of the crap you're about to put me through means that I'll feel less bad if you fail and I end up killing you."

Chapter 5

Isaac Nazir
I-55
Western Tennessee

I didn't realize just how much Ash was still holding out on me until the next night. We'd been tooling around the Midwest all day, clocking a lot of miles but not really getting anywhere. Ash and Kristin spent the day watching to make sure that we hadn't picked up a tail. I spent the day putting together a plan of attack on every major database I could think of.

There was a limit to what I could do on my tablet with no internet connection. I couldn't even scout to see what kind of security I was going to be up against, but in a way that was good because it forced me to think much more big picture than I normally did. It was actually kind of liberating to come up with a plan of attack and not have to worry about how we were going to make the specifics work.

I was pretty good, but I wasn't world-class, not like the guys Alec had on the payroll these days. I couldn't hack the State Department, but Ash was right, I knew enough to keep the guys who could hack the big targets mostly honest. It was still basically tilting at windmills, but I was willing to give it a chance for as long as Ash was willing to fund the kind of talent we would need if we were going to have any chance of succeeding.

Kristin had moved back to the back seat before falling asleep so that I'd have better access for my power adapter. My tablet was a wonderful piece of engineering, but even it couldn't go for twenty hours at a stretch without being recharged. The fact that I was in the front passenger seat meant that I was perfectly positioned to notice when Ash turned south rather than north as I'd been expecting him to when we hit the west edge of Tennessee.

"What are you doing? I thought your safe house was up in Montana somewhere."

"It is—or rather one of them is—but that's where Kristin is expecting us to go. You were the one who was all up in arms about making sure that she couldn't lead Dream Stealer to us. I'm doing the unexpected."

My armrest started to groan and I forced myself to relax before I ripped it free of the chair.

"Montana is a pretty big state; I think that Dream Stealer would have a hard time finding us with nothing more than that to go on, but you know that even better than I do. How about you cut the crap and tell me what's going on before I decide to leave the two of you and go my own way?"

"You don't have the cash to do that, Isaac."

I purposefully made my laugh extra mocking, but I kept it low enough not to wake up Kristin. "You've obviously spent too much time as the only rich boy in the neighborhood. Do you really think that Alec would send us all out without a war chest? The Graves family is worth billions. Not one or two billion dollars, mid to high double digits.

"Every single one of those RV's was loaded with something like half a million dollars in cash and prepaid credit cards. I've got more than enough to get me wherever I need to go and Alec will send more with nothing more than a call. Your money doesn't have any kind of hold over me. Start talking."

Ash took a deep breath and a little ray of warmth shone through me as I realized that I'd managed to get under *his* skin for a change. It was petty, but it was also a sign that he wasn't in complete control of everything like he usually pretended. Our little partnership wasn't going to work unless he was willing to eventually acknowledge that he was just as far in over his head as I was.

"Fine. I've tried to keep this particular card close to my chest because it's not really my secret to be sharing."

"Whose secret is it?"

"My family's. We've got more of them even than you'd expect. It's the only reason that we haven't been run entirely out of the New Orleans pack—that or killed. My sister is still back there, still under Onyx's thumb, and what I'm about to tell you is one of her hole cards. It's the one she'll play when she's out of all other options, so it's vital that none of this make it back to Onyx before then."

Ash waited to make sure that I understood the importance of what he'd just told me, and then cleared his throat.

"What do you know about lamias?"

It was such a non sequitur that it took me a moment to collect my thoughts. "Greek mythological creatures, snakes below the waist, women above the waist. The Old World is even more off limits than the eastern half of the United States, so there is less in the way of confirmation when it comes to whether or not something from over there is based in fact or not, but I haven't seen anything that makes me think they are more than just a legend."

"Yeah, they're real. I mean there is a lot that the myths got wrong, but there's something out in the bayous that I'm pretty sure is based on the same thing as the Greek legends. There are bits and pieces of other stuff that seems to tie back to the same creature. One of the Aztec gods was depicted as a man with snake fangs—I think his name was Tlaloc. That's supposedly closer to the truth."

My stomach was already tying itself into knots. Even my beast wasn't happy about the news that there was yet another thing out there that might end up hunting us at some point.

"The Aztec gods weren't a very warm and cuddly pantheon, Ash. Why are we headed down to see something that had a hand in human sacrifices? Do you know that some sources claim that the Aztecs alone sacrificed a quarter of a million people per year?"

Ash nodded. "I'm not as well read as you are generally speaking, but I think that you'll find that in this area I'm just as informed as you are. The Incan and the Mayan civilizations practiced human sacrifice too, but it does seem like the Aztecs took it to a whole other level. The rededication of the Great Pyramid of Tenochtitlan resulted in somewhere between ten thousand and eighty thousand sacrifices over the course of just four days."

"You know that Strakes originally thought that the presence of human sacrifice in South America was compelling evidence that there were vampires in the New World before the arrival of Columbus?"

Benitone Strakes was the closest thing we shape shifters had to a historian, at least one whose writings had survived and been disseminated beyond just their immediate pack.

My observation earned me a rare smile from Ash. He smiled at Kristin sometimes, but most of the rest of us never saw anything other than his game face.

"Does this mean you're not pissed off at me anymore?"

"No, it means I'm willing to avoid thinking about just how pissed I am for as long as you continue to keep this conversation interesting."

It wasn't completely a lie. I was still kind of mad, but I wasn't as mad as I should have been. Ash looked back at the road and shrugged.

"Yeah, I was aware of that, but you're starting to get to the very edge of my expertise. Strakes has been conclusively disproved on that point from what I understand though. There aren't any records of shape shifters encountering vampires on this continent until well after the Europeans started founding colonies over here. The case is still out when it comes to werewolves—there have been plenty of unexplained disappearances that they might have caused—but unlike vampires, werewolves are pretty good at hiding from us since they don't have as distinctive a smell."

I tapped the edge of my tablet. "Sure, but the mere fact that the lamias have managed to stay a secret over here for tens of thousands of years proves that Strakes was right about there being preternatural species here that were unknown to our people.

"We spent all of that time fighting the jaguars and never realized that there were other threats out there, never even considered that there were other continents out there. Even worse, we never even considered that the humans might someday become so numerous that we'd be forced into hiding to avoid being hunted to extinction."

"You think that we should have fought back, that the packs should have rallied together to push the Europeans back into the ocean?"

"I don't think it was even possible. The packs were all still at each other's throats. It hadn't been all that long, relatively speaking, at that point since the monarchy had been overthrown. If the Coun'hij had tried to put together the kind of massive army that fighting the colonists would have required, they would have lost control. Whoever was put in charge would have almost certainly used the army to establish themselves as the new king."

We drove in silence for a couple of minutes before Ash finally responded. "I think you're probably right. The jaguars in South and Central America tried to fight back. They worked as individuals rather than a unified force, but they had some resounding successes against the second wave of colonists. Despite that, they never really got their heads around the fact that it didn't matter how many people they slaughtered. With the promise of so much gold over here, there was no way they were going to stem the tide of *conquistadores*."

"Yeah, and once the native humans down there realized that the Spanish were generally the less corrupt option, the humans turned on our cousins with a speed that shocked everyone."

I thought maybe Ash was done talking history with me. We drove for five more minutes before he sighed and slouched down in his seat. "The jaguars have never forgotten that betrayal. The ones who were alive when it happened are all long dead, but hatred for humans is endemic down there. All of the corruption in that area can be traced back to the jaguars. If they'd worked together they probably could have won, but they don't see it that way. That's a weakness we all seem to have. Wolves, jaguars, vampires, werewolves, we're all terrible at cooperating with our own kind. If even one of the preternatural races could bring itself to work together like a human nation, we'd be unstoppable."

"Is that why you're so determined to back Alec's play?"

"There isn't a simple answer to that question, but yeah, that's part of it. I made a promise to him that I'd join your pack in return for his help saving us from Anton, but if that was all that was going on I wouldn't have taken some of the risks that I've taken trying to support him.

"The truth is that my ancestors were probably the reason that the monarchy fell. They were so concerned with trying to protect their power base that they let the Coun'hij take over everything. It was the worst decision they could have made. Alec's ancestors weren't perfect—if they had been they wouldn't have lost control in the first place—but they're good, fair leaders. It's like it's in their DNA."

"Alec has made his fair share of mistakes."

"I can't argue with you there, Isaac, but when he does something wrong it is because he's made a mistake rather than because he's some kind of despot who views the rest of us as disposable pieces that exist solely to serve him."

That hit a little too close to home. Once upon a time I'd backed Alec as far or farther than anything Ash had done so far. I'd done it for different reasons, but I'd done it anyway. I'd backed him against James—kept him in power inside of our pack dozens of times after he'd pushed too hard and left himself exposed—and I'd done it with a pretty minimal amount of complaining.

The problem was that I'd done it at least partly because it had been the easiest way to keep my life from taking a turn for the worst.

"I'd like to believe that, but I'm not sure I can give Alec quite that much of the benefit of the doubt. Not after he let Agony's group do what they did to us. Even declaring war on the Coun'hij was suspect. He should have waited, gathered support and then moved against them later when it wasn't as much of a risk."

"It's easy to second-guess the person in the big chair when you're not the one who has to deal with the ultimate consequences of the hard decisions, Isaac. That's something I didn't realize until after I left home. I gave my sister a lot of grief over her policies, and I always felt justified in doing so until I was on my own. That changed my perspective."

"Maybe you're right, but it's going to take more than just a pep talk to convince me to get religion again where Alec is concerned."

"Fair enough. You wanted to know why we're headed south and I only partially answered your question. The lamias...know things. Their queen is supposed to be able to see into the future. It's not as clear as what Kristin gets from her dreams, but they get a much broader picture than she does."

"That doesn't make me feel any calmer where these snake people are concerned, Ash. No wonder nobody knows about them—if the queens know everything that is going to happen in advance then it's a wonder that they haven't taken over the world already. All of the Aztec sacrifices aside, they don't happen to be a bunch of tiny scaly pacifists do they?"

"No, not according to my family's records at least. They're six and a half feet tall and incredibly violent. There's a reason that there aren't many werewolves in Louisiana. The lamias hunt them down—not in packs, singly—because the queen's consorts like the challenge of killing werewolves in single combat."

"You're going to give me a whole new set of nightmares."

"Yeah, that's not the worst part though. One of my ancestors was convinced that the only reason that the lamias hadn't tried to take over the world was that their queen had decided that it wasn't time yet."

"And you're going to just stroll up to the queen and ask her if she can tell us where Dream Stealer is hiding?"

"Something like that. It will have to be Kristin who asks though. Under the right circumstances they'll treat visiting females as honorary queens. You and I just have to convince them that she deserves a hearing. By defeating one of the consorts."

Chapter 6

Isaac Nazir
I-55
Western Tennessee

Our conversation lapsed into silence and we drove for hours in our own little worlds, Ash focused on the road and me continuing to make notes on my tablet. It felt more than a little pointless to continue planning the largest single hacking operation in history now that I knew it probably wasn't going to happen, but I kept grinding away at it regardless.

There was always the possibility that we'd survive combat with something that was capable of bringing down a werewolf by itself. It wasn't a very good possibility, but it might happen, and if it did then we'd need a backup plan in case the lamias didn't know how to find Dream Stealer. Besides, the problem of simultaneously launching attacks on so many different places had captured my imagination.

As I continued working I realized that cracking all of those government and corporate databases was only part of the problem. Given enough time and effort, just about any system could be hacked, but you couldn't guarantee access for any extended period of time.

The real question was what to do with the access once we had it. We needed to conduct the world's biggest data-mining operation, which meant that we needed a data repository where we could store everything we stole.

That was easy enough, but if we just sent the data there then the Feds would be able to track the electronic trail from their systems to the warehouse. We needed a physical cutout, a spot in the process where the data could be copied onto some kind of transportable medium and then physically moved to a new location, preferably a location that didn't have any kind of connectivity to the rest of the world.

The last thing we needed to worry about was some kind of Trojan horse leading the authorities to us the first time that we copied the data over. We needed processing power and we needed a massive storage array, something that could handle petabytes of data and still resolve data requests quickly enough to keep the rest of our infrastructure busy.

That wasn't a trivial task, but now that I'd identified the problem I'd just use more of Ash's money to solve it. The one thing that couldn't be outsourced was figuring out our approach to analyzing the data once we had it.

Banking data could be picked through looking for large cash withdrawals, but I knew that wasn't likely to reveal anything, not with the level of scrutiny that kind of information was already under by the IRS. It took me a while, but as we crossed over the Louisiana border I started to hit on some approaches that might succeed.

Rare art sales might get me something—members of the Coun'hij had been known to occasionally liquidate art that nobody had even known existed—but my money was on gas station data. Coun'hij enforcers tended to travel to and from operations in big SUVs so as to avoid the paper trail that flying unavoidably left behind.

It went without saying that they were using either cash or anonymous prepaid credit cards to buy fuel for those cars, but that was probably something I could still work with.

"Hey, Ash, how long do you think it would take to put together a comprehensive list of times and places that the Coun'hij or their people have made an appearance in the last fifteen years?"

"Normally I'd say we could have something pretty solid in just a day or two. I'm pretty sure that the Chicago pack has been religiously taking notes on that very thing since even before Ulrich came into power."

I sighed. "Alec said that Shawn and Ulrich have gone off of the grid. For all we know there isn't a Chicago pack anymore."

"No way. They might have been forced to scatter, but Ulrich is way too cagey not to have seen that coming. He'll have had contingency plans in place. Even under a worst-case scenario he'll manage to get a good chunk of his people out."

"Maybe, maybe not. Even if he gets out, there's no guarantee that his records will make it out too. Most of the old guard is overly attached to paper records."

"I guess we'll just have to wait and see what he's got access to when he or Shawn resurface. What do you have in mind?"

"I want to track them back using point-of-sale data from the gas stations. If we figure out the range of a typical SUV and then look at all the fuel purchases in that radius around each appearance, one of those purchases will be the guys we want to track."

"They'll be using something untraceable."

"Yeah, I'm actually counting on it. I'll ditch all of the transactions made by regular credit cards, which will get my data set down to something more manageable, and then I'll start massaging the data. If you've got a large enough data sample then you can find all kinds of patterns in there. If we can get a pretty comprehensive list of visitations by guys like Agony and the rest, the data we're looking for will eventually pop up; it will just be a matter of wading through the false positives."

"There's going to be a lot of false positives in that much data, Isaac."

"Yeah, you're right there. I can do a lot to fine-tune the pattern-recognition algorithm, but the real key is going to be getting our hands on the data showing buy times and locations for prepaid credit cards. I'm betting that something will pop up there."

"That just might work. Whoever is bankrolling the Coun'hij's operation isn't going to be buying those things one or two at a time. They'll be picking up dozens of them at once."

"Yep, and they probably won't just stick a hundred bucks on them either, which means that they'll get used to refuel the vehicles more than once before they are depleted and thrown away. By cross-referencing the point-of-sale data and the instances of multiple cards being purchased, we're bound to be able to track them back. Even if they are smart enough to issue each enforcer multiple cards and tell the line grunts to rotate them I'd still bet that some of them get sloppy about that kind of thing and there will still be a pattern there for us to find."

"Sure, that works if they are using prepaid cards, but it doesn't do anything for you if they are using cash."

"Except that if they are using cash then it will still tend to create a pattern. That would mean that I could disregard every electronic payment and just focus on cash transactions above, say, fifty bucks. With search parameters that narrow I just may be able to track them all the way back to their home base despite cash being the perfect anonymous payment method."

Ash looked doubtful. "I know trying to track the Coun'hij down by running a team of hackers was my idea, but if it's really that easy then why hasn't someone already done it?"

"It's not easy. You're going to have to hire a ton of really top-level talent to get the data we need, and that isn't going to come cheap. Credit card companies spend billions every year to make their systems as close to impregnable as possible. At the end of the day we may have to hire someone to physically break into some of these facilities—actually, it wouldn't surprise me if we had to send a team of shape shifters in, normal humans would have an easier time breaking into Fort Knox. Whoever tries to go in there is going to need a serious edge."

"I can make that happen. I know people who specialize in that kind of thing, we could pose as IT auditors from their accounting firm. All of those types of companies are publically held and their external auditors are the one group of people that pretty much have to see every security measure they have in place."

I found myself nodding. "That's not a bad idea, actually, but to answer your question, I don't think that this would have been possible even just a few years ago. Most of the current pack leaders are at least eighty or ninety years old. There are always exceptions, but it's pretty unusual to have someone as young as Alec running a pack. That means that they don't tend to think in terms of cyber-threats. Sure, they hire people to keep them in the loop about the threats that they are most likely to face, but that isn't the same as really understanding the threat yourself.

"Even more than that though, up until recently our national economy was a lot more cash-based than it's become over the last few years. We had a lot of small, independent gas stations who used actual cash registers rather than big national and regional chains that have fancy digital point-of-sale devices that instantly send every transaction off to a central database for long-term storage."

"I see. It wouldn't have been feasible before now because to get the data we need we would have had to find and steal paper documents."

"Right, and even if we managed to get all of the data that we needed we'd still be faced with the impossible task of manually analyzing them, which would have taken decades."

"I'm impressed, Isaac. Alec really was right about you."

"What, that I spend too much time behind my computer?"

"No, that you're the kind of guy who always comes through in a pinch, the kind of guy who can be depended on, which is a lot less common than most people realize."

It was suddenly hard to talk, but I forced my question out. "When did he say that?"

"Right before we all split up in Nevada. I managed to get him off by himself and told him that things were getting a lot worse with Kristin. He told me to bring you along, but I wasn't thrilled by the idea, not after how tense things got between you and me the night of the attack."

"Yeah, you pissed off a lot of people that night. I wouldn't turn your back on Grayson anytime soon."

"I wasn't planning on it, but it's nice to have some independent confirmation of the fact that he's carrying a grudge. It's hard for me to get a good read on that guy most of the time."

That wasn't a line of conversation that I wanted to pursue. It was a short trip from Grayson to Wyatt and Jess.

"So Alec told you to take me and you said no, but he overruled you and here we are."

"No, Alec suggested I take you, I said no, and then he told me that there was a storm coming, the kind of storm where I'd need someone I could trust at my back, someone like you."

"I...thanks. I appreciate the vote of confidence, from both of you I guess, but I especially appreciate you letting me know he said that. It means more than I expected it to after some of the things that have happened lately."

We lapsed back into a silence that was mostly comfortable until Kristin started screaming in the back seat. I bailed out of the passenger seat and back to the rear seat before Ash could even open his mouth to ask me to check on her. Ash flipped on the interior dome light as I reached her.

She was still asleep, but every single muscle in her body was tensed up like they were trying to rip themselves free of her bones. She was screaming nonstop—I wasn't sure how she was keeping it up without stopping to breathe, but she was doing it.

She started thrashing and I pressed down on her shoulder to hold her in place, but it was like pushing an oak tree.

"Get her awake!"

Ash and I had both been screaming her name since the attack started, so I did the only other thing I could think of. I slapped her. Not as hard as I could have, but hard enough that I was riding a fine line between shocking her awake and simply giving her a concussion.

Kristin's head rocked back and to the side and then her eyes snapped open. "Get off of the main road, Ash."

"What?"

"I just had another precognitive dream. Dream Stealer was trying to keep me there so that I couldn't warn you. Get off of the main highway, they know we're driving down this road and they've got a description of our vehicle."

I looked forward at Ash as he looked up at me in the rearview mirror. I could see the same doubt in his eyes that I was thinking of.

"Guys, we really need to get off of the road. I'm telling you, this dream was the real deal, the details were too crisp to be anything other than another prophetic dream."

"This isn't the first time that Dream Stealer has done this to you, Kristin. He knows how your power works now. He knows the mistakes he made back in Sanctuary when he tried to counterfeit one of your dreams."

"I can't believe we're having this discussion. I have no idea where we are or even where we're headed. Ash had to have changed directions when I fell asleep. How could Dream Stealer possibly lure us into some kind of ambush?"

"If he's got satellites under his control and he knows roughly where we were when you fell asleep, then he just looks for a vehicle that exits the interstate shortly after you wake up and tell us about the ambush. One time probably wouldn't be enough, but if he can cross-reference that data with a knowledge of where we are when you go to sleep next it might be enough to narrow his list of suspects down to something he can have his people in the area manually run down."

"That's crazy. Dream Stealer wants me at large for as long as possible in the hopes that you guys will slip up and tell me something he can use. That satellite thing doesn't even sound possible, there's too much area to cover for it to work."

I bit my lip. I didn't actually know whether or not it was possible. Alec had other guys he turned to when it came to the satellite stuff. I needed time to think, but Ash only gave me a couple of seconds.

"Call it, Isaac. You're the expert and you're the one who's back there with her. If she's right then we need to move sooner rather than later if we're going to have any chance of avoiding the net they are setting up for us."

Kristin shot Ash a dirty look, but she didn't say anything before she turned back to me and met my gaze. Her scent wasn't off, at least no more than you'd expect from someone who was convinced that we were just seconds away from being jumped by a superior force. That was the problem, all of the signs that might have told me that she was lying would have been masked by the fact that she was worried about us.

I had no way of being sure. Even if she was telling the truth, Dream Stealer might have figured out how to counterfeit her precognitive dreams.

"Go ahead and get off at the next exit, Ash. We'll have to ditch the car somewhere in New Orleans first thing once the sun rises. If we can do it under an overpass or inside of a parking garage again that should make sure that Dream Stealer loses our trail if this is some kind of trick. Given that we'll be right smack dab in the middle of your old pack's territory, it's a big risk though."

Ash nodded as he pulled onto the off ramp. "Yeah, all it would take is one phone call for him to have Onyx turn out the entire pack to look for us. If they know what we're driving we won't have any chance of getting away."

Kristin motioned me out of the way so that she could go sit next to Ash. "We'll just have to be careful and move quickly. As long as we ditch this car before they realize they lost us, we have a decent chance of making a clean getaway. What were you guys thinking coming down here, by the way?"

I felt like banging my head against the window. All the work trying to keep our location a secret from Kristin and we'd just told her exactly where we were. Even worse, if she realized that we had a compelling reason to be down here then we were completely screwed. Dream Stealer would have an ambush waiting for us the next time we came down to talk to the lamias.

"We just thought it was the last place that anyone would look for us."

Ash said it without any change to his expression. There was a tiny blip in his heart rate, but I might have missed it if I hadn't been paying attention. I mentally added another entry to the list of things that I knew Ash could do. I hadn't realized that he was that good of a liar.

Kristin leaned back in the passenger's seat, rolling her eyes at the way the leather squeaked. "Well, it was a stupid idea. You should have headed to whatever safe house you've got in mind for us. The sooner we can climb into a hole and pull it closed behind us the happier I'll be."

Ash started to respond and then frowned as he looked at the rearview mirror for the third time in as many seconds. Kristin noticed too.

"What's going on, Ash?"

"There's a vehicle back there that got close to us like they were planning on passing, but they just backed way off. It was hard to tell, but it looked like something big, maybe a van or another SUV."

"Crap, they found us; can you lose them?"

He shook his head and then looked back at me. "Please pass my bug-out bag up to Kristin. We need to put silencers on our guns. Trying to run is almost guaranteed to fail. The car behind us will stay just far enough back to radio our position to the rest of the hunters and they'll just slowly tighten the noose around us. If we were in the city maybe we could lose them, but it's too open here, too few places to disappear."

Kristin screwed a silencer onto her gun and then handed it back to me to hold while she reached around Ash so that she could unholster his weapon.

"How are we going to do this?"

Ash looked back at me as if to see whether I wanted to weigh in, but I just waved for him to proceed. This kind of spy stuff was more his bag of tea than mine. If I thought his plan wouldn't work then I could always make my case once he was done explaining his idea.

"If there was any way to be sure those are bad guys back there I'd just drive up next to them and start shooting while they're still in the car and unable to shift. Instead Kristin and I are going to swap seats and then Isaac and I will pile out of the SUV while it's still moving. With any luck we can do it without them seeing. Kristin pulls to a stop fifty yards later and then Isaac and I wait for these guys to stop and get out of their vehicle.

"If they drive on by then we jump back in the car and drive back the way we came. If not, that's a bad sign. If they give off any kind of shape shifter vibe, or anyone recognizes one of them as being a known agent for the Coun'hij, we open fire on them and Isaac intercepts whoever tries to rush either of the shooters."

It wasn't a great plan, but it gave us a chance of taking them by surprise and I didn't have anything better to offer. I gave Ash a nod of agreement as I started stripping out of my clothes, and then he and Kristin swapped places with a smoothness that would have been impossible without cruise control.

"There, the road bends and those cypress trees will partially hide us from view."

Ash and I threw ourselves out of the SUV and hit the ground rolling. I was tempted to shift then and there, but there was too much chance that someone would feel me changing, even through the metal and glass of the other vehicle, and then we'd lose the element of surprise.

Instead I took deep breaths as I crouched behind the tree that Ash had pointed out. The air was full of smells that I'd never encountered before, mostly plant life, but I could smell some animals on the wind too.

"Anything out here I should be worried about?"

"Nothing from downwind of us, but that's not the most reassuring fact since we won't be able to smell if anything comes out of the vegetation behind us."

A smile tugged at my lips despite my best efforts. "You're just a rousing ball of non-stop fun. Remind me again what it is that Kristin sees in you."

"I'm great fun at a party."

"I'd like to see that."

"Isn't that what we're about to do?"

The following car, another black SUV, came even with us and we both hunkered down and shut up in case they had a window down. Kristin had already started slowing down, which caused the other guys to follow suit.

Her timing wasn't perfect, but she managed to bring them to a stop less than twenty yards from us. Ash and I both stood and crept forward, only to freeze as soon as the first door swung open.

"Remember, there's only three of them. Kill Nazir and the girl, but take Hunt alive if at all possible. Onyx wants him to use as leverage against his sister and the boss owes Onyx a favor."

Kristin was already out of our car. She'd angled it slightly so that it would provide her with a little cover, but even from here I could tell that she was nervous.

"Hey, wait a second! She's by herself."

We were out of time. Even if they hadn't been able to see that our vehicle was empty they would have still known something was up when they stopped to count heartbeats.

Ash opened fire and he was every bit as deadly as I'd hoped he would be. There were four of them. Ash put two rounds in the first guy, dropping him before he could change forms.

Kristin got her gun in play before Ash could get his third shot off. There was too much going on for me to be sure who hit the next enforcer, but he was mid-change when the bullets started slamming into him. A fraction of a second sooner and they probably would have put him down as easily as the first guy, but his hybrid body was just too big and damage-resistant to be taken out of action that quickly. He staggered back behind the side of the car, which sheltered him from Ash's shots, and then broke into a fast run towards Kristin.

The other two guys spun back around and charged us. It was probably the sheer volume of Ash's fire that made them pick us over Kristin. Ash got two shots into one of them and then they were on us.

I'd shifted less than a second after the ball dropped and my beast was raring and ready to go. I stepped into the uninjured hybrid, blocking his claws by slashing at his arm a split second before I put my shoulder into his chest.

It was the kind of tactic that wasn't supposed to work, which was why he hadn't been more prepared for it, but I didn't hit him directly in the center of his mass, I hit him a little left of center. That, combined with the fact that I had both sets of talons burrowed deep into the surface of the road, was just enough to allow me not to be leveled by the force of his charge.

His momentum was converted to a spin as he ricocheted off of me, but I managed a deep raking attack across his stomach as he sailed past. I dropped my right hand down to the ground and used the extra traction provided by my claws to regain my balance in the split second before the second hybrid reached me.

More shots rang out, some from behind me, some from Kristin up ahead, but I didn't have time for that. I'd succeeded in giving Ash a target that was off balance and flailing, but it had come at a cost. I was going into the matchup with the second hybrid without the momentum I would have needed to meet him on equal terms.

I darted back to the right and managed to get just far enough to the side to deny my opponent the clinch that he'd been seeking, but he still tore big, long gashes in my left arm. I spun around in an attempt at latching onto his back before he could turn and come at me again, but he was just too fast.

We exchanged blows, each trying for something vital on the other guy while trying to deflect incoming attacks. More shots went off around me as Kristin and Ash both emptied their magazines in a last-ditch attempt to stop the hybrids charging them.

Something heavy hit the ground behind me, and I took a gamble that I wouldn't have taken with too many other people. I went for a clinch with my enforcer before there was anything remotely resembling the kind of opening that I'd need to survive for more than a couple of seconds.

It was suicide, but it was the last thing he'd been expecting me to do given that he had more than an inch of height on me. I made like I was going to feint to the left at the last second, and then just went in full speed. I didn't manage to hit him hard enough to take him to the ground, but I knocked him back on his heels, which let me get inside of his reach and fasten my jaws on his shoulder.

I had control of his hands too, at least for the initial clinch. He'd managed to bury one set of claws into my side, but I wrapped up his wrist, immobilizing him before he could really go to town on me.

It wasn't something I could maintain for long; he was stronger than me and eventually he'd either break free or succeed in sinking his teeth into me, but I was hoping I wasn't going to need to hold him off for more than a second or so.

A heartbeat later I felt the impact of a hundred and eighty pounds of lean badass as Ash literally ran up my back. I was going to have a set of boot-shaped bruises to go along with the gashes and punctures that the enforcer had inflicted on me, but that didn't matter.

Moving faster than any human could have followed, Ash knelt on my shoulders and pressed the barrel of his gun up against the enforcer's forehead. I had just enough presence of mind to close my eyes before Ash's gun went off with what felt like the force of a cannon.

The other hybrid collapsed as Ash leaped off of me and hit the ground running. His gun went off again and again each time his feet left the pavement. In anyone else they would have been wildly uncontrolled shots, but Ash was scoring on the last hybrid with what looked like half of them.

I'd started to fall with the hybrid I'd been tangled up with, but I freed myself from him and started forward still acting on reflex. A distant portion of my mind wondered why Ash was shooting so wildly when each missed shot had a chance of hitting Kristin, but I couldn't dwell on the question, not with how close the other hybrid was.

Ash had a head start on me, but merely human legs could never hope to outrun a hybrid. I was less than half a step behind him now, close enough that I could feel the shockwaves rippling through the air with each shot. We were less than ten feet from the enforcer when Ash squeezed off his last two rounds in such close succession that they almost sounded like one long shot.

The slide on Ash's gun locked back, and the other hybrid dropped his arms now that he no longer needed them to shield his face. Ash's empty magazine was already falling away from his gun as he reached for a fresh magazine.

The enforcer was bleeding from more than a dozen spots, but Ash and Kristin hadn't hit anything vital enough to put that massive body down permanently. Given enough time it was still possible that he'd bleed out, but the fight was going to be over—one way or the other—before that happened.

I saw a set of five claws go slicing through the air and knew that I wasn't going to be close enough to stop the enforcer from slicing Ash in half. I reached forward anyway, hoping my judgment as to Ash's chances of survival were off, but knowing that wasn't the case.

I took one last step forward; I was perfectly positioned now to stop those deadly claws a foot *after* they cut into Ash's chest, but suddenly Ash wasn't where I'd been expecting him to be. Rather than barreling into the enforcer, he threw himself forward, turning mid fall so that he landed on his back as he skidded head-first between our opponent's legs.

It shouldn't have worked, wouldn't have worked if not for the fact that I was just behind him. Normally the other hybrid would have still opened Ash up from one end to the other, but I got my claws in place just in time to save Ash.

I punched my free hand into the side of the enforcer's chest as Ash went skidding across the pavement, his slick leather jacket simultaneously saving his skin and making it possible for him to continue sliding long after he normally would have stopped. The other hybrid dodged to the side just enough that I missed his heart, but it didn't matter. Ash had a new magazine in his pistol and I heard the slide on his gun slam home with a finality that told me he wasn't going to wait for me to get out of the way.

I used my grip to shove the enforcer up and back onto his heels, and then dropped down so that his chest was interposed between my head and Ash. Half a second later the muted hiss of two more silenced shots put an end to the last threat on the road with us.

I dropped the corpse that I'd been supporting and opened my mouth to tell Ash that his last two shots had been unacceptably reckless, but the words never made it past my tongue. Ash's pistol was lying forgotten on the road and he already had both hands inside of Kristin's chest in an attempt to keep her from bleeding to death.

"Get the first-aid kit out of the car!"

I shifted back to human form as I reached the SUV, ripped Ash's bag open, and was back at his side within three seconds. I wasn't as experienced of a surgeon as Donovan or Dominic, but I knew my way around the inside of the human body and what I saw as I knelt down next to Kristin made my stomach knot up.

I wouldn't have bet on anyone surviving those kinds of wounds for more than two or three minutes, not any amount of money, not for any odds.

Chapter 7

Isaac Nazir
Fifteen miles off of I-55
Eastern Louisiana

I'd never seen Ash lose control like that. He'd always been the one guy you could count on to keep his eye on the big picture, but his hands were shaking as he tried to pull out the first roll of gauze from the first-aid kit.

I shouldered him to one side and started working as quickly as I could. The damage wasn't quite as bad as I'd initially thought, but it was still incredibly bad. Somehow the claws that had opened up her chest cavity had managed to miss any of the really major arteries, but she'd already lost a ton of blood.

"Hold pressure there and there, Ash, or she'll bleed out before I can get enough of the smaller arteries sewn shut for her to have any kind of chance."

"This is all my fault. I should have gone with a different plan, should have kept us together instead of splitting us up like that."

There wasn't time for Ash to fall apart on me. I finished tying off the artery I was working on and then backhanded him hard enough to knock him to the pavement.

"Pull yourself together or she's as good as dead. It was a decent plan, a good plan even. She knew the risks. All it would have taken is one or two shots hitting the right spot and that guy never would have even gotten within ten feet of her."

With someone else I probably would have angered their beast enough that they wouldn't have been able to stop themselves from attacking me, but Ash's beast was weaker than most. He rolled back to his knees and then crammed his hands inside her chest exactly as I'd ordered him to.

"That was risky."

I could hear the anger in his voice, but for once my beast didn't rise to the implied challenge. I couldn't help but smile as I tied off a second blood vessel.

"More dangerous than sliding between someone's feet and then shooting the bad guy while your buddy is still in the line of fire?"

"I knew you'd be there, just like you knew that I'd be there when you knocked that first guy off balance and then locked up the second guy. It was the last threat, you didn't have anything else to worry about but him. I knew you were right behind me and it only made sense that you'd deflect his attack away from me."

I wasn't good at the tiny, delicate stitches you needed to hold broken arteries together, but it was too late to do anything but keep going. A normal person wouldn't even have been able to see well enough to have operated under these circumstances, but my vision seemed just barely up to the task. I hadn't ever realized before how much brighter the life-glow was to fresh-spilled blood. It was faint when I was in normal human form, but it still served as a softly glowing beacon that told me exactly where I needed to go to find each torn vein or artery.

"I'm just glad that you didn't hit me with those last two shots."

"There was almost no chance of that. I held the shot until you ducked and then I took him in the head. Do you want me to try to tie up one of these?"

"No, there's only the one needle that was pre-threaded. You'd need both hands to thread it and get started. I'm not sure she can take that much blood loss. I'm just about done here, keep the pressure on her for a few more seconds and then I'll start on one of those. You have any miracles in one of those packs?"

"We've got a couple of saline bags, but that isn't going to do anything to keep her blood oxygen level from crashing."

"No, but it may be enough to keep her heart from stopping. Okay, move your right hand now."

Under normal circumstances the hole revealed as Ash got out of my way would have gushed blood. It was the worst rip I'd tried to repair yet, but her blood pressure was dropping to the point where there wasn't a whole lot left for her to lose.

I got the first stitch in place and started swearing under my breath as I realized that I should have put an IV into her before we started on these last two tears. It was too late to reverse course now; if we put pressure back on the tear now we might rip the stitch out and make things even worse. I had to just finish stitching her up quickly.

The second-to-last stitch went in with less fuss than usual and I started the last stitch with hands that had started to shake a little.

"As soon as I get this tied off you need to run and grab those bags of saline."

"No, you should do it so I don't have to take pressure off of her."

"I suck at running an IV, Ash. Always have, probably always will. Besides, I don't know where you guys have that stuff squirreled away."

"Fine, I'll get it, but we move her first. I'll hold pressure on her, you pick her up, and then I'll run the IV as soon as we have somewhere to hang it from."

I grunted an agreement as I cut the thread and then it was time to lift her into the car. There was so much blood that I almost couldn't believe she was still alive. The fading glow painted across her as red blood cells started dying was beyond eerie. It wasn't until my shaking got worse that I realized that a lot of the blood was mine.

Ash set what I was pretty sure was a world record and had the IV run and a bag of saline hanging from the passenger seat in seconds.

"I'm not sure I can do this last one, Ash. I'm starting to get lightheaded."

"It's just one more set of stitches, Isaac, you can do it and then you can stop and tape yourself up. I'll be back in a minute."

I wanted to argue with him, wanted to tell him that I was too far gone, but I couldn't seem to bring myself to say the words. I must have taken more damage in the fight than I'd realized, even this much blood loss shouldn't have impacted me this quickly.

My whole world narrowed down to the needle, thread, and the hole that I needed to close up. The tremble in my hands made things worse, but Ash had left the interior light on and the better visibility helped compensate for the shake.

Either all of the practice was taking effect already, or someone besides just Ash and I really wanted Kristin to live. The first stitch went in perfectly and the next one was almost as good.

After what felt like forever I pulled the last stitch tight and tied it off.

Ash stuck his head inside the car to check that I was done and then grabbed me by one arm and helped get me up into the back seat as he passed me a gigantic roll of medical tape.

"That will have to be good enough. Get started on yourself before you lose any more blood. We have to get out of here before the fire draws the cops and more of Onyx's people."

I stared dumbly at the tape for a second before looking around. "What fire?"

"The one that is going to start in fifteen minutes when the time-delay fuses on the two incendiary grenades I jammed inside of their car go off."

Ash threw the SUV into gear and took off like we were already being chased by the cops. I wanted to just lie down and close my eyes, but something told me that would be a very bad idea.

I forced myself to start taping up the huge hole in my side. Ash looked back at me and frowned. "How much blood have you lost?"

"Honestly, I have no idea, but it must have been a lot. I can't remember the last time I was this loopy."

For some reason that struck me as being incredibly funny. I started to laugh, but that just pulled on the wound in my side and sent me down a dizzying spiral of pain. I managed to get a hand out and stop myself from falling over, but the motion pulled at something inside my chest and got me started coughing.

"Isaac, you've got to work faster. I can't stop, and not just for Kristin. We've got to get out of this area or Onyx will find us."

I sucked down a couple of big gasps of air to oxygenate my blood enough to keep me from passing out, and then nodded as I ripped off another big strip of tape and used it to hold the edges of my stomach wound closed.

"I know. How long will it take us to get to the nearest hospital?"

"I think I can get us there in twenty minutes, maybe a minute or two faster if everything goes perfectly."

"You know that's the first place that Onyx will check, right?"

"Yeah, I know. We don't have any other choice though. We've got to get some blood inside of Kristin and get her on oxygen or she'll never make it. Honestly, the way you're looking we probably need to get a bag of saline and some oxygen into you too."

The image of Ash trying to sneak a canister of oxygen out of the hospital under his jacket struck me as being so funny that I nearly broke out into laughter again, but I'd learned my lesson the time before.

"I'm not complaining, just trying to make sure you're working on a plan. I'm not going to be good for much of anything once we get there, so I can't bail you out this time."

"Your vote of confidence is absolutely overwhelming, but yes, I'm working on it."

"That's good then. I'm just going to close my eyes then."

"Did you get yourself all taped up?"

"I think so."

I wasn't positive I had, but I couldn't keep my eyes open any longer. Whatever I'd managed to get done was just going to have to be good enough.

"Okay, hold on the best you can. I'll have us there soon. And, Isaac..."

"Yeah?"

"Thanks for taking care of Kristin and helping me keep things together."

"No problem. You would have done the same for me if it had been Jess."

"Yeah, yeah, I would have."

Chapter 8

Isaac Nazir
River Parishes Hospital
New Orleans, Louisiana

I must have fallen asleep at some point. I came back to myself enough to be aware of my surroundings about two minutes before we arrived at the hospital.

The relief in Ash's voice when I asked him how close we were was palpable. I stripped off what was left of my ha'bit and used it to wipe away the worst of the blood before I slipped my clothes back on.

I rolled out of the vehicle as soon as Ash pulled up to the emergency room entrance, and the two of us carried Kristin inside of the hospital. It was like walking into a tidal wave. Within seconds of stepping inside the modern-looking, gray building we were surrounded by people in blue hospital scrubs, all of who were asking us what had happened as they took Kristin out of our arms and placed her on a bed.

Ash handled things much better than I would have. He'd had the benefit of being able to plan out his story while I'd been passed out, but even so I couldn't have done as good of a job throwing everyone off of the truth.

Within seconds he had everyone convinced that Kristin had been attacked by a mountain lion. It wasn't a perfect match to her wounds, not unless someone had run across a new breed of cat that had six-inch claws, but at that point the doctors were more concerned with getting Kristin into an operating room than with poking holes in Ash's story.

He made sure that the surgeon knew that we'd stitched up the worst of the vascular damage, told one of the nurses that I was in shock and in need of some oxygen, and then disappeared back into the night.

I tried to wave the nurse off—by that time I was feeling much steadier than I'd been in the car—but she was pretty insistent. In the end I decided not to fight her. Even shape shifters don't bounce back instantly from that kind of blood loss, so I figured it was only a matter of time before the adrenaline wore off and I'd be back to staggering around like a drunk.

Ash showed back up to my room fifteen minutes later with all three bug-out bags.

"I checked with a nurse on my way back in. They've got her in surgery. It will probably be another couple of hours before we know anything substantial, but from what I could hear from outside the operating room it sounded like they have her on oxygen and are transfusing blood."

"Good, if she's made it this long then she'll be okay. Once they get her hematocrit and blood pressure back up then the only other thing to worry about is infection."

"Yeah, if we can avoid Onyx's people long enough for the doctors to finish stabilizing her then she's got a good chance. One of the doctors was admiring your handiwork, by the way. Craziest thing I've ever seen. You can't run an IV, but you stitched her up like a pro."

"I got lucky. You should see Donovan. He's better than most doctors with ten years of experience under their belts. He's the one who taught me how to sew up an artery like that. He insisted that we all learn what he called 'the basics of first aid.' With the constant low-level conflict between us and Brandon's pack we got lots of chances to practice our skills. It wasn't until I got quite a bit older that I realized that he'd essentially given us a residency as surgeons. I think that Alec realized how much more Donovan was teaching us than he was letting on, but Alec never said anything, never complained or let on that he knew."

Ash nodded. "I can't say that I'm surprised about Alec or Donovan either one. Donovan is one of those rare treasures you don't come across very often. It says a lot about Alec's judgment that he's listened so closely to Donovan's advice for so many years."

"Yeah, I guess you're right. It's hard to think of Donovan as being something unusual. He's just been there for as long as I can remember. He's...well, he's just Donovan."

"That's a common tendency, but in my experience it's a dangerous way to think. It's all too easy to miss out on greatness when you do that. Just because you know someone doesn't mean that they can't be world-class at something. You wouldn't dream of saying that Thanatas or Jaldul were *just* Thanatas and Jaldul, but you think nothing of saying that about Alec."

I was too tired to get really indignant over anything, but I could feel the faintest stirrings of unhappiness from my beast. It was the kind of early-warning system that I had to heed these days.

"I saved your life and your girlfriend's life today. Can you just do me a favor and give the recriminations and sermons a rest for a few hours?"

"Sure thing. Sorry, I guess trying to teach Kristin everything she needed to know over the last few months has me in lecture mode."

We sat in silence for several minutes before I pulled the mask back off and turned off the oxygen.

"So, did you come up with a plan or are we just screwed?"

Ash pulled out a small black box and looked at it for a couple of seconds before stuffing it back into his pocket and turning back to me.

"Just wanted to make sure that nobody's planted a bug in here. In answer to your question, some of both. By now I expect that our SUV is gone. I stripped the plates off of it and then turned it on, left the doors unlocked and walked away. We'll have to buy or steal something when it's time to leave, but that shouldn't be too much of a problem. I can boost most of the older cars in less than two minutes."

"What about the police?"

"I stripped the barrel out of my gun on the way here and tossed it in the bayou. I took care of Kristin's a few minutes ago. I wiped it down and then jammed it down into the grass with my foot. The police will search the scene of the fight and if they track us here they'll search us and any dumpsters, but they'll never think to take a metal detector out there and sweep the lawn."

"Does that mean you're unarmed now?"

Ash shook his head and tapped the magazine he had sitting in his lap. "Spare barrel. It's cheaper than just tossing the weapon and goes a long way towards making it so the police can't tie your weapon to the incident."

"So there's nothing left to tie us to the fight then."

"Some tire tracks, but we used a pseudonym when we purchased the SUV, so even if the police eventually track it down they won't have anything other than Kristin's DNA."

"So we're the evidence then."

"I'm afraid so. I'm not too worried about the cops coming at us from that direction though. Even if they find it tonight they won't do much with the crime scene before the sun comes up. The more urgent worry is that the hospital will call the precinct and let them know that they've got someone here who looks like she might be the victim of a stabbing or other violent crime."

"So what's your brilliant plan there?"

"You're my brilliant plan." Ash gestured at the black bags. "All of your favorite toys are in there. My bet is that nobody will call the police before the surgeons finish up with Kristin because they'll want to have the full story. If you can hack their email and phone system within the next couple of hours then the police won't know we were even here until we're long gone."

"That's your big plan?"

Ash shrugged. "I didn't have a lot to work with. Besides, you said it's easier to do this kind of thing from inside the facility."

I closed my eyes and counted to ten.

"Sure, it would be easier if I had access to one of the nurses' terminals. Working on their public wi-fi isn't going to be any easier than attacking from the outside."

"I don't think it would be a good idea to go walking around in the hopes of sneaking some time on an unlocked terminal. I'm pretty sure that the nurses have instructions to keep an eye on us in case the doctors decide that we are accessories to some kind of crime."

"You think?"

The barest hint of a smile played at the edge of Ash's lips as he closed his eyes. "Be nice, Isaac, or I might not give you the present that I picked up for you just outside the gift shop."

Before I could come up with a suitably biting response Ash pulled a tablet out from where he'd wedged it between the magazine and his gun.

"The unlock code the nurse used is two-four-two-five. Hopefully that will help."

"What are you going to be doing while I desperately try to save our bacon?"

"I'm going to take a nap. If things go as badly as I think they might, then it might be a while before I'll get another chance to sleep."

I almost said something cutting about him being a cold monster if he was really going to be able to sleep while his girlfriend was being operated on, but I thought better of it at the last second. Ash could be cold when the situation warranted it, but he was right. We didn't both need to be awake right now and if we were forced to make a run for it then sleep might get really hard to come by.

I unlocked the nurse's tablet and breathed a silent sigh of relief when I saw that it was one of the operating systems that I was most familiar with. It only took me a couple of minutes to pull the file containing all of the encrypted passwords and transfer it over to my own tablet. I plugged my tablet in and then pulled up my decryption program and hoped that the hospital's IT staff was less paranoid than most.

The decryption program was good—I'd written it myself when I'd found backdoors in both of the off-the-shelf programs that I'd downloaded five years ago—but if it had to brute-force its way to a solution by trying every possible combination then we'd be in for a really, really long wait. Our only hope was that the IT staff used something relatively easy to remember so that they didn't have to enter a long string of random characters each time they got a new batch of thirty or forty tablets that needed to be configured *yesterday*.

While my tablet was beating on the password file, I grabbed the tablet Ash had lifted for me, pulled it out of the hospital-issue cover so that it wouldn't be quite so conspicuous, and started loading it up with all of my favorite utilities.

The port scanner I was running on the hospital tablet finished up about the same time that I started investigating the phone next to my bed. It was a power-over-Ethernet model, which meant that I was going to have less difficulty tracking down the system that ran the phones than I'd been worrying I might.

I took a deep breath and dived into the toughest hack I'd ever attempted. Ash hadn't really understood what he was asking when he'd suggested that I crack a professional-grade system in no more than two or three hours with two tablets and no advance legwork.

It took me forty minutes to penetrate the network deeply enough to bring down the mail servers. I knew there was no way I was going to get root access to the mail system, so I didn't even try. Instead I started suborning all of the desktop computers I could get my hands on.

It took me three tries to figure out which antivirus program the hospital was running, but once I guessed right I started loading up a Trojan horse that convinced the users to enter the right set of keystrokes to turn off their antivirus program. Once that happened, I loaded up another virus which accessed each computer's mail client and started sending emails consisting of varying numbers of random words out of a dictionary to every user in their email address book.

It wasn't anything I'd designed, I just downloaded it from one of the better-known hacker sites and input a few key variables. It wouldn't stop the IT department for long. Once they realized that they had more than a dozen compromised computers they'd just manually turn back on the antivirus software, but given the lateness of the hour and the fact that the emails were just emails, without any kind of malicious component, I was banking on the IT guys waiting to take care of things until the normal day staff arrived.

By then the email servers would be buried in such a large backlog of unsent mail messages that any legitimate traffic would be queued up behind hours of garbage. The police would still eventually get any email notifications sent their way by the hospital, but I'd purchased us several hours.

The phone system was harder to deal with. I considered trying to bring it down with some kind of denial-of-service attack, but that felt like the kind of thing that would prompt a more immediate response from the IT staff. Not only that, it wouldn't do anything about people's cell phones and if I did cut the hospital off from all outside communication then people might die as a result.

It took me another hour and a half of furious effort to hack my way into the phone system. Working under a time crunch was bad enough, but I also had a nurse checking up on me every twenty minutes and she was obviously becoming more suspicious of me each time she stopped by.

Our cover story was that Kristin was my sister and Ash's wife, so I told the nurse that I was corresponding with my parents, who were out of the country and only able to communicate via email, but even I knew my excuse was wearing thin.

Once I finally found a way inside the hospital's phone system I rerouted all outgoing calls to the police department over to the phone beside my bed. I collapsed back against the pillows, exhausted, a couple of minutes before the surgeon finished up with Kristin and came to find us.

I heard him talking to the nurse out in the hall and went out to meet them so that we wouldn't wake Ash up. I knew Ash would probably be pissed that I hadn't shaken him awake, but it served him right after dumping such a difficult hack in my lap.

"Excuse me, doctor. Is there any word on my sister? She's the redhead who was attacked by the mountain lion."

"Yes, Mr. Parks. She's out of surgery and seems to be stable. We had to redo a couple of the sutures to make sure that she wouldn't have circulatory issues later on, but I have to say that she's a lucky woman. I think she's going to make a full recovery. The nurses said that you were the one who sewed her up?"

I nodded and tried for the right combination of relief combined with crushing exhaustion. It wasn't hard, as that was exactly what I was feeling once you filtered out an intense fear that

Onyx or the Coun'hij were going to show up at any minute.

"Yeah. I was doing a surgical residency in Maine, but my parents got sick last year and I had to take a leave of absence."

"Are you planning on returning and finishing up your residency?"

"I'm not sure. Before I left, the pressure was really getting to me. It's a pretty sad state of affairs when the first thing you feel upon hearing that your parents are severely sick is relief because you know it will mean that you can get away from the hospital to do something besides just sleeping for the first time in months."

He hadn't been expecting that, I could tell by the way that he stopped to consider his response. "For what it's worth, I think you should go back and finish up. It wasn't that long ago that I was doing my residency; I remember the pressure and you're right about it being brutal, but it's also worth it in the end. You've got a real gift, I can't imagine trying to sew someone up like that with nothing but an interior dome light and a flashlight for illumination."

I mustered an exhausted smile and nodded. "Thanks, I'm just glad that it looks like she's going to be okay. Maybe you're right. I've been leaning that way anyway if for no other reason than I'm not sure how else I'll pay down my student loans. That's going to be hard enough on a doctor's salary, I'm not sure it will even be possible on what I make right now."

I turned to go, but he stopped me with a hand on my arm.

"Mr. Parks, what actually happened out there?"

"I'm sorry?"

"Those wounds weren't inflicted by a mountain lion. They were too deep. I'd say that you and her husband did it to her, but you're obviously hiding injuries yourself and he's got a couple of bruises that I'm not sure your sister could have dished out even if she used a crowbar on him. I've been doing this for long enough to know what the police are going to think if I send this over without more information than I have right now."

The gears inside of my mind spun furiously for several seconds. I'd gone too far in my attempt to bond with the good doctor. I'd figured that my hacks would buy us the time we needed to get Kristin out of the hospital, but if he was becoming personally invested in our situation then he wouldn't just wait for the email backlog to clear out, he'd call the cops himself.

"Honestly? I'm not sure. It started out on four legs—at least I think that was what I saw. It was just so fast. One second it was down close to the ground and then it was tall. It knocked me down and was on top of my sister before any of us could react. Her husband shot it with his gun and it turned and ran away."

For a second there was something in the backs of his eyes that told me I'd struck some kind of nerve with my story, but it only lasted a split second before his professional skepticism reasserted itself.

"Are you trying to tell me that a monster of some kind did this to her?"

A laugh burst out of me and I noticed in passing that it had a nice touch of hysteria to it. "We're screwed. I knew someone would question the wounds. I told him that there wasn't any way real doctors would believe that a mountain lion could inflict wounds that deep, but we didn't know what else to tell people. Saying that some kind of monster did it is like asking to be committed, but he didn't want the cops to know that he'd been carrying a weapon illegally.

"He's got a permit back home, but it's no good for Louisiana. We weren't even planning on stopping. The original plan was to just drive straight through but my sister wanted to get some pictures so we decided to stop and campout for one night..."

Doctor Hamilton held up a hand to interrupt the flow of words. "Okay, the first thing you need to do is calm down. Fortunately for you I'm inclined to believe you. I did my residency down five minutes from the Mexican border. These days it seems like the gangs down there are plenty flush with guns, but a few years ago that wasn't the case. I've seen my share of knife fights and I've never seen anything like this.

"You're a big guy, you could probably take someone apart like this with a sword, even a short one, but I'm not so sure you could do it with a knife as short as this one would have had to have been. I know a guy who does forensic work on cadavers for the FBI. We took extensive pictures while we had your sister opened up."

"So you'll send him the pictures and he may be able to prove that we didn't do it?"

"Yeah, it's not guaranteed, but it's a start and it gives me a reason to wait to call the authorities. With any luck he'll come back with something that will give the police enough of a pause once I do file my report that they'll choose to just keep an eye on you until your sister wakes up and can collaborate your story."

I reached out and took his hand in both of mine, shaking it with the unbridled relief of an innocent man learning he was going to dodge the electric chair.

"Thank you, Doctor Hamilton. I never in a million years thought we'd find someone willing to give us the benefit of the doubt like this. Between that and finding out that Kris is going to be okay, well, I feel like the hall is spinning."

I let myself sway a little, which prompted him to reach back out to steady me.

"Let's get you back to your bed and look at those wounds."

I shook my head as he guided me back into my room and helped me back down onto the bed. "Can you please look in on my sister again and get those photos sent off to your friend first? I'll be fine for a few more minutes and it would mean a lot to know that she was still okay."

He gave me a considering look, but nodded. "All right, but don't go anywhere. I'm worried about your wounds and wouldn't want anything to happen to you."

I gave him my best honest face and relaxed back into the bed in an attempt to put him at ease. He nodded to a familiar-looking blonde nurse as he left my room and turned right to go check up on Kristin, cell phone already out and dialing.

I still had five minutes before my scheduled check-in with my nurse, so I offered this nurse a wan smile in the hopes that she'd move on. It didn't work.

She walked into my room and looked down at her aluminum clipboard as she closed the door. Alarm bells started going off inside of my head a split second before she kicked Ash's feet off of the low table where he'd propped them when he'd fallen asleep.

"It's amazing that you've managed to survive this long on your own if this is the kind of mess you typically make of things."

LOST

I expected Ash to pull a knife on her. Dangerous people are always the most unpredictable when waking up somewhere that isn't completely safe. This seemed like the perfect situation to have Ash go off like a crate of dynamite, only he didn't.

"Hi, Celeste. It's nice to see you, too."

Ash didn't seem surprised that the nurse in our room was ready to rip his head off, but I rolled out of the bed and subtly lowered my center of gravity into something that wasn't quite a crouch, ready to respond if things heated up even more.

I opened my mouth to ask what was going on, but before I got my question out the nurse stepped forward and picked Ash up by the shirt collar, slamming him against the wall with enough force that I wondered if there was anyone in the next room over to hear the impact.

"You piece of trash. Do you have any idea the mess you left behind when you left here? Do you know what I had to do to keep your secret? You put me through nine kinds of hell and never bothered to even call and tell me that you'd survived. Then a few months ago you call and tell me that some Ancient from south of the border is tearing through the western half of the country and please can I figure out a way to stop him before he kills you? Oh, and while I'm at it is there any way I can arrange to keep the fact that you were my anonymous tipster quiet?

Don't you know that you're supposed to grow up to be less of an ass rather than more of one?"

The surge of energy coming off of her put to rest any question as to what we were dealing with. To summon that kind of raw boiling energy she had to be a shape shifter, and she wasn't just a wolf, she was one of the more naturally powerful hybrids I'd ever come up against.

Ash was in terrible danger. She'd positioned herself perfectly to rip his head off with her claws if she shifted forms. I'd taken a step towards the two of them when she grabbed him, but now I froze, not wanting to do anything to push her over the edge into a transformation.

It wasn't until I looked back over at Ash that I realized why he was still eerily calm. Having Celeste kick his feet off of the table like that should have sent the sports magazine on his lap tumbling to the ground. It hadn't because he hadn't been asleep.

Something had woken him up before she walked into the room and he'd anticipated her actions, up to and including the fact that she was going to manhandle him. Ash was calm because he still had a measure of control over the situation.

The magazine hadn't gone crashing to the floor, but more importantly the silenced pistol underneath it hadn't ever left Ash's hand. It was now pressed up against the nurse's chest, silencer and all.

"If it helps, I'm sorry about the way things went down. There are some things I'd probably do differently if I had it all to do over again, but this is the last time you put your hands on me, *sis*. The next time you put yourself in a position where you could kill me, I won't hesitate to pull the trigger."

I felt like I'd been hit by a baseball bat. I should have seen it before she even made it inside of the room. The resemblance was incredible. They both had the same straight blond hair and similar features.

On Ash they looked good, but his sister was nothing less than gorgeous. She had the delicate cheeks and chin of an angel, and a body that, even under stolen hospital scrubs, I could tell was perfect.

Somewhere along the way she'd acquired the toned, hard build of a dedicated athlete without losing the femininity I'd always found so attractive in Jess, but it was her eyes that most captivated me. They were an incredible shade of gray that had depths to it that I'd never seen anywhere else. Right now they were filled with heat, not all of which was directed away from me, but it was still all I could do to pull my gaze away from hers when she glanced back to confirm that I was still outside of striking range.

"You wouldn't dare shoot me, Ashley."

Ash looked like he wanted to flinch when she used his full name, but his hand stayed rock-solid.

"I think that you'd be surprised at what I'd be willing to do, Celeste. I've studied under some people over the last few years who were every bit as hard and unforgiving as you or Mom. Isaac and I just finished killing four of the Coun'hij enforcers Onyx had out looking for us. One of them got their claws into Kristin, but the rest of us all walked away under our own power. That should give you an idea of just how dangerous I've become since we last saw each other."

Celeste looked back at me appraisingly. "He doesn't look that impressive. This Kristin chick must be hell on wheels."

"Isaac would surprise you, but Kristin is a normal human. She's pretty good with a gun, but she didn't uncork some puissant ability and magically eliminate two or three of the opposition hybrids if that is what you're thinking."

For the first time since she'd entered the room, Ash's sister looked uncertain of herself. It had been obvious that Ash hadn't been lying when he said that we'd just finished mopping up a hit squad that would have been capable of taking down some small packs.

"I'm not bluffing, Celeste. If you don't put me down in the next ten seconds I'll shoot you and deal with the consequences of having one more dead body on my hands."

"You're a better liar than you used to be. You'd never get a shot off before I transformed and cut your throat. Even if you did, it would take more than one shot to stop me."

"Maybe, but I can guarantee you won't be beating Isaac with a bullet lodged up against your heart. Two seconds."

It was like watching two trucks filled with explosives slide towards each other across a sheet of ice. Everything was happening in slow motion. It felt like I should have been able to do something to stop the wreck from happening, but I couldn't.

Celeste thought she was still dealing with the same scared teenager who had left home more than a decade before. Even worse, she probably had the same stubborn streak that caused Ash to consistently throw himself into fights that he shouldn't have been able to win.

That was the thing though. He did tend to win them. Ash had learned that the only way to be respected by a dominant was to be willing to put his life on the line to back up his position. This was the most important interaction he was ever going to have with his sister. If he backed down now then he was always going to be working at a disadvantage. It was the first step in a dance that would ultimately lead to her bossing him around for however long they were together.

If there was one thing that I knew about Ash, it was that he would die before he'd become a slave to his sister or anyone else. More

DEAN MURRAY

importantly, he'd kill in order to avoid having his choices taken away like that.

It was surprising in someone trained by spies, but he viewed the world through the same lens as the shape shifters from a thousand years ago. Once he was your man he'd endure terrible things on your behalf, but his loyalty wasn't something that could be taken by force.

For Ash it was all one long, unbreakable chain. If he backed down now then it was just a matter of time before his sister would push him too far and he'd be forced to try and kill her. It was now or never. She had to accept him as an equal, as a possible rival, or all bets were off.

They were frozen for one impossibly long second with Celeste's hands against Ash's throat, suspending him in the air and his gun dimpling the fabric of her scrubs. I was positive that neither of them was going to blink, and then Celeste's phone buzzed with an incoming text. It gave her an excuse, a way of backing down that was external to the two of them and the standoff that they'd locked themselves inside of.

I was watching closely enough to see Ash's finger start to take up the slack on his trigger as his deadline wound down, but his sister set him back down a fraction of a second before her time ran out. As she fished her phone out of her back pocket I wondered if she knew how close he'd come to shooting her. I hoped so. It would probably avoid a lot of issues down the road if she understood that Ash wasn't going to back down.

"One of my people back at the house just texted me to let me know that Onyx received a call a few minutes ago that has him nine different kinds of excited. He jumped in his car and drove away in a hurry. Any bets as to why?"

Ash closed his eyes for a single second. It was his way of preparing himself for what we all knew was coming.

"He just found out we're here. How long do we have before his people start arriving?"

"If I knew that I'd be prescient and I would have killed him off long ago. It all depends on who he's got out helping the enforcers the Coun'hij sent down to look for you and how close they happen to be. My person back at the house would have spent a couple of minutes getting somewhere safe before they texted me. People could show up within the next five minutes. You might have more than that, but he'll be here himself within the next fifteen minutes. What's your escape plan?"

Ash tossed me two of the bug-out bags and headed towards the door with the other one. "I'm not sure; I'll let you know as I figure it out."

Celeste brushed past me, hot on Ash's heels.

"You came here without a plan?" Her question came out in a hiss that was too faint for the humans at the nursing station to hear.

"Of course not. The plan was to talk to the lamias, find out where Dream Stealer is and then go and kill him. We've just run up against some problems that I haven't finished working my way around yet."

"Ashley! What the hell are you thinking? We don't talk about them outside of the family."

Ash stepped up to the nursing station, but he got one last jab in. "It's Ash now, and these days Isaac is more my family than you are—it's been at least a day and a half since he threatened to kill me."

The nurse looked up as Ash put his free hand, the one not buried inside of his bag to hide the fact that he was carrying a huge semi-automatic with a silencer on it, on the counter in front of her.

"I'm sorry to bother you, but where did they take my wife? She's got some allergies that her brother wasn't aware of and I need to make sure that they haven't given her anything that will send her into shock."

"You got married without telling me!"

Celeste's exclamation was nearly loud enough for the nurse to hear, but Ash's expression didn't flicker at all.

"I can pull up her list of medications right here, sir, and make sure that she hasn't been given anything problematic. Then we can enter a note on her file and make sure that nobody gives her anything they shouldn't."

Between the news that Onyx was on his way, probably with half a dozen or more hybrids to back him up, and the tension between Ash and his sister I already had a confused, worried expression on my face. I amped it up to eleven and made sure that the nurse saw it before I turned and started down the hall in the direction her doctor had come from.

"There isn't time; someone could be sticking it in her IV drip right now! I'll start checking rooms down here."

I could hear the nurse's gasp from twenty feet away. She was probably worried about lawsuits and losing her job. Given the ongoing, low-level concerns with terrorism for the last several years, having someone of Middle-Eastern descent running around the hospital screaming was the kind of thing that could start a panic, but Ash didn't give her a chance to think of calling security.

"Crap. He's incredibly protective of her. Quick, which room is she in? It's the only way to stop him from searching the whole hospital."

"Second floor, room 236."

I spied an elevator bank off to my left, but I didn't wait for it. I threw open the heavy gray door to the stairwell and went up the stairs three at a time. Ash and Celeste were only about a second behind me.

"I didn't get married, not yet at least—we are waiting for her to turn eighteen first. It's just a cover story so that they'll keep us in the loop on her status and not go hunting her parents down."

"Wait, your girlfriend is seventeen? Please tell me that she's seventeen. If you're dating a sixteen-year-old I swear I'll kill you myself."

"We don't have time for this, Celeste. How well do you know this hospital?"

"Better than you do."

"Then lead or get out of the way, but either way shut up."

I stopped in the hallway, looking both directions in an effort to figure out the hospital's numbering system, and Celeste brushed past me.

"Intensive care is this way, but this conversation isn't over. Mom and I raised you better than this—I'm not going to just sit around while you date someone half your age. That's statutory...it's just wrong."

It took us less than thirty seconds to get to Kristin's room with Celeste leading the way. We weren't running, but most people would have had to run to keep up with us.

"What's the best way out of here, sis?"

Ash flipped up the thin blanket covering Kristin and slid his bag underneath her bare legs as he waited for a response from Celeste.

"There are only two main entrances with two larger parking lots and half a dozen smaller ones scattered around the periphery of the building. Do you guys have a vehicle?"

I shook my head as I slipped my bags under Kristin and then covered her back up. The bags were only marginally less conspicuous this way, but it was better than nothing.

"We were going to buy or steal one once we knew Kristin was going to be okay. No time for anything other than stealing one now."

Ash already had the wheels on the bed down and was moving the IV bag over so it was suspended from the bed rather than the freestanding rod next to the bed.

"Whoever trained you was an idiot. My car is in the west parking lot, we'll take it."

I grabbed the wires running between Kristin and the bank of expensive monitors next to her and disconnected them with a single powerful pull that would have made Donovan flinch. The computers at the nurse's station started beeping as soon as the monitors were disconnected, but it would be a few seconds before anyone made it over to Kristin's room.

Ash patted the bed as he looked at his sister. "Hop up there and give everyone a show so they don't stop to think about the fact that we're stealing one of their patients."

Celeste didn't look particularly happy to be taking orders from her kid brother, but it wasn't a bad plan, all things considered. She climbed up on the bed, straddled Kristin's chest, pointed to the left, and then we were out in the hall.

I took the front of the bed, but I didn't really need to pull it along at all, Ash provided all of the propulsion anyone could have possibly wanted, all I needed to do was just steer the rocket ship as it went screaming down the hall.

"Call the dialysis unit and tell them we'll be there in four minutes and they need to be ready for us!"

Celeste was a better actor than I would have given her credit for. She managed to sound terrified but in control and anyone watching us from the nursing station wouldn't have been able to tell that she wasn't actually compressing Kristin's chest.

"That should buy us some time assuming that we're actually headed in the direction of the dialysis unit."

Celeste shot her brother a dirty look as she bent down and pretended to give Kristin mouth-to-mouth.

"Of course the dialysis is this direction. Turn left at the next intersection and then hang a right at the end of the hall. The stairs we want are sixty yards further along."

Supernatural strength is nice, but it only lets you do so much without decent traction. At the speed that Ash was moving it was all I could do to keep us from crashing into the wall. My feet slid across six feet of slick linoleum floor before the leading edge of my shoes slammed into the far wall and gave me something substantial to push against.

Celeste wasn't ready for the sudden change in direction and started toppling over as I muscled the bed around and got it headed the right direction again. When Ash slid into the same wall and the back end of the bed changed directions it was too much for her and she nearly took a header into the wall. She saved herself by grabbing a bar on the bed, but it was a close thing and she bent the slender metal in the process.

The deformed bar made me revise my estimate of her strength up a couple notches. You didn't do something like that in human form without having some weight behind you and on her it was obviously all muscle.

"Some warning next time would be good so I don't accidentally put my knee into your girlfriend's chest and start her bleeding again. It would be a pity to have her die in the middle of your heroic escape attempt."

"Yeah, but not as much of a shame as having all of us die because we didn't make it out of here before Onyx showed up with his goons. We're turning now."

Ash hadn't slowed down at all, but I was ready for the turn this time. I started trying to change direction at the earliest possible second and then checked myself with a hand against the wall a split second after my feet slid into it. The extra leverage was enough for me to bring the bed around despite the greater speed that Ash had carried into the second turn.

"Nice trick, but you would have looked kind of stupid if you'd put your hand through the wall."

Ash had taken off all the stops, we were practically flying down the hall as I looked over at Celeste.

"I could see the texture change where they'd put nails through the sheetrock and hit the stud underneath. I hit the wall directly over the stud, so I knew I'd be okay."

She muttered something under her breath that sounded a bit like "speaking of wannabe studs" and then a few seconds later Ash and I started decelerating the bed to make sure that we wouldn't overshoot the door to the stairwell.

"Elevator?"

Ash shook his head at Celeste. "There isn't time. Jump off, we're taking the stairs and we don't need any extra weight in the mix."

Celeste jumped off of the bed with all of the lithe grace I would have expected from that slender, toned body, and made it to the stairwell door before us. She held it open so we didn't even have to slow down until we hit the actual stairs.

The table was heavier than I expected it to be. Between the steel frame, the mattress, bedding, Kristin, and our bags it felt like it was pushing five hundred pounds. Normally I would have said that I couldn't have carried that much weight with my arms extended up above my head, but I managed to take it down the entire flight of stairs without jostling Kristin badly enough to make her fall off of the bed.

Maybe it wasn't as heavy as I thought, or maybe the adrenaline floating through my bloodstream made me stronger than normal. Either way, I was relieved as we exited the stairwell and saw the entrance less than twenty yards away.

We got a couple of odd looks from people as we wheeled Kristin outside, but nobody tried to stop us. Once we left the sidewalks the going got rougher, a lot rougher. The wheels on the bed had been designed with smooth hallways in mind and didn't function nearly as well on the asphalt surface of the parking lot.

Celeste came up to the other side of the bed from me and latched onto the frame. "Just pick it up and carry it. I'm over here on the right."

A muted grunt from Ash signaled that he'd picked up his end, and then things got much smoother. I thought we had it made until I heard footsteps behind us and looked back to see a tall blond guy chasing us.

Celeste saw him too and nearly tripped. "Ash, that's Nicolas. He's Onyx's right-hand man. We're screwed."

Ash's voice had the calm, almost dead, overtones that he picked up when things were at their worst.

"Don't slow down. Get Kristin into the vehicle. I'll deal with this guy."

The back set of wheels hit the ground with enough force to make Kristin's teeth rattle and she groaned in pain despite all of the painkillers in her system, but Celeste and I shifted backwards so that we were carrying the bed from the middle without missing a step.

Ash opened fire on Nicolas as Celeste steered the bed towards a white Pathfinder. The shots were close together but still controlled as Ash slowly backed towards us.

"Help Ash!"

I shook my head at Celeste. "You heard him, he'll handle that guy. We've got to get Kristin and the bags into your car before more of them show up."

"You don't understand, Isaac. You don't just *handle* Nicolas. He's like a force of nature. Ash is in over his head, he just doesn't realize it."

Ash went to rapid fire and I looked back and saw that she was right. Opening fire on someone in a public place, even with a silenced pistol, even at six in the morning, was the kind of thing guaranteed to bring cops swarming over the area, but Nicolas had escalated things faster than I'd expected. He'd shifted into hybrid form and he was using the cars in the parking lot for cover as he worked his way towards Ash.

Nicolas, as a hybrid, was only an inch or two shorter than Jasmin was these days and he was fast, faster than anyone I'd ever seen other than Brandon. I shifted forms, in the middle of the parking lot, surrounded by who knew how many witnesses, and charged back to help Ash.

As Nicolas ducked behind another car I heard the slide on Ash's gun lock back and he turned and sprinted towards me across the black pavement as he reached for a fresh magazine. Ash made it exactly one step before Nicolas stepped out from behind the red car he'd been sheltering behind and chased after Ash with the ground-devouring run of a hybrid moving at full speed.

It took Ash two more steps to get a new magazine seated and spin back around so he could bring his weapon to bear again. I wasn't going to make it in time. I hadn't realized just how much ground Celeste and I had covered after Ash had stopped to engage Nicolas.

Ash's first round from the new magazine hit Nicolas in the chest. It was the perfect shot, his placement was flawless. It should have bored in between two ribs and taken Nicolas right in one of the chambers of his heart.

It didn't. It wasn't until Ash fired his next shot that it registered for me that I'd seen the bullet ricochet off of Nicolas and then strike sparks off of the ground a dozen yards away. I could see where the bullet had ripped a long furrow in his flesh, but it hadn't penetrated—and that shouldn't have been possible.

I'd hit people in that exact same spot and I knew for a fact that hybrids didn't come equipped with anything capable of turning a bullet in that part of their anatomy, but there wasn't any arguing with my own eyes.

I suddenly understood why Celeste had been so terrified.

Ash was still moving backwards, trying to close the distance between the two of us and buy me time to get there and help him. Working together was our only hope—neither of us had a chance of beating a monster like Nicolas was turning out to be.

Ash emptied the rest of his magazine as I took two more steps towards him and then turned back around. They were good shots, more than half of them hit. Nicolas was bleeding from more than a dozen different holes, some of them deep, but none of them were in vital spots.

Moving at a full sprint, Ash was capable of covering a lot of distance, but it was nothing compared to how fast Nicolas was moving. I was still three steps away from Ash when Nicolas reached him and I had a split second to realize that Ash's mistake had been slowing down to fire that last magazine.

Nicolas put his claws into Ash's back and ripped the entire right side of Ash's back and chest open. Ash went down in a spray of blood and then it was my turn.

LOST

I was moving at full tilt, but so was Nicolas so the advantage went to the biggest, heaviest guy, which wasn't me. We hit hard enough that I felt a couple of ribs crack with bright jolts of pain that I knew would turn into a special kind of stabbing agony once I shifted back to human form and didn't have the special benefits of a hybrid's nervous system muting the pain.

I managed to get a set of claws into his stomach before the impact sent me flying backwards. The feel of his flesh tearing underneath my claws was satisfying after what he'd done to Ash, but I knew it wasn't the kind of thing that was going to stop Nicolas.

We both rolled to our feet, but his blinding speed meant that I was only just able to get set before he was on me. I tried to circle to the right, but he just charged in, moving too quick for me to land anything other than glancing blows.

He buried his right hand into my gut all the way to his wrist and I realized that he was playing with me. He'd just marked me with the exact same wound that I'd inflicted on him only deeper and wider.

"I've been hoping I'd get a chance to go up against the best the Sanctuary pack had to offer ever since Graves sent our people home to us in cages. I didn't think I'd get the chance to realize that dream quite so quickly."

"Sorry to disappoint you, but I'm far from the best Sanctuary has to offer."

Before he could respond I did the absolute last thing he expected. It was something that Carson had showed me before he'd been killed fighting a werewolf the night of the assault on the estate.

Most hybrids would do everything they could to keep an opponent from getting around behind them. It was analogous to fighter pilots back in World War II. Once someone got behind you, your options were limited and if they got a good grip on you then you were as good as dead.

Carson had known a counter for that rule, a single instance when it was okay to turn your back on someone who was trying to kill you.

I locked my left hand around Nicolas' right wrist and then spun around, bringing my right arm back around behind him so that it pressed against his back as I pulled him across my hip. It bore a lot of resemblance to a classic judo takedown, just with the added risk that your enemy would rip you to shreds if you were too slow or didn't execute that technique just right.

The move went against every instinct I'd inherited from my beast. It required the kind of total commitment to the attack that I'd marveled at every time I saw Jasmin fight. All good techniques required a degree of commitment, a willingness to risk being hurt in return for hurting your opponent, but I'd always preferred stuff that involved less risk even though it often meant a longer, more drawn-out fight.

LOST

This technique was nothing at all like that. It was in-your-face dangerous for only moderate benefits, but I already knew I couldn't match Nicolas' speed, so fighting using my normal style wasn't going to work.

Unlike the last time I'd tried to use something that Carson had shown me, the throw worked. Nicolas' feet shot straight up into the air as I flipped him over my hip and threw him into the ground with as much force as I could muster.

I'd been hoping to break his neck, but rather than tightening up, he relaxed into the throw and controlled his descent enough that he was able to spread the impact out over one whole side of his body.

I kept hold of his wrist with the intention of throwing a joint lock on it, but he spun around before I could even begin to apply the arm bar. I should have let go of his arm and jumped backwards. I wasn't good enough with Carson's style of fighting to go up against someone who knew what they were doing, but I made the classic beginner's mistake and fixated on what I wanted to do to Nicolas rather than just responding to the fight as it developed.

A split second later I slammed into the ground with enough force to knock the wind out of me. I hadn't even seen his takedown coming.

"Isaac Nazir, second-in-command of the Sanctuary pack. Said to be Alec's strong right hand, a dependable if uninspired fighter who has more experience than you'd expect out of someone who's only seventeen, because he's spent the last several years in a constant series of low-level skirmishes against the other Sanctuary pack."

Nicolas had me in some kind of grappling hold. I tried to muscle my way free, but he manhandled me like I was a child. He had me stretched out with my arms at full extension, talons digging into my right arm and his claws locked on my left arm. His strength was incredible, but it hardly mattered. I'd been there before with Wyatt.

Wyatt, Carson and Grayson had been the only hybrids that I'd ever seen use the odd, grappling style of fighting that Nicolas was using against me now with such devastating results. I'd seen them in action and I knew that once an experienced grappler got hold of someone they were in trouble.

I didn't have the skills to get away from Nicolas now and Ash wasn't in any condition to come save me.

"You don't give yourself enough credit, Nazir. Admittedly, your showing has been pretty pathetic so far, but you're definitely the best the Sanctuary pack has to offer me. I can't fight Graves—not now that he's got a get-out-of-jail-free card—but at least I'll be able to say that I took down his second in command without breaking a sweat.

"I do have to say that you caught me by surprise with that hip throw. When exactly did Carson teach that to you? I never thought that old bag of bones would leave his precious haven."

The pressure on my arms was excruciating. I had to strain against him to stop from having my arms broken, but that was exactly what he wanted me to do. He had all of the leverage and he was just tiring me out so I wouldn't have any chance of breaking free when he finally went for a new hold.

My breath was coming in deep gasps now, but I still managed to respond to him. "Seriously, you need better intelligence. I wish I could be there when you finally go up against Jasmin. She's going to wipe the floor with you."

"The wolf? She's less than nothing."

"Funny, that's exactly what I was thinking of you."

He shifted his grip, flipping me over onto my stomach as he repositioned so he had a clear shot at my neck. I fought him with everything I had left, and it was almost enough. I could feel his arms starting to shake from the effort of containing me, but he was just too strong.

I screamed in pain as his claws sank even more deeply into my flesh. My timing was perfect. It took a very loud sound to mask the roar of an engine under hard acceleration, but I managed it.

Nicolas didn't hear Celeste's Pathfinder until the very last second.

She hit doing somewhere in excess of thirty miles per hour and I heard massive hybrid bones crunch.

He was between me and the vehicle, but a significant amount of the force of the impact was transmitted through his body and into me. We were both thrown across the parking lot, a cartwheeling maelstrom of claws and talons.

We came to rest separated by a distance of more than twenty feet and for nearly a second I couldn't get my body to move. I would have worried that I'd been paralyzed except for the fact that I could still feel my legs and they hurt too bad for the nerves between my head and toes to be anything other than still working normally.

I managed to pull myself up onto my feet and took an unsteady step towards Nicolas, but Celeste pulled me up short with a yell.

"No! There isn't time to finish him off; we have to get out of here before the rest of them get here."

I looked over to where she was pointing and saw four more hybrids headed our way. It was like something out of a nightmare. Under other circumstances nobody would have dared to let a fight escalate like this. The Coun'hij would have had all of our heads for this, but I was already a marked man. Apparently Nicolas and the others figured that killing me would buy them some leniency with Puppeteer and the rest.

Either way, the containment teams were going to have their work cut out for them this time. If the Coun'hij expected to keep this particular incident off of the national stage they were going to have to leave Oblivion down here for the next week or two.

I itched to cover the rest of the distance over to Nicolas and end him once and for all, but Celeste was right, the other four hybrids were just too close. Not only that, Nicolas was starting to stir.

I staggered over to Ash, picked him up, and carried him over to Celeste's Pathfinder. Three seconds later we were tearing out of the parking lot. I looked back and saw the other hybrids gathering around Nicolas just before we rounded a corner that hid them all from view.

As much as I might wish otherwise, I knew that we hadn't managed to kill Nicolas. It was too bad. I was pretty sure that I'd eventually end up fighting him again at some point and the odds were very good that I wouldn't survive our next meeting.

Chapter 9

Isaac Nazir
Highway 310
Eastern Louisiana

Once I was satisfied that the hybrids from the New Orleans pack weren't going to run us down and force me into another fight that I was nearly guaranteed to lose, I turned back to Ash. He still had a pulse and he was still breathing, but he was fading fast.

I tore open the bags we'd smuggled out of the hospital and swore when I found the first-aid kit. Neither Ash nor I had thought to pre thread the second needle after our adventure earlier that night.

"What's going on back there? He's still alive, right?"

The terror I'd heard in Celeste's voice hadn't ever really disappeared, its cause had just morphed as we'd narrowly avoided one catastrophe and plunged towards another.

"He's still alive right now, but he won't be for much longer unless I can get the bleeding under control."

I finally managed to get the needle threaded as Celeste flipped on the dome light. Then, for the second time in less than twenty-four hours, I stuck my hands inside one of my friends hoping that I'd be able to stop them from bleeding to death.

"Where are we headed?"

"Shouldn't you be concentrating on Ashley?"

I'd opened Ash up thinking that Nicolas couldn't have hit any major arteries, but I'd been wrong. Given the placement of the wound it would have been a small miracle for that to have been the case, but that hadn't stopped me from hoping.

"Yeah, I'll be plenty focused on sewing Ash up in about three seconds, but I haven't made it to the tricky part yet. Where are you taking us? They know what we're driving, what's your plan for slipping through whatever net they're trying to set up?"

The kidneys are a bad place to be stabbed or cut. There are a lot of blood vessels there and the main renal artery was capable of bleeding an average person out in something like a minute, with unconsciousness occurring in a quarter of that time.

Ash's right renal artery hadn't been severed or he would have already been dead, but it had been nicked. I went to start my first stitch, but then paused.

"Are we on a straightaway or are you about to throw us into a turn?"

"What? No, we'll be going straight for another minute or two, I'll warn you before that changes."

I slid the needle into Ash's renal artery and angled it so that the needle would come back out just above the tear.

Celeste sounded like she was shaking, but she kept the SUV steady. "I've got a boat about ten minutes from here. We can ditch the car and take the boat. That should give us a chance at losing Onyx's people."

I pulled the first stitch tight while she was talking and started on the second one. The first one had gone in about right, but I was worried about the second one. If I didn't pull it tight enough then Ash would bleed to death. If I pulled it too tight then the tear might not match up correctly and he'd still bleed to death.

"We can't stay on a boat forever. What do we do when it's time to return to dry land?"

"I'm still working on that part of the plan. If nothing else I can arrange to have a different car waiting for us somewhere else when it's time to come out of the swamp."

"So you're making this up as you go then?"

"Do you have a problem with that?"

The second stitch was done and the third one seemed to have the right amount of tension on it. I shook my head without looking up from Ash.

"No, surprisingly enough, I don't seem to have any kind of problem at all with that. I guess my beast sees the family resemblance too."

I could feel her staring daggers at me in the rearview mirror, but that was okay. She'd busted Ash's chops for not having a better plan for getting us out of the hospital, but she was apparently cut from the same cloth. As long as all she did was stare then I didn't care how pissed off she might be.

"Turning now."

Ash didn't have a lot of time to waste by that point. He'd lost a lot of blood already. I'd managed to slow the bleeding from the renal artery to something that was barely more than a trickle, but I was still worried about him.

Despite my concerns, I waited to start the second-to-last stitch until we were through the turn. I didn't want to risk tearing the artery open if we hit a bump—what I was doing was already dangerous enough.

The last two stitches went in without any problem and then I used what was left of his shirt to soak up the blood that had puddled inside of him so I could see where I had additional problems. There were a few, but none of them were as bad as I expected them to be.

We drove in silence for a couple more minutes as I tried to take care of all of the other places where blood was leaking out of his body. The fight seemed to have taken even more out of me than I'd realized, my vision was going blurry.

I did some quick math while I closed up a vein and came to a total number of hours since I'd last slept that was only just this side of dangerous. No wonder I was dragging. In the last thirty-six hours I'd been in two major fights, performed two emergency surgeries, hacked two separate systems inside the hospital and done it all without getting any sleep.

"Ash told you about the lamias?"

"Some. He seemed to think that they might be able to tell us where the Coun'hij was based, but he swore me to secrecy. He said the lamias were like the ultimate trump card, something that needed to stay a secret for when you'd played every other card you had."

"Yeah, I think I might be to that point now. A lot has changed since Ashley was here last. Onyx is a fast learner and he's not afraid to play dirty. Are you up to a challenge match if it comes to that? I'd do it myself, but their queens don't fight and this whole thing is one colossal bluff that all depends on them believing that I'm a queen, just like their queen, and therefore due the same rights and privileges."

"Do I have any choice?"

"Not if we want to survive."

"Then I guess I'd better be ready for a fight to the death against something capable of bringing down a werewolf all by itself."

"It won't be as bad as that—don't get me wrong, it will still be bad—but they like their fights more evenly matched than that. They have an incredibly powerful venom that they inject via the tips of their claws that is the primary reason they are able to bring down werewolves. They wouldn't use that on you unless they viewed you as being as big a threat as a werewolf. If you were to survive enough challenge matches you might eventually be classified as an opponent worthy of using venom on, but you'll be safe for a while."

I tied off the last stitch on another blood vessel—this one had been cut all of the way through—and tried to remember how many of them I'd sewn up so far. I'd lost count somewhere around five; I was pretty sure that we'd been driving for more than ten minutes.

"How many fights are we talking?"

"I'm not sure. It depends on how long we're there, but there are other factors. They'll challenge you at irregular intervals throughout our time with them. There is always a challenge when a new queen first shows up, but I don't know what triggers subsequent challenges after that."

As the SUV coasted to a stop I used Ash's shirt again to soak up the blood that had continued to pool while I'd been working.

Looking at the bloody material jogged something in the back of my mind and I suddenly realized that I was naked.

My face heated up instantly. Our pack hadn't ever practiced the kind of casual nudity common in most other packs. It made things go much more smoothly when you didn't have the dominants inside of the pack worrying about who was getting an eyeful of whose girlfriend or boyfriend each time someone changed back to human form.

Normally I would have put a new ha'bit on as soon as I changed out of the ruined one, but I'd been so worried about Kristin on the way to the car that it hadn't even crossed my mind. I decided that Ash was stabilized enough to move and unobtrusively reached for the change of clothes in my bag.

Celeste chuckled as she put her Pathfinder into park. "I was wondering how long it was going to take for you to realize that. Grab your clothes and put them on if you have to, but work fast. There's no telling how long we have before Nicolas' guys show up. There are only so many places we could have been headed."

She slipped out of the vehicle and headed towards the dock and the two dozen boats moored to it. I pulled on my last undamaged ha'bit and then covered it up with jeans and a t-shirt so that I wouldn't stand out any more than necessary.

LOST

The daggers I'd felt her staring at me during the drive had suddenly taken on a different significance altogether. I was pretty sure if the shoe had been on the other foot and I'd been checking her out while she hadn't even realized she wasn't wearing clothes that there would have been hell to pay.

Part of me wanted to challenge her right then and there, but the situation was more complex than that. The question of dominance needed to be established between us, but I was already hurt so I'd be starting out at a disadvantage.

Even if I did win, the price might very well be our lives. Even if Onyx's people didn't happen on us before the fight was over, it would just make it that much harder to beat the lamias in an hour or two.

Now wasn't the time, but the time would eventually come, and when it did I was going to hit her so hard her head would spin.

I gently picked Ash up and carried him down to the aluminum boat, realizing in the process that it probably didn't matter much what I looked like while I was carrying a limp body in my arms. So much for being unobtrusive.

"Go get Kristin and the bags while I finish up with Ash."

Celeste turned towards me with fire in her eyes. "You don't tell me what to do."

"Consider it a down payment on the show you got earlier. Unless you want to try your hand at a little vascular surgery while I fetch our things."

Her mouth tightened and she picked up a fine tremble in her arms like she was having a hard time keeping her beast in check enough to maintain her shape. I looked down at Ash, turning my back on her the way you would do with an enemy who wasn't worth worrying about. I knew it would piss her off, which was part of why I'd done it, but I was also still worried about Ash.

I'd had him all sewn up by the time we'd stopped, but there was a possibility that moving him had ripped some of his stitches. I started carefully probing the long gashes in his back while I waited to see what Celeste was going to do.

"This isn't over. Damn Sanctuary prima donna. We're going to have a knock-down dragout once we get somewhere safe."

"I look forward to it; now hurry up before we have company."

Less than five minutes later Kristin and all three bags had been moved to the boat and we'd pushed off from the dock. The boat was one of the shallow-bottomed fan boats that were primarily used in swamps and bayous, which hadn't been a surprise, but I was shocked at just how loud the prop turned out to be.

I finished checking Ash's internal injuries, taped all of the gashes up to stop them from seeping blood from hundreds of smaller blood vessels, and checked over Kristin before staggering to the other chair.

It felt odd to be sitting in something that put me four feet above the bottom of the boat when Ash and Kristin were lying at my feet, but I put the discomfort out of my mind, much like I'd done with the incessant droning of the motor behind us, and looked around at our surroundings.

It was more than five minutes later that I happened to look up at Celeste just as a gust of wind pushed her hair out of the way enough for me to see the bright green earplugs in her ears.

I tapped her shoulder and then pointed to the earplugs. "I want some too."

"Tough."

I'd noticed a small black bag affixed to the bottom of her seat with Velcro when I'd been working on Kristin and Ash. I hadn't heard her unzip it, but that might just mean she'd waited to fish out her earplugs until after the prop was spinning.

I waited until she was focused on the water ahead of us again and then reached down and pulled the bag away from her seat. She shot me another angry look as I unzipped the bag and found that it did indeed contain additional sets of earplugs along with clothes made out of stretchy, soft black cloth.

I was pushing her too hard, but she wasn't going to do anything about it until after we were all out of danger. Once that was the case, I would welcome the chance to see who was really dominant to whom.

I'd already checked over my wounds and taped up the worst of them, but I was still exhausted.

"How long until we arrive in the lamias' territory?"

"An hour, give or take. Why?"

"I haven't slept in almost a day and a half. If there's any way to stretch out the trip maybe I could get caught up on my sleep and have a chance at winning that fight."

Her face softened slightly. "You didn't say anything about being that tired when I first told you we were headed towards the lamias. How are you keeping control of your beast?"

I shrugged. "I didn't mention anything because it doesn't matter. We would either have time to rest before we got there or we wouldn't. Either way I'll still go through with the fight and do my best to save Ash and Kristin. As for the other, I can't really explain it. My beast has been more difficult to control lately, not less. When you throw in the way that you and I have been playing dominance-chicken, I should be struggling a lot more than I am to keep him leashed."

"The lamias aren't going to be fighting our kind of challenge match, Isaac. This is for real; they will be trying to kill you."

"I know, I gathered as much already. It doesn't matter though, I've been in fights like that before. I'm not looking to die, even though that sounds like the most likely outcome, but if it happens it happens. I'll have given it my best shot and there are worse fates than dying cleanly in battle."

"I think you'll do better against the lamias than you think. I've never seen anyone stand up against Nicolas even half as well as you did."

"That wasn't anything to be impressed with. I got in a single lucky shot, but other than that he controlled the entire fight."

"One lucky shot is more than I've ever seen anyone else manage. Go ahead and take a nap. I'll buy you an extra hour. Go on, I'll wake you up with plenty of time to prepare for your match."

The abrupt change in Celeste's manner, the sudden softening of her expression, was dizzying. I got the feeling that we were still going to end up fighting each other before all was said and done, but neither of us was looking forward to it quite as much as we had been.

Chapter 10

Isaac Nazir
Bayou Perot
Eastern Louisiana

I awoke to a different world. We'd still been within sight of the ocean when I'd closed my eyes, but now we were deep inside the bayou.

The Cyprus trees looked like something out of a horror film. Their trunks branched out as they disappeared into the water. It was almost like they'd become confused and started growing roots above ground. As we slowly coasted past a particularly large specimen I wondered if it was pulling more of its nutrients from the water than was normal in other locations.

The water was a muddy morass that was so full of algae that in some sections the brown of the dirt had been overpowered by green.

In places the Spanish moss hanging down from the trees was long enough to touch the water, creating an odd, barely moving veil of vegetation that made me nervous for some reason. It wasn't until we'd been slowly gliding forward for a couple of minutes that I realized what had me so on edge.

I could smell something out there in the water, something big and reptilian, and the moss was making it so I couldn't locate whatever it was.

"Do you smell that?"

Celeste nodded. "It's an alligator, a big one."

"Should I be worried?"

She shot me an uncertain smile. "I don't know. In most parts of the bayou I'd say no, but we're at the outer edge of the lamias' hunting territory. Things get weirder and weirder the further in you get. All of the predators get bigger. I've seen alligators almost twice as big as what I've seen anywhere else, bull sharks the size of a great white, and water moccasins that are bigger around than your arm."

"You're pulling my leg, right?"

Celeste pointed up ahead and I got my first look at a deep-bayou alligator. To say it was huge would have been an understatement. It looked like it was twenty feet long and pushing fifteen hundred pounds. Before seeing it I wouldn't have thought there was anything in the bayou other than the lamias that could threaten a full-grown hybrid. I would have been wrong. Down in the water where the hybrid's mobility would be hampered, there wasn't any guarantee that a hybrid could take down a monster like that.

Its sheer size would make it harder to get at anything vital and I had a suspicion that its thick skin would be resistant even to my hybrid claws. As if that wasn't enough, it weighed enough that I wouldn't be able to manhandle it like I could have a smaller creature. Lifting something like that, while it was thrashing and struggling would be like trying to lift a ton and a half of dead weight.

"Do we have to worry about one of those things attacking us when we're inside the boat?"

"Possibly. All of the big predators are going to view Ash and Kristin as wounded, easy prey. The boat usually scares everything away, it's one of the benefits of it being so loud, but some of those things are bigger than the boat is."

"Just great. No wonder nobody else has found the lamias. The native wildlife eats them before they make it far enough in to see anything they aren't supposed to see."

"You're not wrong."

We both laughed, but it was gallows humor.

Celeste turned the boat in a long, slow arc around a large stand of trees and it was as if we'd entered yet another world. The long, unmoving waterway had given way to a series of low islands. Some were the result of the ground sloping up out of the water, some were because several trees had come together and established a spot above the water that was just sufficient for other plants to have a chance at survival.

The effect was astonishing. The ground and water seemed to merge together without any real rhyme or reason. Celeste slowed the boat even more as the terrain around us became more dangerous.

"I was actually just about to wake you. I'll try to keep us out of reach of anything dangerous, but if you can keep an eye out that would be good. I'd hate to have a water moccasin come over the side of the boat."

"Okay, is this boat going to capsize if I suddenly put a few hundred extra pounds on?"

"I hope not, but I don't know for sure, I've never shifted forms on one. Try to stay towards the center of the boat until you've actually changed, if it comes to that, and you'll probably be okay."

We journeyed on in near silence for another half hour, the giant propeller on the back of the boat turned down to the point where I pulled out my earplugs so I'd have a chance to hear if something tried to sneak up on us. I was surprised when we didn't arrive at our destination within a few minutes of my having woken up.

"How long was I out for?"

"A tad more than two hours. Why?"

"I was just adding things up. You bought me more than just an hour if the whole trip was only supposed to take an hour."

She looked...not embarrassed exactly, but definitely uncomfortable. "You looked like you needed the sleep so I took a less direct route. I figured it couldn't hurt, it might even throw Onyx a bit further off of our trail."

"Thanks. I appreciate it."

"Yeah, just try not to get yourself killed. I'd hate for all of that effort to end up being wasted."

We hit another stretch of water that was more open, so I risked looking away from our surroundings to check on Ash and Kristin. They were both unchanged, which was a good sign. If either of them had been suffering from serious internal bleeding then they would have probably died while I'd been asleep.

It didn't mean that they were out of the woods yet, but they had a chance still despite the fact that we were miles away from any medical help.

I looked back up and nearly shifted forms out of sheer reflex when I saw more than a dozen huge, simply-clothed forms standing in the water less than thirty feet ahead of us. I hadn't been looking down for that long, it shouldn't have been possible for them to have appeared in the middle of the channel like that.

Even if I hadn't been expecting to run into lamias I still would have known that there was something off about the figures ahead of us. They were tall. It was hard to say just how tall since I didn't know how deep the water was, but it looked like they were somewhere between the size of a hybrid and a werewolf.

That, combined with the fact that none of them seemed worried about standing in the middle of a bayou filled with giant snakes and alligators, would have been enough to tell me that I'd just seen my first group of lamias, but the real shocker was the way that their forms seemed to flicker whenever I looked at them out of the corner of my eyes.

None of their forms were quite right. On one the eyes were wrong—he had the slit-like pupils of a snake. Another had skin that gave off the smooth sheen of scales, and another opened his mouth and displayed fangs like a rattlesnake.

Celeste cut the engine back to almost nothing so that we approached the group at something less than a walk. My beast was wide awake and pacing back and forth inside of my mind. He hadn't liked the presence of the monstrous alligator from before, but that had nothing on how he felt about the lamias.

He knew they were threats and he was throwing off energy in hissing, burning waves that were being mirrored by Celeste. She cut the engine completely and we coasted up to the middle lamia, one with fangs that were visible even when his mouth was closed. He reached out and stopped our forward motion without any apparent effort.

"Why are you here?"

His voice could have almost passed for human except for the undertone of dry scales sliding across sand. They weren't snakes in the traditional sense, they had two arms and two legs with no tails, but I could understand why the ancient peoples had painted them as being half human and half snake. It was the only way to depict something that was almost human but reminded you of a snake at every turn.

I almost responded, but Celeste beat me to it. "I've come to talk to your queen, one queen to another."

The lamia blinked at her before turning to look over Kristin, Ash and me. It had happened too quickly for me to be sure, but I thought that his eyelids had closed from the sides rather than from the tops and bottoms.

"Your...people, your...escort is small and sickly. What kind of queen travels away from her enclave with so little protection?"

He held his s's for the barest fraction of a second too long. It was unnerving, but Celeste took it in stride. She'd probably had a good idea of what to expect from her family's oral histories.

"A queen who comes as a supplicant, one asking help from one greater than herself. My champion is ready to face your champion and prove his worth."

"No, not his worth, the worth of you all. As a consort reflects the glory of his queen, so too does the queen stand illuminated in the light of her people. You risked much to come here with so few. You do us great honor in displaying such trust in our honor... our hospitality. You know more of the way than most of the energy ones...the sun people. You will be granted the right of combat."

I half expected him to attack me then and there, but he simply turned our boat towards a nearby island and gave us a push towards it. Any scholar would have been beside themselves at the idea of interacting with a previously undiscovered culture. I was no exception. I already had half a dozen questions that I was itching to ask the lamias.

He'd called us 'sun people', which almost sounded analogous to the dayborn, but we'd always referred to the humans as dayborn. It hinted at a mythology different than our own while still suggesting the possibility of some kind of common origin. I'd already had plenty of reason to try and survive the coming fight, but I figured that it couldn't hurt to add one more reason into the mix.

If I survived then maybe I would have a chance to ask some of my questions.

The lamias had collapsed around us, forming a long double line. As we pulled even with each set of lamias, they reached out and grabbed the side of our boat for just long enough to give us a push towards the island. The resulting journey was much smoother than I would have expected.

Their pushes were deceptively graceful and by the end we'd built up a lot more speed than I'd realized or I would have tried to cushion the impact when we hit the island.

We hit with enough force that Ash and Kristin were both sent sliding forward toward the front of the boat. They didn't hit the gunwale, but being pushed across the bottom of the boat, which wasn't perfectly smooth, drew a ragged groan out of Ash.

I reached down to check on him, but Celeste was already there, her fingers on his pulse.

"I think he's okay still. His pulse is still about as strong as it was when I checked him earlier while you were asleep."

"Okay, keep an eye on him. It wouldn't take much to open some of those tears back up and he hasn't been topped up with fresh blood like they did with Kristin before we broke her out of the hospital."

I got a distracted nod in response, which caused me to turn and look. The lamias had all left the water and gathered on the far side of the island, which meant I was able to get my first clear view of their size. I was surprised to see that there were two different groups. The one who had been talking to us—the one with the non-retracting fangs—and two others were only a couple of inches shy of seven feet tall, but all of the rest of the lamias looked like they couldn't be more than six-two or six-three.

LOST

Knowing my luck I was going to have to fight one of the big ones, but there wasn't anything I could do about it. This was their home, which meant that we were going to be playing by their rules. I was running out of clothes so I stripped down to my ha'bit, took a deep breath, and then stepped off of the boat onto the squishy mud of the island.

I walked up to the lamia in the center, the one we'd been talking to, and gave him a respectful nod that I hoped translated between species.

"My name is Isaac and I'm ready to begin. Who am I challenging?"

The lamia before me gave me a slow nod in return. "Welcome, Isaac. I am known as Set. Your manner does you credit."

"Thank you. Will I be fighting you, then?"

He looked me over, eyes stopping at each of the spots where I'd been injured, despite the fact that my ha'bit covered up all of the tape.

"You're injured. While it does you credit that you are willing to face me…honor does not demand such a match yet. You are free to face a…lesser opponent if you so desire. Any of those present would be considered worthy opponents, but the other two consorts would likewise be considered beyond the bounds of what honor requires."

I looked around at the rest of the lamia who were waiting to either side of Set. None of them seemed unhappy with having been called lesser opponents; in fact, none of them seemed to have any feelings one way or another about the fight.

When you were dealing with a shape shifter pack in any kind of challenge situation you could always count on them throwing someone at you whom they were confident could beat you. Preferably that wasn't the alpha of the pack as it set a bad precedent, but if he was the only one the pack was confident would come out on top then he was the one you faced off against. It was only when nobody in the pack was good enough to be sure of beating you that they threw the submissives into the rotation in an effort to wear the challenger down to the point where one of the dominants could be sure of winning.

Everything about this challenge felt wrong. Set had just indicated that he could wipe the floor with me, but instead of taking me on himself so as to make sure that none of the others in his party would be killed, he was offering to let me go up against someone he thought I had a chance of beating.

If I knew enough to pick the right opponent then I could maximize my chances of winning, but I had no way of knowing who the weakest fighter was. There wasn't any surge of energy as they prepared themselves to fight, nobody was moving back and forth with pre-fight jitters, it was just one long line of impassive lamias who didn't seem to care whether or not I picked them.

"Honored Set, I have no way of knowing who would be the most appropriate opponent for me. I would defer to your judgment, if honor allows such a thing."

It was a risk. Set could always set me up against a ringer I couldn't possibly beat, but it seemed like the right risk to take.

"Such a thing is indeed permitted, although it puts me in a difficult position. The *snnelt*...the worker on the far end is the youngest and least able fighter. You may fight him without any fear of dishonor. You show uncommon wisdom for one not of the people, for a sun person."

I bowed my head to him in respect. "I thank you for your guidance and apologize for any discomfort my request might have occasioned. I will do as you have counseled."

"Very well. You may shift to your sun form now if you wish. The contest will commence when your opponent steps toward you."

The change tore through me without any effort on my part. I'd had my beast leashed as tightly as I'd ever managed before and I'd still nearly started shaking as my beast tried to force a transformation. As soon as I relaxed the grip I was maintaining on my beast, he pushed me into hybrid form.

My added weight once I was a hybrid forced my feet deeper into the mud. I moved side to side, shifting my feet to pack down enough mud that I'd be able to move without getting stuck.

The lamia I'd chosen as my opponent remained motionless for several seconds and then sprang towards me with the kind of speed that I'd only ever seen out of hybrids or werewolves previously. He was fast, but not so fast that I didn't have a chance at beating him.

I dodged to the left, avoiding a slash from the claws on his hand, and raked my claws down the outside of his arm. The texture was all wrong, it felt like my claws were skidding off of scales. I should have scored a long gash down the length of his arm, instead there wasn't anything more than a thin, intermittent line of blood.

We both recovered and started circling. Set had indicated that my opponent was young, which hopefully also indicated that he was less experienced, more easily tricked, and prone to simple, direct attacks.

I moved forward, trying to draw his arms out of position, but he saw through my attack and blocked my claws with his. I'd hoped that his claws might not be as hard as mine, but that wasn't the case. They were made out of something different, something almost crystalline in feel, but they seemed more than able to withstand the punishment of hitting my claws if we were both going after each other for real.

The next exchange sent me reeling back with blood running down my right arm. He hadn't gotten to the inside of my arm, so it wasn't bleeding like it could have been, but it was still a sign that he'd read my attack and been prepared for me.

I set myself and then charged forward. My enemy was fast, but he hadn't seen just how quickly a hybrid's reverse-articulated legs could launch me forward. He tried to plant himself at the same time he brought his arms back into position to intercept me, but I'd caught him off guard and his arms were too far to the outside.

I led with my shoulder and hit him hard enough that most hybrids would have gone tumbling backwards, but he was heavier than I'd expected. I still knocked him down, but it was a close thing.

I'd been hoping for the kind of bone-rattling collision that would disorient him and tip the balance of the fight firmly in my direction, but I hadn't been depending on it. I hit him with my shoulder, but my right hand had been only a couple of inches behind and the fact that he hadn't given as much as expected meant that the tips of my claws hit even harder than I'd been expecting.

His scales had stood up well against raking attacks, but they were no match for a straight stabbing attack with my full weight behind it. There was only the barest amount of resistance and then my claws punched through his scales and buried themselves inside of his flesh.

I rode him to the ground as my momentum carried him over backwards. I was so worried about his claws that I didn't pay enough attention to his feet. Somehow he managed to get them up between us and he straightened them with a single explosive movement at the exact instant when his back hit the ground.

He launched me more than twenty feet backwards, tearing my claws out of his chest a split-second before his feet lost contact with my chest. The impact was bruising. I was frankly surprised that he hadn't cracked some of my ribs, but for the first time this fight I felt a smile pulling my lips back so my teeth showed.

He was fast—nearly as fast as I was—and he was much stronger than I was, but he wasn't indestructible. I'd just hurt him and by my calculations I was up on points and feeling pretty good about things. Even my chest wounds weren't hurting like they had been.

There was a quiet murmur from the watching lamia, which made me incredibly nervous. Other than Set, none of them had said anything before now, but that exchange had apparently caught them by surprise. All I could do was hope that I hadn't broken some kind of unstated rule that was going to cause them all to turn on me.

My opponent pulled himself back to his feet, one arm pressed against his chest where I'd stabbed him, and then stood motionless for several seconds as he waited for me to move and

LOST

I waited to see if Set and the others were going to come after me.

Set made a gesture and the lamia I'd been fighting broke into a run towards me. I made as though planning on meeting his charge head on, but I knew he would level me if I actually tried that. Instead of meeting brute force with brute force, I dodged to the side at the last possible instant.

I'd almost waited too long. His arms were longer than I'd realized and he managed to slice the top of my right shoulder. I spun back around to slash him before he made it too far past me, but he was already gone and my right arm wasn't working quite right anymore. I still had good lateral movement and strength, but I couldn't raise it as high as I normally could.

The confidence I'd just been feeling evaporated as the lamia turned back around and charged me again. If anything he was even faster and more committed than he'd been before. I started my dodge sooner this time, but he was expecting me to do exactly that and he had just enough time to compensate for my dodge. This time his claws tore into my side in almost the exact same spot where Nicolas had injured me just hours before.

Once again the lamia was past me before I could do more than connect with a half-hearted, ineffectual swipe that skittered off of his scales.

I was bleeding heavily from my side and my right arm was only at seventy percent. I had to come up with something soon or I was a dead man. One or two more passes like that would wear me down to the point where he could dispatch me at his leisure. No wonder these things hunted werewolves for sport. They were the next best thing to indestructible and the one I was fighting wasn't even using his venom on me.

There wasn't any question—he was going to charge me again, but I didn't wait for him. Instead, I charged forward at the exact same time, blurring into motion in the hopes that I could throw off his timing.

I made as if to meet him head on again, but we both knew that would be foolish, so he was once again expecting me to dodge aside at the last possible second. I gave him exactly what he was expecting. I'd dodged to my left twice now and failed to get away cleanly both times, so this time I went right.

Which was exactly what he wanted me to do. The speed and ease with which he adjusted as I started my dodge told me that he'd let his weight shift to my right even before I'd started moving.

There was no possible way to get far enough to the right to avoid his claws. I'd started moving too early, even sooner than I had on the last pass, and he had plenty of time to veer as far right as he needed to in order to mow me down.

Everything was developing exactly as I'd hoped. I planted my right foot in the mud and pushed off as hard as I could, dodging to the left after he'd already committed himself to going right. Even my best dodge wasn't quite up to getting me completely out of his path, but that was okay too. I ducked under his right arm and then I hit him.

This time I didn't lead with my shoulder, I led with my claws. All five claws slid home and then I splayed them out in an effort to stop them from ripping out through his side. My duck to avoid his right arm, combined with the fact that my shoulder wasn't working quite right, meant that I hadn't been able to take him up high enough to hit anything vital.

I hadn't taken him in the heart and I didn't seem to have hit any major arteries, but my hand in his guts served as a kind of moving, fleshy anchor and I used it to flip myself around behind him.

His speed was still breathtaking, but this time, aided by the grip my right hand had on him, I managed to get around fast enough to slam my left hand home in his back roughly where the left kidney would have been on a human. It almost wasn't enough. He was already slowing, his hands were both coming down and back and I was low enough that he wasn't going to have any problems scraping me off of his back.

I did the only other thing I could do. I wrapped my left hand around a couple of his ribs, and then I pulled myself up with my arms far enough that I could whip both of my legs forward and sink both sets of talons into the meat of his calves.

He was strong enough to bear my weight along with his own, but the force of me pushing on his right leg as he tried to pick it up was enough to trip him up and both of us went crashing to the ground. Fortunately I was on top this time and I scrambled forward, repositioning to where I could get at his neck.

Less than five seconds later he was dead.

Chapter 11

Isaac Nazir
Unknown Bayou
Eastern Louisiana

I stumbled away from the corpse of the lamia I'd been fighting and looked over to Set, trying to judge his reaction.

"An honorable fight. We will take your group into the enclave so that you may wait upon the queen's pleasure."

Set drew in another breath as if he was going to say something else, but before he could do so Celeste yelled for me.

"Isaac, it's Ash. His pulse is getting weaker; I think he's bleeding internally."

I sprinted back over to the boat, shifting back down to human form as I arrived at the boat.

"Can you save him?"

I shook my head as I tore open the first-aid kit and grabbed the needle. "I don't know. If we had blood for a transfusion then I'd say yes, but he's already lost so much blood that I'm not sure he'll make it."

Set glided forward to within two feet of the boat. "You seem distressed. If you are not confident in your ability to save him, may I suggest an alternative?"

I'd been busy pulling off the long strips of tape I'd used earlier to hold Ash's wounds closed. "You have a way to keep him from dying?"

"I believe so. Your victory in the challenge entitles you to ask a boon from our enclave over and above the normal requirements of hospitality. If your request is that I do my best to keep your companion in arms alive, then I will do so."

"Yes, heal Ash, that is how we want to use the boon!" Celeste's voice was desperate. Despite her tough show back at the hospital, she didn't want to lose her brother now that she'd found him again.

Set turned towards her with an expression of distaste. "It is not for you to decide. Your consort has won you the right to petition my queen for an audience, but the boon is his and his alone. You may not usurp his rights in this area without declaring yourself…unclean."

Celeste swelled up like she was ready to give Set a piece of her mind, but I waved my arms at the two of them.

LOST

"That is my choice, made of my own free will, to save a friend—a companion in arms. If there is anything you can do to help Ash, then please do so."

Set examined me for a second and then nodded. "Very well."

He took one more step forward and then placed his hand over Ash's wound. His hands looked like they always had, but out beyond the ends of them, Ash's skin dimpled slightly as though the tips of invisible claws were resting on him.

It was a disturbing sight on several levels and I found myself wondering if I would ever see the lamias' real form. The thought of seeing them with their illusions stripped away was simultaneously tempting and repulsive. I got the feeling that I wasn't ready for the sight of their actual form, that I might not ever be ready.

Set closed his eyes and a second later his hand got hot enough that I could feel the heat radiating off of him from several inches away. That meant he was hot enough to burn unprotected flesh and it was all I could do not to tear his hand away from Ash's back. Only there wasn't any need. Not only was Ash not being burned, it almost seemed like he was radiating the same kind of heat.

Nearly a full minute passed and then Set pushed on Ash's wound with one side of his hand, compressing the flesh underneath with an exactness that was too precise to be happenstance. I tried to visualize the effect the pressure would have on the organs underneath Set's hand and decided that he'd just pushed the edges of the tear in Ash's renal artery a little closer together.

Two minutes later Set stepped back. "It is done."

I picked up Ash's wrist and checked his pulse. It still felt weak. "Would it be considered impolite for me to ask what it is that you did to help him?"

Set cocked his head to one side. "Such a question does not violate the guidelines of honor, but this language does not have all of the words necessary for a proper explanation."

I nodded my understanding as I realized that I'd been overlooking the most exciting aspect of meeting the lamia. They had a language of their very own, the first known non-human language anyone had ever encountered. It was enough to make me salivate.

Satisfied that I really did understand the difficulty of what I was asking for, Set pointed to Ash. "His life-fluid...the blood, as you call it, was leaking out of its proper pathways. Once too much blood is lost, he would have moved on...he would have died, so I took steps to stop the leak."

My mind was whirling at the possibility. Celeste had said that Ash was bleeding internally, which was one piece of evidence that

Set hadn't diagnosed Ash without seeing inside of him, but he'd compressed Ash's renal artery, which I was pretty sure had been the source of the internal bleeding.

"You were able to see the leak, the tear, in his artery without opening him up?"

"Yes, one merely follows the circulation of the life-fluid and looks for places where it pools instead of continuing back to the throne...the heart."

"And then you were able to stitch it together from outside of his body?"

That earned me a frown. "No, I did not heal it. I merely slowed the leak. The breach is still there, blood still leaves through it, but much less. His body now has time to replenish what was lost, but there is danger still. The breach is still healing itself, but it has been likewise slowed. The...change is not stable or...permanent. When it lapses he will resume bleeding and if his body cannot seal the leak quickly enough he will still move on."

It almost sounded like he was saying that he'd slowed down *time*, which was impossible—except that Ash hadn't died yet. His pulse was still weak, but it hadn't gotten any weaker and given just how much blood Ash had lost, even a small tear should have killed him by now.

Ash was a shape shifter, so his body healed faster than a normal human's, but he was one of the weakest wolves I'd ever met. He was fast and deadly with the weapons he'd spent so much time mastering, but his makeup lacked something that most of the rest of us took for granted.

His beast was so quiet that I wasn't sure he really believed the rest of us when we described how hard it was to master the being that took up residence inside of us the first time we shifted forms. There were times that I envied him in that area, but it seemed linked to the fact that in human form he was only slightly stronger than someone with his general build normally would have been, and his constitution was unusually weak by shape shifter standards.

If it had been Jasmin lying there with a time bomb inside of her I wouldn't have worried. Assuming that she started with a normal amount of blood in her, her body, especially now that she was a hybrid, could have easily healed a small tear in an artery before she bled out. It was a completely different ballgame when it was Ash lying there.

There wasn't anything to do but hope that Set's solution would work. I couldn't open Ash back up right now without killing him. Maybe in a few days I could go in and sew the hole closed if Ash made it that long.

"Thank you, Set. I appreciate you doing that."

"It was no more than your successful challenge had earned you."

"That may be so, but I'm thankful nonetheless."

LOST

The massive lamia bowed his head in acknowledgement. "Very well. Come, we should be going now if we're going to make it to the enclave before the entrance moves."

Chapter 12

Isaac Nazir
Unknown Bayou
Eastern Louisiana

Two of the smaller lamias wordlessly helped me drag Celeste's silver boat further up onto the island. Based on the waterline on some of the nearby trees, it looked like we'd pulled it far enough up to avoid having it wash away. I hoped that was the case. I hated the thought of having to wade back to civilization through thirty miles of alligator-infested, chest-deep swamp water.

None of the lamias seemed to think it odd that Celeste didn't help move the boat. Apparently queens weren't expected to get their hands dirty with manual labor any more than they were expected to deal with challengers.

I'd shifted forms to help move the boat, but once the boat was safely tucked away between two large trees, I wasn't particularly excited about the idea of shifting again. I'd already worn far too many forms over the last forty-eight hours.

I'd resigned myself to the fact that I was going to be dealing with a horrific set of cramps in my arms and legs within the next few hours, but I was hoping to put off dealing with them until we'd made it to the lamias' enclave. Another shift back to human form and then again to hybrid form so that I wasn't walking through the bayou in human form would almost guarantee that I wouldn't make it through the next hour without writhing around on the ground in agony.

Celeste saw me looking at the bags and understood the quandary I was faced with. She came over to the boat and picked up one of the large, black duffle bags.

"Here, bend down and I'll loop it across your chest."

"I don't want to have you do anything to undermine your position with our new friends."

"I'll be fine, Isaac. Bend down so we can get moving. I don't want to have to march halfway through the bayou looking for a new portal."

My beast was apparently adjusting to the presence of the lamia enough that he was ready and willing to expend energy fighting over more mundane offenses. He took a run at the mental cage where I'd locked him away and gave it a good shaking. It was an unsubtle reminder that we still needed to settle the issue of who was the top dog around here.

If we'd been somewhere else where I didn't have to worry about what the lamia would consider lèse-majesté, I would have reminded her that she didn't have any place giving me orders. That wasn't an option, so I just shot her a dirty look and then did exactly as she'd ordered.

About the time she got the first bag situated across my shoulder, two of the smaller lamias stepped forward and took up positions to either side of me with their heads bowed.

"Bearers for you to use as you see fit, Eminence."

Set's voice had an edge of something that I thought might be impatience. Once the first of the bearers had the second black duffle slung across his back, he bent down and carefully lifted Ash. The lamia cradled Ash against his chest like he was worried any sudden move would break him.

Satisfied that the lamia was going to do his best to avoid reopening Ash's wounds, I reached down and picked Kristin up. Part of me wanted to leave her for the other lamia—my beast most definitely didn't like the idea of having my arms full around creatures like the one that we'd been fighting just minutes before—but I knew how I would have felt if Ash and I had swapped positions and it had been me unconscious and unable to watch over Jess.

LOST

I would have wanted for Ash to carry my girlfriend rather than leave her in the arms of something that was capable of accidentally injecting her with werewolf-killing venom. I still felt that way despite the fact that Jess wasn't my girlfriend and hadn't been in months.

Kristin normally wasn't very heavy, but now, after an injury that had come within minutes of killing her, she seemed as light as a feather to my hybrid arms. I shifted her around, careful not to cut her with my claws, until I was happy with how I'd positioned her and then turned back to Celeste.

I caught her partway through stripping out of her clothes. Everything important was still covered up, but she'd already unzipped her pants and had started sliding them down over her hips. She caught me eyeing the black lace panties that she'd just revealed, and went bright red.

"Turn around."

Normally I would have turned without her even having to ask me to, but I hadn't forgotten about the fact that she hadn't bothered averting her eyes when the shoe had been on the other foot.

"Didn't you say something about all of us from the Sanctuary pack being a bunch of prudes? You're the last person on earth I would have expected to be bothered by the thought of flashing a little skin." I said it in something less than a whisper, pitched so that it would carry to her ears, but not make it to the lamias who'd retreated back to rejoin their fellows as soon as they'd been given their burdens.

"Isaac, turn around. This isn't the time to be pushing. We can talk about it once we are by ourselves." It came out as a hiss, quiet enough that there was a chance that the lamias couldn't hear her, but loaded with plenty of indignation.

She'd just ordered me around two more times in less than five seconds. I'd expected my beast to respond with a flare of rage, but my beast wasn't mad...he was curious. I was still all wrapped around an axle over what had happened with Jess, but my beast seemed to have already moved on. Maybe not all the way, but enough that he'd noticed that Celeste was a very attractive female.

She wasn't trying to assert dominance, she was embarrassed. She was demonstrating vulnerability. With another guy it might not have mattered, but with a girl, with Celeste at least, my beast was willing to cut her some slack.

I captured her eyes for several long seconds before nodding and turning around. The lamia had already turned their backs to her. "So what changed, Celeste? I know how things work in most other packs. You guys don't wear ha'bits, this isn't the first time you've been naked around someone."

She'd only waited the barest fraction of a second after I'd turned around to resume pulling her clothes off, but the rustle of fabric sliding across skin stopped as she considered my question.

"I'm not sure. You guys don't do casual nudity and I know you get mocked for it a lot, but it's not a bad idea. If I was running the New Orleans pack and hadn't had to worry about blowback from the Coun'hij, then I probably would have implemented a similar policy, but I guess that's just a smokescreen."

For several seconds she didn't say anything else and I'd almost given up on getting anything else out of her. When she started speaking again her voice was different, more vulnerable, less guarded.

"I guess it matters to me because it matters to you. You guys don't do casual nudity, so showing skin around you feels like it should be a big deal. Sorry, it's not a great explanation, but it's all I have to give you right now."

I tried to come up with something to say that wouldn't sound stupid, but I took too long. She resumed undressing and the sound of her clothes dropping down to the bottom of the boat was too distracting to allow me to continue thinking about anything else.

A second later I heard her bend down and pick up the discarded articles of clothing. The sound of Velcro pulling apart as she tore the tiny black bag she'd had mounted to the bottom of the captain's chair free of its mounting was followed by the swish of her hair as she walked towards me. Only it was all wrong. It wasn't the sound of hybrid talons on the aluminum of the boat, it was bare soles.

"Don't turn around yet."

I knew it was my imagination, but I could almost feel her behind me, scant inches away from my body as she unzipped the duffle bag hanging across my back and stuffed her things into it.

"Sorry, I didn't really come prepared for an extended trip. I don't want to risk catching the material on my claws and ruining my clothes."

I had to clear my throat to get it to work. "There's always Kristin's clothes if nothing else."

Celeste chuckled once before shifting in a cool rush of power. When she spoke again her voice had dropped by more than an octave but it still somehow managed to sound feminine. "Borrowing another girl's clothes without asking is the kind of thing some girls never forgive. I'd like to hope that Ash picked better than that, but I'd really like to avoid pissing her off before we've even been introduced. It seems like the most...prudent route if I'm going to have any chance of Ash talking to me after all this is said and done."

"That's the first time that you've called him Ash."

"Yeah, I guess you're right. I need to get used to the fact that he's a different person than the one I remember."

"Not completely different. He hasn't forgotten where he came from. It still drives him, still pushes him to be tough enough to make sure that he doesn't have to be in someone else's power ever again."

There was sadness in her voice now. "If that's true then you're right, he hasn't changed entirely, he's still got that in common with the little brother who used to push me to take a harder stance against Onyx. That's where he and I are different. I gave up those dreams decades ago."

Celeste nodded to Set, who had turned around—along with the rest of his people—as soon as she'd shifted forms. "Let's get moving. We need to make up for lost time."

Set motioned for two of his people to pick up the body of the lamia I'd killed and then we all shook out into a loose line that had all three consorts at the front and Celeste, Ash, Kristin and me in the middle.

The trip went by more quickly than I'd feared. Neither the bags nor carrying Ash and Kristin slowed any of us down appreciably and Set led with a pace that was just enough less than a run to avoid jostling Ash and Kristin.

Our course took us over a variety of islands and across more than a dozen channels, none of which was deeper than mid-thigh for a hybrid, which I was grateful for. Not only did I have several thousand dollars' worth of electronics in my bag, I also couldn't get past the image of a two-ton shark lunging out of the water to attack us.

We didn't see any sharks, but we did see three or four more giant alligators. The alligators eyed us as we went past, and I got the feeling that if it had been just Celeste and me they might have come after us, but each of the alligators kept their distance.

Apparently the denizens of the bayou knew who occupied the top spot in the food chain. I couldn't blame them. I wouldn't have wanted to tangle with eleven lamias, not at the same time and not under circumstances where they had no compunction about using their venom. They were plenty deadly enough even without it.

Gradually—so gradually that I almost didn't notice—the islands got taller and dryer while the water-filled channels disappeared. After just over an hour of walking we came to a twenty-foot-tall rock cliff broken by a single narrow crack that was just barely wide enough for a lamia or hybrid to walk through without turning sideways.

We walked along the cave for several dozen yards in near darkness before it widened out into a circular valley with red, rock walls much, much taller than the twenty feet we'd just seen on the other side when we'd started into the cave. I turned back to Celeste, who was only half a step behind me.

"Those cliffs have to be four hundred feet tall. Are there any rock formations that tall in this area?"

"In this area, yes, but not in Louisiana within an hour's walk of the bayou. We aren't in Louisiana anymore, at least not the version you and I are familiar with."

"How is that even possible?"

"Honestly? I have no idea. My ancestors thought that the lamias were able to manipulate time and space the same way that you or I would use sand to build a sand castle. They are unique in ways that nothing else on our planet is unique."

"Are you trying to say that they aren't from our planet? Do you know how crazy that sounds?"

"Yeah, but I think it's the least scary answer."

I dropped my voice even lower so as not to offend our hosts. "What's scarier than giant snake people from another planet?"

"Giant snake people from this planet but from another dimension. If that doesn't do it for you then you could try giant snake people from the future, or maybe the past. No matter how you slice things I'm pretty sure they didn't evolve from the same gene pool as the rest of us."

"That's quite the sentiment coming from someone who changes into a giant, furry monster whenever the fancy takes her."

"Yeah, I know. It doesn't make it any less true though."

I shook my head at her. "This is like stepping into an episode of *The Twilight Zone*."

The valley we were standing in was like a little piece of paradise. It wasn't that big—it looked like I could run across the entire valley in less than five minutes—but the sheer amount of vegetation blocked off most of the sightlines and made it feel like it was two or three times as big as it actually was. We'd been walking through the valley, following one of the narrow, winding pathways, for ten minutes before I realized that it wasn't just the plant life that smelled different than anything else I'd ever encountered—the soil smelled odd too. There was an odd, faint blue cast to the dirt. It was the kind of thing that you didn't even notice unless you were looking closely at the ground, but it was definitely there.

I shook my head and added that fact to the list of things that I couldn't explain along with the strange, stalky plants with triangular leaves and the way that the sun looked too red. The dirt could have some kind of cobalt compound in it and the color of the sun could be due to high levels of smoke in the air, but I had a sneaking suspicion that Celeste was right. We weren't in Louisiana any more.

A couple of minutes after that we came to another opening in the sheer rock wall. Set turned to us as the other two consorts stepped into the darkness.

"You will wait here while we seek the queen's will."

Celeste looked unhappy, but I just nodded. Maybe it was a benefit in some ways that I had no idea what we were getting into. Unlike her, I had no idea what to expect next. The one thing that I knew was that we didn't have any control over our fates.

I was starting to suspect that Celeste hadn't realized yet just how fully we were at the mercy of Set and the rest of the lamias. My suspicion was confirmed when Set returned twenty minutes later.

"The queen will see you when she's ready. For now I suggest that you take refreshment in the chambers that have been prepared for you."

Unlike me, Celeste hadn't chosen to sit down while we waited for Set to return. She turned towards him with all of the fury a six-and-a-half-foot-tall hybrid could generate.

"No, we need to talk to her now. We don't have time to wait."

I was pretty sure that Celeste hadn't been planning on actually assaulting Set, but the response was instantaneous. Four of the smaller lamias moved in front of Set to shield him while two others stepped to within striking distance of Kristin and me.

Celeste was too focused on Set to notice, but the lamia holding Ash had moved too. He'd stepped several yards away from us and repositioned one of his hands so that his claws were poised above Ash's heart.

I left Kristin on the ground where I'd set her when we'd arrived and grabbed Celeste by her shoulder before she could take another step towards Set.

"Stop! Look at Ash. Are you really so stupid as to think you can force any of them to do something they don't want to do? We are completely at their mercy."

She turned on me with hot gray eyes that looked like they would welcome an excuse to rip my heart out of my chest and feed it to me.

"Get your hand off of me."

"Gladly, as soon as you're in control of yourself."

Whatever she was about to say was cut off by Set. "Your consort is only partly right. We would not kill a visiting queen regardless of the provocation, but if you indeed prove yourself to be without honor then we will kill the men and the little queen so as to free them from the shame of your service. You would be physically removed from our enclave and deposited back in your...place. You would die in the swamp or survive to return to your people, but either way you would not be welcome back here."

Celeste tore herself free of my grip, leaving blood and skin on my claws, and then stalked off back up the path. My beast was raging. I had to close my eyes for a count of five to bring him back under control enough not to chase her down and have things out with her then and there.

LOST

Once I'd calmed myself down enough that I wasn't radiating a hissing corona of metaphysical energy, I turned back to Set.

"I'm sorry for any offense caused by my...queen."

"The offense is not yours to require apology. The ways of the queens are...unpredictable and oftentimes difficult. These two will show you the way to the quarters that have been prepared for you. I ask your leave to retire. Dealing with queens is exhausting and arrangements still need to be made for the defeated worker."

With everything else that had just happened, I'd completely forgotten about the smaller lamia, the one I'd killed, who had been carried into the valley with us. My eyes drifted over to the corpse of their own accord and I couldn't seem to make myself look away.

I'd killed before. Werewolves, vampires, even a couple of the members of the other Sanctuary pack when they'd tried to go after Jess' dad and James' mom, but this was the first time I'd killed someone who hadn't been bad, someone who hadn't been out to hurt my friends and family. This was the first time that I'd killed someone and then stuck around to talk to *his* friends and family.

Saying it was a weird feeling didn't even begin to do it justice. My beast didn't look at things quite the same way. For him things were a lot more black and white. If we hadn't killed the lamia then we would have been killed. Case

DEAN MURRAY

closed, end of story. Now that I'd come down
from the thrill of surviving the fight and my
beast was focused on Celeste, I wasn't so sure.

It was true that we'd been fighting for our
lives, but we never would have been compelled
to fight if we hadn't sought the lamias out in the
first place. We'd come to them knowing that the
price of securing an audience with their queen
was to kill at least one of her people.

It was one thing to agree to that plan when it
was a matter of life and death. Back then, I'd
looked at it as being a question of killing one of
the lamia in order to save Kristin's life, but that
wasn't the truth.

We should have pursued the possibility of
tracking the Coun'hij down with the hackers
before throwing in the towel and coming here.
I'd been confident that my plan would work, but
I'd let first Ash, and then his sister, convince me
to come here and murder another sentient being.

It was a lot easier to justify that in the abstract
than it was once I was staring at a corpse.

"I...I'm sorry. I wish we had tried other
avenues, wish we hadn't come here and killed
your friend."

Set bowed his head. "Now is not the time to
discuss such things. It is not the place of one
such as you or me to question the actions of our
queens. The stream moves as it moves and it is
for us to be the *tssath*...the strong raft for our
queens to guide to the safe haven."

LOST

Set stepped forward and clasped me on the shoulder with a hand that could have easily ended my life with a single injection of venom. "Again, your sentiment shows much honor if little understanding of the way the world works. Go see to your queen and I will go see to mine."

Chapter 13

Isaac Nazir
The Lamia Enclave

I did eventually go to Celeste, but first I asked the workers to lead me to our quarters. We followed another winding, seemingly aimless set of paths and five minutes later I followed the workers into another cave, only calling it a cave didn't do it justice.

Two steps into the mouth of the cave the passageway took a sharp turn to the right. Directly after the bend a curtain of vines blocked off the passage so completely that they seemed to divide two different worlds. On the outside of the curtain was a dimly-lit passage that, other than being exceptionally clean, looked much like any other cave. On the inside was a series of rooms lit by organic-looking bulbs that seemed to grow into the surface of the rock.

LOST

The floor was carpeted with something that looked like an extremely short, extremely dense kind of grass. There were three stone beds that were little more than raised platforms carpeted by more of the soft green vegetation that made up the carpet.

I hesitantly set Kristin down on the large bed in one of the rooms, but I was surprised to find that the 'mattress' was soft and springy. I bent down and poked at the carpet and was amazed at the complete lack of insect life. I was able to shear the end off of one of the blades of grass, but the clear liquid that leaked out was more like water than anything else.

It was an environmentalist's fever dream. There wasn't anything artificial anywhere. There was even a bathroom that seemed to dispose of wastes by having some kind of plant absorb them. The kitchen didn't have any kind of refrigerator, but there were long vines hanging down one wall that had a variety of fruit growing off of them.

The vines were simply too small to grow the crazy amount of fruit I was seeing, so I was pretty sure that the main body of the plants must be somewhere else. Presumably that was where they got the sunlight, water, and nutrients that they needed.

After giving myself a quick tour I came back out to the main room to find that my escorts had remained exactly where I'd left them.

"Please carefully set Ash down next to Kristin. The bags can go wherever."

The lamias nodded and did as requested before returning to a kind of parade rest as if waiting for additional orders. I searched my brain trying to come up with all of the questions that I might need answered before dismissing them.

"Are we safe here, are there any threats that we need to worry about?"

A nod followed by a shake of the closest one's head, and then he walked over to the curtain and pointed to it.

"So the curtain keeps everything undesirable out?"

Another nod.

"What about outside? Do we have to worry about dangerous insects? Spiders? Snakes?"

Three more shakes.

"Can we eat the food or will it make us sick?"

Once I was satisfied that we were indeed safe and that we had food and water enough to make sure that we weren't going to starve, I dismissed the workers with my thanks for their help, and then went looking for Celeste.

I was still in hybrid form, so it was easy to pick her scent out. I didn't want to go crashing through the walls of vegetation though, so it took me a few minutes to find the correct path.

When I finally found her she was sitting on a large rock that had been carved into the shape of a bench, dangling her hybrid feet in the stream that ran through the center of the small clearing. She stood as I came into sight and then stalked over to confront me.

"What did you do, Isaac?"

"What do you mean, what did I do? I took care of Ash and Kristin. What else was I supposed to do, go off and pout like a spoiled child?"

She wanted to hit me. I could see it in her eyes, but something stopped her from taking that step. It didn't stop her from hurling insults at me though.

"No, you oaf. What did you do to ruin things with the lamias? It's never happened like this before. We were supposed to win one challenge match and then be granted access to their queen. You screwed things up somehow, offended them by asking for help deciding who to fight."

Anger had been building in a slow burn in the back of my mind for months now. First Oblivion had stolen Jess' memory, which had destroyed the life I'd struggled so hard to build with her.

Then Alec had made a ton of bad decisions that had nearly gotten us all killed, until Adri came back, at which point we were supposed to just forgive and forget months of hell. Then Alec had started freezing me out, replacing me with Ash and a bunch of pack leaders who'd never lifted a finger to help us when Brandon had been half a step away from killing our dominants and absorbing the submissives.

That was all old anger that I knew all too well, but it had been joined by new anger. Anger at Ash for not turning and running sooner so that we could have worked as a team rather than him getting nearly cut in half. He'd left me alone with no help other than Celeste to try and keep him and Kristin alive, and neither of the Hunts had bothered telling me the full truth of what we were getting into by going to the lamias for help.

Even worse, they'd both acted like they had all of the answers when the truth was that they didn't know much more than they'd already told me. And now to top it all off, Celeste was blaming me for the mess that we were in.

"How many times?"

"What?"

"How many times did your ancestors come here and ask the queen for help? Twice? Three times?"

"Three times, why?"

"Because you're behaving like a child. Of course things aren't going the way that you planned. You know next to nothing about what we're dealing with. You have a bunch of lame theories passed down from ancestors who came here before humans even understood how electricity worked. We're dealing with an entirely different species here, one with its own culture, one that doesn't seem to have much, if any, cross-contamination with modern human culture. We have no idea what's going to happen next."

"What, and you're better placed to know how to get us out of here alive? Maybe I only have a handful of stories passed down over hundreds of years, but that's more than you've got. You should be grateful that I came and bailed the three of you out rather than just leaving you at the hospital to die."

"Oh, so I should just shut up and soldier? Is that it?"

"Yeah, basically. You have your role to play and I have mine. All you have to do is hit people. I have to figure out what changed this time around and get us back on track so we can get our answers and get out of here before you go up against their real fighters and get your head handed to you."

"That's the biggest crock of crap I've heard in a long time, but you're right about one thing. You're going to end up sitting around on your butt while I risk my life over and over again killing people I don't have any quarrel with so a pair of *queens* can have some kind of pissing match over whose boyfriend can beat the other one's boyfriend up. The least you can do is not make my job harder by coming within inches of getting us all executed out of hand."

It had been a mistake to come looking for Celeste. I still wasn't sure why I'd done so, but one thing was certain. I didn't particularly care whether I ever saw her again.

I turned and stalked back to the cave where I'd left Ash and Kristin without looking back.

Chapter 14

Isaac Nazir
The Lamia Enclave

It wasn't a very good excuse, but with all of the craziness that had happened since we'd arrived in Louisiana, I completely forgot just how many different shapes I'd worn in such a short time. It was all the more ironic considering that I'd been worried about that very thing less than two hours before, but once I made it back to the cave, instead of settling down for a long stretching session to minimize the inevitable cramps, I just flopped down on one of the empty beds and let myself fall asleep.

The cramps blindsided me. I woke up to excruciating pain as every muscle in my body simultaneously tried to rip itself free from the bones it was connected to. I'd pushed the envelope before and transformed too many times in too short of a time period, but the cramps had never been this bad before.

Maybe it was the result of being wounded, or maybe I really hadn't ever pushed quite so many transformations in such a short time. Either way, two seconds after the cramps began I started wishing I was dead. Trying not to scream never even entered into my mind, the pain was simply too intense to allow for rational thought.

I writhed on my bed for what felt like forever before the pain started to subside enough for me to register anything else. Even at that point I was still hurting pretty badly, but I was able to at least open my eyes enough to see that I wasn't alone inside of my room.

Celeste had slipped into my room and was busy stretching and rubbing my legs in an effort to shorten the duration of the muscle spasms. It was still hard to think of much else other than the pain, but I noticed that she was exceptionally good with her hands.

I'd fallen asleep on my stomach and the muscles in my neck had pulled my chin all of the way down to my chest, so it was all I could do to breathe, let alone turn my head to the point where I could see Celeste, but I knew it was her based on her scent. After another micro-eternity of pain she finished up with my second leg and moved around to my right arm.

The arms went faster. Nearly everyone's strongest muscles are in their legs, and I was no exception to that rule. The muscles in my arms were still impossibly strong compared to most humans, but then again Celeste had the same kind of preternatural strength and she was able to rub out the spasms and knots in both arms in about half the time she'd taken with the legs.

By that point the pain had lessened substantially, but the muscles in my core were still fighting against each other like they wanted to rip me in half.

"Sorry, Isaac, but these beds weren't exactly made with human bodies in mind. You're up too high for me to get the rest of you from here. I'm going to have to climb up there and straddle you."

She was right. I hadn't paid it much attention, but everything inside of our cave was sized for seven-foot tall lamia rather than for sub-six-foot-tall females. The lamia apparently liked their beds taller, wider, and longer than I was used to.

A few seconds later Celeste was up on the bed with me, kneeling with her legs on either side of my waist as she tried to relax the muscles in my back and shoulders. The pain was getting down to manageable levels, but I still couldn't speak, and fighting my own muscles to make them unknot enough for me to breathe had tired me out more than I'd realized. Even as the pain decreased, I found that I was having more and more difficulty breathing.

Celeste was apparently listening closely enough to realize what was going on.

"I'm not done with your shoulders yet, but we'd better get you flipped over or you're going to be in real trouble soon."

Celeste hopped back down off of the bed and then pulled me to the very edge of the bed before climbing back up next to me and turning me over. This time she straddled me just above my knees and went to work on my diaphragm, pushing in on my upper stomach when the muscles seemed to want to contract, and then pulling back away to give them a chance to relax again.

It wasn't as efficient when it came to relaxing the muscles in my abdomen, but the sheer amount of pressure she was putting on my stomach compressed my lungs even beyond what my diaphragm was doing. It hurt more than the cramps, but she was effectively breathing for me because whenever she let off the pressure my lungs naturally expanded, at least a little, even when the muscles had other ideas.

Over the next few minutes my abdominals slowly started to relax and I was able to breathe at least a little on my own. Once I wasn't in any danger of suffocating, I stopped panicking and Celeste moved up so she was straddling my stomach. She wasn't sitting on it, her weight was all on her knees so as not to make it difficult for me to breathe, but I was relaxed enough that I could start processing other things now as she started on the muscles of my chest.

Her hands were firm, but surprisingly soft. She was too focused on her task to look up and meet my gaze, but that was probably a good thing. Before I'd gone to sleep I'd showered. Once the swamp water, blood and dirt had all been cleaned off I hadn't been able to bring myself to put one of my dirty, bloody ha'bits back on, so I'd just pulled on a pair of jeans and fallen asleep without a shirt on.

Apparently Celeste had felt much the same way. She'd showered while I'd been asleep, and then slipped into the clothes from the boat. She was wearing a soft, black tube dress that trailed across my skin as she leaned forward to work the last of the spasms out of my pectorals, and I could feel her bare legs rubbing against my sides.

It was the kind of situation that I'd never expected to find myself in, and I felt a kind of paralysis take hold of me. Celeste was undeniably beautiful, but I wasn't some mindless animal to act without concern for the consequences of my actions.

I'd spent months pursuing Jess without any success, but my lack of headway didn't necessarily mean that I was prepared to give up. We had a history together that went back almost as long as I could remember. We'd grown up as friends and then later it had turned into something more than just friendship.

Jess and I had been together for something like four years and I wasn't ready to throw that away if there was still any chance of getting back together with her. Even if I was, pursuing any kind of relationship with Celeste was a bad idea on almost every level.

She was Ash's sister. Ash and I didn't particularly get along as it was, the last thing we needed to throw into that dynamic was for me to date the sister he'd been estranged from for more than ten years.

All of that was true, but they were the kinds of things that you think about after the fact to justify a decision that you'd made originally without even thinking about them. The truth was that I wasn't going to make a move on Celeste because I barely knew her. I didn't know if I could trust her, and I certainly didn't know her well enough to decide whether I liked her.

I needed to keep her at arm's length for the foreseeable future, needed to fish or cut bait where Jess was concerned before I even thought about anyone else, but I was having a very hard time pulling my eyes away from her.

The light from the plant globes above us had dimmed down sometime when I'd been asleep so the light hitting her was achingly soft. Her hair was a loose blond tangle and her bare shoulders were exactly the kind of delicate perfection that

I'd imagined dwelt underneath her clothes the first time I saw her.

She caught me looking at her legs, bare up to mid-thigh where her dress ended, and her hands slowed.

"Are you okay now?"

I wasn't sure I trusted my voice to not give away more than I wanted it to, but refusing to speak would be just as bad.

"Yes, thank you. If you hadn't come when you did then I'm not sure that I would have made it."

"You're welcome. I don't know that I've ever seen cramps that bad. You had me really worried there for a while. Does that happen often?"

I shook my head. "No, it's never been that bad before. I'd say that I lost track of how many times I'd shifted, but that wouldn't be true. I knew I was riding the ragged edge of what I could manage, but the threats just kept coming. I should have stretched rather than just falling asleep like that, but by then I wasn't thinking very clearly."

Celeste looked at me with eyes that I couldn't begin to read and I was struck again by the fact that her human eyes—the deep gray eyes looking at me at that moment—were the same eyes she had in her hybrid form. That wasn't unheard of, Alec and Jasmin had blue eyes in both their hybrid and human forms, but their hybrid eyes were a paler shade of blue than they had as humans.

It was as if she'd cast some kind of pagan spell on me with her eyes. She was still kneeling over my stomach and she showed no sign of moving other than to pull her hands back away from my chest.

"You've been through more in the last two days than I gave you credit for. Ash and Kristin are lucky to have a friend like you. Not everyone would put everything on the line like that for their friends."

That drew a chuckle out of me. "I'm not sure you can say that Ash and I are friends. More like comrades in arms. To be honest, it wasn't as though I had any other choice; the Coun'hij and Onyx were all after me too."

She cocked her head. "You could have dropped Ash off at the hospital and made a run for it."

"It was Ash's car."

"Which he discarded without a second thought after the three of you arrived."

She had me there. I hadn't been bluffing when I'd told Ash that I had enough cash to go my own way. There hadn't been a compelling reason that I couldn't have left Ash and Kristin. I didn't want to admit that though, not to her, even if I wasn't sure exactly why.

"It's okay, Isaac. You don't have to say anything. Just spend some time thinking about what you'll do when you don't *have* to be the dependable rock." Celeste suddenly shifted back a little further away from me. "Listen to me, I don't even know what I'm saying. This isn't what I was hoping to say to you."

"What did you want to say to me, then?"

"I wanted to apologize for how I treated you earlier. You didn't deserve that. You've done nothing but deliver despite all of the things working against you. I should be better than that, I just...well, I just know better. I'm sorry."

"Apology accepted, and thanks again for coming in to save my bacon just now. I understand that probably wasn't the easiest thing you've ever done."

"Thanks. I'm also sorry about the fact that Ash and I dragged you here. I can understand your frustrations. Just remember that once we know where Dream Stealer and the rest of the Coun'hij are we can finally take them down. Over the long run that will save a lot of lives."

She looked away from me—apparently embarrassed, although I couldn't tell whether her sudden bashfulness was driven by our conversation or the fact that she'd been sitting on top of me—and then jumped off of the bed. I grabbed her arm before she could make her escape.

"Don't worry. I'll see this through. We'll get their queen to tell us what we need to know and then Ash will be willing to give you a chance. The two of you can work things out, it will just take some time."

LOST

She looked at me like I'd just grown a second head and then ran out of my room. One second she was less than a foot from my bed and then all that was left of her was a single bare leg disappearing around the corner.

Apparently I still had a lot more to learn about women than I'd realized.

Chapter 15

Isaac Nazir
The Lamia Enclave

Celeste and I kind of tiptoed around each other for the next two days. Neither of us seemed quite sure how to handle the moment that we'd shared our first night in the enclave.

We worked together well enough to make sure that Ash and Kristin were taken care of, but beyond that we avoided each other whenever possible. I was actually grateful to have some time to myself to think. I couldn't remember the last time that I'd had more than a few hours away from the constant, intrusive stress of pack life.

Celeste still seemed to be holding to our original bargain of not settling the issue of who was dominant to whom, which meant that, for the first time since I'd first shifted forms, I wasn't worried about protecting myself from someone higher up the food chain or keeping whomever was submissive to me from taking a run at me.

It was pleasant in a way that was hard to describe, but I figured it was probably how most people felt on vacation. For a short time I was able to forget about all of the things that usually drove me and just enjoy the moment. The only bad part was that I knew it wasn't going to last. Eventually I was going to have to go back.

I slept a lot more than normal, which was odd, but when I mentioned it in passing to Celeste she told me that she thought it was a side effect of the food. Her ancestors had reported similar changes during their visits to the lamia, along with an increased ability to heal quickly from wounds, which would have been nice except that it didn't seem to be happening for any of us who'd entered the enclave injured.

I chalked it up as just one more instance where the rules had changed since the last time the enclave had hosted visitors, and hoped that Ash and Kristin would wake up soon. It seemed to bother Celeste a lot more than it bothered me, but I already knew that there was something going on there that I didn't understand.

Usually when I had free time on my hands I spent it with my nose buried in a book or online trying to keep up with the latest developments in IT security. Neither option was available inside the enclave. I turned on my tablet the morning of our first full day in the enclave and confirmed that it worked, but then just turned it back off when it failed to register any GPS satellites. There wasn't any point in running down the battery when I didn't have any way of recharging it.

I ended up spending a lot of time out in the valley sitting next to the stream and thinking. I must have gone back through the first few days after Oblivion left Jess without any memories a hundred times while sitting on a rock and listening to the stream.

I'd made such a mess of things. I guess the biggest problem had been that I hadn't been able to believe deep down inside that the Jess I'd known for so long was really gone. She'd changed—she obviously didn't remember any of us—but I kept seeing glimmers of the old Jess peeking through the amnesia.

The way she held her head when she was confused and trying not to admit it, the fact that she loved vanilla bean ice cream more than any other flavor, the way that she sometimes still smiled at her dad, they all pointed to the same thing. I'd been thinking that I just needed to jog her memory, that I needed to keep exposing her to old places and people until the old Jess came back to us. It had made sense to me at the time, but now I wasn't so sure.

The old Jess would never have thrown herself into the arms of some dashing, mysterious stranger she'd known for less than a month, but that was exactly what the new Jess—what Jessica—had done. I'd spent months wooing Jess when we were younger. Even back then she'd been such a tightly coiled ball of hurt that she'd been extremely slow to trust.

Even after Jess had chosen to go off with Wyatt rather than staying with Andrew and me, I'd been convinced that she'd been tricked, that he'd fast-talked his way into her heart. The more I thought about it though, the less I believed that had actually been what happened. If anything, I'd pushed her into his arms.

She'd walked around the estate for months knowing that she had a history with everyone there, a history that she couldn't remember, but most of them had at least left her alone to decide when and how she wanted to proceed with them. Not me though. I'd pushed and pushed, never happy with the tiny measures of progress when she'd opened up to me, always wanting more, wanting things to be just like they'd been before. It was no wonder that she'd latched onto the first new guy who had shown an interest in her.

The freedom to just be herself must have been intoxicating. No need to worry about a shadowy shared history, no sense that she was competing against the old Jess, it must have felt like paradise.

I was still turning all of that over inside of my mind, but that process of self-reflection had to take a back seat on the morning of the third day when Set came calling. Set was the only lamia that had spoken to me so far. I'd been hoping to be able to ask him more about his people and their culture, but when I'd approached the entrance to the main cave and asked the two lamia guards there if Set was available they had just waved me away with threatening looks in their eyes.

Seeing Set waiting outside the cave he'd assigned me was simultaneously a relief and cause for alarm. I'd been wanting to talk to him, but I suspected that he wasn't there to talk to me about lamia history or culture.

"Are you ready for your next challenge match, sun person?"

"Do I have a choice in the matter?"

"There is always a choice. Your queen could withdraw her request for hospitality and you could all withdraw."

A part of me wanted to agree with him. I wanted to tell him that we would pack up and go within the next five minutes, but I knew I couldn't do that.

Kristin still hadn't woken up, but as soon as the morphine they'd given her at the hospital had worn off she'd gone back to thrashing and moaning in her sleep. She wasn't my girlfriend, but that didn't mean that I didn't understand why Ash was willing to do whatever it took to save her.

Besides, Celeste was right about how many lives we would save if we could find the Coun'hij's base and take them all down. If it had been up to me I would have tried the hacking route first, but now that we were here I needed to keep winning fights as long as I could, to give Ash and Kristin time to heal if for no other reason.

"There are other choices, but none with consequences that I can live with. I will meet whatever challenger you judge most appropriate. May I go get my queen before we begin?"

Five minutes later Celeste and I had been led to a large cave on the far side of the valley that had a sandy circle in its center. Conscious of the fact that there wasn't any way to get hold of replacement clothes here in the enclave, I stripped down to my ha'bit and shifted forms with an explosion of power that told me that my beast was ready and willing for another fight.

I stepped into the circle and sank my talons as far down as they would go, testing the depth of the white sand. It was deep, much deeper than I would have expected. The lamias hadn't just poured some sand on top of the floor, they'd bored down into the rock, creating a depression at least a foot deep before hauling in sand to fill it up.

Assuming that it had all been done by hand—I hadn't seen any kind of machinery since we'd arrived—that was a lot of work. The lamias obviously took their challenge matches very seriously.

There were enough glow bulbs hanging from the ceiling to illuminate the cavern with the bright, white light of an operating room. Every detail was thrown into stark relief so that those watching wouldn't miss any of the fight's nuances.

I stretched my massive hybrid arms, making sure that I didn't have any residual stiffness from my most recent injuries. Everything seemed to be in working order, which was good, because my opponent had just stepped into the far end of the circle.

Based on his height, I was up against another worker, but he was more muscular than my first opponent had been. All of the lamia were muscular, but this one was built more like a consort than a worker.

It wasn't something designed to make me enthused about the fight. They'd picked out someone more dangerous to fight me this time, but there had been a healthy dose of luck involved in my last victory. I wasn't sure that I could win a fight against someone who was even faster and stronger.

Set looked back and forth between the two of us to make sure that we were ready and then clapped his hands. My opponent didn't charge forward. I was pretty sure that this lamia hadn't been there for my last fight, but apparently news of my tactics had made the rounds and this guy was adjusting his tactics accordingly.

We moved slowly towards the center of the sandy ring, mirroring each other's movements and I started working my way through a threat assessment. He was big, nearly as tall as me, but massive in a way that told me I couldn't hope to match him in a straight-up contest of strength. He moved well too, obviously comfortable with the sand and unintimidated by being in a fight for his life, but his step was a shade heavier than I'd expected.

That was probably a bad sign. It probably meant he was even heavier and stronger than I'd realized, but it did give me the barest beginnings of an idea.

Our first exchange was tentative. He jabbed at me, leading with the claws of his right hand while I batted the blow away. Against another hybrid I would have drawn a decent amount of blood—nothing crippling, but something to begin weakening him. Instead I got only the smallest trickle of red to show for my efforts.

I darted towards the lamia and then shifted to the side at the last second. I wasn't trying to actually score on him, although I did manage to nick him in the side. I wanted to force some motion into the fight and test out his footwork.

He was good, but then I wouldn't have expected anything less from the second opponent Set had selected for me. He shifted his feet exactly like he needed to. He didn't cross his feet or do anything else *wrong*, but he wasn't as fast as he should have been.

He was used to fighting two-thousand-pound alligators and werewolves. Against enemies like that he needed to be fast, but even more importantly, he needed to make sure he didn't get bowled over in the first few seconds of the fight. If he could get even just one shot with his venom in then keep his feet, it would be just a matter of time before he would come out on top.

I couldn't go toe to toe with him. Maybe Jasmin could have, but I knew that would just get me killed. Instead I needed to make him fight the kind of fight that he wasn't used to fighting. I needed to work the perimeter and make him move around as much as possible.

I started circling him, varying my speed and tempo, always trying to stay just close enough that he could almost reach me if he lunged. At first he was content to just turn in place so that he could keep me from getting around behind him.

That lasted until the first time that I started to sprint left and then planted and went right instead. He'd already anticipated that I'd keep going left and he committed himself too heavily.

I darted in close, knocking his left hand away with my right, and then I slammed the claws on my left hand into the meat of his thigh. I hadn't expected to be quite so successful, or I might have passed up the chance to stab him in the thigh and just gone for a clinch from behind.

I still tried to get behind him, but now I wasn't quite fast enough to make it happen and he connected with his elbow to the back of my head. The blow sent me flying, but I hit the ground in a roll and came back up in time to just barely avoid being impaled through the chest by his claws.

He still managed to catch me with a long, raking attack across the ribs, but I moved laterally and kept him from landing anything else while I blinked away the spots in my vision. It had been a long time since I'd taken that much blunt trauma to the head in a fight and I'd forgotten the sheer shock of being hit unexpectedly.

My opponent was feeling his oats and he charged me again, trying to keep me off balance, but I broke to his left and he couldn't quite keep up with me with the added stress on his injured leg. Realizing that wasn't working, he slowed down and stopped in the center of the circle again, waiting for me to make the next move.

I resumed circling, feeling out his footwork and response speed now that he was injured. He was compensating, but I could tell there was a difference. He darted forward and managed to slice me across the outside of my arm before I twisted away, but I didn't riposte with an attack of my own.

It was tempting to try to make him pay for the blood that was now coursing down my arm, but I couldn't afford to get sucked into the kind of close-quarters pounding match that favored him. I needed to stay mobile and figure out why his footwork seemed different than it had been a few moments before.

We traded two more sets of lightning-fast blows, little more than jabs really, before I figured out what was going on. I was bleeding from my left arm and the right side of my chest now, but it had been worth it.

The lamia was compensating for the wound on his leg by anticipating that I would go to his weak side again the next time I made a move. He was good, he wasn't committing too drastically, but even so he was a little bit slower now going either direction than he'd been before.

Part of me wanted to go towards his weak side again. I'd beaten him off the mark once before he'd been injured and there was a good chance that I could do it again. If I could, there was a chance that I could cripple that leg once and for all, which would end the fight.

It was a powerful lure. I moved the slightest bit closer, circling to the lamia's right, to his strong side, and then I sped up nearly to full speed. He was tracking me right up until I did a stutter step. He was banking on the fact that I was going to change direction, but instead I threw myself forward, continuing around his strong side and slamming the claws on my right hand home in his right leg.

I didn't try to block his right hand as it came around in an attempt to claw my neck as I went past. There wasn't time, not if I wanted to land the blow to his leg, but it was the riskiest thing I'd done up to that point in the fight.

LOST

It's one thing to duck a punch in a human-style boxing match and know that they might clip you as they bring their fist back in. It's a completely different situation when your opponent might rip your throat out on the backswing.

My gamble paid off. I managed to stay half a step ahead of him, just far enough away that the tips of his claws went whistling past my ear, and then I was back to circling. He was definitely slower now. He was having a hard time tracking fast enough to keep me in sight, which meant that I should be able to get much cleaner shots at his legs now if I wanted them.

I reversed direction, more to test out his footwork again than because I expected to generate some kind of opening, and my opponent tripped himself up when one of his legs caught on the sand rather than lifting up high enough to cleanly respond to my movements. I didn't even think about what came next.

I charged in and rammed him with my shoulder, knocking him off balance even further, and then I slashed the outside of his right leg with everything I had. The semi-impenetrable scales that had been so effective turning my attacks when he was able to angle his body to turn them into glancing blows weren't up to the challenge now and my claws tore through flesh with an ease that would have been sickening if not for the bloodlust bleeding into my mind from my beast.

I jumped backwards to avoid the lamia's attack, and managed to sink the tips of my claws into his arm as it went whipping past my face. He was as good as done and we both knew it. Even now he was trying to get his collapsed leg underneath himself so that he could face me again.

I looped around behind him, moving fast enough that he didn't have any chance of keeping up with me, and then I darted in and savaged his other leg. He would have fallen to the ground then, but I grabbed him by one shoulder, steadying him before his legs could completely give way.

"I've won. He's at my mercy. Go ahead and declare me the victor."

Set met my eyes with something that looked like sadness in his expression and shook his head. "I'm sorry, but honor doesn't allow for such a thing. We've been commanded by our queen to fight to the death."

I opened my mouth, but before I could get the words out, Set hissed something to the worker and my opponent thrashed around in my grip. I thought for a second that the wounded lamia was trying to get one last blow in and I tightened my grip on him, but the precaution proved to be unnecessary.

Rather than trying to hurt me the worker reached up and shoved his own hand into his chest. I looked at the corpse that had been a person, albeit a strange one, a few seconds previously and then slowly lowered him to the ground. I was in shock. I'd never seen anything like it, and hoped to never see anything similar ever again.

"You are victorious, Isaac Nazir. Are you ready to claim the boon that tradition provides for you?"

I shifted back to human form and shook my head before turning to go, sickened by the whole proceeding, but Celeste grabbed my hand before I made it to the entrance of the cave.

"Don't waste this, Isaac. You may not get many more shots at having the lamia offer you anything in their power."

She wanted to tell me what to ask for. I could see the desire in her eyes, but she didn't say anything else. She just sat there, my hand in hers, and waited for me to make a decision. There was no way of telling what made her stop short of actually suggesting a particular request. It was possible that my words from our first day inside the enclave had finally sunk in and she didn't want to generate any more ill will with Set and the rest, but I didn't think that was the reason—at least not all of it.

The boon was something that I had earned, something that I'd risked my life to obtain even if it hadn't been the primary reason for agreeing to fight. I'd earned it and it was mine to choose.

Even more, she was right. That had been another close fight; there wasn't any guarantee that I'd win the next one, not if the opponents kept getting tougher and tougher.

I stopped and looked back at Set for several seconds as I considered what it was that I most wanted in the entire world. Jess certainly, but the lamias couldn't give her to me anymore than anyone else could. Only Jess could give herself to someone.

An end to the war, victory for Alec and the rest of us rebels, but that felt like it was beyond what the male lamias could provide me. The thought of scores of lamias descending on the Coun'hij and wiping out Puppeteer's werewolves with their venom, was tempting, but I was fairly sure that only their queen could decide to enter the war.

I wanted to talk to my friends and family, I wanted to learn more about the lamias, but none of that mattered if I didn't survive the next challenge match. It hit me like a wrecking ball. That was it, I needed an edge, some way to survive however many fights I had left before the queen finally agreed to see us.

"I want you to train me. That is the boon that I request. I want you to do everything you can to give me an edge in the coming challenges."

Set looked at me for several long seconds and I got the feeling I'd asked for something that didn't mean what I thought it meant by the time he finally nodded his agreement.

"Very well, I will come find you tomorrow morning and begin your training."

Chapter 16

Isaac Nazir
The Lamia Enclave

Ash and Kristin were still sleeping when I rolled out of bed the next morning. I could hear Celeste breathing in her room, but I didn't disturb her. She wasn't sleeping as much as I was, but she was still sleeping more than normal.

I couldn't blame her. Until we were finally granted an audience with the lamia queen there wasn't anything for her to do other than sit around and take care of Ash and Kristin.

Boredom had started setting in a long time ago, but it was more than that. Having time to think was helping me start to put some of my demons to rest, which was something that was long overdue. All of that time seemed to be having the opposite effect for Celeste. There had been a couple of times recently where I'd been woken up by screams and assumed it was Kristin again before realizing it was Celeste.

I hadn't said anything to her about it yet. She didn't seem like the type to welcome prying questions and I didn't want to trigger any kind of confrontation between us. Things had been going well enough ever since she'd helped me out that first night and I didn't want to rock the boat.

I rolled out of bed, grabbed a light breakfast of one of the more citrusy fruits growing in the kitchen, and then headed outside to see if I could find Set. The transition to an all-fruit diet had gone better than I'd expected.

Normally a shape shifter had to keep plenty of protein in their diet if they wanted to keep control over their beast. All I could figure was that one or more of the odd varieties of fruit that we'd been eating must have decent amounts of protein in it.

My beast had actually been quite a bit easier than normal to keep under control since we'd arrived at the enclave, which made me wonder if part of the issue over the last several months had been that I'd been missing something key from my diet. It was something to keep in mind for when I went back to the normal world, assuming I survived that long.

I went to the entrance to the main lamia cave and asked the guards if they knew when Set would be looking for me. They didn't answer, but one of them hissed something to someone inside the cave and five minutes later Set came outside.

"You are ready, Isaac Nazir?"

"Yes, but we don't need to start right now if it's not convenient for you. I was just trying to find out when to expect you."

"Now is an appropriate time."

I followed Set to the circular cave where I'd fought the day before and then transformed and stretched to loosen up some of the knots. I'd been expecting Set to jump right into teaching me techniques. He'd never been overly verbose before, but this time he assumed a kind of parade rest and examined me for several seconds.

"I was perhaps hasty in my agreement to train you, Isaac Nazir. I am still willing to do so to the best of my ability, but honor compels me to tell you that I may not be able to deliver that which you requested."

"I don't understand."

"You did not ask for only training, you asked for an edge in the challenges you may face in the future. I can provide training, but the act of doing so will skew my perception of your abilities, causing you to qualify to face stronger opponents. It is a problem that is...circular in nature."

I cocked my head to one side, interested in seeing where he was going.

"That would be challenge enough, but there are other considerations. If you continue to defeat your other challengers, you and I will face each other in this very circle. If that were to occur, my having trained you would possibly make you less likely to defeat me."

Looking at Set's massive bulk and knowing that his own people considered him one of their best fighters, I almost told him that I didn't expect to last long enough for that to be an issue, but something stopped me.

"You seem the kind of man not to present a problem without first arriving at a solution, Set. What do you suggest?"

He bowed his head slightly as though in appreciation of a compliment. That made me wonder how many of his mannerisms were copied from his interactions with humans and shape shifters previously and how many were the result of actual parallels between our races.

"In this instance I have not been able to see a solution that satisfies the full demands of honor. I have just come from speaking with my queen in the hopes that she would be able to illuminate my path."

My pulse sped up. The lamia queen was an enigma. She was the reason that we were here cooling our heels. I'd already killed two of her people for no good reason that I could see. If she had agreed to talk to us then the deaths wouldn't have needed to take place, but I saw no indication from Set or the others that she cared about the deaths of her people.

That could indicate someone who was so caught up in her power that she no longer viewed her subjects as real people, but that didn't seem to match up with the fact that Set had gone to her for advice when stumped on a question of honor. Even more confounding was the fact that she was supposed to be capable of seeing things the rest of us couldn't.

Celeste's ancestors had stopped short of claiming that the queen was some kind of omniscient deity, but they'd walked right up to that line. How could someone like that allow unnecessary deaths when she knew how the challenge matches were likely to end even before they started?

"How was your conversation with her?"

"Disquieting. There are other considerations where you are concerned that make it harder than normal to assign you a proper opponent. I believe that she recommended that I stop picking your opponents and instead allow the others to volunteer. You will fight the weakest of all the combatants who volunteer for any particular challenge."

I mulled that over. As long as the lamias were all able to watch each fight then they would have a decent idea of how good I was. In a shape shifter pack that would just mean that only the very best fighters in the pack, the ones who were virtually guaranteed to win, would volunteer to face off against me, but the lamias would probably be compelled by their honor to *all* volunteer unless they were absolutely positive that they couldn't beat me.

Once again I was basing my chances of survival on the goodwill and honor of a race of beings that I knew next to nothing about, but by now I should have been used to that. I would agree to his proposal, but I was most curious about his comments about his queen.

"Disquieting?"

"Yes...I'm afraid I lack the words to adequately explain further."

I wanted to press him on that point, but he'd gone completely still, which I was pretty sure was a sign that he was uncomfortable. I'd seen the guards outside the main lamia cavern freeze up in the exact same manner each time that I'd approached them.

"You feel that the course of action...suggested by the queen satisfies the requirements of your personal honor then?"

There was a long pause as though Set was translating a particularly difficult problem or possibly just that he didn't know how to answer.

"She is the queen. She is beyond concepts such as honor. If she orders me to take a particular course then I have no choice. One might say that there is more honor in following the mandates of one's queen than in any other action. She supersedes individual honor."

That wasn't very reassuring. My survival depended in no small part on the honor of Set and the others, but they could be ordered to set their honor aside at any point by their queen. I still didn't understand the other considerations Set had referenced, but he was giving the vibe of someone who had been pressed as far as he was willing to be pressed.

"I am satisfied that you have done all that can be expected to uphold honor, Set. If you are willing, then I am ready to begin my instruction."

Chapter 17

Isaac Nazir
The Lamia Enclave

By the time that Set released me for the day I was tired and sore in a way that rarely happened to a shape shifter after we manifested our first alternate form. Despite my injuries, Set had worked me as hard as I could ever remember being worked. I was actually glad that I wasn't at one hundred percent. I wasn't sure that I would have survived the training session that Set would have put me through if I'd been healthy.

I stumbled into our cave a little after what felt like noon, and found Celeste pacing back and forth through the kitchen. She acknowledged me with a nod, but didn't even slow down.

Neither of us said anything for nearly a full minute while she continued to pace, and then my hunger finally got the best of me. I waited until she was on the far end of her circuit and then darted in and grabbed one of the biggest yellow melons.

"You could have said something; I would have waited for you."

I stopped mid-bite and looked longingly at the fruit in my hand before looking up at her. "I didn't want to spoil your crazy cabin fever motif. You seem to be putting a lot of work into it."

For the briefest of instants I thought she was going to get mad at me, but then she smiled.

"I guess you're right. I've been stuck inside here for days and I'm starting to go a little stir-crazy."

"So leave. Nobody is stopping you. Ash and Kristin will be fine for an hour while you go out and stretch your legs. If you're really that worried about them I can always stay here with them."

She looked a little guilty. "I wasn't even thinking of them, actually. You're right, they would be fine. It's the lamias. I'm not sure what they expect out of a queen. Their queen never seems to leave that cave, and I'm worried that if I go out into the valley that they will decide I'm not...queenly enough and it will ruin our chances of talking to their queen."

"That's silly. They aren't going to decide that. Besides, it isn't even their call. The queen will decide when she wants to talk to us. The consorts and workers don't have anything to do with it."

"How can you be so sure? The queen doesn't work in a vacuum. I'm sure she talks to the consorts at least. Who's to say that she's not going to be influenced by them if they decide that I'm not acting the part?"

I wanted to argue with her, but I was the one with the most to lose if she was right. Given that I could lose the next challenge match at any point, it didn't seem smart to risk anything that might stretch our stay here out any longer than absolutely necessary.

"What about if I go out there with you? The lamias said that there wasn't anything dangerous that would go past the curtain, so Ash and Kristin will be safe while we're gone. The lamias were okay with you coming here in the first place, they can hardly get up in arms about you going out to the valley as long as you have a proper escort."

"I'm sure you have better things to do, Isaac. You look like you're about to fall over at any minute."

I filled a large cup with water from the faucet that I was pretty sure came from some kind of overhead cistern as I shook my head.

"I'll be okay, I'm just a little tired. Let me bring something to eat and I'll be fine. Besides, what else am I going to do? I can't take a nap yet and it's not like I can fire up my tablet and do research or anything."

LOST

After a few seconds she hesitantly nodded. "Thanks, Isaac. That would be nice."

We set out on one of the larger paths. It was nearly big enough for two lamia to walk alongside each other, so the two of us had no problem walking side by side in human form. The melon at my side was a reassuring weight and I found myself wondering how long it would be before she found a place to stop so that I could eat.

"Why don't you lead the way, Isaac? You probably know of a place where we could stop and sit down."

I nodded and steered her towards a large clearing off to one side of the valley. A tiny tributary of the stream trickled through one side, but other than that it was fully enclosed except for the path that connected it to the rest of the valley.

The privacy would hopefully mean that Celeste would be able to relax a little. It looked for a moment as though she still wasn't going to be able to let her hair down, but then she took a deep breath and walked over to the stream.

As she sat down and rolled up her jeans to mid-calf so that she could put her feet in the stream, I sat down on a nearby rock and bit into the melon I'd brought along with me.

Celeste waded in the cold water for a couple of minutes and then about the time that I finished up with my lunch, she came over to a nearby slab of rock and sat down.

"So you were Alec's right-hand man for the last four or five years. What's he like?"

For a second I thought she wasn't serious, but when I looked over at her, there wasn't any indication that she was trying to be funny. She wasn't grinning at me, she wasn't even watching to see my expression. She'd stretched out on the rock with her eyes closed and her shirt pulled up so her bare stomach could get some sunlight.

"He's okay."

"Really? You've known him basically your entire life and that's the best you can manage?"

I felt a spark of something from my beast, but he was too tired and well-fed to get worked up over anything right now.

"Alec is everything you would expect out of the heir to the monarchy."

"A power-hungry fiend who will sacrifice anyone and anything to expand his sphere of influence?"

I frowned at her despite the fact that her eyes were closed. "No, he's nothing at all like that."

She opened her eyes a crack to look at me and then shrugged and closed them again. "Sorry, the monarchy represents different things to different people. My family felt like his ancestors screwed them out of their position in the old order. Before the monarchy was established we were one of the preeminent packs in North America. His family and mine both had a history of producing hybrids with exceptional abilities, but unlike his ancestors, mine never used their abilities to take over the rest of North America."

"I've been through all of this with Ash. I did some research after the last time we talked and there were some very well-respected pack leaders who contradicted the history that your ancestors passed down to you."

"The victors always rewrite history to make themselves look better. You should know that, Isaac."

"Why is it that *I* should know that?"

She looked over at me again and shook her head. "You don't really think that you're some kind of anonymous face in the crowd, do you? Every single wolf pack, regardless of whether they come down for or against the Coun'hij, maintains a file on the dominant personalities in every other pack. We all have a big dossier on Alec Graves and most of us have at least a small file with your name on it."

"Why? I'm basically nobody."

"We both know that isn't the truth. You have to know how uncommon it is for any hybrid to back up their alpha like you did for all of those years. It happens, but not often. In a lot of packs it's only the lowest-of-the-low subordinates who display that level of loyalty to the pack leader. They know that the alpha is their natural ally against the other dominants inside the pack, the ones who tend to make their lives miserable.

"Then again, maybe you don't know all of that. Sometimes I forget. I grew up in a pretty messed-up situation, but in some ways your pack has always been even unhealthier than mine. You were always half a step from being devoured by the other Sanctuary pack."

"Yeah, we were. Brandon nearly killed us all half a dozen times and nobody else even lifted a hand to help us out."

I didn't even try to keep the bitterness from my voice. Celeste had lain back down and closed her eyes, but she reached over and patted me on the leg.

"Welcome to the club. My family has been clawing tooth and nail for centuries in an effort to keep the New Orleans pack from being taken away from them. We've had hundreds of millions of dollars extorted from us and most of us die before we hit middle age. As soon as there is a couple of spare Hunts walking around, whoever is running the pack arranges for some kind of accident to befall the older generation and then starts hammering away on the younger pair of Hunts.

"Nobody has helped us out either, everything we've accomplished has been on our own, but I think that's something to be proud of. *I* take care of the submissives inside of my pack. *I* shield them from the worst of Onyx's excesses."

Her eyes were closed still, so I took advantage of that fact to really look at her again. She was still gorgeous, nothing had changed there.

Someone else might have registered the flawless skin and perfect body and stopped there, but I already knew there was more to her than just her beauty.

It was there all of the time if you knew what to look for, but it was especially obvious now that she was talking about her pack. There was a fierceness to her that was breathtaking. It was the kind of thing that made me want to spend hours watching her. That protectiveness was the perfect complement to her unearthly physical perfection. It completed her in ways that I'd never even realized were possible.

"You're very loyal to your people back in New Orleans."

"Damn straight I am. It's Onyx's pack to everyone in the outside world, but it's me who keeps the wheels from coming off. I'm the one they turn to when there's some kind of disaster and they are loyal to me in return. If Onyx wasn't so powerful I would have overthrown him long ago and taken my pack back."

I believed her. She seemed like someone who wouldn't be stopped if there was a way to achieve what she wanted.

"What is Onyx's power? Back in the day we didn't have much information on the other packs. Alec and Donovan were mostly just focused on trying to keep one step ahead of Brandon. They're getting up to speed on the rest of the world now that Brandon is out of the way, but I haven't been in a position to see any of the reports that they've been reading."

"Pain. Onyx's power is the ability to create the kind of all-consuming pain that makes even a hybrid wish they were dead. It's completely debilitating. What's worse, he sucks something away from you while he's using it. I've seen him kill people with nothing more than the extended application of his ability."

A low whistle escaped me. "That's pretty world-class. That makes him more dangerous than Agony was, more deadly than Jaclyn Annikov or any of half a dozen other tier one or two hybrids who come to mind. How is he not on the Coun'hij as one of the inner circle already?"

I'd almost said that Onyx was more deadly than Grayson, but I'd remembered at the last second that most of the rest of the world didn't know that he'd been working for Alec. It wasn't that I didn't trust Celeste, but if she was possibly going to be hanging around someone like Onyx after this then it would be better for her not to know certain things. What she didn't know couldn't be tortured out of her.

"He could have taken a place on the Coun'hij at almost any time, but he doesn't want one. In his mind, ruling the New Orleans pack is a better route to power than what he would get by joining in with Puppeteer and the rest. He still stays on good terms with them, but so far he's retained his independence."

"Because of the money. He's staying with your pack because of the money he hopes to steal from you."

"Yeah, only you'd be more correct if you were to say that he's staying because of the money that he's hoping to *continue* to steal from us. The rate of decline in our family's wealth has more than quadrupled since Onyx took over the pack. He's got a real gift for finding weaknesses and using them against people. Just since Ash left, Onyx has made himself more than half a billion dollars richer just off of what he's taken from me.

"That doesn't include the tithe from the pack or the investment returns that he's made on the rest of his money. At the rate he's going he'll be able to challenge Alec Graves on the financial front before too much longer."

I chuckled. I couldn't help myself, the thought of an upstart thief like Onyx trying to buy and sell the combined team of Alec and Donovan was just so funny.

"Sorry, I'm not making light of what you've been through. You'd just have to know...it's not really my place to say, but trust me—Onyx has a long, long way to go before he'll be in a position where he can threaten Alec on a financial level. Alec and Donovan are in a class all by themselves."

Celeste had started to sit up, obviously ready to give me a piece of her mind, but my explanation mollified her enough to avoid a fight.

"That doesn't really make me feel any better, but it's nice to know that there are bigger fish than Onyx out there. I've been stuck inside the same tiny little pond for so long that sometimes it seems like Onyx is the biggest threat conceivable."

My mirth died instantly. "I can understand that. That's the way that I used to feel about Brandon. It's hard when you're in those kinds of situations to worry about the bigger picture. That was part of the difference between Alec and me. He always kept one eye out for the stuff that none of the rest of us figured we'd ever live long enough to have to worry about.

"Even now, it's hard sometimes for me to believe that Brandon is really dead. He was like a force of nature. Alec didn't see it because he was the one who was usually mixing it up with Brandon, but there were times when I'd be in the middle of a fight of my own and I'd catch bits and pieces of their fight. I think Brandon was holding back on everyone all along. I think that as deadly as he was, he was still keeping people from seeing his real potential because he was worried that it would scare the Coun'hij badly enough for them to have Puppeteer show up with two dozen hybrids."

Celeste was silent for a while as she digested what I'd said. I realized that was one of the things that I liked about her. She was as capable of rattling off a response in anger as anyone else, but most of the time she considered what she heard and made sure that she understood what it really meant before she responded.

"I wasn't there, I didn't see the body, but all indications are that Worthingfield really is dead. He's not the kind of person to keep a low profile for months to convince everyone that he's gone. He was too narcissistic for something like that."

I nodded. "I know. I did actually see his body before we buried him, and you're right about the fact that he isn't the kind of person to go to ground, but even so it still feels like this impossible thing."

"You guys accomplished something great. You should be proud to have brought him down. Everything I ever heard about him indicated that Worthingfield was no good."

"I didn't have anything to do with it. That was all Alec. It was the very first time that his ability manifested. One second Brandon was about to kill Alec and then everyone collapsed to the ground. I was positive that we were all about to die, but Alec came through for us."

"I think that you aren't giving yourself enough credit, Isaac. I said earlier that the kind of loyalty you displayed to Alec was rare, but the reason it is so significant is that when an alpha has that kind of support they invariably accomplish a lot more than they would have without it. Knowing that they've got the second strongest fighter in the pack backing them up means that they can do things other pack leaders couldn't even consider, it means that they can take risks that nobody else can take. It makes a difference."

"That's not making me feel any better."

"Now you're not making any sense. I just basically told you that Alec and the rest of your pack wouldn't have survived long enough for him to manifest his power if not for you supporting him like you did. Indirectly or otherwise, you saved all of your friends and family. You should feel like a million bucks right now."

I couldn't remain seated any longer. I stood and started pacing, making a circuit around the clearing while Celeste watched me.

"You would think so, but the truth is that I haven't been that guy—the one who was ready to back Alec no matter what—for a long time."

"What changed?"

"I guess you could say that I had a crisis of faith. Alec made some decisions that I didn't agree with, decisions that hurt me—that hurt people that I cared about—and suddenly I didn't know what to believe or who to trust anymore."

"That doesn't sound unreasonable, Isaac."

"Yeah, I know. I've been telling myself that for a while, but it's started to ring hollow lately. I'm not sure that my reasons were as pure as I originally thought. I realized a few days ago that I supported Alec at least partially because I didn't want to be the one leading the pack. Being submissive to anyone can suck, but Alec was better about that than almost anyone. By supporting him I got to enjoy the power of being the number two hybrid in the pack without the stress of trying to come up with a way to keep Brandon from rolling over the top of us."

Celeste reached out and grabbed my hand as I walked past. She gently pulled me down onto the rock next to her.

"That isn't something to be ashamed of."

"Isn't it? It seems like it to me. You asked what Alec is like. Well, the truth is that he's everything you could want in a leader. He isn't perfect, but he tries hard to do the right thing and when he screws up he is willing to admit it and try to make things right.

"Alec is the kind of guy who cares about other people. He does whatever he can to fight injustice. Even when he's falling apart he still does a better job taking care of his pack than most alphas. He's the real deal, and now that he's manifested his ability he has a chance to make a real difference, not just for his pack, but for everyone. That's why Ash agreed to join us. He came in without all of the baggage that the rest of us had and realized that Alec is the kind of guy people should want to hitch their wagons to."

"If you really believe that then why haven't you hitched your wagon to him, Isaac?"

"If you'd asked me this morning, I would have told you that I was resentful of the way that Alec was confiding in other people. Ash, Jaclyn, Rebekka—none of them had the history with him that I had, but they were all replacing me."

"But you don't believe that now?"

I shrugged uncomfortably. She hadn't let go of my hand yet, which was nice, but it felt wrong. At this point Jess—Jessica— didn't care what I did or who I saw, but it still felt disloyal to what she and I had had together before she'd lost her memories.

"I think that all of that stuff is just a bunch of symptoms. The real problem is that I'm scared of stepping up and taking responsibility. It's easy when I don't have any choice, but it's a lot harder to do when I have other options. Being the alpha, means that there isn't anyone else to step in and fix things if you screw up.

"A guy like Alec is the final arbiter, he doesn't have any peers, not really. I need to make a decision, I need to either step up and be who I have the potential to be, or I need to own up to the fact that I've been a fraud this entire time. Alec has moved beyond the point where he has use for someone like me. He needs someone who's all in."

I hadn't planned on making such a heavy confession, especially not to Celeste, who seemed like she didn't know how to back down from any kind of challenge. She was so dominant that she took care of her people even after being overthrown by someone like Onyx.

What I felt was something beyond embarrassment and all I could think of was the fact that I needed to get away from her, that I needed to hide until some of the pain had worn away. I stood to go, but Celeste still hadn't let go of my hand. She slipped in behind me and pressed up against my back as though trying to hug someone who didn't want to be hugged.

"I think you still aren't giving yourself enough credit, Isaac. I think you're already most of the way to where you want to be. You're already taking the responsibility; you just aren't acknowledging the choice."

Chapter 18

Isaac Nazir
The Lamia Enclave

Celeste had slipped away, walking up the trail before I could say anything in response to her assertion. I was so surprised by what she'd said that I just sat there trying to make sense of her words for several seconds.

I felt like I was almost there, like I could almost see the point she was trying to make, and then I realized that I'd let her leave the clearing without the escort that I'd promised her. I hadn't thought much of her concerns back in our rooms, but it wasn't the kind of thing that we should be leaving to chance.

I took off at a sprint, trying to catch up with her, and my attempts to reconcile what she'd said with my view of the world were pushed to the back of my mind.

LOST

Even at a sprint I wasn't fast enough to catch her. By the time I made it back to our rooms she'd already slipped behind the curtain to her bedroom. The vines and leaves that made up the curtains were unusually good at blocking sounds. I stood just a few feet from the curtain and imagined that I could hear her heartbeat from inside her room, but the truth was that I couldn't.

I couldn't bring myself to go into her room and she was obviously not going to come out. She might as well have been on a different continent.

After the better part of five minutes I forced myself to turn around and go into my room. I knew I wouldn't be able to sleep, but I dropped down onto my bed regardless. I closed my eyes but the scenes from the clearing kept playing through my mind.

I could see her on the back of my eyelids, stretched out on the slab of rock taking in the sun as though we were a couple of normal teenagers out at the beach. The image changed and I could see her the way she'd looked the first night we'd arrived at the enclave, pale skin showing above and below the soft black material of her dress.

The images started speeding up to the point where she seemed to run and jump—like a character from one of the old stop-motion films. It was as though my subconscious mind had been taking pictures of her at random times for days now without my conscious mind being aware of what was happening.

My left hand was tingling from where she'd touched me earlier. It was intense almost to the point of being uncomfortable, much like the actual experience had been. It was as much a relief as it was a surprise when I fell asleep a few minutes later.

Celeste was still in her room when I woke the next morning. I was pretty sure she wasn't asleep, but again I couldn't bring myself to break the silence between us. My feelings, about Jess and Celeste both, were just too confused for me to want to wade any deeper into that particular pool than I had to right now.

I showered, grabbed something to eat on the way and then left our rooms as fast as possible so that Celeste wouldn't have to continue hiding in her rooms.

Set found me walking down the path towards the main lamia cavern and accompanied me to the challenge ring without saying a word. Once we arrived, he waited only long enough for me to shift forms and stretch before beginning the training session.

We started out with actual techniques again and I found myself learning a system of fighting that seemed to favor short, raking slashes, knees, and elbows, all of which were executed from extremely close range.

LOST

It was an interesting style of combat, but partway through the session I started wondering why anyone as large as Set would want to fight at such close range and use striking surfaces that didn't allow him to use the venom in his claws that was the lamias' single greatest asset. The close-in blocks and attacks that I was learning were the kind of techniques that a small person would use against a much larger individual, but I couldn't think of any enemies other than the werewolves who were significantly larger than a lamia consort.

Even werewolves weren't that much larger than a lamia. Definitely not enough larger to justify developing a completely different style of combat.

"Set, this kind of fighting doesn't fit with what I would expect from your people."

He looked at me for several seconds before nodding in agreement. Once again, I got the feeling that he was trying to translate difficult concepts into English.

"You know that we aren't from this place?"

I pursed my lips. "There are legends among the people in South and Central America that I believe were spawned by interactions with your people. Is that what you mean?"

"You mean the Aztec people?"

I nodded, excited that we seemed to have found a common frame of reference, but he just frowned.

"No, that wasn't our enclave. Before we were here, near the territory of your queen, we were somewhere else. With the...I think you call them pharaohs?"

My eyes practically bugged out of my head. "How did you move your entire enclave? My understanding from Celeste, from my queen, is that you arrived here on this continent before its discovery by the Old World. How did you travel across the ocean when sailing technology was still so primitive?"

"No, we didn't move. The enclave remains in the same place, only the portals move."

My mind was spinning. It was the clearest proof yet that the enclave wasn't in Louisiana. When they wanted to move away from Egypt they apparently had just changed the position of the enclave as compared to what I thought of as the real world.

"Okay, I think I understand, not how that is possible, but the fact that you did it. How does being in Egypt, being with the pharaohs, explain a fighting system that is best suited for fighting someone much bigger than you?"

"No. Different move. Before we were here near your queen we were with the pharaohs. Before we were with the pharaohs we were somewhere *else*."

Things that historians had wondered about for centuries suddenly clicked into place for me. The pyramids. The lamias were somehow responsible for them. There had been pyramids in Egypt, but there had also been pyramids in the Americas and in parts of Asia.

LOST

Various historians had tried to prove a link between the different ancient cultures that had built pyramids, but nobody had been able to come up with a hypothesis that worked.

All of those man-hours wasted. They'd never had any chance of figuring the link out, not without being willing to believe in things like werewolves, vampires and lamias. The sad thing was that we wolves could have put the pieces together if we'd ever managed to expand beyond North America.

We had such a long life expectancy that we could have easily tied some of those disparate threads together, but the jaguars had been solidly in control of everything from current-day Mexico down, and Europe and the rest of the Old World was such a vampire and werewolf cesspit that nobody had gone over there and come back to report their findings.

The lamias probably even explained the myths in Asia when it came to hydras and dragons. The lamias had taught them how to construct pyramids and in the process they'd spawned legends of giant, snake-like creatures that served as sources of knowledge and enlightenment.

Set moved impatiently and I realized that I'd spent too long lost in the ramifications of what I thought he was telling me.

"Sorry. Before you were with the pharaohs you were somewhere else. I think it was probably Asia—Thailand or Cambodia? I don't remember exactly where the pyramids over there are located."

Set looked even more frustrated now. "No, that was another enclave. We were somewhere different. Not Louisiana, not Egypt. Not here..."

He lapsed back into his native tongue for several words before looking at me expectantly. I had a feeling that we weren't going to make much progress now, but I decided to try one last time.

"You weren't here? In the enclave?"

"No. Enclave came later."

"Where was your enclave before this one?"

Set bent down and drew a circle in the sand that I thought was supposed to represent the Earth. Once I indicated that I understood, he wiped the circle away with his foot.

"Not an enclave. Home. Enclave came later."

I didn't think he was telling me that his people were from outer space, but I was drawing a blank on what else it could all mean.

"You came from somewhere else."

"Yes, but other things came here with us. Hunters. Much bigger than lamias, very dangerous. We call them-it the Consumed."

It was hard, but I temporarily put aside the question of where his people had come from and focused on what he was telling me now.

"So this is the style of fighting that you use when you are fighting the Consumed?"

"Yes. That."

LOST

It was interesting that Set's language skills seemed to degenerate so much when we got into more abstract questions. He obviously wasn't stupid, the only logical explanation seemed to be that we were touching on things that were important to him, things that he wasn't entirely comfortable discussing.

"Are the Consumed the reason that you left Egypt, Set?"

"Yes, and no. There were complications. It was the order of the queen."

The things that I was learning were incredible, but they wouldn't keep me alive in the next challenge match, a match that was getting closer with each second. Still, there was a part of me that couldn't bear to let such an incredible source of information go.

"Set, would it be possible for me to come here sometime later? After I've left with my queen? I wouldn't be coming back to ask for an audience with your queen, I'd be coming to talk to you."

Set looked at me as though I'd lost my mind. "You have many strange ideas, Isaac Nazir. Men do not visit another enclave without their queen. Such a thing is without honor. How could you leave your queen without assistance?"

I struggled for a way to explain things in a way that matched up with Set's world view. "My...queen may not be able to return. She has commitments that may not allow her to visit again, but she does not always need my help.

What if I were to return with a different queen? Possibly the tiny queen who accompanied me here with my queen and the other sun person. Is there a way for me to return and not have to face challengers?"

I was pretty sure that the concept of changing queens, of shifting one's loyalty between women would be anathema to Set, but I was hoping that I could muddy the waters by throwing Kristin into the mix. Surely they occasionally had new queens born in the enclave, and when that happened it was only logical that some of the lamias from the original enclave would be allowed to accompany the adolescent queen when she left to set up a new enclave.

Set considered my question for several long moments.

"I start to wonder if some of my brethren might not be right. Our very presence here exposes us to things that workers and consorts are not meant to know. These are questions and ideas that are meant for queens. I fear that our people will not recognize us when we return home."

Fearing that I'd inadvertently pushed too hard, I started to apologize, but Set stopped me with a gesture.

"With someone else it might be possible. It would be a question for my queen, but it would not be possible for you to return, Isaac Nazir. You stress the way of things too much."

"I'm sorry that my questions are so disruptive, Set. I meant no harm by them. I merely wish to learn more about your people."

"You misunderstand me. Your questions and ideas are concerning, but they are not the reason that you wouldn't be able to return. Your sun is too bright and it grows brighter still."

"I don't understand what you mean."

Set waved at the cavern we were standing in. "It grows smaller with every passing day. Surely you have noticed this."

I looked around and realized for the first time that he was right. The change was very small, but during my last fight there had been a ring of lamias watching us that had been two deep in spots. Now there wasn't enough space between the wall and the circle for two lamias to stand.

"How is this possible?"

Set shrugged. "It is the queen. She shapes the world stuff, but we consorts and workers hide the enclave from the Consumed. Fewer workers mean the enclave has to be smaller to hide it, but the presence of sun people always makes it harder to hide."

"So shape shifters create some kind of...beacon that lures the Consumed to your home?"

"Yes, and no. Sun people make hiding difficult. Lure the Consumed to enclave, not home. You are special case, nearly ready to expand, bigger...lure."

I couldn't decide if he was saying that my shifting shapes was what was causing the problems or if he was trying to reference something else. I started to ask another question, but Set waved me back into the center of the circle.

Apparently he was done answering questions.

Chapter 19

Isaac Nazir
The Lamia Enclave

The next fight was a real doozy. I was starting to suspect that Set waited for me to heal from the last fight before throwing me back in the ring. If that was the case, then the sheer amount of punishment I took training with him bought me an extra day or so.

My next opponent was another worker, roughly the same size as my previous challenger, but faster on his feet than anyone I'd faced up to that point. I tried every trick I knew and still thought several times that I wasn't going to beat him.

Despite my best efforts, I couldn't manage to control the tempo and terms of the fight. He was just too good for that. He came in close and went to town on me. He wasn't using the style of fighting that Set had been teaching me though. It was more just the result of him being slightly shorter than me. It was only natural for him to close and try to get inside of my reach.

The fight turned into the kind of battering match that I knew at the start I wasn't likely to win. Neither of us was getting anything vital with the blows that we were landing, but we were still each bleeding from a couple of dozen spots within seconds.

I kept trying to back away and get myself room to maneuver, but he stayed right inside of my reach and kept landing blows on me at the rate of three for every two hits I managed. He landed a particularly vicious blow to the right side of my chest towards the end of the second minute and something snapped inside of me.

The lamia I was fighting pulled his hand out of my chest and then threw a short, hooking slash at my neck. All of the hours of training with Set hadn't been enough to wire enough reflexes to go toe-to-toe with a consort using nothing but their preferred fighting style, but it had been enough to make a couple of very elementary blocks reflexive.

My elbow slammed into his arm with enough force to make his arm go numb, and then I rammed another elbow home into the side of his neck. It was a telling blow, the kind of hit that would have brought most lesser foes to their knees, but my opponent was already bringing his other arm around for a shot at my kidney.

I couldn't match him in a straight-up contest of strength, but rather than backing away in an attempt to get out of his range, I charged forward with everything I had left. It shouldn't have worked, it probably wouldn't have worked if not for the fact that I bit down on the side of his neck a split second before I crashed into him.

I could feel his shock, feel the way his body tensed up as my teeth latched onto him. It only lasted for an instant, but it was enough. He was off balance and unprepared when my full weight crashed into him.

I've never particularly liked biting as an offensive tactic, but my beast was enough in control of me this time that I didn't even notice all of the blood other than to thrill at the fact that I'd hit something important. I knew it was only a matter of time before the lamia would bleed out, but until then I needed to stop him from doing more damage to me.

I had hold of his wrists, but he was just too strong for me to control like that. His claws were shredding my back despite my best efforts.

Instead of continuing to battle where I was weak, I spun around so I could get my legs into the fight. I sank my talons into his left arm, and then once I had that arm immobilized I moved my left hand up to his right wrist. Even he wasn't strong enough to out muscle me when it was just his arms against nearly every muscle in my body.

Despite my advantages, I could feel myself tiring. He was strong in the way that a werewolf was strong, and between that and the amount of blood that I'd already lost, I knew he would eventually wear me down enough to break free.

I clamped down even harder on his neck, trying to exert enough pressure to snap it, but in the end simple blood loss did what all of the rest of my efforts hadn't been able to. I pulled myself up to my feet and stumbled towards the mouth of the cave.

I knew that later on I'd regret the fact that I'd been forced to kill yet another lamia for no good reason, but right then I just felt numb. Even the normal high I'd grown to expect from surviving a fight to the death was absent. I made it less than two steps into the valley before I collapsed to the ground in a slowly growing pool of blood.

Chapter 20

Isaac Nazir
The Lamia Enclave

For several days I drifted in and out of consciousness. Celeste must have been taking care of me, but I couldn't remember any of that. Mostly there was just the black oblivion of deep sleep interspersed with dreams about training with Set. Even in my dreams he was a harsh taskmaster. I ran through everything he'd ever shown me—even things that I'd thought I'd forgotten from the first training session.

It didn't make for restful sleep and I was grateful when the void finally started to lose its grip on me. Nobody else was in my room when I opened my eyes, but there was a cup of water and a small melon on one edge of my bed.

The water went down my throat like pure joy. I couldn't remember any other time when I'd been as thirsty, or when the taste of clean, slightly warm water had been quite so satisfying. I'd pulled myself up to a sitting position to drink the water, and from there it seemed silly not to test out my legs.

I grabbed the fruit—my curiosity was stronger than my hunger, but that didn't mean that I wasn't starving—and swung my feet down onto the soft carpet. It turned out to be a good thing that the bed wasn't very far from the wall. I almost fell down after just my first two steps and it was only the presence of the wall that allowed me to make it the rest of the way to my door.

I pushed through the heavy green curtain and found Set standing only a couple of feet away. The sight of an enormous lamia waiting just outside of my room should have freaked me out. Celeste was standing over by the fruit vines and she seemed plenty unnerved by having Set in our rooms, but for some reason it didn't bother me at all that he was there.

"Welcome back to the enclave, Isaac Nazir. Will you make a full recovery?"

Somehow I'd forgotten to check myself over for injuries. I wanted to blame it on being fuzzy after having been asleep for so long, but I didn't think that was the answer. The first thing out of my mouth should have been a question as to how long I'd been asleep, but I already knew that it had been approximately two days.

That wasn't something that I should have known, but I let that question drift away and instead patted myself down in search of bandages. I could feel them on my back still, and there seemed to be a lot of tape across my stomach and the right side of my chest, but the fact that I was standing there, with all of my appendages still working, was pretty good evidence that I was going to eventually be back to full strength.

Set wrapped his hand around my arm, propping me up as I made my unsteady way towards the vegetation-covered slab of rock that served as our couch.

"Thank you, Set. Yes, I believe that I'll be okay. How did you know that I would be getting up today?"

"The queen told me it would be today that she let you return, and I could see your sun glow strengthening again."

I looked over at Celeste, confused. Had she been drugging me? I didn't remember seeing anything in any of the first-aid kits that would have been capable of keeping me out for more than a few hours.

Set shook his head. "No, not your queen, my queen."

"Set, how would your queen know that I was going to wake up now? I haven't been anywhere. At least not under my own power."

That earned me another frown, almost as though I was a particularly dense student who'd just failed some kind of test.

"Not here," said Set as he tapped me on the forehead. "Down here." He pointed at my chest, at my heart, for several seconds until I nodded. I didn't understand, but I had a feeling that further questions at this point were only going to frustrate all of us.

I wasn't sure if it was a breach of etiquette to eat around the lamias, but by that point my hunger had gotten bad enough that I couldn't stop myself from taking a bite from the fruit that Celeste had left for me.

Set waited patiently while I chewed and then sat down on another chunk of rock that served as the lamia equivalent of an easy chair.

"You were the victor in your last fight. I've come to ask you what boon you would like to ask of the men here in the enclave."

Somehow I'd forgotten that I still had that coming to me. I looked over at Celeste, hoping that she would give me an idea of what she thought I should ask for, but she steadfastly refused to meet my gaze.

I knew that things had been tense between us before my last match, but I couldn't put my finger on what had set us off. Even if I'd had a clear memory of whatever it had been that had set us off, I got the feeling that it wouldn't have seemed important now.

I almost said something to her right then despite the fact that Set was there, but I bit back the words at the last second. Internal divisions might cause the lamias to take us less seriously, but the very act of not saying anything just increased the bitterness that had been preying on the back of my mind for days.

It was bad enough that I was stuck in some kind of weird pocket dimension where I was forced to fight for my life every few days. I was surrounded by creatures I didn't understand and my friends were still both in comas. To top it all off, the only other one of my kind here was refusing to talk to me.

Celeste was the one person I should have been able to talk to. Even if we didn't like each other, this experience should have brought us closer together rather than setting us at each other's throats.

In that moment I wanted nothing so much as a friend, but that was the one thing that nobody could give me. Set couldn't compel Celeste to stop ignoring me anymore than he could magically get past the cultural and species barriers that kept him and me from truly becoming friends.

I had an idea that I thought might get me what I wanted, but it felt like a waste to use the gift that I'd fought for, that I'd killed for and very nearly died for, on something so simple. It would just be giving into the weakness inside of me, weakness that had driven Jess away from me.

"Set, if I'm unable to think of something I desire right now can I wait to name the boon?"

"I'm sorry, Isaac Nazir, but that is not how honor works. If no boon is named now you will forfeit the opportunity and we consorts will consider that we've done our duty in easing your stay here."

"Very well, then. I'd like to have my electronics work here so that I'll be able to call home. I have family and friends I'm worried about, people who are likely worried about Ash, Kristin and me. I'd like to be able to talk to them as soon as possible. I don't know if that is within your power or not, but that is what I want."

The responses I got from Celeste and Set were both baffling. Celeste looked like she'd just been told that her family had all been killed in a hit and run accident. She closed her eyes and grabbed the table to stop herself from collapsing.

I opened my mouth to ask her what was wrong, but she opened her eyes and shot me a look that told me in no uncertain terms that she wasn't going to be answering any of my questions.

As odd as that was, Set's response was just as atypical. He looked confused. I would have said that it was a language problem again, but after just a couple of seconds he held his hand out and asked for my phone.

"I'll get it."

Celeste disappeared into my room and was back a short time later with not just my phone, but also my tablet.

LOST

"You did say that you wanted your electronics to work."

Now it was Set's turn to look unhappy, but he nodded and took both devices. He didn't seem to be doing anything with them. He just sat there in the chair with his eyes closed, one hand on my gear, the other on the 'arm' of the chair he was sitting in.

Five minutes later he opened his eyes and put the tablet on the arm of the chair. I started to ask him to be careful, but the words died in my throat when I saw that the charge light on the tablet was glowing. It was impossible. I'd seen cable-free chargers before, but none of my electronics was set up for that.

There was no denying my eyes though or the fact that as he set my phone down on top of the tablet that it also lit up with the glow of an active power feed. If I'd still had any doubt as to the fact that the lamias were capable of astonishing things, that would have cured me of my disbelief then and there.

Set handed me my phone and when I turned it on it was showing that it had a network. A huge grin split my face right up until I remembered the issues that Ash, Kristin and I had experienced on our way across the continent.

"Set, there isn't any way to trace this, is there? We have powerful enemies and I wouldn't want to have them track us back here and create problems for you."

Something flashed across Set's face, almost too quick for me to catch. In a human I would have said it was bitter irony, but I didn't think that Set had spent enough time around humans to have absorbed our mannerisms to the point where they would become unconscious like that.

"I normally wouldn't have brought this up, Isaac Nazir. It stinks of dishonor, of giving a boon and then trying to take the boon away, but your concerns have moved me to talk. Your enemies won't be able to use your phone to find you while you are here, but your use of the phone will make it easier for our enemies to find us."

"the Consumed?"

Set nodded. "the Consumed is always searching for us, always trying to find a chink in our armor that it can use to come here to the enclave. The phone by itself won't cause problems and therefore honor demanded that I grant you that request, but along with other...factors it makes it that much harder for the enclave to remain hidden."

Apparently I wasn't the only one whose mind was whirling as it tried to absorb what Set had said...and what he hadn't. Celeste couldn't remain silent in the face of such a juicy piece of information.

"Wait, who are the Consumed and why is one of you talking about them in the plural and the other in the singular? Are there multiple Consumed or is there just one?"

Set nodded. "Yes."

"That isn't an answer. It's an either-or question, not a yes-or-no question."

I held a hand up, stopping her before she could press Set further. He'd already gone completely still in the way that he did when he didn't know how to respond to something.

"It's not that simple, Celeste. There are concepts that don't translate well from Set's native tongue to English. He's trying to answer us, but I suspect that we aren't asking him the right questions."

For a moment Celeste just sat there looking at me. I could smell the shock coming off of her. I wasn't sure how to proceed. I didn't want to make things worse by further contradicting her in front of Set, but the situation seemed to call for some kind of additional response.

Before I could decide which was the safer path Celeste stomped past Set and disappeared into her room. She hadn't just been embarrassed, she'd been shaking the way shape shifters only did when they were mere heartbeats from being forced into a change by their beast.

I waited for the rush of power that would have told me that she'd lost the battle for control of her own body, but it never came. Relieved that I wouldn't have to throw my battered body between Celeste's hybrid form and Set, I turned back to him and apologized.

"I'm very sorry, Set."

He held up a hand. "No apology is necessary between the two of us, Isaac Nazir. Honor does not require such from someone given the lot to have a difficult queen. It speaks to your honor that you choose to remain at her side and fight as her champion."

I nodded as I powered my phone down and reached over to do the same with my tablet. Set frowned at my actions.

"If you fail to use the phone then the others will say that I have failed to uphold honor, Isaac Nazir. I would not have that. Please use the phone as freely as you would have if I hadn't told you of the Consumed. It is our problem, our concern, not yours."

I nodded, not necessarily because I agreed with his view that the possible arrival of the Consumed wasn't any of my concern, but because I needed to buy myself some time to think.

"I did not state earlier the number of times that I wanted to use my phone, Set. What if I only wanted to make one or two calls?"

"Honor is not something to be trifled with, Isaac Nazir. We would be poor hosts to give you back the ability to communicate with your home enclave and then limit its usage."

"I understand that, but what if I choose to voluntarily limit my use of the phone? What if I asked for something else in exchange for keeping my phone off most of the time?"

LOST

"It seems a poor bargain for you to make. I was able to see how much you desired to talk to them. For you to choose not to talk to them would only be a sign that I have incurred dishonor."

"Unless I have thought of something else, something that I want more than I desire to talk to my friends back home. Then it might be possible for us to modify the terms of our agreement, right?"

Set looked doubtful. I didn't blame him. I was playing with something very important to him. The lamias seemed willing to die rather than risk dishonor, but Set wasn't just some grunt, he was one of the consorts, possibly even the highest-ranking consort. He had to worry about more than just his personal honor, he had to worry about the survival of the enclave.

I needed something important to me, something he could be convinced would be doing me a favor at the same time that he got what he secretly wanted, which was to protect his people. It was a tall order. The need to hear a friendly voice, to talk to someone who missed me, who was glad to hear from me was still overpowering.

The temptation to just admit defeat was strong, but then I realized that I was looking at things wrong. Set couldn't force Celeste to be my friend, but that was still a worthy goal. A friend here in the enclave would be just as valuable as being able to talk to Andrew or any of the rest of the pack. You could even make the case that it would improve my life beyond being able to talk to my friends just because Celeste and I wouldn't be constantly one step away from ripping each other's heads off.

I laboriously levered myself up off of the couch and motioned Set to follow me outside where there wouldn't be any chance of Celeste overhearing us. He steadied me with a hand on my arm and a few minutes later he'd guided me over to a rock in one of the meadows that bordered the stream.

"You spoke truly earlier, Set. My queen is very difficult at times. Being away from her enclave wears at her in ways I didn't anticipate and she then takes out her displeasure on me. The speed of our...journey here did not allow for her to bring all of the possessions that she would have liked to have brought for such an extended stay."

"I do not understand. Has our hospitality been lacking?"

I hadn't anticipated that interpretation of what I was saying. I needed to head him off before he decided that he'd failed in yet another way.

"No, your hospitality has been beyond reproach. Truly we have everything we need, but sometimes it is our nature to want things that we don't need. I don't know if it is the same way for your people, but surely that cannot be construed as a lack of hospitality. I do not think honor would demand that a host meet every unbridled want of their guests."

Set's nod was a hesitant, begrudging kind of motion, but he nodded. "It is true, that is why honor circumscribes the requirements of a hosting enclave. It stops the visiting queen from becoming an undue burden on the enclave. What are you trying to say, Isaac Nazir? What is it that you lack?"

"Clothes, Set. My queen has only one change of clothes and I think it puts her in an ill mood. If you could provide us with some additional clothes then I think it would make my service to her easier and eliminate the need for me to call back to my pack, my enclave."

I put every bit of belief I could into that statement. I didn't have any idea how Set had known how much I'd wanted to talk to my friends, to Jess, but the best way to convince him of what I was saying now was to really feel it. I couldn't fully convince myself that some new jeans and a shirt or two would make all of the difference between Celeste and me, but I came close.

Once I finished talking, Set went still again. I could tell that he was considering my words, but I'd obviously made him uneasy. After several minutes he sighed and turned back towards me.

"I never thought I would find myself bargaining over the requirements of honor like a common *zsst*, Isaac Nazir. Still, I cannot deny that I am worried about the circumstances that we now find ourselves in. I will accept part of your bargain. If you will leave your phone off other than when you are using it, then I will alert you when someone from your enclave is trying to communicate with you."

"How will you know when I've got an incoming call, Set?"

He shrugged. "It is the way of things. I will know."

The things he was implying were on the edge of blowing my mind. I kept telling myself that it wasn't that much more incredible than Kristin's dreams, but he seemed to be saying that he controlled his knowledge rather than just having it come at unpredictable times.

Even if he was wrong, presumably if someone called and my phone was off it would still go to voicemail. If I'd known that it was the ongoing carrier signal that was the most concerning to him then we probably could have avoided a lot of worry on both sides.

"I accept, Set. That seems a good bargain to me."

He shook his head. "Not so easily will you trick me, Isaac Nazir. I will do these things and amend your boon, but I will only do so if we are allowed to provide your party with clothes. I will be said to be a poor bargainer, the other consorts will say that I gave away too much to you, but I will accept that rather than risk the enclave. They will say it is a different kind of dishonor, but it is better this way. Sometimes the right course is the most difficult one."

Chapter 21

Isaac Nazir
The Lamia Enclave

After Set had departed I sat there on the rock for half an hour before I finally turned my phone back on and started making my calls. I tried Alec's phone first. I didn't really *want* to talk to him, but I felt like I *needed* to talk to him.

It was hard to explain—I didn't really understand it all myself—but I was starting to see his actions in a different light. We'd been...well, not exactly friends, but on the same team for a long time. I didn't want to die here in some challenge match without at least telling him that I didn't hate his guts.

Some alphas wouldn't have cared if I hated them as long as I did what I was told to do, but that was part of what made Alec special. He'd still do whatever he felt he had to do, even if it meant that everyone was going to hate him, but he'd feel bad about it. It would eat at him and make it harder for him to continue to make the hard decisions.

I didn't want that. Not for Alec's sake and not for the sake of everyone who was depending on him to pull us through the war he'd started with the Coun'hij.

I dialed Alec's number and listened to the phone ring, counting the attempts until it went through to voicemail. After the beep I cleared my throat and left the most difficult message I'd ever left.

"Alec, it's me, Isaac. I'm not surprised that you let it go through to voicemail. I've been kind of a jerk lately and I just wanted to call and tell you that I was sorry. I...well, I've had a lot of time on my hands to just sit and think lately and I'm starting to think that I should have given you the benefit of the doubt over the last little while instead of just making things harder for you."

Before I'd started talking I'd hoped that he'd let the call go through to voicemail because it had seemed like it would be easier to apologize that way, but now I wasn't so sure. Saying some of these things was a lot harder than I'd realized it was going to be and it would have been nice to be able to have some kind of feedback from him as I went along.

"I guess I'm starting to realize things about myself that have shed a new light on the last few months and I could use someone to talk to. I know you're busy, what with trying to keep the rebellion from being crushed and all, but you've already had to think through some of this stuff and while I haven't always agreed with everything you've done I can see now that there might have been aspects to the situations that I couldn't see at the time."

I cleared my throat again and took a deep breath. "I'm worried about making mistakes. It's like there is this pressure building around me and I'm worried about where I'm headed. I'm not sure if some of the things I'm doing are justified by the end I'm pursuing. That's all. If you can find a few minutes to talk, then I'd appreciate it, but even if you can't I still want you to know that I'm sorry.

"The apology wasn't just because I wanted something out of you. I mean it independent of all of that other stuff. Good luck and be careful."

I hung the phone up and almost turned it off, but if I did that I might not ever turn it back on. It was a temptation, but that wouldn't be fair. I had two more calls that I needed to make still, one for someone else and one for me.

I dialed the second number on my list and a wave of relief washed over me as Andrew answered the phone.

"Isaac, is that you? Are you okay?"

"Hi, Andrew. Yeah, it's me. I'm fine, how are you?"

"Better now that I know you're still alive. I've tried calling you half a dozen times, but it just keeps going through to voicemail."

"Yeah, I'm sorry. Ash and Alec agreed that we were going to keep our phones off for a little while for operational security reasons. I'll be available a little more now, at least for a while."

"Are Ash and Kristin okay?"

"I'm not sure."

"Have the three of you become separated?" The worry edging back into Andrew's voice was unmistakable. It was the worry of a parent who knew that they couldn't shield one of their children from what life was throwing at them. There was a special kind of agony there that I'd never had to experience, but I knew it was very real.

I'd seen Andrew deal with being confined to a wheelchair for as long as I could remember. He'd been in a constant state of low-level pain, but that hadn't ever seemed to bother him as much as when Jess or I had been struggling for some reason or another.

Andrew wasn't my biological father, but he was my parent in every way that mattered.

"No, we haven't been separated. They're still here with me, but they're hurt. We tangled with the Coun'hij a couple of times and Kristin got hurt. Then Ash got hurt at the hospital when we were trying to get Kristin patched up. I think they'll both be okay, but they've been asleep for a long time—I guess it's some kind of coma."

I was actually less sure than I was letting on to Andrew, but I didn't want him to worry.

"It's not safe to be wandering around by yourself, Isaac. I'll give Alec a call and ask him to send someone down to watch your back."

"No, there's no need, Andrew. We're holed up somewhere safe and we seem to have fallen off of the Coun'hij's radar. If Alec sends someone down they'll be in danger the entire trip down here, and even if they make it to us, they might just end up leading the bad guys to us. I'll be fine. Besides, I actually do have someone to watch my back. I'd rather have you down here with me, but she's not so bad."

There was a catch in Andrew's voice. "I'm afraid that I wouldn't do you any good, Isaac. I'm still confined to this blasted chair. As long as whoever you've got down there is trustworthy, you're much better off with them than you would be with me. I'd just be a burden."

My beast woke from the quiet corner of my mind where he'd been sleeping. Andrew was ours and he didn't like anyone insulting something that was ours, not even when it was Andrew insulting himself.

"You should be out of that chair by now. Dom healed Donovan's limp, she shouldn't have any problem healing you too. Is it James? Is he forcing her to extort stuff from people before she heals them? If so I'll go up there and rip him in half."

"Calm down, Isaac. James isn't the problem. If anything, he's gone above and beyond when it comes to protecting our little group. He and Dominic are running themselves ragged taking care of Addison, Samantha and me. We're constantly in motion to make sure that we aren't in any one place long enough for the Coun'hij to track us down."

There was a pause as Andrew tried to mask the pain and longing he was feeling, but it still leaked through his voice if you knew what to listen for.

"It seems as though Dominic's healing of Donovan and all of the wounded was something in the way of a fluke. I don't think her ability has truly vanished, but for now she's unable to access it. It's not really surprising. There aren't any other records of one of her people manifesting this kind of power, it's only reasonable to expect some false starts along the way, but I have every confidence that I'll walk again someday soon."

Not very many people could get away with telling me what to do like that. Alec usually could, and occasionally Jess depending on the situation and how unreasonable I was being, but Andrew always got away with it when he was in parenting mode. Some people would have said that it was some kind of survival instinct designed to let the young of our species survive long enough to learn the things we needed to from our parents, but I'd always felt like it was something else.

My beast let Andrew the parent order me around because he'd realized that while we were dominant to Andrew physically, and had been since before I'd shifted forms my very first time, he was our superior in age, experience and wisdom. My beast listened to Andrew because he respected the man Andrew had always been.

It was hard to talk around the lump in my throat, but I forced the words out. "I'm sure that you're right. You'll be walking around again before you know it and then we'll go running across the estate together."

"Maybe not the estate, I'm afraid that's not going to be possible for a long time, but yes, I look forward to running at your side someday soon."

"Alec is going to win this war sooner than you realize, Andrew, and once it's over he'll go back and rebuild. You'll see."

"I hope so, Isaac, but I'd be lying if I said that I didn't have my share of worries there. I don't know if you've managed to get through to Alec lately, but the number of updates from his group have slowed to the tiniest of trickles recently. It's not the kind of thing you would expect to see if the war was going well. Alec has a lot of things going for him, not the least of which is that he is on the side of justice, but the Coun'hij has had centuries to lay contingency plans for this exact eventuality."

I closed my eyes and tried to fight off the crushing despair that Andrew's words conjured. Alec needed all of the help he could get, and I was stuck here with the lamias, fighting to the death in a series of useless challenges. I wanted to be out actively fighting the Coun'hij, wanted to be hunting down that piece of garbage Oblivion who had stolen Jess' memories.

The only thing that kept me from screaming in frustration was the fact that the potential payoff for what I was doing was huge. If I could find out where the Coun'hij was based, then Alec could assemble his forces and wipe the bad guys out in a single afternoon of fighting.

"I guess that means that we'll all have to work a little harder. This isn't the kind of fight you back down from."

I chuckled at the absurdity of me giving Andrew a pep talk. I guess it was a sign I was starting to cross over into adulthood. When I was younger it always seemed like Andrew had all of the answers.

"What's so funny, Isaac? I could use a good laugh right about now."

I couldn't tell him the truth so I offered up the next funniest thing I could think of.

"I called Alec a few minutes ago to apologize for being such a jerk lately and ask for help, but it turns out he's in over his head too. It's kind of funny that we can't ever get on the same page."

Andrew let the silence between the two of us grow nearly to the point of being uncomfortable before he spoke again.

"I'm proud of you, Isaac. I know that had to have been hard. You've had to deal with a lot of difficult problems lately, but I want you to know how impressed I've been with how you've handled them. I don't know that anyone could have done better."

It would have been nice to just bask in his approval, but a stubborn core of honesty inside of me wouldn't let that comment stand.

"Maybe I'm starting to handle some of them better, but the truth is that I've been doing a pretty lousy job up until now, and things with Alec aren't even the worst part of it."

"That's not true, Isaac. The things that have happened recently aren't the kinds of things that you can just expect a person to shake off immediately."

"Maybe, maybe not, but you can't deny that I created most of my own problems with Jess since Agony's visit."

Andrew was silent for a minute. "I tried to tell you that dozens of times, but you weren't ready to hear it."

"I'm still not ready to hear it, but I think I finally understand where I went wrong. I kept thinking that Jess was still inside of Jessica, that if I kept trying I'd be able to get her to come out and everything would go back to how it was before. That's not going to happen though, is it?"

"I don't think so. Sometimes I felt the same way. There were days where the way that Jessica would smile or laugh would make me ache for my little girl, but I honestly believe that she's gone now. Jessica is a different person. She doesn't have all of the hurts that Jess carried around inside her. I loved that Jess was such a fighter, but now she doesn't remember any of that. She doesn't have to battle all of the time to deal with what Vincent tried to do to her, and I think that's probably for the best."

"I wish I'd been the one to rip his throat out. I came so close a couple of times, but he always managed to squirm out of my reach at the last second."

"I can understand your desire for vengeance, but I'm actually glad that it was Agony who disposed of him. I wanted to kill Vincent myself back when it first happened, but even if I'd been young and healthy I still wouldn't have been any kind of match for him. No, this way is for the best. It's best for all of us."

"Have you talked to her since she left with…since she left?"

"Yes, she's called a couple of times."

"Is she okay?"

I could tell that Andrew was picking out his words very carefully. He didn't want to lie, but he also didn't want to hurt me any more than I'd already been hurt.

"I believe so. I think that she's feeling a little homesick or she wouldn't have called me at all. She's being even more evasive about what's going on and where she's at than you are, but I think she's doing okay, especially for being out on her own for the first time."

"Is that all she said?"

"No, she did tell me that almost everything that we've believed for all of these years is wrong. She made it sound like there was some grand conspiracy, but I think she's still very young and she's had even less experience out in the world on her own than she realizes."

I almost said something about Wyatt. I didn't trust him, didn't think that anything he was involved in could be anything other than sinister, but I managed to stop myself.

"Is she happy? More than just okay, is she really happy?"

"I'm not sure how to answer that question, Isaac."

"Just tell me the truth—I think I'm ready to hear it now."

He didn't want to say it, but I needed to hear it from him if I was ever going to get to the point where I could move on, where I could stop chasing Jess and making things harder for her.

"Yes, she's happy. Things are different than they were before. What she and Wyatt have isn't like what the two of you had. It's not mature, it hasn't stood the test of time. It's like the first bloom of springtime rather than being an ancient oak with roots that sink deep into the earth."

"But she's happy even so?"

"Yes. Jess was so strong that sometimes I think that both you and I forgot how hard she had to fight some days. That's all gone now and it's made all of the difference for her. She was happy with you, she really was, but this is something else. It goes all the way through her. It's like she's free again."

I sighed. "I think I knew that, but I just couldn't stop hoping that she'd come back."

"She can't come back, Isaac. Jess is gone, and as much as we both miss her, the best we can do is just make the best accommodation possible with Jessica. It's time to let go."

"I know, it's just so hard. I loved her so much."

"I know you did. We both did, but at least we can take solace in the fact that she's not dead. She's different and she doesn't remember us, but at least there is some small part of her inside of Jessica. If we play our cards right then we still have a chance to see her grow into someone amazing, but things won't ever be like they were before."

"Thank you, Andrew. I needed to hear that. I know it wasn't easy for you to tell me that, but it will make things better in the long run."

"Are you going to be okay? I know you said that you're worried about someone leading the Coun'hij to you, but if you need me to be there for you right now then I'll chance the trip. I'll buy a car that is set up so that I can drive it with just my hands, and I'll be there within the next forty-eight hours if that is what you want."

"No, I'll be fine. You need to stay there with Dom and James. She's going to get her healing ability figured out sooner or later and when she does you're going to get the use of your legs back so that you can help me hunt Oblivion down."

"Vengeance isn't the answer, Isaac."

"I know. It's not about vengeance. The Coun'hij all need to be put down though, and I'd just as soon it be us who make sure he's stopped."

"Okay, I can respect that. If you change your mind about having me out there just let me know."

"I will. I'll call you if I can't handle things myself."

After the call with Andrew I wanted to just curl up in a dark corner and lick my wounds, but I couldn't do that yet. I still had one more thing to do and I knew that I had to do it then, before I lost my nerve.

I dialed the last number and let it ring. She sent me to voicemail after only two rings, but that wasn't a surprise.

"Hi, it's me. I just wanted to apologize. I know that I've handled pretty much everything wrong and I'm sorry. I've been thinking a lot for the last several days and I realized that I've been lying to myself.

"I thought that I just wanted what was best for you, but really I wanted what was best for me. You're an adult, you know what you want, and that's what is important. I'll respect that from here on out.

"The truth is that I've been pretty critical of the way that Alec fell apart after Adri left him, but I haven't been doing any better. It's not an excuse, just a realization that I need to be better, that I need to let you go be whoever you want to be.

"I hope that you and Wyatt are happy together. I know that you're not my Jess anymore, but that doesn't mean I don't want you to be happy. I do. Sometimes I just have a hard time separating what's best for you from whatever I want.

"I won't bother you anymore."

Chapter 22

Isaac Nazir
The Lamia Enclave

I turned my phone off and then sank down next to the rock I'd been sitting on.

Somewhere along the way I lost some time. It seemed like I blinked and it was dark outside. Part of me wanted to just stay there hugging that rock all night, but I knew that would be stupid. It wouldn't make any difference to Jessica or Andrew, all it would do was guarantee that I'd be tired and weak the next time that I ended up inside the challenge circle.

That practical part of me refused to be silenced no matter how hard I tried to shut him up. It felt like a betrayal of everything I'd felt for the old Jess, but finally, about an hour after dark, I pulled myself up and stumbled back towards our cave.

It turned out I'd been mourning Jess for months now. I just hadn't admitted it to myself because I'd been so busy trying to convince Jessica to take Jess' place. Now that everything was out in the open and I'd started to accept the fact that Jessica wasn't going to fill the hole inside of my chest, I'd realized something else.

By focusing on Jessica rather than on Jess, I'd missed out on my own grieving process. The wild, crazy extreme of emotion that the death of someone you loved deserved wasn't the kind of thing that could be sustained for very long. Eventually you ran out of emotional energy and settled into an exhausted state where you still missed the person you lost and you felt guilty for not being able to sustain the same depth of grief.

I'd missed that surge of emotion, or more accurately I'd sublimated it into pursuing Jessica. Now that it was gone I didn't seem to have much left inside of me with which to grieve. All the guilt in the world wasn't enough to fill back up the internal reservoirs that had been emptied over the last few months.

Celeste tried to talk to me when I arrived back at our quarters, but I just stepped around her and went into my room. I thought for a moment that she was going to come into my room and confront me, but she didn't. I fell asleep as soon as I climbed into bed.

I woke to more noise than usual the next morning and for a few seconds I worried that I was going to have to go back into the ring again. It was the sound of Celeste singing to herself that convinced me Set wasn't out there waiting for me. The entire time that we'd been at the enclave I hadn't seen her relax at all around any of the lamias.

The knowledge that I didn't have another fight waiting for me gave me the strength to roll out of bed and stumble into the bathroom. Celeste said something as I dropped the curtain, but I couldn't make it out.

As the warm water from the gravity-fed shower ran down my body I realized that I couldn't quite remember my dreams from the night before. I thought that they had involved Jessica, or maybe Jess, but I wasn't sure. Everything was a distorted blur, like I was looking back at the dreams through dirty, bubbly glass.

It was hardly a surprise that I would dream about Jess after everything that had just happened, but I was surprised at just how calm I was about everything now that I had a full night's sleep behind me. There was still a sense of loss there inside of me and I still felt a little guilty that I wasn't sadder, but there was enough distance between me and all of those negative feelings that I felt like I could function again.

Once I was dry, I pulled on my last set of clean clothes and made a mental note that I needed to hand-wash the rest of my clothes again. I steeled myself with a deep breath and then walked out of the bathroom ready to face the music. Only Celeste wasn't mad.

"What did you tell Set to get him to bring all of these clothes over?"

It took me a couple of seconds to understand what she was talking about. That was mostly because I had to tear my eyes away from her in order to take in the rest of the room. She was gorgeous. In fairness she was always gorgeous, but right then she was even more beautiful than normal.

The jeans, t-shirt and black tube dress that she'd been cycling through had been discarded for a white sun dress that looked like it was made out of layers of Egyptian cotton, and her hair was pulled back into a ponytail that caressed her neck and shoulders with every movement of her body.

She pointed at the couch and I finally turned and looked at the mammoth pile of clothes that had taken over the couch and both easy chairs. Shorts, jeans, skirts, dresses, every article of clothing I could think of was there and while most of it was white or black, there was a scattering of other colors mixed in, enough that I figured Celeste could probably go for at least a couple months without having to wear the same outfit twice.

"Set brought that over?"

"Yes, he and a small army of workers. I'm amazed that you were able to sleep through all of the noise. He said he'd be back later today with a load of clothes for you. Seriously, did you sell your soul or something to get your hands on all of this?"

I'd asked Set for some clothes for Celeste, but we hadn't actually stipulated how much 'some' was. I'd been expecting him to stop by with a couple of pairs of jeans and three or four t-shirts. This was way more than anything I would have considered necessary to balance out the fact that I was going to leave my phone powered down whenever I wasn't using it.

I was so shell-shocked that I said the first thing that came to mind. "I told him that you've been difficult and that giving you some clothes would make you easier to live with."

Celeste looked at me in amazement for a couple of seconds. I half expected her good humor to evaporate, but instead she burst out into laughter.

"I guess I deserved that."

I shrugged. "Not really. I just needed a reason to not have my phone on all the time without offending the requirements of his honor. He was obviously worried that it was going to lead one of the Consumed—or the Consumed—to the enclave, but once I asked for it he was set on me having it on all of the time.

"You disappearing into your room gave me an idea so I told him that I'd only wanted to call home because I felt so isolated here. He agreed to get some clothes so that you'd be less unhappy."

"The idea being that if I was less...unhappy, then you'd have a friend here or at least not be quite so miserable?"

I was suddenly uncomfortable. I'd had to tell Set the truth—mostly—about my situation, which meant that I was now telling Celeste more than I really wanted to.

"Yeah, I guess. The important thing being that I managed to convince him to not be offended if I kept my phone off most of the time."

"Well, thanks for thinking of me in your moment of need. I don't mind taking the fall if it means I can finally change into something else. I'm surprised though that you were able to convince him to alter the original terms. He seems to be a real stickler about his honor."

"I'm not sure that I would have managed it if not for the fact that he's super worried about the Consumed. There is so much about them that I still don't know. Have you noticed that our rooms are getting smaller?"

She looked at me like she thought I was pulling her leg for a few seconds before shaking her head. "I hadn't noticed. Are you sure about that?"

"Yeah, I put my bag exactly one cubit from the wall a few days ago and the wall is closer than that now. Set mentioned it the other day when he told me about the Consumed. It sounds like they can only hide the enclave as long as it stays under a certain size, but now that we are here something about our presence makes it harder to hide."

"So they are shrinking it down to stay hidden."

I nodded. "It seems that way, but it isn't just a one-time thing, the enclave seems to be shrinking on a consistent basis."

"That is pretty interesting in a so-terrifying-I'd-rather-not-think-about-it way. These Consumed must be really dangerous if the lamias are hiding from it. They are pretty scary all by themselves."

"Yeah, you're not wrong. Still, setting aside the fact that we are in mortal danger, I wish I could stay here for years. I don't know how you managed to keep their existence a secret for so long. I wouldn't have been able to stay away. You've got an incredible amount of willpower to have never come looking for them until now."

Celeste actually started to fidget. After several seconds she sighed. "This isn't the first time that I've had a brush with the lamia. I actually went out into the swamp looking for them right after Ash left home."

"I don't understand. I thought that Ash said they were your trump card, the thing that you were saving until you didn't have any other choice but to use them."

"Yeah, that sounds like Ash. He was always pushing for me to be more aggressive, for me to lead some kind of glorious charge against Onyx.

Back then Nicolas hadn't arrived yet, but it still would have been suicide to try and stand up to Onyx. I told Ash no, told him that I wasn't going to use the lamias until we'd exhausted every other option.

"He didn't like that answer so he faked his own death and disappeared, leaving me wondering whether he was really dead for an entire decade, and he never even looked back."

"So you went looking for the lamia."

"Yeah, I went looking for the lamia. I thought it was my fault that Ashley—that Ash—had died. I thought that he'd given up hope of things ever getting better because I told him that I wouldn't go to the lamia queen and ask her for an army of lamia to come out of the swamp and kill Onyx and his men. It seemed like going to the lamia was the only way to honor Ash's memory."

"But you couldn't go to the lamia without a champion…"

"Yeah, back in the day Ash wanted to be my champion. Ash might be able to take on a lamia if they let him use his weapons and gave him plenty of room, but the old Ash—Ashley—wouldn't have lasted three seconds against someone like Set."

"So what did you do?"

"I had a guy, Bennet was his name. He was on my payroll, a dispossessed hybrid my people found and offered a ridiculous amount of money to join the pack and pretend to be working for

Onyx. He was pretty good in a fight so I thought we had a chance of getting in to see the queen."

Everything about her from her posture to her tone of voice told me that the story didn't have a happy ending.

"So what happened?"

"Ash hated Bennet. Onyx figured that Ash was the weak link in the family. He was just a wolf, and a weak one at that, so Onyx ordered his guys to rough Ash up every chance they got. I tried to protect him, but I couldn't be there all of the time and Ash made things harder than they needed to be."

"He resented the fact that he had to rely on you for protection."

"Yeah, you could say that. He used to run off by himself, but every so often they would catch him and bring him back to the house half dead. That last time Bennet was with one of Onyx's other guys when they found Ash. Bennet kicked his ribs in—he nearly killed him. The other times had been bad, but it wasn't anything like what Bennet did to him."

"So Ash faked his own death."

"Yeah, but he didn't just fake his death, he used Bennet as his patsy. I don't know what he was thinking. Maybe he just wanted to get back at me for hiring Bennet, for bringing one more person into the pack to beat up on him."

Celeste was silent for several heartbeats while she tried to regain control of herself. "Bennet and I had been dating—very quietly—for a few months before that. I think out of everything, that was the one thing that Ash couldn't forgive. He thought I was dating the enemy, but it wasn't like that. Initially I thought it would be one more thing to tie Bennet to me, but as time went on I started to feel things for him.

"It…well, it was nice to have someone else to back me up. With Bennet, I didn't have to always be *on*. Having him around meant that if things went south I'd have at least one other person around who I could count on to help me fight my way out of New Orleans. It wouldn't have mattered against Onyx, but it would have made all of the difference against his guys if Onyx wasn't around."

Celeste put the palms of her hands against her forehead and closed her eyes. "Ash and I had a deal. With every generation our family has fallen a little further from power so we decided that there weren't going to be any more kids. I stuck to our deal, but Ash didn't believe me. He said such horrible things."

She opened her eyes and stood so that she could start pacing. "Whatever his reasons, Ash screwed things up. Bennet didn't have any proof that Ash wasn't dead, but we didn't have a body and Ash had been acting weird all day."

"He went to Onyx with his suspicions."

Celeste shook her head. "No, although it would have been easier in some ways if he had.

He didn't tell Onyx, but he was getting sloppy. He was going off of script a lot. I had bugs in the house back then that Onyx hadn't found yet. I heard Bennet trying to set Onyx up for some kind of long con. It was dangerous. I'd tried to tell him half a dozen times that he needed to get back to the plan that we'd agreed on, but I couldn't just come right out and say it, not without revealing that I had bugs all over the house."

"What happened?"

"I decided to get my money's worth out of him before it became too late. I decided that I would take him to the lamia and have him fight so that I could get the help I needed from their queen. Then we could go back and kick Onyx out of the city. As long as Onyx was out of the picture it wouldn't matter that Bennet had been disobeying orders. I knew I could depend on him to fight when things got rough, and that was the most important thing."

My shock must have made it onto my face. Celeste mistook it for disbelief.

"Don't give me that look. There are plenty of alphas who keep control of their pack through financial means. You just need to find people who remain bought once you buy them off. Once you hit a certain size things become self-sustaining. The upper-tier hybrids who initially joined you for the money realize that they like the security of being towards the top of a pack a lot better than being one of the dispossessed.

Ulrich has reformed half a dozen hybrids just in the last couple of decades who everyone else said couldn't function inside of a healthy pack. Raynor has done the same thing, just on a smaller scale."

"Your plan didn't work though? I mean Onyx is still around, right?"

"I never carried it out. We were headed here, but I stopped to make sure that nobody was following us. That was when Bennet told me his suspicions about Ash. It was like having my brain jammed inside of a blender. On the one hand, I was overjoyed to find out that my brother might still be alive. On the other hand, it meant that I'd been abandoned by my own flesh and blood. Ash left me in New Orleans to rot, and he used Bennet to do it."

"I'm sorry, Celeste, but I don't understand. Why did it matter that he used Bennet as his witness when he staged his death?"

"Because it meant that Bennet was even more compromised than I'd thought. Bennet was already taking chances that he shouldn't have been taking, and now there was one more piece of information that I had to worry about him letting slip if Onyx strapped him to a table and started torturing him."

I didn't want to believe it, didn't want to think that Celeste was capable of doing what I thought she'd done, but all of the signs were pointing to one conclusion.

"You killed him, didn't you?"

"I...I injected him with a tranquilizer and left him at the edge of the lamias' hunting ground. It was just a matter of time before he got himself into trouble and I kept thinking that my plan was all well and good if the lamia queen sent us back with an army, but everything would fall apart if she sent us back empty-handed. I couldn't risk it, not when Ash's life was on the line."

Celeste looked away from me. "If Onyx had known that Ash was alive he would have never stopped looking for him. I had to control the situation, had to tie up the loose ends before Onyx used them to strangle me."

Part of me knew that I wasn't holding Celeste to the same standard I was using for myself, but I couldn't help the wave of horror that crashed through me. I'd killed, but only people who'd been able to defend themselves.

"Why, Celeste? You could have sent him away. Your family had surely been in situations that were just as dangerous over the years. Why didn't you regroup and give yourself time to think?"

"Because the money was starting to run out! We were starting to run out of money and I'm the only thing that stands between Onyx and a dozen good men and women whose only crime is that they aren't strong enough to stand up for themselves. They're only wolves, just like Ash. Among humans they're practically demigods, but inside of a pack run by someone like Onyx they're just bargaining chips."

Celeste had started out yelling, but by the end she was whispering.

"We weren't out of money yet, but I could see the day coming. Before Onyx arrived the bribes my family paid out mostly just came out of the interest payments from our investments. Onyx has changed all of that. At the time that Ash disappeared I figured that we had another twenty years before Onyx bled us dry."

"I thought Kristin said that Ash made off with a huge chunk of your working capital."

"He did. Half of the money that I had under management disappeared overnight."

"Didn't that cut into how long you were able to make it before you ran out of cash?"

"Yeah. It turns out that necessity really is the mother of invention. Over the last few years I've come up with some creative ways to keep Onyx's take from growing as fast as it otherwise would have, but I'm still essentially out. If you scraped together everything left in all of the numbered accounts you might have enough left to buy a summer house in a nice part of Arizona, but there wouldn't be enough left over to furnish it.

"I'm at the end of my rope. Onyx is convinced that I'm holding out on him because, up until a short time ago, he didn't know that Ash was still alive. I couldn't exactly tell him that my brother, who was supposed to be dead, had taken half of everything. The only thing that has kept me alive this long is that Onyx thought that I still had money he could squeeze out of me, and I was the last living Hunt, so if he pushed me too far he'd be out of options for getting at the money."

"Now that he knows Ash is still alive you're worried that he'll kill you and just torture Ash for the money."

"Maybe. I think he'll try to keep both of us alive, but once he's got a backup there isn't as much need to be careful about what he does to us. Actual physical torture wasn't much of an option before, Onyx had to rely on threatening people I cared about instead, but it would definitely be on the table if he had both Ash and me."

I could tell that there was a lot that she wasn't telling me, but I didn't press for more details. I didn't want to subject Celeste to any more than she'd already been through.

"Why did you tell me all of this, Celeste?"

"Because I'm tired of lying to everyone. I'm good enough at lying that I can get away with almost any lie imaginable, but I want a different life than that. The only way for that to happen is to come clean. You're the first person I've ever told about Bennet. Everyone back in New Orleans thinks that he just vanished into the swamp one day while trying to find me."

"But why me? Why not Ash or someone else?"

"Because you deserve to know that I'm using you too. You and Ash are here trying to help Kristin, but that isn't why I'm here. I came here to convince the lamia queen to kill Onyx for me. If I only get one question then that's the question that I'm going to ask her. I keep telling myself that I'm doing it for the submissives back in New Orleans, but that is just another lie. I'm doing it to rid myself of Onyx so that my life doesn't get even worse. Now you know. Not everything, but the worst parts, the things that I'm most ashamed of."

She met my eyes with defiance, daring me to turn my back on her, and for a second I wanted to do exactly that. She'd never explicitly said that she was here to help Kristin, but it had been implied in dozens of interactions since even before we'd arrived in the enclave.

I'd already been uncomfortable enough killing the lamias in order to save Kristin and bring down the Coun'hij. The idea of killing people on behalf of a small pack that I'd never even met was even more disturbing.

By almost any measure I could think of Celeste was bad news, but I couldn't dispute one thing. She was a leader. I might not agree with her methods, but it was obvious that she was at least partially motivated by concern for the wolves in her pack and she was willing to stand up and deal with the consequences of her actions in a way that very few people ever did.

"Go on. Turn around and walk away from me. I can see it in your eyes; I know it's what you want to do. I'm damaged goods, you can't trust me."

"You're scary as hell, Celeste. I'm not going to lie about that, but I'm no more perfect than anyone else. How much do you know about Agony's visit to Sanctuary last year?"

"Not as much as I should. I've had to cut back on payments to informants or I'd know more. He came through and made a lot of noise, but in the end he failed. He killed a few submissives and Oblivion sucked someone's memories dry, but the core of the pack, the dominants who were the real threat, walked away from the confrontation. Most people viewed it as a win for Alec because it meant that the threat of his power was enough to stop Agony from just executing you all out of hand."

Nothing she'd just said was wrong, but hearing those events rattled off like they were dry facts out of some dusty textbook woke a torrent of rage from my beast that only barely exceeded the anger I was feeling on my own.

Mastering that fury was almost more than I could manage, but it helped that there wasn't a valid target for it. Oblivion wasn't here where I could get my claws on him, and Agony and Vincent were both dead already. I forced the anger down to a slow simmer in the back of my mind and looked up to find that Celeste had taken several steps backwards to buy herself time and space if I lost control.

"Whatever I just said, I'm sorry. I thought James was the hothead from your pack. If you're the controlled one then I seriously need to remember to stay away from Utah."

"Your information is a few months old. I used to be the controlled one, but Agony's visit changed all of that. The wolf Oblivion wiped was my girlfriend. He grabbed her at the same time that Agony killed Vincent and the rest of his guys took down the three wolves we'd absorbed from what was left of Brandon's pack."

"I'm sorry, Isaac. I didn't know."

"I wouldn't have expected for you to know, to everyone else she was just another submissive, but to me she was everything. The week before she had finally agreed to marry me. We hadn't told anyone else yet, not even her father. One moment she was the girl I was going to spend the rest of my life with and then in the next she became a stranger who just happened to walk around wearing my girlfriend's body."

Celeste was obviously struggling to find something to say but I couldn't blame her for coming up blank. I wouldn't have known what to tell me either.

"You don't have to say anything, Celeste. The real kick in the teeth is that I stood by and didn't do anything."

"That's not what I heard."

"Yeah, Alec knocked me down, but he couldn't have stopped me if I'd really been committed to going after Oblivion. Even now, after months spent hating Alec, I still don't think that he would have killed me to stop me from attacking Oblivion.

"To be honest, I think that if I'd gone after Oblivion, Alec might have joined in the fight. We probably would have all died, but if it had come down to a choice between watching me die along with the three wolves or fighting, I don't think Alec would have been able to just sit there.

"I'm the biggest fraud ever. All I needed was an excuse not to try to save Jess, and by knocking me down, Alec provided me with it. I failed Jess, and then I spent the next few months following the person who replaced her around in an attempt to recreate the thing that I let slip through my fingers. Maybe you are a terrible person, but at least you know what you want and you're willing to pay the price for it. I have no right to judge you, Celeste."

I turned to walk away, but she reached out and grabbed my arm. "I'm sorry for your loss, Isaac, truly I am."

I expected her to let go of me, but she didn't. Instead her grip got even tighter. "I don't expect you to care about my opinion, but I think you were in an impossible situation and you did the only thing you could. Oblivion could have wiped out half your pack all by himself. When you throw in Agony and the rest, your side had zero chance of coming out on top."

"That doesn't change the fact that Jess is gone."

"No, it doesn't, but it also doesn't make you worthless for not throwing your life away. You need to let go of Jess and move on with your life."

I pulled my arm free of her hand and turned to go, but she stopped me with one last parting shot.

"I lied earlier. I said that every pack had an extensive file on you and Alec, but the truth is that for most of them you're a footnote. I studied you every chance I could. I've hated everything that Alec Graves has stood for since before he was even born, but despite how I felt about him, he continued to survive against hopeless odds."

"What does that have to do with me?"

"Everything! I analyzed every scrap of information looking for the secret that has let the Graves family succeed where we Hunts have failed and it always comes back to the fact that they command a loyalty beyond what anyone could reasonably expect from a bunch of moonborn.

"Alec's family has survived this long because they always have one or more Isaac Nazirs standing behind them. Other packs, when put in similar kinds of circumstances always splinter, but yours doesn't. *You* are the secret to Alec's power, Isaac. I don't know what could have caused someone who could have led his own pack to decide he wanted to back Alec's play like that, but it's a special kind of miracle and I would have given anything during the last decade and a half to have had you at my side instead of his."

Something in her voice brought me back around despite myself. There was a naked need in her expression that I'd never seen anywhere else before. She'd said she was a good liar, but I couldn't believe she was that good. In that instant I knew that she didn't just want an ally, she wanted a confidant, someone who would back her play no matter what simply because they believed in her.

Part of me wanted to respond in kind, wanted to open up to her and reward the guts she'd shown by coming clean, but I couldn't bring myself to do that.

"You want to know Alec's secret? It's that he's better than all of the rest of us. There's only been one time when he was ever tempted to put himself ahead of his friends and family, and even then in the end he did the right thing. Alec wins people's loyalty because he's worthy of it. That's the only way you can really win loyalty. Anything else is just an illusion."

Chapter 23

Isaac Nazir
The Lamia Enclave

Celeste and I avoided each other for the rest of the day. I would have said such a thing wasn't possible in such a tiny space, but we were each careful to make plenty of noise anytime we left our rooms. The sound-deadening nature of the curtains hanging in our doorways was impressive, but even they couldn't stop shape shifter ears from being able to tell when the other person was outside of their room.

We took turns taking care of Ash and Kristin, and ate in shifts, all without discussing the arrangements with each other. I half expected Set to come back by so he could continue my training, but I never saw him. At one point I went out into the main room and found that there was a new pile of clothes waiting for me on the couch.

LOST

I mostly passed the time working on my tablet with the keyboard plugged into it. I had a difficult decision coming up and I couldn't make an informed choice without finishing up the plan for using Ash's money to hire hackers in an attempt to find Dream Stealer.

It felt good to be working on something again. The time in the enclave had been nice, and being forced to be alone with my thoughts so much had been good for me, but long moments of boredom interspersed with terrifying fights for your life is a hard way to live. I liked the feeling of being able to work towards something again.

The plan came together much more smoothly than I'd expected. It wouldn't have surprised me if it had taken another two or three days to get to the point where it was ready for Ash to start contracting with hackers. Instead I finished the final details up and saved off the document just a few hours after sunset.

The catharsis of having made real progress had relaxed me in ways that I hadn't anticipated, and as I powered off my tablet I was tempted to go apologize to Celeste. I still didn't feel like I could trust her, but I'd been more brutal with her than I'd needed to be.

I even went so far as to leave my room and go stand outside her doorway, but I could faintly hear the sound of deep, even breathing and I decided against waking her up to offer some vague, halting apology that probably wouldn't make her feel any better.

I went back to my room and fell asleep within seconds of lying down. My dreams were filled with vivid instances of fighting. I wasn't just training with Set this time around; I was fighting werewolves, lamia and even other shape shifters. I was outmatched in almost every fight, but they were too real for me to realize that they were just dreams.

I clawed, bit, and bled dozens of times over the course of the night, and each and every fight that I won was done so using one of the techniques that Set had shown me. I chained elbow strikes and close-quarters blocks together in one long, whirling frenzy of combat that didn't let go of me until after sunrise.

When I finally woke up the next morning, Celeste wasn't anywhere to be found. I followed her scent trail far enough to verify that she'd left the cave, and then went back and checked on Ash and Kristin. I was getting really worried about the two of them. Kristin had started thrashing around so much in her sleep that I'd had to restrain her in order to make sure that she wouldn't open Ash's injuries back up.

They should have woken back up by now, but I couldn't do anything for them here and I wasn't quite ready to tell Set that we were leaving. I'd just finished up breakfast when Set arrived at our doorstep and asked if I could come out and speak with him.

"I'm sorry to disturb your rest, Isaac Nazir."

"You're fine, Set. Are we getting started with our training early today?"

"Alas, I must beg your pardon on that point as well. I wanted to continue your studies yesterday, but my queen required my services on another matter. I tried explaining that it was a debt of honor, but she merely indicated that she would satisfy the debt for the day herself. Has she satisfied the debt, Isaac Nazir?"

I had no idea what he was talking about. I certainly would have remembered if the lamia queen had dropped by for a little unarmed combat sparring, but I wasn't about to tell Set that he'd come up deficient in any way, not and risk him over-reacting in one way or another.

"The debt remains satisfied, Set. Please put your mind at ease regarding the matter."

He bowed his head in relief. "It pleases me to hear it. I'm afraid that we will have to postpone our time together until after I return."

"Can I ask where you are going, Set?"

"I will be leaving on the enclave's business, but in this instance you may know, as I've come to seek a boon from you. I will be taking all of the enclave's workers and most of the consorts with me. I seek a promise from you that you won't attempt to bypass the few guards who will be remaining behind."

Someone else might have agreed thinking that it was the perfect opportunity to force their way in to see the queen, but it never even crossed my mind. It was only afterwards that I realized the level of trust Set was placing on my shoulders.

"Of course. For me you have a solemn promise, but I cannot speak for my queen."

"Such is always the way of things, Isaac Nazir, but a promise from you is sufficient. Your queen would not be able to force her way in unaided, and surely she would not force you to betray your honor in this matter."

He seemed awfully certain for a guy who had just been worried that his queen hadn't fulfilled her end of their bargain, but then again, maybe he had more faith in Celeste than he did in his own queen. I wasn't quite as sure that Celeste was completely trustworthy, but it didn't seem like the time to tell him that.

"Are you off to fight the Consumed?"

"Thankfully no, but we must head off a different problem or we will be paid a visit by the Consumed very soon. Many of the sun people have entered our hunting territory. Their presence will serve to make the enclave more noticeable. They must be encouraged to leave if we are to remain hidden."

I could only think of one pack that had a reason to be out in the swamp right now.

"Set, are the sun people from nearby? Are they from New Orleans?"

He looked confused for the first time in a while. "They are, but my queen indicated that we should prepare for battle. How can this be, Isaac Nazir? Can your queen not simply order them away?"

"I'm afraid not, Set. There are...many enclaves of my people in the city near here. Not all of them serve my queen. If these sun people are the ones that I think they are, then you and your men will be in grave danger. May I come with you and help defend the enclave?"

Set blinked several times—the odd serpentine blink that started from the corners of his eyes and worked inward—and then nodded.

"Your assistance would be appreciated, Isaac Nazir. The time-stream will be most advantageous in one hour, we will leave then."

Before Set was even out of sight I heard Celeste approaching. I nearly followed Set just so I wouldn't have to talk to her, but she deserved to know what was going on.

"Was that Set? You don't have to go fight another challenge match, do you?"

"No, not yet."

It wasn't my imagination, there was real relief in her eyes at the knowledge I wasn't going to be risking my life again. It was so hard to reconcile the two different sides of Celeste that I'd seen so far. How could a cold-blooded killer care whether I died? Was it just because my death would represent the end of her chance at getting the lamias to fight her battles for her?

"I don't have a challenge match, but Set has informed me that some of Onyx's men are prowling around the swamp. He's taking a party to warn them off and I've asked to go along."

She shook her head. "No, that's a terrible idea."

"I thought that is what you wanted, Celeste. We leave in an hour. Two hours from now the lamia might end up wiping out most of Onyx's forces, leaving you in a vastly stronger position than you've ever been in before."

Celeste spun around, nostrils flaring, and then she started down the path that Set had just taken. "You don't understand, Isaac. You don't just throw bodies at someone like Onyx. I wanted the lamias to help, yes, but it wasn't just about obtaining more foot soldiers. I want the queen's help. If there's a way to beat Onyx then she'll know it, but it will involve stealth and guile."

"She's the one sending Set and the others out, if she can really see the future like you think she can, then we'll be fine."

"Is she really behind this? Are you certain? Because I don't get the feeling that she's a very hands-on kind of ruler. Set is tough and smart, but he doesn't have any idea what he's up against. If Onyx is with those men then he'll kill all of you in minutes. Even if he isn't and you massacre the guys he's sent into the swamp it will just mean that he'll come here himself next time."

She was moving quickly, I had to jog to keep up with her. I tried to get a word in edgewise, but she was talking too quickly for that.

"If this isn't handled just right the lamias are going to have the Coun'hij down here searching for them. Is Set really ready to have dozens of werewolves crawling all over the swamp? The lamias need to stay a secret or they don't stand a chance."

"Don't you mean that they need to stay a secret until you're ready to use them?"

She stumbled, but she didn't answer me, not when Set was now in sight.

"Set, wait. Don't go out there. You can't beat the shape shifters you're going to run into out there. You need to keep your people hidden, keep the portal closed if you can."

Set turned and gave her a look that would have frozen water. "This is not your business, queen."

Apparently she hadn't made enough of an effort to make small talk with him, that or he was still unhappy about her having nearly lost control her first day here. She'd started shaking, but I grabbed her arm and hauled her back a couple of steps.

"Set, she doesn't mean to cross any lines, she's just worried about you and your men. She's had dealings with the...queen who most likely commands the shape shifters, the sun people, we're about to go confront. Their leader is indeed very powerful. Celeste has seen people paralyzed with pain from a distance of dozens of yards. Would it be possible to avoid them, to hide as she has suggested until the sun people have moved on?"

Set puffed up as though he was about to tell me to get lost too, but in the end he just shook his head. "No, Isaac Nazir. Under other circumstances maybe, but not today. The sun people are too many and too powerful. We are already shrinking the enclave as quickly as we are able and still it will not be enough. They will illuminate the enclave for the Consumed. He will pick us out of the void and appear without warning."

I felt like I was being torn in three different directions at once, but there was only one remaining option that had any chance of keeping everyone out of trouble.

"Then let us leave. If we were gone it would allow you to hide regardless of how many shape shifters were running around in the swamp. It's the best solution."

"No, Isaac!"

I turned to Celeste and stopped her before she could say anything else. "It doesn't have to be this way. We'll get Ash and Kristin and we'll leave. I've got a plan that has a good chance of finding Dream Stealer, so that takes care of the reason that Ash wanted to be here, and as soon as we're back in Louisiana I'll call Alec and beg him to come down here. He can neutralize Onyx and the entire rest of the pack if he needs to. We can free your people and nobody other than Onyx and his guys needs to get hurt."

"At what price? So we can all become Alec's lap dogs?"

"Yeah, if it comes to that. I don't think it will, but even if it did, would that really be so bad? Even at his worst Alec has never been even a tenth as bad as Onyx. Is swearing fealty really too big a price to pay for the safety of your people?"

It was one of those moments when you know someone has to decide whether or not they were going to put up or shut up. Celeste had already done some terrible things in the name of protecting her people. This was nothing in comparison. All it required was that she let go of her pride and trust someone she had been taught since she was a child was evil.

"All right, Isaac. If that is what you want, if you really think that's the best way forward, then I'll go along. We can leave right now as long as Set can put us down somewhere far enough away from Onyx's men that we have a chance of surviving."

Set was already shaking his head. "To do this thing you are proposing would dishonor our entire enclave. I will not do it."

"Unless you are going to attack us, and violate your duty as host, there isn't any way to stop us. Isaac and I can go get Ash and Kristin and then just walk back out of here the same way we came. The portal might not put us back in the exact same place, but it will be close enough that we'll eventually be able to make it back to civilization."

"That may be true, but it won't stop me from leading my people out to deal with the sun people in the swamp."

Celeste looked like she was going to explode. "What kind of passive-aggressive crap is this? Are you trying to guilt us into doing what you want us to do?"

"I have no choice. Honor compels me to provide for the safety of the enclave's guests."

There was something about the set of his expression that told me he wasn't giving us the full story.

"What aren't you telling us, Set?"

"Over time, your being out of the enclave will make it easier to conceal ourselves, but the sun energies dissipate only slowly. Even if you leave I will still be forced to go disperse the sun people or we will be found."

Celeste looked back and forth between us. "Do you believe him, Isaac?"

"Yes. Set hasn't ever lied to me."

"Then I suppose we'd better go help them attack Onyx's guys."

I shook my head. "No, you need to stay here. Onyx is coming to get you and Ash, which means that you two need to stay here safely out of reach."

She wanted to argue with me, I could see it in her eyes. She wasn't some pampered princess, unwilling to stand up and defend herself, but she knew I was right.

"Fine, but you all need to be careful. Onyx is incredibly dangerous."

Less than an hour later I followed Set and more than a dozen of his men through the crack in the wall that led back to the outside world. Most of the lamias accepted my presence without any sign of unhappiness, but one of them, a huge consort, bared his fangs at me when I walked up to their group.

My beast let out a pulse of power in return that made me feel like I was in the eye of a hurricane, and for a second I thought we were about to come to blows, but Set hissed something indecipherable at the other lamia. The hostile consort eventually turned away from me and stalked further down the tunnel, but I got the impression that it hadn't been a foregone conclusion that he was going to obey.

"What just happened, Set?"

Set looked around and then said something else in his own language to the other two consorts with us. They sped up their pace and were soon out of hearing range.

"All is not well at the enclave, Isaac Nazir. It is unusual for a visiting queen to stay for such a long time. The fact that you are all sun people makes things difficult and Pal questions my judgment in allowing you to stay."

Kristin wasn't actually a shape shifter, but I wasn't going to interrupt him.

"Because we are making it harder to hide from the Consumed?"

"Yes. Also some worry that your presence will corrupt us, make us unsuitable to return to our home when the time comes."

"What do you think, Set?"

"I think that their concerns are not without validity, but they risk completely abandoning honor. I trust in the judgment of my queen. She would not let us go that far astray. I will not become as dust and abandon honor despite what others may do. As long as I continue as the first consort they will not succeed in their plans."

There was something in his tone that told me that he wasn't entirely sure he would be able to maintain his position, which was especially ominous given what he'd just finished telling me.

"What would have to happen for someone else to become the first consort?"

"Honor would require that they defeat me in single combat and receive the blessing of the queen, but...there have been instances in the past where under-consorts have abandoned honor. Under trying circumstances they have been known to forgo single combat and instead attack the first consort en masse. They did not receive their queen's blessing and chaos ensued."

"What happened after that?"

I didn't want to pry, but I also felt like I needed to have an idea of just how much trouble we were likely to be in if things started going downhill.

"The workers have very little of what you would call free will. They will follow whatever orders they are given, whether by queen or consorts. In both cases the consorts denied their queen food in an attempt make her concede to their will. In one instance a neighboring enclave was able to send a force to free the queen."

"What about the second queen?"

"She ultimately died. The enclave is a shadow of what it once was, a few surviving consorts and less than a dozen workers. It was a terrible loss, one that caused severe disruptions to the plan."

"The plan?"

"The plan to return us to our home. The shadow enclave is lost to us forever. Its queen will never work for the good of our race through the plan again. The queen who was rescued and the enclave that rescued her were unable to continue their work for a long time. We can only relocate our enclaves very infrequently. The work has suffered. The queen is less than she once was."

"The one who was starved?"

Set shook his head. "All the queen. You would say all of the queens, but they are all one, reflections of a larger whole."

We were getting into territory that was almost religious, but there was one more pressing question that I needed answered. I'd never adequately understood the degree to which the consorts had free will. I'd thought their honor constrained them, but it was apparent to me now that they could choose to abandon it as easily as any human or shape shifter.

"Set, why didn't the queens who were overthrown act to stop it from happening? Your queens can see the future, can't they?"

"You would say they can."

"But if your queens can see the future, why would anyone disobey them?"

Set stopped at the mouth of the cave and let the workers pass us by. For several long seconds he refused to meet my eyes.

"This business of seeing the time stream is not a solution to all problems, it is merely a different kind of complication. The queens see much, but they do not see all anymore than you see everything around you."

"But I do see everything around me."

Set pointed at a huge tree that dominated the western vista. "What is behind the tree, Isaac Nazir?"

I was silent for nearly a minute as I absorbed his ingenious object lesson.

"I understand—a little at least. So some of the consorts rebel because they don't trust the queens' judgment."

"Yes, but that is only part of it. The goal of the queens is to return our people as a whole to our home, but there will be individuals lost along the way. The goal of the people is survival, but the goal of the individual is also survival. Many will not sacrifice individual survival in exchange for the survival of the species. It is not an easy choice even for my people."

"So the consorts worried that the queens were going to sacrifice them for a larger goal. Is there precedent for that?"

Set hesitated before nodding again. "Yes. Long ago entire enclaves were sacrificed in the pursuit of the work. We were once a much more numerous people than we are now, Isaac Nazir. With each queen lost the queens become less than they once were. Each one lost limits the vision of the others and creates additional doubt in the minds of some consorts."

He was painting a chilling picture, one that I was having a hard time wrapping my mind around. Their entire race had dedicated itself to one mission, a mission that had spanned thousands of years, a mission that they might never realize because of the sacrifices they'd made along the way.

"Set, if the queens become less with each loss and can't see as clearly as they once could, how do you know that it's even possible to achieve your great work still and return home?"

"You ask the same questions as many of my fellows, Isaac. I do not answer them because I've been sworn to secrecy and because knowing the answer for them would just raise more questions, but if you will promise to keep this secret then I will tell you the answer."

"Of course. I will not tell anyone else."

"If we placed a mountain behind that tree would you be able to see it still?"

"Yes."

"There is your answer. My queen tells me that some things are so momentous that they can be seen even from a great distance away, even when other things are hidden. Our return is not guaranteed, but in all of the paths that lead to it, there is no mistaking the fact that it is there."

It was a strange kind of answer, the kind that didn't prove anything, but that was a world that I wasn't completely unfamiliar with. I'd drifted away from that kind of blind trust over the last few months, but it was a place I was still surprisingly comfortable with.

"Faith. You know because of faith in a higher power, in this case faith in your queen."

"Indeed, Isaac Nazir. Possibly that is why she has instructed me to tell you many of these things that have remained hidden from most of your people and mine for so many years."

Set waited to confirm that he'd answered my question sufficiently, and then headed out after the rest of his men. I shifted forms and followed him.

LOST

Less than twenty minutes later our group slowed to a stop, alerted by something I couldn't sense that we were nearly to Onyx's men. The lamias all had their eyes closed and they were all facing the same direction, but they didn't seem to be smelling the air.

I slowly fidgeted, shifting my weight from one foot to the other as I resisted the urge to ask Set what was going on. Just when I wasn't sure that I could keep my mouth closed any longer, he opened his eyes and turned towards me.

"They come from that direction. They'll be here in another fifteen of your minutes, maybe a little less. What should we know about them before we engage?"

If the other consorts hadn't been around I probably would have told him that it was stupid to have left this briefing until the last second like this. I'd somehow been assuming that we still had hours of travel time before we would run into Onyx's men.

Finding out that we had less than fifteen minutes to come up with a workable plan against someone who could strike us down from yards away was the kind of shock that I could do without, but I didn't want to undercut his authority with the other consorts. We would just have to do the best we could.

"Most of them will just be other hybrids like me. Dangerous, but not as dangerous as a werewolf. You should be able to make short work of them with your venom. Some of them will be less skilled in combat than I am, others will be more skilled, but there is one who is very dangerous.

"Celeste, my queen, said that she has seen him strike down several men at once, overpowering them with an incredible pain that if left unchecked can cause death. I'm afraid I don't have much advice for beating him other than trying to take him by surprise. If we strike from behind before he realizes that we were there, then we might be able to kill him before he can bring us all down."

"Your pardon, Isaac Nazir, but there are not many of them like you in the group. Like your queen, yes, but not like you. There is only one based on the sun from that direction. It is good, I think."

I wasn't sure what to make of that. Was he trying to say that Onyx had brought an army of female hybrids to hunt us down? I hadn't asked Celeste about Onyx's people other than to confirm that he was the only one with an ability, but I'd just assumed that most women wouldn't be willing to work with someone like Onyx.

Set nodded, apparently pleased with his conclusion. "The prevailing wind is good, is it not?"

I set my questions aside for a moment and took a deep breath. Just in the time that we'd been talking Onyx's men had gotten closer. I couldn't exactly smell them, but there were hints on the wind that something had changed.

"Yeah, actually, the wind is just about perfect. We need to move quickly if we're going to set this up though."

Set patted me on the shoulder, a feat anyone other than a seven-foot-tall lamia would have found difficult given that I was in my hybrid form. "Don't fear, Isaac Nazir. Our queen provides. We will ambush them right here."

"Is it a good idea to do that so close to the portal? If we are defeated, there won't be anything to stop them from continuing on to the enclave."

If Set's actions earlier hadn't convinced me that at least some of the other consorts understood English, what happened next would have done the trick. One of the consorts let out a soft hissing laugh. I was pretty sure that it was Pal, the one who had been giving me the evil eye earlier.

My beast tried to cut loose with a titanic flare of power on an attempt to put the other consort on notice that we weren't amused, but I suppressed the energy, bleeding it out slowly to keep from sending up a signal flare to Onyx and his people.

Set hissed something menacing at the consort and then gently turned me so that I could look back the way that we'd come from and register the fact that our surroundings had changed.

"The portal has closed already, Isaac Nazir. Come, let us set this ambush."

I got the feeling that the lamias had done this kind of thing before. Set had indicated that they'd been located in Egypt before this, but apparently they hadn't let any grass grow underneath them over the last few centuries when it came to learning about their new, wetter environment.

Set dispersed his people with a rapid series of gestures and verbal instructions, and thirty seconds later all of the lamias other than Set had disappeared underneath the dark, green water. They'd formed a large circle in the center of the channel before submerging themselves.

One of the consorts, I was pretty sure it was Pal again, didn't seem happy to be putting himself in a position where he couldn't see or hear what was going on outside of the water, but in the end he dropped out of sight just like all of the rest.

"Try to lure the sun people into that circle, Isaac Nazir. We have about twenty of your minutes' worth of air before we'll have to surface."

Set pointed at the empty space that was in the middle of a dozen sets of rapidly expanding ripples, as if to remind me of the appropriate spot, and then he too disappeared into the water. I sat there, watching the ripples fade away to nothing, and had to suppress a shiver of discomfort at the idea of getting into water deeper than my head knowing that there were giant snakes, sharks and alligators swimming around with me.

The trap was set, so there wasn't any reason to continue to maintain a low profile. I could smell them now, the scent of gasoline and engine lubricant, mixed with people. The timing was about right if I was the kind to panic, so I reached deep down inside and coaxed my beast up to the surface with a roar of power that was shockingly strong.

They were close enough that I knew they would be bound to feel the surge, now it was just a matter of unobtrusively guiding them into the right spot. The motor on the boat sped up and less than a minute later the boat came into view.

There were three guys on it, one of whom was chained to the boat, and roughly ten hybrids on foot moving from island to island in an effort to increase their party's overall footprint. I was pretty sure that one of the guys in the boat was Onyx, and my bet would have been that he was the one who wasn't steering the boat, but there wasn't any way to be sure until the fur started flying.

I didn't recognize any of the hybrids except one. Nicolas was cheerfully slogging through the water. I couldn't tell whether he was just happy to have finally found me, but he had blood on his hands, so it looked like he'd already tangled with one of the swamp's denizens and come out unscathed.

I looked around as though scared and just realizing how badly outnumbered I was, and made as if to break across their line of travel. It wasn't the best route to go if I was truly trying to get away from them, but it did provide a more or less solid line of islands and, more importantly, I figured it would pull the boat the direction that it needed to go if the ambush was going to have any chance of succeeding.

My first step went off without a hitch, but then the most excruciating pain I'd ever felt tore through me. I hit the ground hard and slid nearly five feet through the mud, but I was in too much pain to even worry about whether or not I'd managed to lure the boat into position.

The pounding of my pulse in my ears was so loud that it drowned out almost every other sound. It was like standing under a waterfall, but one that came in irregular surges, one that seemed to stretch the surges out for an impossibly long time.

"...don't kill him, we need him..."

That was all I caught in between heartbeats and then the pain cut off as quickly as it had started up. I managed to get my head up in time to see the boat capsize, but even that didn't go according to plan.

Only half of the lamias had surfaced. The half of the circle behind the boat had grabbed it and ripped it into pieces as they tried to get their claws into Onyx and the driver, but the other half of the circle, the half closest to me, was nothing more than furiously bubbling water.

As fast as the lamias had been, Onyx was even faster. He sprang from the boat before anyone managed to get hold of him and transformed in midflight. He hit the muddy ground of the island as I rolled to my feet and saw the rest of his men rushing into the battle.

The boat's driver was already dead, but the lamia who had destroyed the boat suddenly convulsed in pain and dropped back down into the water. I thought everything was over at that point. I'd never imagined that Onyx's gift was strong enough to keep twelve lamias paralyzed under the water where they would eventually drown, but given that there still wasn't any sign of the first set of lamias, it looked like that was exactly what he was doing.

Two of the hybrids peeled off from the main group to come deal with me, but everyone else waded knee deep into the water to form a loose circle around the channel that contained what was left of the boat.

As I prepared to sell myself as dearly as possible, the most amazing thing I'd ever seen happened. The water near the hybrids exploded with lamias who'd somehow managed to use the turbulence caused by the boat sinking to get within striking distance of most of the hybrids clustered along the shore.

It was nothing less than miraculous, but it still wasn't quite perfect. There were twelve lamias, and Onyx had brought twelve other guys with him, but the driver of the boat was dead already, and the guy who had been chained to the boat still hadn't surfaced. When you added in the fact that two guys were almost within striking distance of me and Onyx was well outside of melee engagement range, the lamias outnumbered the hybrids twelve to eight.

With the lamias' venom and the element of surprise, the hybrids should have been massacred. They probably would have been, notwithstanding Onyx's presence, but for the fact that the lamias hadn't matched themselves up perfectly against the waiting hybrids.

A number of lamias matched themselves up in one-on-one battles against the New Orleans hybrids. One consort—I was pretty sure it was Pal again—put his opponent down with a single thrust to the chest. The wound shouldn't have been fatal, but the hybrid instantly started screaming and dropped to the ground before he could even finish up the attempted counterstrike that would have taken the consort's head off.

I saw another couple of workers, each trading blows with a single hybrid, but it wasn't readily apparent who held the upper hand there. That was fine, under normal circumstances they would have just needed to last for long enough for another lamia to help them out, but this wasn't the kind of fight that they were used to.

There were some places where two or three lamias attacked a single hybrid and felled them with ease, but there were other places where one lamia ended up squaring off against more than one hybrid. I saw one of the other consorts—not Set—sink his claws into the stomach of his enemy and then fall to an attack that Nicolas delivered unexpectedly from one side.

We lost a couple of lamias in those first few seconds, but we still could have easily won except for the fact that an instant later Onyx reentered the fight.

Unfortunately, I missed his opening salvo because the two hybrids who had been approaching me finally arrived. I dodged to one side in an effort to keep one guy between me and the other guy, but they had obviously worked together before.

The closest guy trusted his teammate to back him up, and simply threw himself at me without even pausing. The move wasn't the kind of thing you usually saw out of a bunch of anti-social hybrids, so it caught me by surprise, but I still managed to block his swipe.

It wasn't pretty—rather than checking his attack with a blow of my own, I just threw my arm up. It was good enough to protect my chest, but it didn't stop him from cutting bloody furrows in my back and the outside of my arm. I'd acted out of reflex and didn't even realize initially that the block was something Set had taught me.

It was way too soon for me to be trying that kind of stuff in an actual fight, my aberrant success in my recent challenge fight notwithstanding. I hadn't even begun to have put enough time into wiring up a new set of reflexes, let alone the time required to integrate Set's stuff with what I already knew, but apparently my subconscious didn't agree.

Rather than backing away, I stepped forward and sank my right foot into my opponent's leg. I didn't hit anything critical with my talons and I wasn't trying to knock him over. Instead I simply used my grip to launch myself upwards.

I got my left leg up just high enough to take a slash, that otherwise would have disemboweled me, on the outside of my leg and then I sank my left hand in his stomach. Normally I would have said that the distance and angle was all wrong, but this time I capitalized on my momentum to do way more damage than I'd ever seen done before with what should have been a minor blow.

I tried to keep half an eye on the rest of the battle as I backed away from my first opponent. He wasn't dead, but his core had been badly damaged and he was having a hard time getting himself back to his feet.

The rest of the fight wasn't going as well as my little corner. Onyx had used his ability on nearly all of the lamias at the same time and the effect had been disastrous. It was impossible to fight when you were in that much pain, which meant that any lamia who had been within arm's reach of one of the few surviving hybrids had been savaged. More than half of the lamias were down on the ground, dead or dying, and only the fact that there hadn't been very many hybrids still alive by the time that Onyx had reentered the fight had allowed any of our guys to slip back into deeper water, out of sight and therefore safe from Onyx's power.

I was hurt, but my injuries were relatively minor and I was ready to take my chances against the other bruiser Onyx had detached to take me down. I started forward with a well-timed slash to my opponent's neck that was designed to test his reaction time, but Onyx hit me with another tidal wave of pain before I could even get within half a foot of his guy.

The ground reached up and hit me. I was in too much pain to even realize that Onyx's guy had backhanded me nearly hard enough to break my neck. He could have just as easily torn my throat out, but apparently he hadn't forgotten that Onyx wanted me alive.

I was still seeing double when Onyx's ability cut back off, but my guy was standing too close to me when it happened and I managed to reach up and nearly hamstring his right leg. He stumbled back away from me, obviously not willing to engage without more help now that his mobility had been compromised.

I took stock of what was going on around me while I tried to get the world to stop spinning. There was one less hybrid standing on the island next to Onyx now. Somewhere along the way the rest of his guys had fallen back to surround him, that or maybe he'd only been able to save the guys closest to him. After that last knock to the head I was too shaken up to be sure.

Onyx's guys all looked pretty uneasy considering that they had him backing them up, but then again I couldn't really blame them. Set and the others were downright creepy. They must have ambushed another of the hybrids from the edge of the water. There was blood in the water and big gashes in the mud that hadn't been there a few seconds before.

I figured that was what had forced Onyx to break off and use his power elsewhere. I was going to buy Set and his guys whatever the lamia equivalent to a drink was once we got back to the enclave.

Another round of splashing as something came up out of the water on Onyx's island brought everyone's head around, but I didn't bother waiting to see who or what it was. I lunged at the hybrid who had nearly knocked me out, and he wasn't fast enough to avoid me.

I went in not planning on doing anything fancy. I hit him with more than enough momentum to drive him to the ground, but he managed to get a slash in while he was falling that should have taken me across the kidney and mirrored what Nicolas had done to Ash back at the hospital.

By that time I was committed, there was no dodging the attack and my hands were out of position to stop him as well. Once again I acted out of reflexes that I shouldn't have had. My elbow shot out and caught him on the inside of his arm. It wasn't enough to completely stop his blow, but it served to rob his claws of most of their momentum.

I still took some deep gashes to my back and side, but they weren't enough to kill me and as his claws recoiled backwards from the force of my elbow strike, I slammed my right hand forward, taking him in the chest.

We hit the ground a fraction of a second later. I rolled back to my feet, leaving a corpse in the mud in front of me, but my thrill of success was short-lived because Onyx hit me again, locking up every muscle in my body as the pain made me try to rip my arms free of their sockets.

It felt like I was screaming in pain for hours, but it couldn't have been more than a few seconds. I dimly heard another outbreak of splashing and then the pain vanished and I weakly got my hands back underneath me enough to lift myself up to where I could see what was going on.

The earlier set of splashes had been the scrawny guy who had been chained to the boat. I wouldn't have thought he could survive that long under water, but somehow he'd gone all the way down to the bottom of the channel and then dragged his piece of the boat up onto Onyx's island.

He looked half dead and he was obviously having trouble emptying the water out of his lungs, but I was impressed. He was a fighter, not that you would have known it by the way that the rest of Onyx's men were looking at him. They obviously would have been happier if he'd stayed at the bottom of the bayou.

The second round of splashes looked to have been an unsuccessful attempt by Set and the others to get their hands on another hybrid. The number of hybrids hadn't decreased any, but it also looked like Onyx hadn't managed to stop the lamias from making it back into the water before the rest of his guys got to them.

Onyx hit me with his ability and for a couple of seconds my world shrank down to nothing more than pain and the screams that I couldn't manage to contain. Once he let off of me, it was all I could do to turn over enough to look at him. I couldn't get myself to my feet, couldn't even sit up.

"I can do this all day, Nazir. Maybe you should tell your weird friends that it's time to come out of the water and just give me what I want. Take me to Celeste Hunt and none of the rest of you have to die."

"We aren't taking you anywhere, Onyx, but I'll give you an alternative. Turn around and walk back to New Orleans and my friends and I won't kill you."

"You're hardly in a position to be making threats. How much longer can you take the pain before your body just shuts down? Ten seconds? Twenty? It's obvious you're getting close to the end. I can kill you without even moving, and then I'll just wait here until your friends have to surface for air and I'll kill them too.

"Once you're all dead I'll track you back to whatever hole you've hidden Celeste in, and then I'll take her and her brother back to New Orleans and torture them until they hand over what's left of their family's fortune."

"That's a nice theory, but my friends can spend longer than you would believe underwater. They can easily go out of sight in shifts to breathe somewhere you can't get at them. It's uncanny the way that they can move under the water without creating ripples, but there you have it. They'll just wait you out. Eventually you'll get sloppy and they'll take another of your guys down. It's really just a matter of time."

I hadn't managed to crack Onyx's towering certainty of his own invulnerability, but I could tell that his remaining men were starting to get nervous. That would eventually get to Onyx even if nothing else did.

"Even if you manage to stay far enough from the water to stop them from snatching you one at a time, that won't save you. Eventually you'll have to move and once you're in the water they can take you all at once. Did you see the way your one guy died? He was poisoned."

Onyx's guys were all shifting around now, trying not to be obvious about it, but doing whatever they could to put extra distance between them and the water.

"I know what you're all thinking. Poison doesn't work on hybrids, right? Don't ask me how, but this poison does. Pretty painful way to go too, based on the way your buddy screamed before he died. That means that my friends don't have to fight fair. They don't have to trade blows with you, they just need to break the skin. One stab, and you're a goner."

"You're bluffing. They don't all have that ability, or none of us would have survived your ambush."

"No, you're right, not all of them can do that, but enough of them can. Besides, they don't have to kill you all with poison. They still outnumber you. They just need to kill *you* with poison, Onyx. Inject you with a dose of hybrid-killing venom and then the rest of you will be easy pickings."

LOST

I waited a second to see if any of his people would crack, but they seemed too scared to make a move on their own.

"The best part of it is that even if you do manage by some miracle to beat my friends, it still won't do you any good. I'm telling you the truth when I say that you won't be able to track us back to where we came from. You came all of the way out here for no reason."

"You're lying. You wouldn't have ambushed us if we weren't a threat."

"Oh, you're a threat all right, just not for the reason you think. You were never going to find us—you never will, not until my friends are ready for us to be found—but there are plenty of other reasons for us to come after you. Do you really think that Celeste would pass up a chance to take you down, Onyx? We almost got you, too. If you'd been a split second slower or if your boat had been a little more to one side then you would have spent your last few seconds writhing in agony as the poison burned its way through your chest. Heck, I shouldn't get ahead of myself, that's still the most likely result of all of this. It's kind of exciting, isn't it?"

Some of his guys were looking back at Onyx now rather than at the water like they were supposed to be. They wanted him to take my deal. It was always possible that I was one of those rare people who could lie even to another shape shifter without being caught, but it wasn't likely. Besides, the lamias had already been under the water for more than six minutes and they'd seen their friend go down from the venom. It was hard to argue with facts like that. I decided it was time to play my last card.

"Of course I could be lying about all of this—I'm not, but it's always a possibility. But even if you manage to kill us all, you're still going to have to make your way back through the bayou on foot. Have you seen the size of the alligators around here? Do you really want to be another man or two down as you try to swim past those monsters? There are really big snakes too. It might be interesting to see what the venom of a thirty-foot water moccasin would do to a hybrid. It probably still wouldn't kill you, but I'll bet it would put you down for several hours at least."

That did it. Every single one of Onyx's men knew that he wouldn't stop in enemy territory for them if they got bitten. He'd leave them behind which would mean that the alligators would get them before they fought off the poison enough to be able to defend themselves again.

"I think we should take his deal."

"Me too!"

The chorus of voices that piped up once the first of Onyx's bruisers broke the silence made it sound like there were two or three times as many people standing around him as there actually were. I had Onyx, and we both knew it. His power was nothing short of impressive, but without some foot soldiers to watch his back even he wouldn't be able to take on more than half a dozen lamia. They'd wait until he was focused in one direction and then they'd rush him from all sides.

He could still kill me and I could see that he wanted to, but that wouldn't guarantee his safety and might even cause his men to turn on him. For a second I played with that idea. If I told his guys that I'd give them safe passage in exchange for taking Onyx down it might be enough to convince them to attack him en masse, but there was no guarantee of that and I didn't want to overplay my hand.

"How do we know that you won't just kill us as soon as we step into the water regardless of what you say?"

I shook my head at him. "Careful, if you keep that up you're going to start insulting the honor of my friends. They don't like that. If you push them too far, then they'll refuse to negotiate with you."

I was riding the ragged edge of what I could get away with from the standpoint of misdirection. That was the biggest reason that I wasn't trying to get them to turn on each other.

It wasn't a lie to say that Set and the others would take a dim view of Onyx calling them liars, but I was very carefully not telling Onyx that the lamias were particularly sensitive to losses right now because each fallen lamia was one less who would be able to help cloak the enclave from the Consumed.

Onyx and I locked gazes for nearly a full minute before he finally nodded. "Fine. This is how things are going to go down. I want your friends to promise that they will let us go, and then they are going to all move back behind you and show themselves so that we know we have a clear shot out of here."

"Set, is that agreeable to you?"

There was a second there where I was afraid that he hadn't been able to hear us, and then Set stood in the water, appearing less than three feet from the edge of the island I was on, in a spot where I would have sworn the water wasn't deep enough to hide a seven-foot-tall lamia.

"Broadly, yes. They must turn around and head back the way that they came. They must not stop, they must not return. If they do, we will know and we will ambush them again. Next time we will not fail."

Onyx looked like he wanted to use his power on Set to put the lamia in his place, but everyone there knew that would just result in Set disappearing underneath the water again. What was more, I was pretty sure that one or more of the other lamias were already creeping forward, preparing to strike from behind if Onyx took the bait Set was offering him.

"Fine, move your people back out of range and we'll leave."

Set nodded, hissed something more complex than I was expecting, and then sank back down into the water. Five minutes later he reappeared more than twenty yards away from where he'd last shown himself. He pointed off to his left and then slapped the water.

Fifty yards away the first lamia rose out of the water at the same time that Set dropped back out of sight. As soon as that lamia was sure Onyx and the rest had seen him, he in turn slapped the water and then sank out of sight as another lamia stood up.

I counted them all, one by one as they each revealed themselves and then disappeared again. They'd stationed themselves in one long arc that covered nearly a hundred yards. As the last surviving lamia dropped back out of sight, Onyx turned back to me.

"I was going to ask you to give Celeste a message for me."

"What message would that be?"

He pointed at the slender guy who had just pulled himself out of the water minutes before. "That piece of trash belongs to her. If she doesn't show back up at the house in three days, I'll start killing one of her people each day. It shouldn't take me much more than a week and a half to kill every man, woman, and child she's tried to protect from me for the last two decades. After that I'll pack up my things and leave town. She can have her freedom or she can have her pack, but she can't have both."

"What made you change your mind about that message?"

"I realized that the snakes can pass it along just as well as you can."

Onyx hit me with his power again and the pain was even more intense than the other times he'd used it on me. I would have said that wasn't possible, but this time the pain wasn't the only thing on my mind.

I'd been expecting him to use his power on me again. A guy like Onyx was almost incapable of passing up a chance to double-cross someone. Even more important, he had to be itching to reestablish his authority with the rest of the surviving hybrids from his pack.

Even before the lamias had moved back out of ambush range, I'd started moving. I'd made a big show—which had only involved a little in the way of theatrics—of staggering around as I forced myself back up onto my feet.

That moved me several feet closer to the shoreline and I sprang towards the water a split second before Onyx had stopped talking, but even as I went flying through the air I knew I'd failed. I hit the water, inch-deep though it was, with my shoulder, but that wasn't enough. My hip and feet landed in mud, which meant that almost all of my body was still out where Onyx could see me.

LOST

Even more ironic was the fact that as I bounced once and then came to a stop—still not far enough out into the water—I realized that my plan never could have worked in the first place. The pain had driven all of the air out of my lungs, so I wouldn't have been able to stay under the water for any stretch of time even if I'd made it as far as I'd been hoping.

I could feel the end approaching. Onyx had overestimated just how much strength I had left. Once again, there was no good way to tell time once all of the external stimuli disappeared. My pulse had gone thready and irregular; I figured that I only had a few more beats before my heart was going to give out entirely.

Dying didn't feel anything like I expected it to. One second I was there consumed by pain, covered in mud, and then something was pulling me down into the darkness, a lukewarm, terrifying black that pressed in on me from all sides.

It took me nearly two full seconds to realize that the pain was gone. My lungs were now the only part of me screaming for relief.

Something had grabbed me and pulled me under the water, only it hadn't let go of me. It was still dragging me through the water at such a fast speed that I couldn't seem to get my feet underneath me. Visions of giant alligators burst over me and I reached forward with my free hand, raking my claws across something hard in an attempt to free myself.

It was the feel of my claws scraping across lamia claws that helped me start to regain a measure of control over myself, but even that might not have been enough to stop me from fighting if the lamia towing me hadn't picked that instant to shove me hard towards the surface of the water.

I surfaced coughing and gasping for air, and would have gone back under if Set hadn't surfaced at nearly the same time. He grabbed hold of me, steadying me at the same time that he looked at Onyx. We'd come up far enough away from where we'd gone under the water that Onyx didn't see us immediately.

Onyx looked at the two of us, and I saw his eyes start to tighten as he summoned up his ability, but before he could send another jolt of pain through my body, his eyes went wide in understanding. I should have been too disoriented to understand what was going through his mind, but it was as though I could read his thoughts.

The time between when Set had slapped the water and when the last of the lamias had risen to show themselves for a split second before disappearing again hadn't been long. Maybe a minute and a half at the most. That shouldn't have been enough time for Set to cover the twenty yards between where he'd been and where I'd been without making enough turbulence in the water to be seen.

LOST

It should have been impossible, and yet Set had done it. Even worse, it was proof that the lamias were much faster than Onyx had believed. It meant that he had no way of guaranteeing that the rest of Set's people weren't mere seconds from reaching Onyx's island again.

Onyx could easily kill me if that was what he wanted to do, but doing that would require precious seconds he couldn't afford to spare. He turned and ran, the rest of his people mere feet behind him.

I collapsed two seconds later.

Chapter 24

Isaac Nazir
The Lamia Enclave

I woke up a few hours later battered and more exhausted than I should have been, but still alive and once again safely back inside the enclave. After everything I'd been through, I just wanted to go back to sleep and put off dealing with whatever the universe was going to throw at me next, but after fifteen minutes of trying to sleep, I finally threw in the towel and rolled out of bed.

I wouldn't have thought that the introduction of just one more person into our living space could have made any kind of huge difference in the look and feel of the room, but I would have been completely wrong. The wolf who had been with Onyx, the one who'd been chained by his wrists to the boat and almost drowned earlier, was stretched out on our couch and looking even worse than when I'd last seen him.

Now that I was close enough to really study him I was struck by the fact that he looked undernourished in a way that was hard to achieve for a shape shifter. Usually if we weren't getting enough food we were in constant danger of losing control of our beasts. The fact that someone had gotten away with starving him like that was pretty strong evidence that he was about as submissive as they came.

As interesting as that particular tidbit was, it was the bandages across his chest that were the most astonishing. I didn't remember him taking a claw to the chest, so that probably meant that Onyx had cut him while I'd been under the water. Apparently Onyx had figured that a dead wolf would serve just as well as a live wolf when it came to sending Celeste the message that he wanted her back in New Orleans.

I took one more quiet step into the room which put me in a position where I was able to see Celeste for the first time. She was sprawled out on one of the stone chairs and she looked as bad as I'd ever seen her look.

Much like starving a shape shifter takes a lot of doing if you wanted to avoid having your head bitten off, it takes a lot to put bags under our eyes. There were bags underneath Celeste's eyes, dark ones that said she hadn't been sleeping well, or possibly even at all, for days. Her hair looked like it hadn't been washed for the better part of a week, and she was wearing the jeans and t-shirt that she'd worn underneath her scrubs when she'd come to the hospital to pick us up. That wasn't a big deal other than the fact they looked like they hadn't been washed recently.

All of it was out of character and I didn't have an explanation for any of it. There was no reason for her to have fallen apart so completely in such a short time.

My stomach reminded me that it had been a while since my last meal, so I started making my stealthy way past Celeste and her pack mate. I only made it a couple of steps before his eyes snapped open and he shot me a sickly smile.

"She just dropped off half an hour ago. I had my eyes closed for an hour before that trying to convince her that it was okay for her to sleep. My name is Jax, by the way."

His voice was pitched, just loud enough to carry to me, but still quiet enough that it didn't wake Celeste. I wasn't sure that I could have managed that, but then again, I hadn't spent the last couple of decades doing everything I could to avoid the attention of the dominants in my pack.

Every pack had submissives and there was no arguing with the fact that it sucked taking orders, but only the worst kind of monster would turn actual people into timid animals that were scared of even their own shadows. Jax wasn't in quite that bad of shape, but he was close. Based on the smile he'd flashed and the eye roll he'd used to punctuate how obsessive-compulsive Celeste had been when it came to trying to take care of him, I was pretty sure that only his native good humor had saved him from being pushed down that path.

I would have said that it wasn't possible for me to dislike Onyx any more than I already did. I would have been wrong. The more I learned about Onyx, the more I wished that Alec had already made a trip down to New Orleans and put the pack's alpha down.

I shook myself, forcing my mind back to the present. I returned Jax's smile and pitched my voice as close as possible to the same range he'd used.

"Hey, my name is Isaac. How did she get so tired so quickly? We were only gone for a couple of hours and I was pretty sure that she was sleeping okay before I left."

"Yeah, about that...she started filling me in while she was bandaging me up. There are probably things about the lamias that she hasn't gotten around to telling me, but it's looking like there are even more things that nobody knew. For you, your trip only lasted a few hours. For her you were gone nearly a week. She was totally freaking out because she had no idea what had happened to your group."

My mind was still trying to process what Jax had just said, but he didn't wait for me to catch up.

"She said that she went to the guards outside of the main cave and asked them for answers something like a hundred times, but none of them would admit to speaking any English."

I nodded. "Yeah, that actually makes sense. Only the consorts speak our language and I'm pretty sure that Set brought them all with us. They are the best fighters the enclave has. Not only that, he probably wasn't entirely comfortable with the idea of leaving both Celeste and his queen here alone with one of them. There have been some...problems in that area recently."

"Are you like some kind of lamia whisperer or something? How did you even know that?"

I shrugged uncomfortably. It didn't seem right to accept any kind of praise for what little I knew about the lamias.

"Set is actually very willing to explain stuff. Usually the biggest problem is figuring out what you need to know."

Even as I said it I realized that my answer wasn't strictly true. Set had said something about his queen telling him to answer all of my questions. I thought about elaborating, but I didn't know Jax well enough to just tell him everything I knew about the lamias. Besides, it seemed like he'd already moved on.

"Still, I'm impressed. That's very cool that you've got such a good in with them."

I gave him what I hoped was a humble nod and then neither of us seemed to have anything else to say. I was eyeing one of the fruits still hanging from the vines on the far wall when Jax started to sit up and then grimaced in pain.

"That will teach me to get excited about something right now. Sorry, I was going to say that there is one more thing I should tell you. Celeste talked like you guys have been here for a while, but back in the real world it's only been two days since you disappeared."

"Interesting. So there are multiple instances where time doesn't seem to be behaving the way it should. Every time I think that I have a decent idea of what the lamias are capable of they turn around and do something else I can't even begin to explain."

"Yeah, that's pretty much what Celeste said too."

I shook my head in disbelief and then looked back over at Jax. "Are you doing okay? Do you need anything before I leave? I'd stay and keep an eye on you, but I should go find Set and see if he will shed any light on all of this craziness."

"Don't worry about me. I'm doing pretty well for a guy who nearly drowned and then had Onyx do a half-hearted job of trying to rip his heart out of his chest. I don't need anything, but if you have a second could you grab a blanket for Celeste? She's been shivering off and on ever since she fell asleep."

"Sure thing, I'll be right back."

It didn't even cross my mind that I might be violating Celeste's privacy by ducking into her room to grab the thin blanket from her bed. I was only two steps into her room when I saw the pictures. There were six of them, all wallet-sized, of nine or ten different people.

I'd never seen any of the pictures and Celeste hadn't had any luggage when we'd jumped into the boat, so all I could figure was that she must have been carrying them in her jeans when she'd left to go to the hospital.

Jax was in one of the shots, but he was the only one I recognized. A few of the people in the photos were obviously related to each other by blood, but the only other common denominator was the fact that they all had the furtive look of people whom life had been especially unkind to, people who weren't entirely sure that they would see next month.

I studied the pictures for nearly a minute before I pulled the blanket off of the bed and carried it back out to Jax.

"You seem pretty concerned about Celeste."

Jax looked confused for a moment before nodding. "I guess you're right. Mostly we just do the absolute minimum we can get away with for the dominants, but that's not how we think of Celeste. She gets kicked around just as much as we do, she's one of us in a way that most hybrids never could be, begging your pardon."

"No offense taken here. Can you tell me more about what things are like inside of your pack?"

"Not much to tell. Onyx and his guys make life a living hell for all of the rest of us on their good days. When they have a bad day they tend to put people in the hospital as a way of blowing off steam. Half of the submissives inside of the pack probably would have died five years ago if Celeste hadn't laid down the law back before her brother disappeared."

"How'd she lay down the law to someone like Onyx? He's completely out of her league."

"She used the one advantage she has over him. He wants her alive more than she wants to be alive. Back when she was still in her twenties, a year or so after Onyx killed her mother, one of Onyx's guys got carried away and accidentally killed Patty. Celeste challenged that guy to a fight and killed him. It was an amazing fight—she was younger, less experienced, and she gave up more than sixty pounds to him, but she ripped his heart out of his chest and threw it down at Onyx's feet."

"That can't have gone over well."

"Nope, Onyx beat her to within an inch of her life. We were all terrified, none of us thought she was going to recover from the beating he'd given her, but she did. Once she recovered he told her he'd do the same thing again if she killed another one of his guys. She just looked at him without blinking and then told him, loud enough that his guys could all hear, that the next time one of his people killed or maimed one of us she wouldn't even give them the formality of a challenge match. She'd just kill them one night when they weren't expecting it."

"She called his bluff."

"Yeah. She knew he didn't want to kill her and risk losing out on all of that money. After that, things got a little better. There was still a lot of bad stuff that happened, but the dominants all knew that there were *some* things that they couldn't get away with."

"She never had to kill any of the other dominants after that?"

Jax looked supremely uncomfortable. "I shouldn't be saying anything, but some of us think she killed another of the dominants a short time after her brother disappeared. I think Onyx suspected as much too, but he never had any proof. If she did, then I say good riddance.

"Bennet was no good. He was scared of her, that much was obvious. He was careful to strut just like all of the rest when he was around the other dominants, but if it was just her and him he didn't engage in the same kind of excesses that the rest of them did."

"That doesn't sound like someone you'd want to see out of the picture."

"Yeah, at least not until you know that he was worse than the rest of the hybrids when it was just us and him. He was really sick."

"You guys never told Celeste?"

"No. He was bad, but not bad enough that any of us wanted to see her get beaten like that again. We kept our mouths shut, but there were signs that she knew. I think she was just having a hard time admitting to herself that she was going to have to kill again. That kind of thing is easier when you're full of rage from finding out that one of your friends has been killed. It's a lot harder to come at it cold. We used to hear her crying occasionally after she killed the first guy."

"She cried like that again after Bennet disappeared?"

"Yeah, but it could have just been because her brother was gone. We all thought he was gone until recently. Some thought that Bennet had killed him, but others thought he'd killed himself like Bennet had claimed. Bennet was a good liar, but masking your pulse and scent only go so far. Eventually those around you figure out whether you can be trusted or not regardless of all that. That's why con men always move on eventually."

"And Celeste? She's a good liar."

"That she is, but we all figured out a long time ago that she's got a good heart underneath all of that."

Jax yawned and then grimaced at the way that the motion pulled at his bandages. "Sorry, but I think I'm done played out. I can barely keep my eyes open."

"That's fine, Jax. Don't stay awake on my account. You need your sleep."

His eyes started moving around in the classic sign of someone in REM sleep even before I'd finished talking. I tiptoed over to the food and carefully ripped a large piece of fruit free of its vine before going outside.

I ate as I walked towards the main cave where the queen was located. There were two guards, just the same as always, but this time one of the guards was a consort. I didn't need him to show me his fangs to recognize Pal, but he opened his mouth and hissed at me regardless.

"I'd like to talk to Set."

"Go away. Set doesn't want to talk to you, sun person."

"Please go tell him that I'm here and would like to talk to him if he has a few minutes to spare."

"I said go away!"

I cocked my head to one side and gave the consort my best nonchalant smile. "We both know that I'm eventually going to run into Set again, and when I do I'm going to tell him about this conversation. If Set really left instructions not to bother him, then you don't have anything to worry about. If you're lying to me, then you'll have interfered with his promise to teach me. Do you really want to cause him to break his promise and act in a dishonorable way?"

The lamia shot me a look that said he would have liked nothing quite so much as the chance to bury his claws in my chest, but he hissed something to the worker standing next to him. The worker disappeared into the cave, leaving the consort and me to exchange glowers.

Five minutes later the worker, or another one that looked similar enough that I couldn't tell them apart, returned with Set following a few steps behind.

"I'm sorry if I'm disturbing something important, Set."

"No, Isaac Nazir, nothing in more important than my promise to see to your instruction. Come, let us retire to the challenge circle."

It wasn't until we reached the sand-filled cave that I realized why Set was moving so gingerly. He had a sizable gash across his right leg and what looked like a nasty puncture wound in the bottom quadrant of the left side of his chest.

I couldn't see the actual wounds, but I could see where the bandages were breaking the line of his simple white clothes. He'd taken much more damage than I'd realized in the early stages of the fight with Onyx's guys, and yet he'd still saved my life there at the end of everything.

"I'm sorry, Set, I didn't realize that you were hurt. I would not have asked you to come teach me if I'd known."

"It's fine, Isaac Nazir. It is within your rights to ask for the assistance that you have earned. I will not be able to spar with you, but I can still show you some new techniques."

We worked together for half an hour before it became apparent that even just showing me the different blocks and strikes was becoming difficult for Set. Lamias were tough, at least as tough as hybrids, but I didn't want to put him through any unnecessary pain, so I looked around for a reason to stop and talk.

It didn't take long to recall one of the reasons that I had gone looking for him in the first place. I probably would have already started asking him why time wasn't behaving itself if I hadn't been so concerned about his injuries. Still, I decided to lead with something else.

"Set, you brought back Onyx's prisoner. Isn't that going to cause you problems? Won't he further shrink the amount of time before the Consumed find the enclave?"

"Again you go right to the heart of the matter, Isaac Nazir. Yes, his presence is already causing us problems. We returned to the enclave significantly later than the point in the time stream where we left it, so some of the difficulties caused by your presence have been able to dissipate, but it is a temporary measure at best and even that causes more difficulties."

"What kind of difficulties?"

"It is lamia business, nothing that you should have to concern yourself about."

He turned as if to end the conversation and return to our training, but I put a hand out and gently gripped his shoulder.

"You saved my life, Set, when nobody could have blamed you for not being able to save me. Letting me die would have made many of your problems go away. With me gone, Celeste would have lacked the challenger she needed to stay here and the enclave would have been safe."

"Honor compelled me to do all that I could to save you. You joined my men to fight for the safety of the enclave. I could do no less for you than I would have done for one of them."

I nodded. "I understand that, Set. My honor also compels me to ask about the difficulties that our presence is creating for you. I would not cause harm to your people without at least knowing the effects of my actions."

Set was quiet for a moment and I realized in a moment of insight that it was hardest for him to talk about himself. I didn't know enough to tell whether that was a cultural thing or just part of Set's personality, but it was something that I needed to remember.

"The problems are many, Isaac Nazir. The loss of so many lamias has made the enclave even weaker and more susceptible to the Consumed's efforts to find us. I had no choice but to bring us back here later or the Consumed would have found us within the month. That was not a popular decision.

"The other consorts did not like leaving our queen so defenseless for such a long period of time, and they blame you and me for our losses. You for bringing the sun people to our territory and me for not abandoning honor and forcing you out of the enclave."

"I am sorry, Set. I would not occasion such difficulties if the need of my people, of my queen, were not great. Are these troubles the kind that will...dissipate over time, do you think?"

Set was silent for so long that I'd almost decided that he wasn't going to answer me. "It is hard to say. My wounds mean that I have three more days of immunity before I can be challenged. If things have cooled off by then, then I should be fine. If they have not, then I fear that I will be going into a challenge against Pal, the angriest of the others, at less than full strength."

Chapter 25

Isaac Nazir
The Lamia Enclave

It was obvious that Set just wanted to be alone to lick his wounds. I wanted to do more, to fix the mess that I'd made of the lamias' internal dynamic, but we both knew that there wasn't anything I could do. I came up with an excuse to end the practice session and promised myself that I'd find a way to convince Set to leave off of training for the next few days.

I didn't know enough about lamia physiology to understand why it was going to take him so long to heal from the injuries he'd sustained, but it was obvious that he wasn't convinced that he was going to be back to full strength by the time his immunity wore off. A hybrid was capable of healing back from almost anything that didn't kill him within three days, but lamias apparently had some offsetting weaknesses to compensate for venom that was capable of dropping even werewolves in seconds.

Celeste and Jax were still in the living room when I got back to our rooms. Jax was still asleep, but Celeste had apparently left his side for long enough to shower and change her clothes. Even just a couple of hours of sleep had done wonders for her. If I hadn't woken up when I had, I never would have realized how worried she'd been.

I suspected that would have been her preference, but I couldn't un-see what I'd seen any more than I could un-hear the things that Jax had told me. I nodded to her as I walked through the living room, headed towards my bedroom, but she stood up and followed me.

If I'd had my choice, I would have chosen for this particular conversation to happen later, preferably a few days later, so that I could have some time to think over everything I'd just heard. Celeste apparently had other ideas.

She stepped inside my room so that the curtain of vines would block the sound of conversation from reaching Jax, and then leaned against the smooth rock of my wall.

"I'm glad that you survived, Isaac. I had a lot of time to think about stuff while you were gone."

I wanted to avoid her eyes, wanted to look anywhere but at her. Looking at her felt dangerous, but I forced myself to do it, to really examine her like I hadn't done since I'd first met her.

Her blond hair fell in loose waves down just past her bare shoulders. It looked so soft that I wanted to reach out and touch it, but I forced myself to stay right where I was.

She was still just as fit and muscular as always. She had the exquisite build of a professional dancer and skin that was flawless, but that wasn't what was dangerous about her.

My gaze, or maybe my lack of response, made her uncomfortable enough that she adjusted the white tube dress that had been among the clothes that Set had given us. I thought about teasing her for wearing the exact same thing she'd been complaining about just when we'd arrived, but I didn't. It wasn't the right time for teasing. Besides, she looked good in white.

Black made her look hard and in control, which had its place and time, but she'd been wearing a lot of white lately and it suited her even better. In that dress, made out of a material that looked soft and touchable, she looked young and vulnerable.

Ash was older than me, which meant that Celeste had to be older still, but she wasn't human. She didn't look her age, whatever it might be. On a normal day she looked all of twenty-two. Today she looked my age, seventeen or eighteen, but that still wasn't the real danger.

I finally looked at her eyes—her soft, gray eyes—and I saw exactly what I'd been afraid of. She really had been worried about me, and not just because she needed me to fight the challenge matches that allowed her to stay in the enclave in the hopes of being able to talk to the lamia queen.

She was developing feelings for me, and despite her best efforts, she wasn't hiding that fact very well. Celeste, the perfect liar, the girl who'd fought an extended shadow war against Onyx where she had to always keep her true emotions hidden, had let her mask slip and that terrified me.

It terrified me because I knew how badly I wanted to reciprocate those feelings. On some level I was even to the point where I could see myself letting go of my feelings for Jess. Nothing I currently felt for Celeste was going to change the fact that I'd desperately loved Jess while she'd been with us, or the fact that I still missed her every day. Despite all of that, Jess was gone and she wasn't going to come back.

I'd been chasing Jessica, who was a completely different person, was it really that different if I let myself feel something for Celeste? Jessica, the new person who'd spent the last few months doing everything she could to keep me at arm's length, wouldn't care—in fact she'd be overjoyed at the idea of me moving on. She wasn't a concern, not now.

LOST

Jess, my beloved Jess who'd stood at my side through half a decade of hell as Brandon tried to grind our pack into the dust, wouldn't have wanted me to go through the rest of my life pining for her. She'd been insanely possessive and even occasionally jealous when she'd been alive, but that had been a function of what she'd been through. If she'd known that I was going to be forced to go on without her, she would have told me to be happy, to find someone I could trust, respect, and love.

No, none of that was a valid reason to hold back from what I wanted to feel for Celeste. The only valid reason was the fact that I didn't know if I could trust her. She was falling for me, but I wasn't sure that there was room in her heart for a boyfriend, didn't know if she was even capable of a healthy relationship after what she'd done to Bennet.

"I guess that is all I wanted to say. I'm glad that you're okay. Thank you for insisting that Set and the others bring Jax back."

Her voice was low and rough, she was holding back tears, but I couldn't let that sway me. If I was going to act on my feelings then it needed to be because I was ready to accept what being with Celeste would mean, not because she'd netted me with her tears.

"I didn't. Set brought him back of his own free will because Jax was one of your people."

"Oh. I guess I owe him my thanks."

She turned to go, but I reached out and wrapped my hand around the bare skin of her arm. She was warm in a way that I hadn't realized I missed quite so much.

"We can't keep doing this."

"Can't keep doing what, Isaac?"

She hadn't torn her arm free from my grasp, instead she'd stepped into me, looking up at me with her lips slightly parted.

"We're destroying the enclave. Having Jax here now too would have been bad enough all by itself, but when you combine that with the fact that we lost another consort and some more workers in the fight against Onyx, it spells disaster. The enclave can't remain hidden for very much longer."

There was a flash of something in her eyes that I didn't initially understand. It wasn't that I couldn't categorize it, it was that I didn't want to believe it of her. She'd been glad to hear that the lamias were reaching the end of their rope.

"Does that really make you happy, Celeste?"

"Yes, but it's not like you think. I don't want them all dead, but this is the one thing that's guaranteed to bring their queen to the table. She's refused to see me up until now, but she won't risk the complete destruction of her people just to avoid answering my questions. This is all just one gigantic game of chicken. If you can win just one more fight we're guaranteed to get what we want."

I shook my head at her, but I couldn't bring myself to step back. Having her so close, occasionally brushing up against each other as we swayed, was intoxicating and part of me was sure that she would change her mind if I could just explain the cost she was imposing on the lamias.

"No, you'll be guaranteed to get what *you* want. Remember? You said that you wouldn't ask about where the Coun'hij was. You're going to ask for a way to save your people. This isn't about us, it's about you, and it's about them."

She was mad now. I didn't step back away from her, but she ripped her arm free of my hand.

"Someone needs to take care of them, Isaac. You've met Jax. Can you really look at me and say that you don't care what happens to him? You're actually going to abandon him and the others like him by refusing to fight *one* more damn match?"

"If we stay here they are going to kill Set. The other consorts are mad that he's let us stay. They want us gone and in a few days one of them is going to challenge him and probably kill him because he's still recovering from the wounds he took saving me and Jax both."

"In *less* than a few days Onyx is going to start killing my friends. He's going to execute them one at a time if I'm not there to stop him by letting him torture me. *Those* people are my family, Isaac, not Ash. He ran away, but they stayed. They've stood by me through thick and thin, I'm not abandoning them to save one lamia, regardless of how nice he's been to us."

"He's the only reason we've made it this far, Celeste. Without him Ash would be dead already. Without him I would have died during my last match, or while we were fighting Onyx. He's a good person. He doesn't deserve to die like this, killed by his own people because he's so honorable."

She stabbed me in the chest with one finger. If she'd been in hybrid form she would have speared me through the heart, but her human finger merely hit me hard enough to leave a bruise.

"I didn't force him to be that way, Isaac. I can't change that, all I can do is play the hand that is dealt me. His honor is something good, but it's also something that I can use to save my people, people who are just as good."

She was so mad she was shaking, but it wasn't the kind of shake that would have presaged a transformation. It was nothing more than human emotions running hot. I knew because I was feeling the same way.

The desire to push past her and avoid the logical conclusion of this fight was strong, but I forced the words out that needed to be said.

"What if I had another way? What if there was someone else who could come take Onyx down. I could get them down here faster than you would believe. Do you trust me enough to leave the enclave with me and go back to New Orleans?"

She looked at me for several long seconds. I could see that she wanted to believe just as badly as I wanted her to believe, but in the end she shook her head.

"Maybe you're right. Maybe the answer is just to call Alec up and have him take away all of our problems, but I just can't believe it will work. That sounds like a fairytale, and my life doesn't have room for fairytales. I trust *you*, Isaac, not somebody a thousand miles away who I've never met. You will do the right thing because it's who you are. I just need you to win one more fight for me and then this will be all over."

"I'm sorry, Celeste, but I'm not going to be the reason that Set dies. The longer we stay here the less likely it is that Set can talk himself out of the pickle that we've put him in. I leave tomorrow morning, and I'll be taking Ash and Kristin with me. I doubt that Set and the others will let you stay here without us, so I think you should pack tonight."

Her hand came up almost like she was going to slap me, but in the end she just turned and ran out of my room.

I would have liked to stay and pack, but there was something I had to do first. I picked my phone up off of the stone shelf where I'd left it, and headed outside as I waited for it to finish powering on.

No sooner did it finish coming up than it started vibrating with an incoming call. I didn't recognize the number, but I didn't have anything to lose by answering it, so I clicked the accept button.

"Who is this?"

"Ah, that was what I was going to ask you. Wait, are you reading my mind?"

The voice on the other end of the line was female and she sounded flirty and cheerful. It took me a second to realize why I was having a hard time placing her. I'd never heard Rachel sound like this, but it was definitely Rachel.

"Rach, is that you?"

"I don't know—which Isaac am I talking to?"

I wanted to throw my phone into the side of the cliff. I wasn't in the mood for more of Rachel's crazy delusions, but I forced a measure of calm into my voice.

"It's me, Isaac Nazir. Does Alec know where you are?"

"Well duh. Of course it's Isaac Nazir, but which Isaac Nazir am I talking to?"

"It's me Rachel, you only know one Isaac. Where are you? I'll call Alec and he can have someone pick you up within a few hours."

"Why would I want to do that, Isaac Nazir? The flowers are so lovely this time of year."

Something about the way she said my name sent shivers racing up my spine. It was still Rachel's voice, but the inflection and cadence was a perfect match for Set.

"Why did you say that, Rachel? Who have you been talking to?"

"I said it because you assured me that there was only one Isaac Nazir. I haven't been so sure lately, but you promised, so I'm willing to take you on faith. Wait, I'm still talking to you, aren't I?"

It took me a second to follow the twisty almost-logic that she seemed to be using, and by the time I'd decided that she really was just talking nonsense I'd missed my chance to get a word in edgewise.

"I hear you're back on the market, so I wanted to make a run at you early on—you know, before all of the girls started lining up."

"Rach, you've lost me again."

"You *are* back on the market aren't you? You know—knight-errantry, dragon slaying, maiden rescuing, all that? Is it still knight-errantry if you slay the dragon before they actually threaten the maiden?"

"Rachel Graves, you really need to tell me where you are so that someone can go get you. You're not well."

"Oh, that's a good one. Is the disease still bad if it hasn't hurt you yet? I like that one even better. Do butterflies get sick?"

"Rachel, I can't keep talking to you if you're not going to make sense. Are you going to let me help you or not?"

"I don't know, Isaac. Are you going to let me help you?"

"Probably not. I don't think you can get me out of this particular problem."

"Hmm, I think I'd like to withdraw my request for your hand. There are other maidens who are ready to let me help them. Don't worry though, it's not you, it's me...or whatever the kids are saying these days."

That actually made me laugh. "I thought that I was the knight and you were the maiden."

"It's all relative, Isaac. If you want to be the knight then be the knight, but don't come running to me complaining that you're getting saddle-sore and your armor is too hot and heavy."

There was something there buried underneath all of the flirting, but before I could latch onto it and give it the analysis it deserved, Rachel sighed.

"Sorry, Isaac. It looks like it's time for me to go. We really could have been great together, but try not to let it get you down too much. Some things just aren't meant to be. Tell Alec and Adri hi for me."

She hung up before I could respond and I was left looking at my phone in bemusement. The old Rachel never would have managed to dominate a conversation so completely. Maybe being crazy had some benefits after all. It meant everyone was too busy trying to figure out what you were saying to actually get a word in edgewise.

I shook myself and then dialed the number that I'd been planning on calling in the first place. I was hoping against hope that Alec had listened to my voicemail and forgiven me for being so erratic lately, but once again he didn't pick up.

"Hey, Alec. If you get this I really need to talk to you. I…well, I guess I need a favor. I know I don't have any right to ask you for anything, but there it is. Ash, Kristin and I are all down in New Orleans and things are every bit as bad as Ash kept telling us they were.

"This Onyx guy is seriously bad news and I'm not sure that anyone but you can stop him. I would if I could, but I can't. I'm in over my head. I'd just pack up and go home, but that wouldn't be right. It would hurt people I care about."

Once again, it was even harder to do this kind of thing via message than I'd thought it would be. In person Alec was pretty forgiving and understanding, but this way I didn't have any of the verbal or nonverbal clues that would have told me that I was getting through to him.

Apparently in my imagination Alec was even more remote and unforgiving than he'd been back when he and Adri had been on the outs.

"I guess that's it. If you won't do it for me, can you at least come down for Ash? You said you'd be willing to come down if Celeste and the submissives in the pack wanted an out. She wants an out now, but we will need your help. Even Grayson or Jaclyn wouldn't be enough to dig us out of this hole.

"Oh, and Rachel called me. I'll text you her number in a second. I tried to get her to tell me where she was, but she refused. I'd get online and look it up myself, but I don't have internet access right now."

I couldn't help the chuckle that escaped me. "I know right? Who would have thought I could survive for more than a few hours without some kind of access to the rest of the world? I guess some things do change after all. Please give me a call as soon as you can. I need to make some decisions and knowing that you're going to be able to come down and put Onyx down would make some of them easier."

I hung up and powered my phone down. Jax was still asleep and Celeste ducked into her bedroom as soon as she heard me coming. It was going to be a long night.

Chapter 26

Isaac Nazir
The Lamia Enclave

It ended up being a long night for reasons I hadn't anticipated. Celeste didn't give me any more grief, but my dreams were so vivid that I felt like I never actually got to sleep. More dreams where I was fighting. They lasted all night and I slept for more than eight hours, which had to be some kind of record for a shape shifter.

I'd needed every minute of it though, because battling lamias, werewolves and other hybrids isn't the kind of thing that leaves you feeling refreshed afterwards, even when it's just happening inside of a dream. Surprisingly, I seemed to be fully recovered from all of the effects of the fight with Onyx, which had to be a side effect of having slept for so long.

Under other circumstances I would have missed the extra free time that I'd lost by sleeping so much, but that didn't bother me as much inside of the enclave. There wasn't much to do other than talk, sleep or fight, so it was actually kind of nice to spend more of each day unconscious.

Even so, I was starting to get a little worried by how much I was sleeping. Hopefully it was just a side effect of all of the weird time and space manipulation that was an inherent part of being inside of the enclave.

It wasn't until I stepped into the shower that I realized that I hadn't spent the whole night fighting, or rather that I hadn't been *just* fighting. Bits and pieces of the conversation with Rachel had played through my head too.

It had left me with a weird collage of memories. A werewolf coming at me while Rachel asked me which Isaac I was. A lamia sticking its claws into my gut as Rachel told me that it was okay to kill a dragon even if it hadn't hurt me yet. Even as the water ran down my body it still felt like Rachel's words were still playing through my mind. Not the memory of our conversation, but the actual conversation, happening again and again.

It was surprisingly disturbing.

I'd expected to find Jax and Celeste both waiting for me. I didn't expect to see Set likewise waiting for me to leave the shower.

LOST

"Greeting, Isaac Nazir. I'm afraid that it is time for another challenge if you all wish to stay here."

I opened my mouth to tell him that we were leaving, but the words stuck in my throat. I heard Rachel's voice in my head again, but I couldn't remember what she'd told me. It was all mixed up for me now, but the one thing that kept coming through was that I had a choice.

That was what I'd been missing all of this time. I had a choice. I'd always had a choice; I just hadn't always been willing to live with the consequences of some of the paths available to me.

If we left now, it would mean that Set might be able to talk himself out of a challenge. If we stayed and I killed another one of his men, then it would almost certainly mean that he'd end up fighting Pal, and he would lose.

There was another option, but even just a couple of days ago I probably wouldn't have been willing to take it. I was ready now.

"Set, if Pal was out of the picture, if he was dead, would anyone else challenge you for the position of first consort?"

"What do you mean, Isaac Nazir?"

"Please just answer the question. Are any of the others likely to try and kill you if Pal is out of the picture?"

"No, Isaac Nazir. There is only one other remaining consort other than Pal and me. I do not believe that Rast will challenge if Pal is not around to stir things up."

"And how much would the loss of Pal impact your ability to keep the enclave hidden?"

"It would reduce the time that we can safely shelter you by a day or two. We lamias are only able to do so much to mask your presence. Mostly the length of time you can be hidden is a function of the...reservoir."

I nodded. I'd hoped that his answer would be something like that. It was only logical given that Pal was ready to kill Set. He wouldn't have been considering that course of action if the loss of another consort would result in the enclave instantly being found by the Consumed.

"I know that I've been having you pick out my opponents, but is it still permissible for me to pick out my own opponent if I so desire."

Set shook his head. "Isaac Nazir, please don't do this."

It seemed impossible for Set not to have realized where my line of questioning was headed. Maybe he'd known all along but just not wanted to admit it to himself. He knew now.

"That's a yes, then. Set, I accept the challenge but I would select Pal as my opponent."

Celeste was at my side, but I didn't remember her crossing the length of the room to get there.

"Isaac, what are you thinking? The consorts are a whole different ball game than fighting a worker. Pal won't be able to use his venom, but that's not going to matter. If he's looking at challenging Set then he's got to be their number two fighter."

LOST

"Yeah, I figured as much."

"You don't have to do this. You've made your point. Let's go back to New Orleans and call your friend."

Even through all of the anger and disappointment she was still concerned about me. Even if her actions hadn't said as much, I still would have been able to see it in her breathtaking gray eyes. I wanted to tell her the truth, that Alec hadn't called me back, that he wasn't going to come save us, but I couldn't bring myself to tell her.

Alec was mad at me, but that didn't mean that he was a bad person. There was still a chance that he'd change his mind, and even if he didn't, I wasn't going to let the fact that he and I had been fighting ruin Celeste's opinion of him.

If the worst came to pass and I died at Pal's hands, then I wanted Celeste to accept Alec's help when he came around offering her his friendship. It was the only real chance that she and her people had, but she was stubborn enough to turn him away if she thought that he was the reason that I'd died.

"I'm sorry, Celeste, this is something that I have to do."

Set was still shaking his head. "It does not have to be like this, Isaac Nazir. You can change your mind right now, but once I go tell Pal of your challenge there will be no going back."

367

"I understand, Set. Please let him know that I'm ready to meet him inside of the challenge circle at his earliest convenience."

Set bowed his head in acknowledgement and then turned and left. I already knew that Celeste wasn't going to be as easy to convince, but then again I didn't have to convince her. She couldn't stop me any more than I could stop her from going to the queen and asking about a way to save her pack rather than asking for the location of the Coun'hij's base.

"You're a fool, Isaac. You don't have to do this. You don't need to prove anything to me. I already know that you're good and moral and fearless."

"I'm sorry, Celeste. This isn't about proving anything to you; it's about proving something to myself. Besides, if I win it will mean that we both get what we want. I'll have saved Set and you'll get a few more days to try and get your audience with his queen."

"I don't want you to throw your life away in a fight you can't win."

"I owe Set this."

"He doesn't want this."

"I know, but that doesn't change the fact that it's exactly what he needs. I might win, but even if I don't I can still guarantee that Pal isn't going to be challenging Set by the time I'm done with him. He's going to be hurt, which means that Set is going to have a chance to recover before Pal takes him on."

She looked like she was going to cry, which just made me realize how much I still had to learn about women. She turned away from me as though planning on running to her room, but I grabbed her elbow.

"Do me a favor if I don't make it?"

"Maybe, depends on what it is."

Her tone drew a smile out of me despite the seriousness of what I was about to go do.

"You're a terrible liar, you know that? You should have just told me yes and then not done it if it was that distasteful."

"Maybe, but I don't want to break my streak. I haven't lied to you yet, Isaac. I haven't told you everything, but I haven't knowingly said anything that wasn't true."

"I appreciate that."

Tears were starting to leak out of the corners of her eyes, but she turned her head so I couldn't see her face.

"What do you want, Isaac?"

"Tell Ash that I'm sorry I couldn't save Kristin for him. There's a file on my tablet with his name on it. It's got all of my notes on it. I think it will be enough for him to be able to run the hack that the two of us discussed. Donovan and Alec can help him run the team. It won't be quite the same, but I think it will still work."

"Is that all?"

"No. Kristin isn't the only one I'm sorry I can't save."

"Whatever. Words are cheap. Don't expect me to be there watching today."

I let her go and headed outside. It wasn't how I'd wanted to end things with her, but there wasn't anything I could say to make her okay with what I was about to do. Besides, I didn't dare stay there with her for much longer or there was a chance that I'd lose my nerve.

It wouldn't change anything. By now Pal had already been informed of the fact that I wanted to fight him, but losing my nerve would make it that much harder to win.

I pulled my clothes off as I walked, and then shifted into my hybrid form as I reached the cave that held the challenge circle. Nobody else was there yet, but that was fine. I knelt down in the sand and closed my eyes in an attempt to clear my mind.

It must have worked because I didn't hear everyone arrive. One moment I was floating in silence and then in the next I heard Set saying my name.

"Are you ready, Isaac Nazir?"

I nodded and opened my eyes as I stood. The cave was smaller than it had ever been before, but the size of the circle hadn't changed. Despite their smaller numbers, the spectators filled the cave up to capacity.

Most surprisingly, Celeste was there. I gave her a sad smile, but she refused to meet my eyes. I shrugged and put her out of my mind. It wasn't easy, but it was something that had to be done.

Pal stepped into the circle and hissed at me.

"I know what you're trying to do, beast. You hope to beat me and thereby save Set from having to face me himself, but all you've done is give me the pleasure of killing you days before it would have otherwise happened. You'll still be dead, and Set will still have been dishonored by having turned to you to save his miserable life."

I shook my head. "Set didn't ask me to do this. In fact, he would much prefer that I not fight you, but my honor is of a different sort. I will not stand by and see him killed for doing the bidding of your queen. You're nothing more than a traitor. We know how to deal with traitors where I'm from."

I stepped into the circle before I'd even finished speaking, and Pal charged me.

He was fast and he was bigger and stronger than I was, which meant that he was holding all of the important cards. All that was left was for me to try to take him by surprise.

We exchanged fast, probing strikes and both reeled away bleeding. No surprises there. His scales gave him a decided advantage against raking attacks, and he was scary fast for someone so big. Going just off of who was bleeding the most he was already ahead.

If we kept on like we were doing so far he'd win simply by bleeding me out. I needed to manufacture some kind of opportunity, which was going to be difficult to do without opening up a dangerous vulnerability on my side.

"Is that the best you can do, mutt?"

I didn't bother responding, saving my breath as I tried to work around the perimeter and tire him out. I managed a nice slash across the same spot that I'd hit earlier and smiled as his arm started really bleeding.

It wasn't going to bleed him out quickly, but it was a start and I'd just managed to confirm that his scales had been weakened in the process of deflecting my first attack. We were back to being even.

I picked the pace up even more in an attempt to stress him, but slowed down after just a few seconds. He didn't have the shoddy footwork that had allowed me to take down one of my earlier opponents, which meant that I couldn't count on bringing him down that way either.

He stepped into me with even more speed than he'd shown so far, and slammed the claws on his right hand home in my stomach. I flowed into a technique that Carson had showed me. It was an arm bar designed to take an opponent down to the ground and hold him there.

I'd executed it correctly—I could feel that much as I grabbed the outside of Pal's hand and flipped it over so that I could apply pressure above his elbow—but something went wrong. Maybe it was because Pal was just too fast for me, or maybe the pain, dull though it was because of my hybrid nervous system, just slowed me down. It was even possible that Pal was just too strong.

Whatever the reason, I felt the hold start to go sour a split second after I started to apply it, so I changed courses instantly and rammed the claws on my left hand into his back where his kidney would have been located if he'd been a human.

I still had control of his wrist, but I didn't make a clean escape once he tore his hand out of my grasp. All he managed was another shallow slash on my arm though, so I counted it as a fair trade. He was probably still ahead, but I was hanging in the fight much better than I'd been worried I might.

We danced back and forth again, but while he was still fast, the blinding speed he'd shown earlier didn't make another appearance until the next time that he stepped into me and slammed his hand home again.

This time he tore a scream out of me. His claws had penetrated a lot deeper, deep enough that even as a hybrid the blow had been excruciating. Despite the pain I reacted with a smoothness that surprised even me.

I dropped my inside knee slightly and brought my full weight down on the inside of his arm in an elbow strike that could have splintered a small tree. The force of my blow brought him down and slightly forward, so I turned into him and threw him into the ground with everything I had.

It was the same hip throw that I'd used against Nicolas, but this time I was using it against someone who'd never learned how to take a fall. Pal hit hard, a lot harder than I expected, but apparently lamias were built even more solidly than I'd realized.

Hitting the ground that hard would have snapped a hybrid's neck. Maybe it would have done the same thing if I'd used it on a worker, but Pal simply bounced and then rolled back to his feet.

"Is that all you've got? A real fighter would have killed me rather than throwing me at the ground."

Pal's words were full of contempt, but I could see the worry in his eyes. I'd just hit him with a technique that was completely outside of his experience and we both knew that if he'd landed a little differently the fight would have been over.

More importantly, I'd just realized that he was a glory hound. He wasn't interested in *being* a better fighter as much as *looking* like a better fighter. He was fast and strong, and his technique was good, but he'd honed that one technique—stepping into his opponent and driving his claws into their stomach or chest—to blinding perfection, and I was pretty sure that he'd done it solely to be able to drop werewolves with a speed that nobody else could match.

It worked perfectly if you were injecting someone with poison, but otherwise it wasn't as effective. He would have been better off hitting me somewhere else that last time, but his reflexes were too wired into that one attack to deviate from it. He probably didn't even consciously think about throwing that punch, he just launched it whenever he saw the opportunity.

I could use that.

We slowly moved back towards each other and I smiled at the way he was opening and closing his right fist. He was trying to work feeling back into his arm. My elbow strike might not have shattered the bones there, but it had still affected him.

I let my hands drift ever so slightly apart and he reacted just as he had twice already. He blurred forward, claws seeking my guts, but this time I wasn't where he expected me to be. I'd already started moving to the right and turning my body counterclockwise. It left my back exposed to his left hand, but he never got a chance to take advantage of that fact.

My right hand shot forward and I took him in the forearm, spearing him with my claws as I stepped into him. The pain made him pull his arm back, but that was exactly what I wanted him to do. I latched on with my left hand as well and pulled against him as I sank the talons on my feet into his legs and side.

It was the exact same attack that I'd tried to use against the Coun'hij enforcer back in the first fight we'd had after leaving Alec and the others, but this time it worked. I straddled his arm with one foot buried in his chest and the other deep in the meat of his shoulder, and wrenched his arm with every ounce of strength I possessed.

He tried to resist, but he failed. Maybe it was the numbness from my elbow strike, maybe it was the fact that blood was still pouring out of his arms where I'd stabbed him. In the end it didn't actually matter that much because the net result was the same.

I kicked off of him, propelling myself a safe distance away from him, and hit the ground rolling. I came back to my feet to find that his right arm was hanging limply at his side.

"It's over. You can't beat me now, not with your arm dislocated like that. Yield so that I don't have to kill you; the enclave can't afford to lose another consort right now."

Pal shook his head at me and hissed something unintelligible at me before responding in English. "I'm not going to give Set the satisfaction of executing me for failing to finish the fight. You'll have to come kill me yourself."

"Is that true, Set?"

I asked the question without taking my eyes off of Pal, but Pal attacked anyway in the hopes that I'd be too distracted to stop him. He was wrong. I knocked his claws away, forcing them across his body as I stepped forward.

The momentum of his charge tried to carry him past me, but I didn't let him get far. I checked him with a glancing blow from my shoulder to slow him down slightly and knock him off balance, and then I stepped around behind him and wrapped my right arm around his neck at the same time that I wrapped up his left arm.

This wasn't something that Set had taught me, it was pure old-fashioned hybrid combat. It was a textbook kill position, and I felt Pal go instantly still as he realized that I could easily open up all of the major veins along the side of his neck with a flick of my wrist.

"Is it true, Set? Are you going to kill him if he surrenders?"

"I'm sorry, Isaac Nazir. I can see what you are trying to do, but it is our way."

I opened my mouth to tell him that their practice was wasteful and bloodthirsty, but I never managed to get the words out.

I'd wrapped Pal's left arm up, but I'd wrapped it up the way that I would have wrapped up a hybrid. For this hold with another hybrid the primary concern was stopping them from raking your other arm. The way that our shoulders were hinged made it almost impossible for us to strike down and back around our own bulk, but apparently lamias didn't face the same kind of restriction.

Pal reached back and slammed the claws on his left hand into my leg. At first I didn't think anything of it. It wasn't a killing blow, and it didn't change my desire to find a way for us to both walk away from this fight.

I started to readjust my hold on his left arm, and then stopped as fire entered my bloodstream from the place where he'd just stabbed me. I screamed in pain, but the agony wasn't enough to completely shut my mind down.

He'd violated the code of the fight and used poison on me. I was as good as dead.

Pal tried to break free of me, but I hadn't lost control of my voluntary muscles yet and I wasn't going to let him win like this. My claws cut into the side of his neck, and then the two of us collapsed to the sand together.

The poison was incredibly fast-acting. It had already reached my chest, burning my heart at the same time that it consumed everything else from my shoulders down, but the thing that really surprised me was the fact that I was already hallucinating.

Set was moving toward me, but that somehow paled in significance compared to the soothing heat that was moving up my arms. I had a split second to wonder why my venom-addled brain had picked a different kind of heat as an escape from what I was going through and then Set reached me and plunged his claws into my chest.

As the blackness claimed me I wondered at the sheer scope of my foolishness. In the end even Set had turned on me.

Chapter 27

Isaac Nazir
The Lamia Enclave

Death wasn't anything like I expected it to be. Despite my best efforts, I was gradually pulled out of the quiet, numb void that had been cradling me and into a different kind of darkness.

It was cold here and hot, all at the same time, but the really terrifying thing was the sheer amount of pain. Onyx's ability had been a constant, all-consuming thing that had left no room for feeling anything other than agony.

This was different. It came in waves. I always hurt, but there were times when the pain was small enough that I could still think. Those moments of lucidity were few and far between though. Instead I spent most of my time in such torment that I felt like I couldn't even breathe.

LOST

Just when I thought I'd taken all of the suffering I could endure, the pain would ramp up even higher and I would find out that my capacity to endure was somehow greater than I'd thought.

Knowing that there was even more pain waiting for me made it even worse than what I'd endured at Onyx's hands. There had been a limit to how long he could hurt me before I would just finally die. There didn't seem to be any such limit inside of my new existence. I was in some kind of afterlife of suffering and no matter how hard I tried I couldn't remember anything that I'd done that was bad enough to merit this.

I hadn't been some kind of mass murderer. I hadn't molested children or robbed anyone. It didn't seem right that my eternal reward was this, but then again I couldn't seem to remember anything truly great that I'd accomplished during my time on Earth. I'd been as strong and powerful as any superhero, but somehow that hadn't been enough for me, not when faced with villains every bit as strong and deadly as I was.

Maybe that was the reason I was cast off into the blackness. All of the superheroes I'd grown up reading about had been up against villains who were their match in almost every way, but that hadn't stopped them from trying to make the world a better place. I'd had the ability to make a difference, a real difference, but I hadn't.

Maybe I'd misunderstood all of the religions that I'd studied as little more than an academic exercise. It wasn't just about doing no harm, that wasn't enough to earn you nirvana or paradise. You had to accomplish something worthwhile before you died.

It felt like I'd been floating in the darkness for forever, but eventually I realized that the lucid times were growing longer and more frequent. They'd been filled with clips of violence that were only fractions of a second long before, but now they became case studies in fighting. I saw every possible way there was to throw a punch and learned what made a good punch in almost any conceivable situation. The same with the use of my claws, talons, and feet. It was like when professional athletes watched themselves on slow-motion film.

There is a limit to how much violence a human, or shape shifter, mind can watch without becoming desensitized to it, and I passed that limit long before the blackness finally let me go. It should have turned me into some kind of psychopath, but it didn't. It didn't because somewhere along the way I realized that I could feel someone's hand on my arm.

That contact reminded me that there was more to existence than just violence. Those long, gentle touches anchored me with the knowledge that violence wasn't an end, it was a means. Violence was a way of dealing with those who refused to honor the natural law that all sentient beings had a right to survive and be free.

LOST

As time went by, I worried that I'd lose contact with whoever was touching me, that they would leave or I would lose the ability to feel, but that wasn't what happened. The feeling that there was someone at my side continued to get stronger until I finally felt the urge to open my eyes.

I'd somehow forgotten that I'd ever had eyes—that I hadn't been blind from birth—but when I finally opened them I found that I was back on my bed in my room in the enclave. That surprised me for some reason. I'd somehow thought that Set and the others would just leave me there in the sand where I'd fallen.

Even more astonishing was the fact that I wasn't alone. I was sitting on the far edge of my bed and Celeste was there with me, curled up next to me with her hand on my arm. She looked terrible and perfect all at the same time.

She looked like she'd showered and changed her clothes recently, but she was obviously exhausted. There were deep worry lines on her forehead that hadn't been there before Pal had poisoned me, and she looked like she'd aged more than a decade since then.

Jax was right. It didn't matter how good a liar someone was, if you spent enough time around them you could eventually put the pieces together and start to see what they were like underneath all of the false pretenses. Celeste was worried about me, she cared about me—much more even than I'd realized.

That new understanding of the depths of her feelings made me wonder how many of her past actions would lend themselves to a new interpretation now if I were to go back through them in my mind.

I resolved to do that the first chance I got, but it would have to wait until after I finished studying her. It was hard to say whether I was more overcome by the fact that I was still alive, or if Celeste being at my side was more shocking.

I drank in every square centimeter of her features and marveled at the fact that she could look so different and still be gorgeous. Her brow furrowed in concern, and I found myself reaching over to smooth away the wrinkles without thinking.

Amazingly, it didn't hurt when I moved, and even more amazing, Celeste didn't wake up when I touched her. Instead she relaxed so completely that the wrinkles smoothed away. She instantly looked nineteen again.

Satisfied that I hadn't robbed her of the sleep that she so obviously needed, I relaxed back onto my back and took a few deep, experimental breaths. Everything seemed to be working correctly. The massive hole that I'd been expecting to find on the right side of my abdomen wasn't there; I seemed to be fully healed and rested.

As much as I wanted to stay there with Celeste forever, I knew that the world wasn't going to just stop turning while we rested. I needed to find Set and find out how long I'd been out.

I started to move off of the bed, trying not to disturb Celeste, but as soon as I tried to slide my arm out from under her hand I got an unexpected response. She grabbed hold of my arm with all of her strength and then a second later her beautiful gray eyes popped open. She looked at me with a sleepy kind of astonishment.

"Isaac. I just dreamed that someone was trying to take you away from me."

"No, I'm still here. You can go back to sleep and we can talk later if you want."

"Screw that. How are you feeling?"

She was entirely awake now. She sat up on the bed and tugged at her top to get it back situated like she wanted it.

"On the whole, surprisingly good. What did I miss out on?"

"Pal poisoned you, but you killed him before his venom started throwing you into convulsions. Set ran over to you and injected you with some kind of anti-venom, but I'm pretty sure none of the lamias expected that to work."

I rubbed my forehead as I tried to get past the memories of fighting that had been a recurring theme while I'd been unconscious. It was hard to pierce the veil of darkness, but I remembered at least some of what had happened.

"I thought he was trying to pump even more poison into my system."

"Nope. The consorts produce an anti-venom in the glands that drain into their pinkie fingers. He stabbed you, but that was just so that he could deliver the anti-venom as quickly as possible into the area directly around your heart. He saved your life."

I nodded. "I should have known that he had my best interests at heart. He's always come through for me."

"Yeah. He and I have spent some time talking over the last few days. I can see why you're so attached to him."

I started to nod, but then the full implication of what she'd just said sank in. "Wait, how long have I been unconscious?"

"I'm not sure, more than a week, maybe nine days now."

She said it with such casualness that I knew she was lying to me. She knew exactly how long I'd been asleep for, she was just hoping that I wouldn't know what it meant.

"I thought you said you didn't want to lie to me."

One instant she was sitting on my bed facing me, completely collected and calm, and in the next she crumbled into my arms.

"You're right, I just didn't want you to feel guilty too. Onyx has been killing my people for days, but I didn't know what to do. Set has been administering the anti-venom to you at least a couple of times per day. I was going to just go back by myself to stop Onyx from hurting my friends, but Set told me that any males left here without a queen would be killed. I begged him to make an exception for you. He seemed genuinely sad, he even went to his queen to see if she would overrule tradition, but she refused and he wasn't willing to dishonor himself, even for you."

"You stayed for me."

She wiped away tears with the back of her hand and then nodded. "I don't know what I was thinking. I know that you don't love me, that you can't love me as long as I'm willing to surrender your friends to save my own, but I couldn't bring myself to let you die."

The magnitude of her sacrifice was almost incomprehensible to me. She'd sacrificed everything she was, everything she had, in an effort to protect the submissives in the New Orleans pack. She could have fled just like Ash had, but she hadn't. She'd stayed because they were *her people*. They were hers in a way that most people didn't understand, but I understood. In a way she was saying that I was hers too. She probably didn't even understand that yet herself, but after all this time I knew her at least that well. She'd stayed for me because she loved me, but even more than that, she'd stayed because I was hers.

While I was thinking all of the ramifications of what she'd gone through, she continued on.

"Even now I can't bring myself to go back there. You're safe now, we could all leave. The three of you could make a clean getaway and I could go back to save whomever is left, but the thought of meeting their eyes and having to tell them that I sacrificed their friends makes me want to curl up on the floor and die.

"I can't believe that I've done this, but by the same measure, I couldn't make myself leave. Every moment that passed I considered leaving, but I couldn't do it. I kept thinking that you could wake up at any point. I kept hoping that you'd wake up in time for me to get back, and then suddenly I realized that it was too late, Onyx had surely killed his first victim.

"And then it was too late to do anything about whomever was dead, there was just you here and another twenty-four hours spent hoping you'd wake up before it was too late for me to return and prevent any more deaths."

I pulled her in tight against my chest and hugged her. "I'm sorry, Celeste. I'm glad to be alive, but I'm sorry to have put you through that."

"It's not your fault. You were right, you know. Every step you took was the right one to have taken. I can see that now. I wish that you'd just killed Pal without giving him a chance to poison you, but you were right to fight him, right to save Set and the rest of the enclave by extension. You seem to always do the right thing. I wish I was like that.

"No, that's not right. I wish I could want to be like that, but the price is too high for me. There was never any other way to save my friends other than what I did."

I lifted her chin so that she would have to meet my eyes. "We are like two sides of the same coin. I never thought that I had any choices. You always saw nothing but choices. I never took enough responsibility, you always took too much. I'm glad I met you, Celeste Hunt. There were things that I needed to learn from you."

"You sound like you're leaving."

She wanted to be kissed, I could feel it. The desire to give her what she wanted was almost overpowering, but I forced myself not to act on it. I hadn't earned that yet.

"I have something that I need to go do…"

I started to untangle myself from her, but she grabbed me with the kind of desperate strength that I hadn't been sure she was capable of. That required more emotion than she'd shown up until recently.

"Is it because of Jess? You cried out for her a few times while you were asleep. I know you said that you'd started moving on, but if that's all that's stopping you then I can wait. I've traded in everything I've spent the last thirty years working towards for you, Isaac. Don't cast me aside; I don't think I could survive that."

"It's not because of Jess. I really have moved on. It took me a while to realize it, but she really is gone. I still love her, but she's not coming back and I've come to accept that. There's nothing there to stop me from becoming...close...to someone else."

Even as I said it, I realized just how true it was. I had vague memories of Jess being inside my dreams during the last week, but it had been Jess that I'd been dreaming of, not Jessica. I was sad she was gone, but I wasn't pining anymore after the girl wearing her body.

"What is it then?"

There it was, the one question I couldn't answer. If she thought back over our past conversations she'd know what it was, but right now she didn't remember the reason. Maybe that wasn't fair to her. Her whole world had changed so completely over the last few days that it was only natural that she would feel like my world had shifted just as dramatically.

She could see that I had feelings for her, and for some people that was enough. Love changed everything for those kinds of people. They weren't wrong, love really did change everything, but it also changed nothing, all at the same time. She was going to have to figure out the answer on her own. If I just came out and told her, she'd have to make a decision, one she'd already made, but this time I'd be holding a gun to her head. I wanted her to do the right thing because it *was* the right thing, not because she thought it was the only way to win my affections.

"Do you trust me?"

She looked at me for several seconds before finally nodding. The nod was hesitant, almost as though I'd dragged it out of her in spite of her better judgment, but she nodded all the same.

"Everything in my past tells me that I shouldn't trust you—that I shouldn't trust anyone—but I do trust you, Isaac. How did you manage that?"

"I'm not sure, but I'm very glad that I did. I promise you that I'll tell you as much as I can as soon as I can. I can't promise that everything will work out perfectly, but I'll do the best I can for you, Celeste."

"Okay. I already know that's the best I'm going to get out of you. I can accept it for now. Go do what you have to do, I'll be here waiting when you get back."

I took her hand and pulled her up off of my bed. "You don't have to wait, you can come with me if you want to."

We walked out to the living room like that, holding hands even though I wasn't sure that was a good idea. I didn't want to make promises to her that I couldn't keep. Holding hands wasn't the same kind of promise as kissing, but it was still a promise. In the end I didn't pull away because I sensed that she already knew what I was thinking, and despite that she was still holding onto me with that same brittle, determined strength.

I got yet another major shock when we stepped out into the living room and I saw Ash sitting a few feet away from Jax. I was so excited to see him with his eyes open that I pulled Celeste towards him. He stood as we crossed over to him. He took in the fact that we were holding hands, and I saw his lips tighten slightly before he finally relaxed and clasped me on the shoulders.

"Celeste has been filling me in on your exploits. I owe you one for keeping Nicolas from finishing the job he started on me, and another one for getting us all here and keeping us safe for so long."

"You would have done the same thing in my shoes."

Ash shook his head. "No, I would have tried to do the same thing, but I would have failed. You made it happen against all odds. I'm grateful, and more than just for my own sake."

Jax gave me a lazy wave. "Don't mind me, I'm just still in shock. Not only did I dodge a bullet by getting out of New Orleans, I also get to see Ashley...I mean Ash...again. It seems like it was just yesterday that he was running around, getting underfoot and playing pranks on people.

If I were going to pick two people to try and reestablish the pack with than I could have done a lot worse than Ash and Celeste."

My mind skipped a track at the idea of super-serious Ash ever engaging in pranks, but the astonishment only lasted until I had a chance to register the last half of what he'd said.

"Actually, that's why I came out here. It's time to go see if I can do something about all of that. You can come or stay as you'd like."

Ash and Celeste shot each other confused looks, but my words didn't seem to have even registered for Jax. I headed towards the door out into the valley, and Celeste was only one step behind me, still clutching my hand for all she was worth.

Ash asked Jax to keep an eye on Kristin and then he was jogging to catch up with us before the curtain closed.

"What are you talking about, Isaac? There isn't anything that can be done about the past."

I didn't look back at Ash as I continued to lead Celeste down the winding path that led towards the main lamia cavern.

"I'm not so sure about that anymore, Ash. It's time to see if the lamias have yet another trick that none of us have thought to ask them about."

The two workers stationed outside the cavern entrance saw us coming and one of them turned and hissed something to someone deeper inside the cave. Set arrived just seconds after we did.

"Isaac Nazir! I am very glad to see that you have survived. I have worried much about you these last several days. Had you died we would have had a great honor debt to your enclave. Even more than that though, I would have missed your presence here in the enclave."

"I understand that I have you to thank for my survival, Set. I appreciate you moving so quickly to inject me with the anti-venom. I didn't know that there was such a thing when it comes to lamia poison."

Set gave me an uncomfortable smile and looked back and forth at Ash and Celeste before responding. Evidently his queen's order to answer all of my questions was still in effect even if there were other shape shifters present.

"The poison drives most things when it comes to my kind. It is the development of poison glands that allows a worker to become a consort. It is a...painful...transition. There is always some poison that leaks out of the glands and some of the workers do not survive the transformation. Even when we get older the leaks continue."

"Is that why you heal slower than a hybrid would?"

Set nodded. "The workers heal at a similar rate as you sun people, but the older a consort gets the more potent his venom becomes and the slower he heals from most injuries. Luckily our anti-venom becomes more potent as well or the leaks from the venom would eventually kill us."

LOST

It was an amazing insight into their physiology. They were organisms that were in a constant state of war with themselves. If at any point their production of anti-venom were to drop they would sicken and die in short order.

I opened my mouth to thank Set again, and noticed for the first time how worn-down he looked. Celeste had looked briefly like she'd aged a decade; Set looked like he'd aged a century. Whatever illusion kept their full nature from showing through was masking at least part of how much he'd changed, but he had definitely changed. His face was now lined and his skin had turned an ashy shade of white that didn't seem to bode well for his continued health.

"Injecting me with the anti-venom put you at risk, didn't it, Set?"

He didn't want to answer that one, but he wasn't going to lie and he knew that I wasn't going to just let this question go.

"Yes, Isaac Nazir. There was some risk, but it was controllable. The anti-venom does more than just keep us alive, it is also a safety measure in case a consort accidentally injects another consort or worker with venom. For our kind, a quick injection of anti-venom from the consort who accidentally poisoned the worker or consort in question is enough to combat the effects of the poison.

"I did not think it would be enough for you though, Isaac Nazir. Your kind lacks our natural resistance to our own venom. As much as I am overjoyed that you survived, you should be dead."

I waved his comment away. "How much risk are we talking, Set? How dangerous is what you just did for me?"

"Under normal circumstances the consort who injects someone with anti-venom is the same consort who injected the individual with poison in the first place. In those cases there is no risk because the decrease of anti-venom in the consort's system is balanced by a corresponding reduction in the amount of venom leaking into their body."

"But that wasn't the case for you."

"No, it was not I who injected you initially, but I cleared my glands of poison shortly after using my anti-venom on you. The risk did not arise until I had been injecting you for several days. The anti-venom only leaks into the body when the glands are full, but the poison leaks into the body, albeit at a lesser rate, even when the glands are empty. There has been some pain, and my normal regenerative abilities have been weakened temporarily as a result."

I had to close my eyes and take a few deep breaths to maintain control of myself. I'd been poisoned myself, I had a pretty good idea of the amount of pain he'd been in—that he was probably still in. It wasn't a minor thing for all that he was doing his best to underplay it.

He'd been slowly poisoning himself in an effort to keep me alive, and he'd been in excruciating pain nearly the entire time. Set had never called me friend, but I couldn't think of any surer sign of friendship.

I reached up my puny human hands and clasped him on his arms. The gesture probably looked ludicrous given the sheer disparity in our sizes, but that didn't stop me from doing it.

"There was no one else who could share the burden with you?"

"No, Isaac Nazir. The burden was mine alone to carry. With Pal gone there are only two consorts to protect the enclave. I could not allow my brother to empty himself of venom and leave our queen defenseless from the greater threats in the world. Even doing so myself was a risk that I should not have taken, but my queen gave me permission to proceed regardless."

"I thank you once again, Set. Though you have never called me such, I consider you my friend and feel that I am in your debt."

"It was nothing less than what honor required, Isaac Nazir."

"I know, but even among your own people honor is not always followed. I name you exceptional despite your protests, my friend."

After a second, Set finally bowed his head in acknowledgment and clasped me on the shoulders. "I'm very glad that you survived, Isaac Nazir. Much more grateful than I imagined

I could be when you first arrived here in the enclave."

After a minute we released each other and stepped back. I forced out my question. If it had just been for me then I wouldn't have said anything, but it wasn't for me. There was a lot depending on his answer.

"I'm sorry to ask this given the fact that I'm already in your debt, Set, but am I owed a boon for having survived the fight with Pal?"

He didn't move, but I could feel him withdrawing slightly. I didn't blame him—I knew how it looked, knew that he thought I'd just been buttering him up, but I had to ask.

"Yes, Isaac Nazir. Honor demands that you be granted a boon if you choose to ask for one."

"As much as I would like to stay here with you, Set, I will be leaving soon and I think that my queen and the rest of her people will be coming along too."

Celeste gripped my hand harder, but she didn't say anything despite how hard it must have been to know that our entire trip had been a waste. Ash stepped forward as if he was about to say something, but I shot him a look that let him know that he was out of his depth and that—at least for now— I was the one calling the shots.

"I'm sorry to see you go, Isaac Nazir, but I can't deny that it will make many things much easier to have you gone."

"I understand. Is it possible for you to manipulate the exact time of our return? If so, this is the boon that I would ask of you. I don't want to return to Louisiana weeks after our departure, I want us to return as close to when we fought Onyx as possible."

Set relaxed slightly as though the thing that I'd asked from him wasn't as bad as what he'd been expecting.

"Yes, Isaac Nazir. What you ask for is possible. If you leave in the next little while there is an opening in the time stream that I can use to drop you off very close to your boat only a few of your minutes after we left our territory."

"This is indeed what I want."

"I will go make the arrangements, Isaac Nazir. Please have all of your party ready to go before one of your hours has passed."

Celeste's hand had relaxed in mine and there was a sense of wonder on her face. I'd just bought her a chance to get back to New Orleans in time to stop Onyx from killing any of her people. Ash didn't look as happy, but I knew I could bring him around if I could get a few minutes alone with him.

As Set turned to go, a worker hurried up to him and hissed something complex. I'd just looked up, so I had a chance to see Set's reaction to whatever he'd just been told. His shoulders bent forward as though he'd just been handed an enormous burden, and his skin went even more ashen.

Set looked off into space, motionless and silent, for nearly a full minute before he finally turned back to us. The expression on his face was the look of a man who'd just been betrayed by his family and deity all at the same time.

"Isaac Nazir, my queen commands that I relay a message."

I tried to stop him; I knew that whatever he had to say wasn't good, but he talked over me.

"She bids me to tell you that if you'll stay for one last challenge match, this one to start immediately, that she'll meet with your queen immediately after the fight and tell your queen all that she wishes to know."

He didn't have to tell me who my opponent would be. I could see it in every line of his face and posture.

"Against you?"

"Yes. Those are her terms."

The next second seemed to stretch out to eternity. I heard Celeste gasp in astonishment and felt her hand tighten in mine as she realized that there was a chance for her to get everything she'd set out for. I'd just finished doing the deal she needed to get back earlier than she'd believed possible, and now she was being offered the opportunity to talk to Set's queen.

Ash had gone completely still. In that way he was like the lamias. He probably hadn't realized yet that Celeste wasn't planning on using her question to save Kristin, so for him this also felt like a chance at the dream he'd been sure he was going to have to give up.

None of us had any illusions about Set's ability to fight me. Normally I would have been virtually guaranteed to lose a match against him, but right then he could barely move.

It was all there for the taking. Everything we'd been fighting and bleeding for. Talking to the queen had become a kind of Holy Grail for all of us, but the price was too high. At least for me it was too high.

I wasn't going to murder the man who'd saved my life not just once but twice. I wasn't going to take advantage of the fact that he'd nearly put himself in a coma to save me. I didn't know what kind of game his queen was playing at, but I wasn't going to be a pawn on her board. I was finally ready to admit that there was an endless array of possibilities before me.

The only limiting factor was what I was willing to sacrifice to get the outcome I wanted. For every person the sacrifices they were willing to make were going to be different, but for me those sacrifices weren't going to be paid by innocent people. I wasn't going to sacrifice Set, his life wasn't mine to discard on a whim like that.

"Please tell your queen that we decline her offer to converse with her. The price she asks for her counsel is too dear."

Ash stepped forward. "Isaac, think this through. This isn't just about Kristin. This is our opportunity to bring down the entire Coun'hij. That's the first step towards the kind of golden age our people experienced under Alec's ancestors.

"Alec could unite the packs. We could hunt the vampires to extinction. We could even bring order to the cats south of the border. That wouldn't just benefit our kind, that would represent a turning point for the humans in those countries too. I've been down there and met some of those people. They are good people stuck in a system that is corrupt. They deserve better."

For a moment I was tempted to tell Ash that his dream had been dead before it had even started, that his sister was planning on using her question to save her people rather than saving Kristin, but at the last second I thought better of that.

"I have a plan, Ash. The hack that we talked about on the way down here could work. If you're still willing to fund the attempt then I think you can get what you want, what we all want, without Set needing to die."

"And if I'm unwilling to just walk away like that?"

"I don't think that you're a match for Set, not without your weapons, but if you do manage to kill him somehow, then I'll kill you in turn."

"You'd do that? After all that we've been through together? You'd do that knowing that you'd be sentencing Kristin to insanity and death?"

"Yes, Ash, I would. Alec was right. I've been confused for a while now, but I back my friends up. It's just what I do. You and Set are both my friends. You've both saved my life and I'd like for nothing more than the two of you to get along, but if one of you attacks the other without cause than I'll kill the one who instigates the fight."

Ash gave me a hard look, the kind of look that told me he was seriously considering his odds of surviving both fights, but after a second he nodded.

"You honestly believe that this plan of yours can work?"

"Absolutely. Everything you'll need in order to carry it out is on a file on my tablet with your name on it."

"Okay, I hope you're right, and I'll back your play on this one."

Celeste probably would have said something too, but she knew that the decision was out of her hands. Set and the rest wouldn't let her fight, and Ash had just agreed to abide by my decision, which meant that her only other option would be to throw Jax into the ring, and we all knew that would be like tossing a baby chick into a pool filled with piranhas. Even in his current state, Set would make short work of Jax.

My decision was going to stand. Set might still die as a result of us having come to his enclave, but it wouldn't be at my hand.

"We'll be at the path to the portal within the next half hour, Set."

Set gave me a tired, thankful smile and then turned to go, but before he could even take a step another worker came running out of their cavern. It took less than a second for the agitated lamia to deliver his message and then Set turned back to us.

"My queen bids you attend her immediately, both of you. She says no further challenge is necessary."

Chapter 28

Isaac Nazir
The Lamia Enclave

There was no question which two of us he was referring to. Ash wasn't happy at being excluded, but he agreed to go back to our rooms and help Jax get everything packed up and ready for our departure.

As soon as Ash was gone, Celeste and I followed Set inside the lamia cave. I couldn't have said for sure what I was expecting, but I was left with a vague sense of disappointment. It looked a lot like our quarters.

The chairs were subtly different, like they'd been designed for bodies that didn't quite match up with what I saw each time I looked at a lamia, but that wasn't really a surprise. I already knew that something was messing with my perceptions there.

The rooms and halls that we walked through were well-lit with the same softly-glowing spheres that I was used to seeing in our rooms. Their caves were just a much bigger version of ours.

If I'd been expecting something more alien in their habitat and been disappointed, my expectations were more than fulfilled where their queen was concerned. We walked around a bend in the corridor and then suddenly there she was, a tiny woman no bigger than Celeste or I, whose power filled the room she was in to capacity and then beyond.

Her skin glowed, but not with the normal glow that I was used to seeing from all living things. In this form, with eyes that were only a little better than what a normal human was born with, I shouldn't have been able to see any more than a very faint glow. Instead she lit up the room.

There were still half a dozen of the glowing melons hanging from the ceiling, so I couldn't be sure whether Set and the rest of the lamias saw the same kind of cool, white radiance coming off of her that we did, but I got the feeling that Celeste and I could have easily read a book with nothing more than her as a light source.

"Welcome, Isaac Nazir and Celeste Hunt. You have done well. You have earned your question. I will answer in the best way I am able."

Her voice was...odd. Her English was crisp and unaccented, but there was something on the trailing end of her words. I couldn't tell if it was just because I was a shape shifter and had better than normal hearing, but it almost sounded like there was a chorus of people repeating her words.

I shook my head in disbelief. Even that wasn't quite the right description for what I was hearing. A chorus of people talking at the same time as her would have rendered her words unintelligible, but that wasn't what was happening. It was only the last few sounds of the last word in any given sentence.

The queen looked over at me and smiled. "Such a questing mind, Isaac Nazir. I wish that you could remain here with my people. I would enjoy filling you up with knowledge the likes of which you can't even begin to imagine, but such a thing is not to be. Your brightness already is nearly blinding. Even now the Consumed would be upon us if not for the fact that your glow dimmed during the time that you struggled on death's door."

"I too regret that I can't return another time. There is much that I would like to learn."

Her smile turned sad. "Yes, you can't stay, and you can't return, but maybe that is for the best. We would have to change you at the same time that we taught you. You would become something different, something greater in some ways and lesser in others. That is always the price of change."

She looked at Set, reaching out a hand to him, and he dropped down to his knees so she could place her hand on his head. "Our poor consorts are the perfect example of that. Changed from what they were into something else, their bodies constantly at war with themselves. I wish that we had been able to see another way."

Set changed before our very eyes. It was like looking at time lapse photography. In a matter of seconds he went from aged and decrepit to being once again the vibrant individual he'd been when we first arrived at the enclave.

"My most faithful of consorts, I regret putting you in such trying circumstances, but it was necessary. You bore it well and I am proud of you. Your honor is intact and you have moved the work forward in important ways."

I found myself wishing that I could transform to my wolf body so that I could see what she looked like with those eyes. Something about Set's queen demanded that she be viewed as a being of pure light.

Set reached up and clasped his queen's hand, holding it against his head as though worried she was going to withdraw from him.

"It is enough for me to know that the work continues. Honor does not demand recognition for my small contribution."

The queen shook her head at him. "There are no small contributions, Set, but yours are greater than most. You offer all that any man or woman can offer. Your energies and loyalty combined with a willingness to sacrifice whatever needs sacrificed to move the work forward. It is upon such things that all works, large or small, move forward."

She was responding to Set, but she was looking at me by the end of her statement and chills raced up and down my spine as I realized that she knew exactly what I was planning. I opened my mouth to ask her how much she knew, but she held a finger up, silencing me.

"It is not proper for consorts to ask questions when queens are present. We get so few opportunities to commune together."

She turned to Celeste and smiled. "Ask your question, child."

It was the kind of thing that could have sounded condescending, but it didn't. Even Celeste didn't seem inclined to take offense.

I looked over at Celeste and realized that she looked more like the queen than she ever had before. The simple white clothing she was wearing soaked up the light from around the room and then re-emitted it, subtly changed so that it was now Celeste's light.

"How do we find the Coun'hij? We need to find them and destroy them so that our people can free themselves. Any help or information that you can provide would be appreciated."

I stopped breathing. I wanted to breathe still, but my lungs refused to function. The oral histories that had been passed down to Celeste all indicated that the queen would answer only one question. Celeste had just used our only question to save Kristin and bring down the Coun'hij.

Somewhere along the way she'd become willing to sacrifice her people to save the rest of our race. Even if that meant putting Alec Graves back into power. It was the one thing that I'd nearly given up hope of ever seeing happen. She'd just removed the one barrier between us.

The queen shook her head at Celeste, but the gesture wasn't scolding. If anything it was just sad. "Freedom isn't what you think it is, and the destruction of overlords just reveals new overlords. Sometimes the new masters are external, sometimes they are internal. Freedom doesn't guarantee happiness."

"No, nothing external guarantees happiness, but there are more reasons to fight than just happiness. Justice is worth fighting for. Ending oppression is worth fighting for."

The queen turned back to me, but I hadn't technically asked a question. "You're right, dear Isaac. If only more of your people and mine understood that."

She turned back to Celeste as she finally withdrew her hand from Set's head. Set looked sad, but didn't protest.

"I cannot answer that question for you, not now at least. Telling you where to find your enemies would lead to the failure of our work, but just as important, it would lead to the failure of yours."

I felt Celeste stiffen next to me and realized that we were holding hands again, that or maybe we'd never stopped.

"So this has all been a waste? Everything we've been through was for nothing?"

"Would you say that the changes you've been through are a waste? You've both learned things about each other and yourselves that were vitally important. If for no other reason, your time here was well-spent."

Celeste was shaking now. She was gripping my hand tight enough that I had to squeeze back in order to avoid being hurt.

"I could have used my question to save my people back in New Orleans. If I'd known this is how you were going to answer me I wouldn't have wasted my question."

The queen pulled back slightly. She didn't actually move, but I felt a difference in the air, a hardening of the energy around us.

"No outcome is ever sure when you undertake it. Your question was not wasted. Eventually you will know the full measure of its value and you will regret your hastiness."

Celeste pulled as though to drag me back towards the surface, but I held my ground.

"Thank you for your wisdom."

The queen's face softened slightly. "I will not promise you what you seek, Isaac Nazir. I will, however, commend you on the feelings and principles that cause you to undertake the course you have already selected."

"Even though you already know exactly how things will end up?"

"That was a question, Isaac Nazir, but some rules were indeed made to be broken. I do not see all, but I do see the results of that which you are most concerned about."

"You make us take you on faith just like you do with Set."

"Perhaps, but that is not the primary cause for my actions. I am not infallible. The path that I have embarked on has required a price. I am less than I was when I embarked on it."

"Then why?"

"Because each action ripples through the time stream forever. Sometimes the ripples are small, sometimes they are large, but they never fully dissipate. There is a cost to everything, Isaac Nazir, and much of what I—my sisters and I—focus on is limiting the costs that must be paid to achieve that which needs to be achieved.

"You have various costs that could be paid, I am merely shepherding you onto a path where the cost you pay will be the best cost."

"Not the smallest cost?"

"Not necessarily. The smallest cost is not always the best cost. Besides, you are already willing to pay the ultimate price, does it matter which price you ultimately end up paying?"

It did. It mattered because I didn't want to die. I wanted a way out, just like anyone else would have, but she was right. I was finally ready to accept the responsibility for my actions.

"Thank you, I think I understand."

"You're welcome. You're wrong. You don't understand it all, but you understand more than most. You understand enough."

As Celeste and I turned to leave, the queen said one more thing. "Your work and our work are not incompatible. In fact, our key is also your key. We won't let you go completely unguided into the darkness that awaits us all.

"Tell your friends about us, tell them that if things become impossible that we will come to them. Tell the key. Tell Alec Graves. He needs to know, everything depends on it."

Chapter 29

Isaac Nazir
The Lamia Enclave

Everyone else had already packed up and left our quarters. Jax was able to walk under his own power, as was Ash. Kristin was awake now, but still worryingly weak. It had been obvious that she wasn't going to be able to walk to the portal. I'd expected for Ash to pick her up and carry her out. He was just a wolf, but that still made him plenty strong enough to carry Kristin however far she needed to be carried.

It had shocked all of us when Set had arrived with three workers a couple of minutes before we were ready to go and offered to carry not only our bags, but Kristin too. For a second I thought that Ash was going to refuse the offer, but something in Set's eyes convinced him to trust the lamias.

LOST

As the workers picked up the bulging black duffle bags, Ash passed Kristin over to Set, who thanked him for the honor of carrying a queen, and everyone started towards the valley. Just before he got to the exterior doorway, Set turned back to me.

"You have calls that will be arriving soon, Isaac Nazir. My queen has agreed to help establish the portal to get you back to the spot in the time stream that you requested, which means you have plenty of time to talk to the friends who are calling you. Stay here where you can have some privacy, we will all be waiting at the portal when you are done."

Kristin mustered up a weak smile for me and then both of them were gone. It was just me and my phone.

Not even five seconds after my phone finished powering on the first call arrived. It was Jasmin of all people.

"Jasmin, is that really you?"

"Hi, Isaac."

Her voice was like a little slice of paradise. She sounded tired and like she was under more stress than normal, but it was still her, and that was one of the best going-away presents that anyone could have given me. It wasn't just chance that had made her call arrive now, just before we left the enclave. I was apparently a much slower learner than I liked to think I was, but I'd at least figured that much out.

Set, probably working hand in hand with his queen, had manipulated things so that I would have a chance to talk to Jasmin now when I most needed the sound of a friendly voice to give me the strength to go through with what I needed to do.

"You have no idea how good it is to hear your voice. Everyone else has pretty much gone dark lately."

Jasmin was quiet for a second. With someone else that might have meant that they were trying to decide how much to tell me, but this was Jasmin. She'd just come right out and tell me what was on her mind. She just needed a minute to fit the fact that I was getting blown off by Alec in with everything else she knew.

"I was afraid of that, I just tried Alec and he didn't pick up. Are you, Ash and Kristin all okay?"

It was the one question that I couldn't answer. Kristin was awake now, but she hadn't managed much more than an occasional weak nod or smile. There wasn't any way to know for sure how much of that was from her injuries and how much was because of Dream Stealer, but it was easy to assume the worst. Ash was obviously still worried about her, but it wasn't my place to fill Jasmin in on all of the gory details.

I was still debating how much to tell her, when she apparently decided that I needed a nudge.

"Tell me the truth, Isaac."

"Things are pretty bad here. Kristin got hurt and lost a lot of blood. I've spent weeks worrying that she was never going to wake up from her coma. We got forced down to the territory claimed by Ash's old pack."

"What the crap were you guys thinking? You have to get out of there right now or Onyx and the others will kill you!"

It was such a simplification that I wanted to scream. My beast didn't appreciate being ordered around, but he'd hardly even stirred since I'd woken up an hour or so before.

It was another thing to worry about. A few days ago I would have given anything to have my beast calm down so that I wasn't always on hair-trigger. Now he'd calmed down and I was worrying that he'd been permanently damaged by the lamia poison that had come so close to killing me.

I was about to head right back into Onyx's territory, and Jasmin was telling me to get out. I wanted to follow her advice. Two months ago I would have just told her that I didn't have any other choice but to go back to New Orleans, but now I knew that wasn't right. I just couldn't live with all of the other choices out there.

Jasmin wasn't privy to what was going on inside of my head and apparently decided that she'd been too aggressive.

"I'm sorry, Isaac, that was out of line. I'm having a harder time keeping control of stuff lately."

I couldn't help the laugh that escaped me. She thought that I was worried about who was dominant to whom, but I couldn't care less. In this instance it was easier just to go along with her.

"Join the club. It seems like I want to rip the head off of anyone who even talks to me lately. The truth is that it's too late. Onyx's people found us within a few hours of our arrival. Ash tried to shoot his way out, but this new guy just shrugged off all of the bullets and practically tore him in two."

"He'll be okay, though, right?"

There was a level of worry in Jasmin's voice that surprised me for a second. She and Ash hadn't ever been very close and I was pretty sure that she and Kristin actively disliked each other, but the more I thought about it the more I realized that I shouldn't be surprised.

There hadn't ever been very many of us to start out with, and the forces arrayed against us hadn't gotten appreciably smaller. Even the loss of just one of Alec's supporters made it that much less likely that the rest of us would make it to see next month.

She was worried about Ash because she could see herself in his place, but I didn't know what to tell her. He was up and moving around, but there still wasn't any guarantee that he was going to make it. Whatever Set had done to seal off the tear in his artery had an expiration date on it. Once that patch disappeared it was just a question of whether or not his body could heal the rip before he bled to death internally. I didn't even know if Celeste had told him that yet.

"I'm not sure. Normally I'd say yes, but you know Ash, he's not a very fast healer."

It was as close to the truth as I could get without telling her everything, without telling her about the lamias and what it was I was about to go off and do.

"I'm sorry to hear that."

"Yeah, me too. How's Ben?"

"Weaker every day. I don't know how much longer he's going to make it, but Rachel seems to finally be helping me rather than just leading me on some kind of cross-continental wild goose chase. Have you heard from any of the others?"

Someone else might have missed the pain in her voice when she talked about Ben, but I could hear it. Jasmin had racked up more practice dealing with pain and pretending that it didn't bother her than anyone else I knew.

Jess was up there with her when it came to dealing with pain, but she'd never been as concerned with presenting a tough front to the rest of the world as Jasmin was. I wished that there was something I could do to save Jasmin from the heartbreak she was in for if Ben didn't wake up soon, but I couldn't shield her from that any more than she could shield me.

It was nice to be able to retreat back to safer subjects.

"Just Andrew. He's okay. We only had a minute to talk, but he told me that Jessica phoned him. He said that she was being really evasive about where they are, but that she's found some kind of big secret."

"I'm not sure whether that's a good thing or a bad thing."

"I'm pretty sure it's a bad thing. Whatever Wyatt is involved in isn't good."

She didn't know what to say about that, but I hadn't been expecting anything different. She probably thought that I was still just hung up on Jessica.

The problem was that I wasn't hung up on Jess anymore, but I still didn't like Wyatt. I'd said all along that there was more going on than met the eye with him, Carson and Grayson, but nobody had believed me. Now I had proof, but still nobody was listening.

Nicolas had fought using the same strange fighting style that Wyatt had used to beat me. All by itself that would have been enough to convince me that he was linked to Wyatt and the others, but when you threw in the fact that Nicolas had known Carson by name, it was solid proof that the power bloc represented by Wyatt's group was trying to play both sides against the middle.

I could hack into government databases, but I didn't know how to function in the world of politics and backroom power-brokering. That had always been Alec's area of expertise and now that I needed him to figure out what was going on, he wasn't even answering my calls.

"I'm serious, Jasmin. I'm starting to feel like I'm playing the wrong game, like I thought we were playing checkers and now it turns out that everyone is playing three-dimensional chess. Onyx has a new guy here, someone I've never heard of before, and he fights like Wyatt used to fight."

"That weird grappling style?"

"Yeah, that alone would pretty much make him unstoppable for the rest of us who don't know that kind of fighting, but that isn't all. Ash shot him—several times, and in all of the right places—but it didn't even slow him down. I saw bullets ricochet off of him after hitting places where I've been cut before. There shouldn't have been bone there, but there was."

Even as I said it, I realized how ridiculous it sounded, but I finally seemed to have Jasmin's full attention.

"Does he have blue eyes?"

"I don't remember for sure, but I don't think so. Why, how does that matter?"

"You need to do everything you can to stay clear of this guy, Isaac. You weren't imagining things. I can't explain, but your suspicions are correct, whoever he is he's going to be faster, stronger, and harder to kill than any hybrid has a right to be."

It had been staring me in the face for years. Alec had always been a good fighter. He'd been so good and it had just been the natural order of things for so long that I'd never stopped to wonder if he was *too* good.

"Like Alec."

She didn't want to let that particular cat out of the bag, but then again, I couldn't blame her. She'd always been much tougher and faster than any normal wolf had any right to be. She paused for nearly a minute before finally responding.

"Yes, like Alec. If you could get around behind him and manage a good clinch you could still kill this guy, but otherwise it will be like fighting someone in armor."

"Where are his weak points?"

"I don't know, Isaac, I swear. I don't...I don't have it. Donovan might be able to tell you, but I'm not sure he'll be willing to give away Alec's secrets like that. Just stay clear of this guy, do whatever it takes."

"I understand, but I don't think that's going to be possible, Jasmin. Thanks for warning me though."

The knowledge that I was going up against someone that had been bred to be even more dangerous than a normal hybrid should have scared me. Actually it did scare me, but it didn't change my determination to do what had to be done. I was already reaching for the disconnect button, but Jasmin surprised me.

"What if I came down there, Isaac? I could be down in New Orleans in a day or so."

It was the kind of thing that made everyone love Jasmin even though she'd spent most of her time as a wolf trying to prove that she was just as dominant as James and me. She had a big heart, and it was hard to hold a grudge after she made those kinds of offers, but that was just who Jasmin was.

Underneath that hard, indifferent exterior that she used to keep the rest of the world at arm's length was a person who would sacrifice just about anything to help her friends. I wanted to take her up on her offer, but I knew I couldn't do that.

It didn't sound like Ben had any time to waste, and even if he did, the two of us plus Ash and Celeste couldn't hope to take on Onyx, Nicolas and what was left of the rest of their hybrids. Letting her come down here to help me would just be signing her death warrant.

"No, it's not worth it, Jas. There's no telling when I'll get backed into fighting this creep. You could arrive down here, and find me dead, and end up in the same position I'm looking at right now. Besides, I couldn't ask you to watch Ben die. You said it yourself. He doesn't have much time left."

"I want to tell you that you're wrong, but I can't seem to force myself to say the words."

That made me smile. I could visualize exactly what she looked like right now, her face dropping into a stubborn set as she tried to force herself to do something she didn't actually want to do.

"I know. It's because I'm right and you know it. Have you found this Geoffrey character yet?"

"Yes, it turns out he's a vampire and I'm going to have to help him before he'll save Ben for me."

That was a development that I hadn't been expecting, but it actually made a lot of sense. We needed to use a vampire to fix the damage the first vampire had done to Ben. Only there wasn't any way to be sure that the second vampire was any better than the first.

"I don't like the sound of that, Jas. Bloodsuckers can't be trusted. Everything I've ever read says that they are all cunning and amoral in ways that sometimes even the Coun'hij can't equal."

She took a deep breath. "I know, but Rachel says it's the only way."

"What do you need from me?"

"We need the location of Puppeteer and the rest of the Coun'hij. You've spent time thinking about where you'd go if you had to leave because of the way things have been going with Jessica. I need a pack with ties to the Coun'hij that is small enough that I have a chance of taking it over."

I hadn't been expecting that. Until Jasmin's words hit my ear I'd forgotten entirely that I'd been so close to running away. The Isaac who'd been contemplating that felt like a different person entirely.

"You knew that? You knew I was looking at leaving the pack and making a run for it?"

"Yeah. I didn't have any evidence, but it's what I would have been doing in your place. I don't blame you."

"I figured if you all found out you would feel like I was betraying you."

"Like I said, I understand why you wanted out. Can you think of a pack that might fit the bill?"

I started mentally running through the list of packs that I'd been compiling based on every drop of information I could squeeze out of the delegates sent to meet with Alec.

"I'm not sure. I was mostly looking for packs that were more independent than that, since the Coun'hij takes a dim view of people coming in and deposing leaders who have an established history of toeing the line. You know, in some ways that could make things easier. The Coun'hij tends to scrape off the cream of the crop out of their allied packs, so there doesn't tend to be as much talent there as what you see in the independent packs."

"Right, a lot of the time they end up being on the smaller side too."

I nodded to myself as a clear winner rose to the top of my mind.

"I think your best bet is Duluth then. Between the cold and the snow it's one of the less desirable territories, so they haven't had anyone challenge up there for a couple of decades. You'll still be up against some stiff competition though. The alpha there isn't anything special, but he's still got more than two hundred years of fighting under his belt. Your biggest problem is going to be a guy named Branson. He's practically an honorary enforcer for the Coun'hij. He's big and fast, not as big and fast as you, but he's good and you haven't been in very many fights as a hybrid yet."

"Yeah, I know. If you've got a better idea for finding the Coun'hij, I'm all ears."

"Sorry, nothing comes to mind. I guess we've both got some impossible fights ahead of us."

"Yeah, I guess we do. I'll see you on the other side."

Chapter 30

Isaac Nazir
The Lamia Enclave

After Jasmin hung up I stared at my phone for nearly a minute. I was stalling, but I wasn't just stalling. I was even more glad than ever that I hadn't fought Set. Not only would his queen not have told us what we needed to know, it was all pointless anyway. Assuming that Jasmin's pet vampire was even slightly trustworthy, she now had a foolproof way of tracking the Coun'hij back to their base.

I really did feel like I was in over my head. There were too many pieces moving around right now for me to fit everything together. Wyatt, Nicolas and the order was just part of it. There was also Jasmin, some secret mission that Jaclyn had been sent on, and probably half a dozen other things that I didn't even know were going on.

The most concerning thing though was the fact that there was something wrong with Alec. Dodging my calls was one thing. Not picking up when Jasmin called was something else entirely. She and Alec were thick as thieves.

That was why I was stalling. As long as I didn't make the call I needed to make to Alec, then there was still a chance that he would pick up the phone and have a magic solution to everything wrong in the world. Once I called and he didn't pick up then I'd be fully committed.

I started to press his speed-dial number, but my phone started ringing a split second before I dialed him. It was Jessica.

"Isaac, are you there?"

For a second I couldn't get any words out, but then my voice started working again.

"Hi, Jessica. I didn't expect to hear from you, is everything okay?"

I was walking a wire that was razor-thin. Every step hurt and I could fall at any moment, but my only chance was to keep walking and hope that there was something left of me to save on the other side of this conversation. I struggled to keep my voice casual, to keep from sounding like the jilted boyfriend that I'd been for so long.

"I'm okay. This is going to sound stupid, but I just wanted to know if you really meant the things you said in your message earlier. Have you really moved on?"

There was something in her voice that I couldn't quite identify. That was proof enough to overcome any doubt I might have had that I was doing the right thing. With Jess there was never a time that I couldn't tell what all of those little signs meant. Jessica was a different person.

"Yeah. I know that's probably hard to believe after the way that I've been acting, but I really did mean every word of it. I'm glad that you're happy now. I'm not going to pretend that I don't still have concerns about Wyatt and the others, but more than anything I just want you to be happy."

There was what I thought was wonder in her voice when she finally responded a few seconds later. "I called up thinking that this was just some ploy to get me to talk to you. I didn't expect to believe you, but I think I do. How did you finally manage to move on? What was it that did the trick for you?"

She'd just finished saying that she believed me, but I sensed traces of what I thought were doubt still in her voice.

"I can understand why you're having a hard time believing that I've moved on, Jessica, but I really have. I think it was two things really. I finally realized that Jess is gone. You really are a different person, there isn't any shared history there, we don't have a flame that we could rekindle under the right circumstances. The relationship I had with Jess is as gone as if her body had died when Oblivion took away your memories."

"What was the other thing?"

Her voice caught oddly, probably in relief that I really did seem to be ready to leave her alone.

"I met someone. It's complicated, but I think she'll be good for me and that I'll be good for her too."

"Do you love her?"

This time I recognized what I was hearing. There was regret there in her voice, but even that was understandable. She'd spent untold hours running away from me, but there had still probably been a sense of security to the arrangement. She'd always known that if all else failed that she could go back to me and I would take her without complaint.

"I'm sorry, Jessica. I don't mean to be insensitive. I'm only telling you this because I want you to know that you can go off and be happy without worrying about me. I'd be lying if I said that I didn't still have some worries where Wyatt is concerned, but to be honest I'd have the same worries even if you weren't dating him. I found some stuff that isn't adding up and it's making me nervous."

She giggled, which was an odd response, but she started talking again before I could ask her what was so funny.

"No, don't worry about me, Isaac. You aren't being hurtful, this was all stuff that I needed to hear. I'm better off knowing what's going on. I'm really happy for you. I know you don't need my blessing, but you have it."

"Thanks, Jessica. That means a lot—I really appreciate it."

"I need to go, Isaac. I'll talk to you another day?"

I knew I was probably undoing most of the progress I'd just made, but I couldn't help it. Something in her voice awakened protective instincts that hadn't really had a chance to start to atrophy yet.

"Jess, there's something wrong, isn't there? Is it Wyatt, is he involved in something that is making you uncomfortable?"

"No, honestly, Wyatt is incredible. I don't know what you've found in the last few days, but he's shown me everything now that we're back here at his home. There isn't anything shady going on, in fact it's the opposite of shady. He's so amazing that I honestly tell myself at least half a dozen times a day that I don't deserve him."

Something there still wasn't right.

"Is it that he's there? Say 'maybe' if there's someone there listening, if there's a reason that you can't tell me the truth."

"No, Isaac, it's not like that, I promise. I'm all by myself right now and nobody has me locked up or anything. You don't need to worry. I'm sorry if I sound like I'm falling apart, I'm just really happy for you. I know that I haven't been very grateful, but I just want you to know that I haven't forgotten the time you saved me from the vampires. You're a pretty great guy and I guess that being out here has made me a little nostalgic for old times."

She took an odd, choking breath. "I'm happy for you, I guess I just miss you and Andrew more than I expected to."

She was telling the truth. I knew even the new Jessica well enough to know when she wasn't lying.

"Okay, now I feel like an idiot. I didn't mean to overreact, I guess some of the stuff that I've seen recently has me even more paranoid than I'd realized."

"You're fine, Isaac. Honestly, your protectiveness is one of your best qualities. I'm sorry that I gave you so much crap about that before."

There was a couple of seconds of silence, but Jessica broke it before it could really get awkward.

"I'm sorry to cut things short, but there is this party that I'm supposed to go to."

"No worries, Jessica. I'll catch up with you later—I'm glad that things are going so well for the two of you and that I turned out to be wrong about Wyatt."

Chapter 31

Isaac Nazir
The Lamia Enclave

As I hung up I felt bad about lying to Jessica, but there wasn't any other way that conversation could have really gone down. If I'd told her that I wasn't planning on ever seeing her again, it would have sounded like some kind of massive sympathy play.

This had been much better. She knew that I was happy and that I wanted her to be happy.

There weren't any more valid reasons to put off my call to Alec, so I dialed him and held my breath until his phone started ringing.

"Isaac, is that you?"

"Adri? Where is Alec? I'm sorry, but I don't have much time and I really need to talk to him."

"I'm sorry, Isaac. Alec isn't available, but he made me promise that I'd pick up no matter what the next time you called."

She sounded worn out in a way that I'd never heard out of her. Adri tended more towards the serious side of things than Jessica, but this was something else entirely. She sounded like she had the weight of the world on her shoulders.

"How long will it be before Alec can call me himself and talk to me?"

"I don't have an answer for you on that one, Isaac. Why don't you just tell me what you need and we'll see what we can pull together for you?"

"What's going on, Adri?"

"The Chicago pack is in ruins. Nobody has heard from Shawn or Ulrich in days. The Coun'hij has kill teams scouring the country for our people and they are scary good at finding people they shouldn't be able to find. My two best weapons are Jaclyn who refuses to pick up her phone, and Grayson who told me directly the last time I called him that he can't help me with any of my problems."

"That's not what I was talking about and you know it."

"Sorry, Isaac, that's all you're going to get unless you're ready to come meet up with us so that I can tell you in person. I'm not saying any more over a phone line regardless of how secure you or anyone else tell me it is."

What she was implying was enough to make my stomach drop away. I could feel a black hole trying to swallow my determination and leave me nothing but a hollow shell, but I refused to give in before I had confirmation for what she was implying.

"Where is Alec?"

"Not another word, Isaac, or I'll hang up on you right now and Alec can just deal with the fact that I broke my promise to him."

"He's not dead."

"No, he's not dead. What do you need? I've got problems here that need to be dealt with."

She wasn't lying, at least I didn't think she was. I would have said that Adri was incapable of keeping a secret from anyone longer than five minutes, but this new Adri was as cold as they came. Still, if Alec wasn't dead then that meant we all still had a chance.

"I'm in Louisiana. Those kill teams chased us here and then Onyx backed us into a corner. I'm about to go fight Onyx, but I know that I can't win. I was hoping that Alec could come put him down for me."

"That's not going to happen, not with everything else that's going on right now, but I might be able to get some hybrids down there to help you out. I think that there are two from the Tucson pack I could shake loose along with four or five wolves."

"No, that isn't going to do the trick. You can't just throw bodies at this guy. He's got an ability that drops people from a dozen yards away. Sending a dozen hybrids wouldn't be enough, you'd just end up with more corpses on our side when all was said and done. I need Alec, he's the only one who can definitely neutralize Onyx."

She was silent for a couple of seconds before sighing. "I'm sorry, Isaac, I really wish there was more that we could do, but there isn't. Are you sure that there isn't some way to get the three of you out of there?"

"Not one that would let me live with myself afterwards. What about if I stall for a day or two?"

I wasn't sure that I could live with that; I knew that Celeste wouldn't be able to, but I needed to know what I was up against.

"It wouldn't make any difference. I wish it would, but there's just no way. Can you think of anything else that we could do from here that would give you a chance of getting out of there?"

I closed my eyes and rested my head in my hand. "Crap. No, there isn't any other way."

"Are you sure, Isaac? I...we could really use your help back here. There aren't very many people I can trust right now."

There it was, the perfect reason to abandon my plan and retreat back to wherever Adri, Alec and the others happened to be. You could even argue that retreating would be doing the most good for the greatest number.

The only problem was that I knew exactly what that would cost me. Celeste wasn't going to walk away from her people, not for a second time, not after knowing just how terrible she'd felt when she'd stayed in the enclave to keep me alive and thought that her people were all dead.

She would stay, and if she stayed, she was going to end up dead. That wasn't a price that I was willing to pay.

"No, Adri, I just can't do that. I'm sorry, but you'll be okay. You seem like you're keeping the wheels on, just don't let on to anyone else the true extent of our problems. I'm not going to tell anyone, but if word gets out we're all going to find ourselves pretty much screwed."

"Go teach your grandma to suck eggs, Isaac. You caught me in a weak moment or I wouldn't have even told you as much as I did."

This time the silence stretched out, but in the end I was the one who broke it.

"Just make sure that you tell Alec that I'm sorry. Oh, and if Ash doesn't manage to bring Onyx down, promise me that you guys will find a way to take him down soon. He needs to be stopped before he can do more damage down here."

"Alec already knows. He wanted to tell you that he's already forgiven anything that needed forgiving. He hopes that you know how sorry he was that he couldn't have done more to save Jess. He still considers you one of his closest friends."

My voice came out rough despite my best efforts.

"I feel the same way. Do I have your promise that you'll see to Onyx?"

"Yeah, even if I have to pull the trigger myself. We're going to bring the Coun'hij and everyone who's been supporting them down or we'll die trying."

"The old Adri wouldn't have approved of assassination."

"Yeah, well, I swore a promise back in Chicago. Besides, it's been a rough couple of weeks. There are worse things than putting a bullet in the head of the kind of people we are fighting. Take care of yourself, Isaac. I'll pass on your message."

"You too, Adri."

Chapter 32

Isaac Nazir
The Lamia Enclave

Everyone was waiting for me at the entrance to the tunnel that led back to our world. Kristin wasn't in any shape to ask me any questions, and Jax was too submissive to pry, but I could see that Ash and Celeste both wanted to know who I'd been talking to.

I motioned everyone into the tunnel without volunteering any information. Apparently I was currently dominant enough to get away with that. Nobody argued, and a few minutes later we exited the tunnel and started our way out onto a series of progressively smaller islands.

They were all close enough together that we were able to step from one to another without getting our feet wet, and then a few minutes after that Set led us around to the other side of a familiar-looking tree that it turned out had been hiding our boat.

Our bags all went into the bottom of the vessel, followed by Kristin with an appropriate amount of fussing on Ash's part as Set gently lowered her onto one of the chairs. The lamias then reached down and picked the boat up so that they could walk it down into the water.

Ash, Jax and Celeste all piled into the boat as soon as it was in the water, but I stopped and turned back to Set before getting in.

"Take care, my friend. I'm sorry for the damage I did to your enclave while I was there. I hope you're able to quickly rebuild and come out stronger in the near future."

"You took the path that honor demanded, Isaac Nazir. I'm glad to have known you. I wish you honor and faith sufficient to accomplish your task."

A minute later we were all on the boat and skimming across the water. I looked back just before we started around a big island that would have cut Set and the others off from view, but they were already gone.

We were moving much faster than we had on the way in, and the drone of the engine and propeller precluded casual conversation, but I managed to communicate well enough with Celeste to convince her to stop when we were still five minutes from our destination.

LOST

Satisfied that I would have time to explain my plan before we arrived back in civilization, I leaned back in my chair and enjoyed zipping across the murky green water. It was over all too soon.

Celeste cut the engine and then turned to me. "Okay, what did you want to tell everyone?"

"I'm going in to New Orleans with you and Jax. We'll drop Ash and Kristin off far enough outside of town that they won't get picked up by Onyx's guys, but close enough that they can buy a car and get to a hospital somewhere out of state."

Ash shook his head. "What are you talking about? Why would we need to go to a hospital?"

"I guess that wasn't one of the things that you and Celeste talked about while I was unconscious. When you got hurt I sewed you up, but one of your stitches popped open after I closed you up. Set slowed the bleeding down, but there is a hole in your right renal artery. You need to get to a doctor and have them open you back up or there is a chance that you'll bleed to death."

He looked over at Celeste for confirmation and received a nod. "Okay, I need to get to a hospital, but that isn't any kind of reason for the three of you to go back to the house in New Orleans."

Celeste cleared her throat. "I'm going back. Jax and Isaac should go with you two, but I have to go back or Onyx will start killing the pack's submissives. I'm not going to let that happen."

Jax jumped into the conversation with an uncharacteristic burst of assertiveness. "I'm going back too. Those are my friends back there. I'm not going to abandon them."

I gave Ash a tired smile. "If Celeste is going back, then I'm going with her."

"That's crazy, Isaac. Just because you have the hots for my sister isn't any reason to throw your life away. You're good, maybe even better than good, but Onyx eats guys like you for breakfast. You can't win."

"I know. My chances aren't spectacular, but by going in there I can put him on notice. I'll tell him that if he hurts Celeste or the others then he'll get a visit from Alec, and once that happens, New Orleans will be under new management."

Celeste shook her head and grabbed my arm. "Isaac, you don't have to do this. It's an incredible gesture, but it won't make any difference. Onyx isn't going to kill me, not as long as he still thinks he can get his hands on my family's money."

She hadn't quite come out and said that there wasn't any money left, but she'd come too close just now. It was one more bit of proof that she wasn't ready to go back to New Orleans on her own.

The old Celeste, the one that had been hardened by decades of high-stakes intrigue against Onyx, might have been able to withstand what she was headed into, but even then I wasn't sure. This new, softer Celeste I'd helped to create wasn't ready to go back into that kind of hell. Onyx would chew her up in a matter of days.

If she did survive, she'd be so scarred that there wouldn't be any coming back this time around. I couldn't let that happen, but I also couldn't tell her that. She was already going to blame herself for my death. If I made her think I'd died because she'd been too weak, that would change her for the worse forever.

"You're still thinking of things like they used to be, Celeste. Onyx knows that Ash is alive now. Not only that, he's going to be smarting from having just lost half of his hybrids to the ambush Set and I put together. If you don't give him exactly what he wants he'll just kill you and go back to looking for Ash."

I had her there, but Ash jumped back in the conversation. "Let's not be stupid about this. I'm not as good from extreme long distances, but it's the obvious solution. Let me get hold of some guys I know. It will take me a couple of days to set it up, but Onyx will go down to a fifty-caliber round just like anyone else."

Celeste looked truly torn now. Ash had just turned this into a choice between *some* of her people and me. I wasn't going to spend the rest of my life with her wondering if she'd made the right choice each time she looked at me.

"You can't guarantee a timeframe on something like that, Ash. Your contacts may not even be in this country. They may have commitments on another job, or Onyx may be so busy killing the submissives that he doesn't stick his head outside of the house until they are all dead. You might be able to put him down within the next twenty-four hours, or it might take a week and a half for all of the pieces to fall into place."

"Fine, but we should at least explore the possibility. I've got a lot of contacts, maybe one of them is already in this state. We don't lose anything by at least checking."

"Yes, we do. The longer Celeste is gone, the more furious Onyx is going to be when she gets back. His reputation is on the line. She needs to be back at the house as soon as possible to defuse the situation."

"Fine, I'll take the shot myself then. I'm not the best out there, but I should be able to hit him from far enough away to make sure that he doesn't see the shot coming."

I shook my head. "This is too important to blow, Ash. You're only going to get one chance to bring him down with snipers. Once that genie is out of the bottle then Onyx and every other piece of garbage that's been sheltering behind the Coun'hij is going to start taking precautions."

"It's worth it to give you a shot at making it out of there alive."

LOST

"What about the rest of the hybrids in the pack? If you kill Onyx with a slug from five hundred yards away then the rest of his guys will tear through half of the submissives and then use the rest as hostages."

"Acceptable losses."

Celeste looked like she was going to rip her brother's head off, but I grabbed her hand so that I could hold her back if necessary.

"And what happens if you bleed out while you're sitting there waiting for Onyx to show himself? You'd never buy off on such a hit-and-miss plan if our roles were reversed, Ash. You need to go get fixed up. Go to a hospital, or at least get your hands on enough blood to survive if you start bleeding again. Once you're not at risk anymore you can reach out to your contacts and start putting a plan together, one that will let you take down Onyx and his guys at the same time that you get Celeste and her people out."

"You're making this an either-or choice, Isaac. Isn't there any way we can get them and you all out?"

"Yeah, I go in and win my fight. It's not a guarantee, but I honestly believe that I have a chance of accomplishing my mission. I learned some things while I was with Set, things that Onyx doesn't understand, things that he won't see coming."

I'd very carefully not said that I had a chance of winning. I wasn't that good a liar. Ash and

445

Celeste both should have seen through my attempt at deception, but desperate people are naturally prone to believe that there is a way out, a magic bullet that will solve all of their problems. They bought it and first Ash and then Celeste finally nodded.

"Okay. If this is really what you want to do, then I won't keep trying to stop you."

I gripped Ash's arm and smiled. "This is definitely what I want to do."

No lie needed there.

Celeste got the boat moving again, and less than five minutes later I was helping offload Kristin and Ash's bags onto an old wooden dock. I unzipped Ash's duffle and slipped my tablet into it.

"Everything you need to get started is in here, but give Jasmin a call before you get started, she might have a plan that will work even better for finding Dream Stealer."

"Thanks, Isaac."

"You're welcome. Are you going to be okay with all of this stuff and Kristin at the same time?"

"Yeah, I'll call a cab and take her over to a motel so she's safe while I go out and secure transportation."

Ash turned to Celeste and looked at her for several seconds before shrugging. "I'm sorry about the way that I left all of those years ago. I couldn't stay there and be everyone's punching bag, but I shouldn't have involved Bennet like I did."

Celeste stepped out of the boat and walked over to where she could give Ash a hug. "I'm not going to lie and say that I didn't hate you for leaving, but it makes it easier to know that you weren't off sipping drinks on a beach somewhere. You've turned yourself into someone who has a chance of taking down an entire pack with the right help and some planning, and that counts for something in my book. I hope that Isaac wins and there's no need for you to put your plan into motion, but it will make things a little easier knowing that you're out there ready to back me up if it comes to it."

Ash watched as we motored off, and then just before the shoreline hid him from view, reached down and picked Kristin back up from the bench where she'd been resting.

The rest of the trip went by in a flash and then we were pulling up to an artificial shoreline of earth behind a retaining wall of rocks. I recognized one of the guys waiting at the floating wooden dock. His scent was the same, even now when he was in human form.

The house was remarkably secluded, which was about what I'd expected to find. It meant that there were fewer nosey neighbors around to notice if someone slipped up and transformed out in plain view. It also meant that Ash would have plenty of spots to pick from when it came to stationing snipers around the perimeter of the property.

I turned to Celeste as she cut the engine and let us coast the rest of the way in.

"Do you trust me?"

"Yeah, more than I should, probably, but so far you've always managed to come through."

I gave her a smile, but maintained my distance. It wouldn't do to give Onyx any idea that we had feelings for each other. He'd be quick to exploit that kind of weakness.

"Just follow my lead then and try not to look surprised."

I turned towards the closest of Onyx's men and tossed him the free end of the mooring rope. "Tie that off and then take us to see Onyx."

He let the rope fall to the wooden dock at his feet. "I don't take orders from you."

I was wearing the jeans and t-shirt that I'd gone into the swamp wearing, which made me happy. I wasn't going to get a chance to wear them again, but I would have hated destroying any of the clothes Set had given me.

I could pick up new jeans anywhere, but the clothes that the lamias had made were one of a kind.

I flashed an easy smile at Onyx's man as I stepped out of the boat and onto the deck. He shot me a frown in return, but even so he wasn't expecting what came next.

LOST

I shifted to hybrid form in a roar of power and shoved my hand into his chest.

Most people, even shape shifters have to work themselves up to a fight. There is a predictable series of steps that anyone other than a psychopath or someone expecting trouble has to go through in order to commit real, bone-shattering violence. There are even more steps that most people have to go through in order to actually kill someone.

That's why normal people are usually so shocked when things turn deadly. If you're not in a frame of mind that would allow you to hurt someone, then on some level it's hard to believe that anyone else is in that state of mind.

I'd moved through all of those steps on the trip to Celeste's house. I didn't have to dehumanize Onyx and his men, I just had to accept the fact that they were evil and the only way to save Celeste and her people was to kill the New Orleans hybrids at the slightest provocation.

My attack caught Onyx's man off guard. He'd only just started shifting when my claws pierced his flesh. I let his body drop down onto the dock and took a step towards the second guy, who'd just finished transforming.

"Are you insane? You're a dead man. Even if Onyx wasn't planning on killing you before he'll make an example of you now. The Coun'hij has forbidden fights out in the open."

"I don't care about the Coun'hij, they're a petty bunch of children who are about to be swept aside and replaced with a new order. I asked to be conducted to Onyx and your fellow refused me. Will you at least deliver a message for me, or must I kill you as well and go looking for your *master* myself?"

"Stay here. I'll go get him."

"Really? I care little for such things myself these days, but you seemed alarmed at the fact that I was in this form. Would you not rather I wait inside of your hovel?"

I waved for Celeste and Jax to follow me and set off towards Celeste's ancestral home, driving Onyx's man ahead of me the way a wolf drives a calf along before it.

Jax tied the boat off and then grabbed my bag before hurrying after Celeste, but I registered all of that based on the sounds coming from behind me. My eyes never left the enemy hybrid, who was still backing away from me so quickly that it was all he could do to avoid tripping over his own feet.

Once we arrived at the massive plantation-style house, the hybrid once again ordered us to stay put as he ran deeper inside to find someone else to help him deal with us.

"Celeste, where am I most likely to find Onyx?"

"He spends most of his time in my father's study."

"Lead the way."

She set off at a pace that was fast enough that I figured we had a chance of making it to the study before more of Onyx's people showed up, but she was careful not to break into a run. That was good, appearances were everything right now.

It turned out that Onyx wasn't in his study when we arrived, so I went in and sat down at his desk, a massive oak number that was the equal of anything I'd seen back at Graves Manor. Celeste's eyes got big, but she didn't say anything. Jax looked like he was about to have a coronary.

Onyx stormed into the room less than two minutes later, eyes flashing.

"Who the hell... Seriously? A piss-ant two-bit hybrid like you is all that I get? My guy was talking like the reincarnation of Jaldul himself had just stormed into the house. I should have known that it was just another stupid poser."

I could see his eyes start to tighten up in a signal that he was about to use his ability on me, but I held up one hand.

"You're going to want to hear what I have to say."

"Why, have you decided to beg for your sorry life?"

"Hardly. I'm here for two reasons. The first is to tell you that Celeste, her brother Ash, Jax and the rest of the submissives in this pack are under the protection of his royal highness, Alec Graves. Any mistreatment of them will bring down judgment upon your head and the heads of your men."

"Surely you're joking. I could kill you all and there wouldn't be a single thing Graves could do to stop me."

"He doesn't need to stop you, he's more than happy to give you the freedom to choose your actions, but if you harm any of us then you'll wish for death when he finally comes for you."

"Torture hardly sounds like something a Graves would do."

"King Alec isn't just any Graves, he's someone whose father was killed by your allies, he's someone whose home was just burned to the ground in a failed attack on him by Puppeteer."

"He doesn't sound like much of a king to me. I wouldn't have lost my house if it had been me."

A trickle of guys had joined the two who had arrived with Onyx. I let my eyes scan past each of them, and then gave Onyx a cold smile.

"I understand that you feel a need to posture in front of your men, but every person here knows that a force of nearly two dozen werewolves accompanied by the same number of Coun'hij enforcers would have torn through your entire pack in minutes. Rather than preen, you should be thinking of the fact that after the initial surprise, King Alec destroyed all of the hybrids and all of the remaining werewolves without losing a single man. Your abilities are considerable, but you're just as powerless against werewolves as any of your men."

I looked around the office and shook my head. "You know, I think if you were to just surrender to him there is even a chance that he'll allow you to keep this house rather than just burning it to the ground."

"I've heard enough."

"Very well, then I challenge you for control of this pack."

That caught him off guard. He'd thought that I was trying to run some kind of colossal bluff in the hopes that he would be scared enough to let me, Celeste and the others go.

I smiled. "I've surprised you. What you fail to understand is that King Alec is my liege. He ordered me to deliver my message in such a way as to make sure that you understood what you are up against."

"How is me effortlessly killing you going to show me anything of importance?"

"I am one of the least of those in the King's court, surely you know this. And yet I am willing to lay my life down simply to deliver a message for him. Surely even you have an idea of the kind of loyalty required to do something like that. If you fail to heed my words then the best-case scenario is that the King is too busy to see to you himself. If that is the case then you will simply be faced with a never-ending stream of steadily more powerful hybrids who are happy to sacrifice themselves if necessary to see the King's justice done."

Something flickered in the back of Onyx's eyes. He didn't understand what was going on, but he could tell that I wasn't lying, and that was frightening to him. He knew how he motivated his men, but he wasn't familiar with anything that would have made his guys willing to die for him in a fight they knew they couldn't win.

That was baffling enough, but I'd just told them that Alec would bring exactly that kind of fight to their doorsteps if they harmed any of us.

I could hear the hybrids in the back of the crowd shifting from one foot to the other. I had them worried. I even thought that maybe I'd managed to succeed in bluffing Onyx right up until Nicolas pushed his way into the room.

"I couldn't care less about his tiny little king, but if you're going to let this one challenge you then I want to have the pleasure of killing him."

It was over. The fear that I'd felt spreading through the rank and file evaporated. As dangerous as Nicolas was, everyone in the room knew that he was nothing compared to Onyx. If Nicolas wasn't scared then there was no reason for Onyx to be scared. As long as they were serving Onyx they were untouchable.

The one remaining hope was that I could manage to beat Nicolas. I knew I couldn't beat Onyx, but if I—self-admittedly the weakest of Alec's hybrids—took Nicolas down then it would put some fear back in them. It might even be enough.

LOST

I hadn't risen from my place behind Onyx's desk. Now I looked up at Nicolas and smiled. "You have no idea how glad I am to be able to kill you in the service of my king."

Another rumble of astonishment crept through the room. They'd probably never seen anyone so unworried at the prospect of fighting Nicolas. In the tiny pond that was New Orleans, he was the man to beat, the guy that was second only to Onyx.

I'd managed to orchestrate nearly everything about our confrontation so far and Onyx knew that he needed to regain a measure of control.

"We have a challenge ring in the center of the house. Follow us there if you're really ready to die."

The tiniest part of me wanted to scream out that I didn't want to die, but it was surprisingly easy to silence those screams. I was going to die no matter what happened at this point. The only remaining question was *how*. I was resolved to die in the way that would do the most good.

I was going to give Celeste and her people whatever measure of protection I could, and maybe in the process I could create a stronger legend for Alec, a legend that might mean at some point people would surrender to him rather than fighting until the bitter end.

I stood with a faint grin and gestured for Onyx and Nicolas to precede me. "By all means.

You will have to lead the way. I couldn't be bothered to memorize the floor plan of a house that will be a charred ruin in just a few days or weeks."

The challenge ring turned out to be a large auditorium set on a massive slab of concrete. Most of the furnishings were of a utilitarian nature, bench seats for the spectators and industrial fixtures for lighting, but there was a raised dais at one end of the room that didn't look like it had been poured at the same time as the floor. The dais and the throne on it were proof that Onyx had grander designs than just ruling a single pack in New Orleans.

He'd probably figured that he could move into town and suck what was left of the Hunt family dry over the course of just a year or two before moving on to establish himself as a major power on the Coun'hij. Instead, Celeste and her mom had held him off for decades. A few decades didn't mean much to a hybrid like Onyx, but the Hunts had bought the rest of us something more precious than money.

They'd bought us time of comparative freedom, a world in which the Coun'hij had one less weapon to hold to our heads.

I'd never shifted back after killing Onyx's man at the dock, but now Nicolas and Onyx both changed forms as well. A few more people trickled in, and I realized that Onyx had ordered the whole pack gathered to see my death.

LOST

The collection of people who formed a tiny ball around Celeste and Jax looked battered and scared, but I gave them all a reassuring smile.

"Your king is aware of your situation. If I fall here it will be only a temporary setback. He will free you. Today, tomorrow, next week, it matters not. His arm is mighty and his reach unending. Even tyrants like Onyx can't hope to escape his justice forever."

Onyx clapped sarcastically. "Ah, yes. More empty promises, more worthless grandstanding. The truth is that Celeste has been a very bad girl. She has been conspiring with our pack's enemies in the hopes of overthrowing me. Unfortunately her would-be allies are so weak that they couldn't send the army she asked for. They sent one hybrid, little more than a child really, as a salve to their conscience so that they can say that they tried to free you.

"The truth is that nobody wants you. You're a group that the rest of the world would simply let starve. *I* protect you. *I* keep you safe from the threats out there in the wider world. *I* am your king, and as your king I've invited you all here to see the pretender's pawn fall to our very own Nicolas."

Onyx dropped his hand and Nicolas blurred towards me. He was every bit as fast as I remembered, but I'd seen this very same attack a thousand times inside my dreams. I acted without thinking, ducking to the right and then reversing back to the left at the last second and raking my claws through his stomach and side as he tried to compensate for my abrupt shift in location.

My claws scraped against a sheath of bone where there shouldn't have been anything other than muscles and organs, but the wound was still surprisingly deep, all things considered.

"That was for my friend Ash. Too bad he doesn't have your…advantages."

Nicolas' eyes narrowed, probably partially because I'd referenced—however obliquely—the fact that he shared a common heritage with Alec and Jasmin, and partially because it had been a very long time since anyone had managed to bleed him like that in a fight without help.

"Apparently Carson taught you more than I gave you credit for. That's good; I've grown weary of fighting incompetents."

He came back towards me, moving with more caution, and we swapped feints for a couple of seconds before he stepped in with the hybrid equivalent to a straight jab. I should have stepped back and tried to slash his arm. That was my normal reaction to those kinds of attacks, but this time I stepped into him, blocking his claw-tipped jab with the side of my arm, and then slamming my right fist into his stomach.

His other arm came at me from my right, but I stepped to the side and slammed his arm with my right elbow before slicing him across the chest and backing away.

Fighting a hybrid was liberating after so long fighting lamias. Nicolas didn't have scales capable of at least partially turning my blows and I'd done such a large amount of damage to him in such a short amount of time that I could scarcely believe it.

He wasn't going to bleed out in the next two minutes, but losing so much blood was going to eventually have an impact even on a hybrid. If I could avoid clinching with him for a minute or two, he would start to slow down slightly and I would have more options. Even better, if I could manage another strike or two like the last two, then he'd start feeling pressure to finish the fight more quickly, which would mean that he would be more likely to make mistakes.

It was too early to start celebrating though. Two minutes was still a lot of time and if he managed to get close enough to put me in one of the holds that Carson had favored, I would still lose.

We circled, gauging each other's reaction times and technique. Even wounded like he was, he was still the slightest bit faster than me, which was extremely bad. He was bigger than me too, which meant that he had the advantage when we were fighting further apart.

His claws licked out once, twice, and then a third time. I was bleeding from three different spots on my arms, and I'd only managed to land one blow on him in return. He was still bleeding faster that I was, but he'd just proved that he was going to win if I tried to wait him out.

His advantages at long range meant that I couldn't afford to keep fighting him out at the distances we'd been fighting at, but by the same measure, I couldn't afford to let him get in close where he could turn this into a grappling match. There was an extremely narrow band of distance where I seemed to have the advantage, but if I erred even by just a couple of inches too close or too far away, then he would make me pay in blood and pain.

I was like an amateur with one trick going up against a seasoned pro with a whole arsenal of techniques, but there wasn't anything to do but try to force the kind of fight that I had at least some chance of winning.

We exchanged a couple of more jabs before I saw my chance. As his fist came towards me I knocked it high and to my left so that his body was uncovered as I stepped in. My right fist shot forward with the speed and force of a piston, but it was too similar to what I'd already done.

As I moved forward in an attempt to get inside of his reach, he'd already turned slightly so that my claws only managed a glancing blow, and then he hit me with way more force than anyone should have been able to generate from such a short charge. None of my normal techniques were going to be able to get me out of this bind. I couldn't move forward without guaranteeing him exactly the kind of clinch he was after, and I wasn't fast enough to get out of his reach, not as fast as he'd come at me. The fight was over at that moment, and I knew it, but some part of my subconscious apparently didn't agree.

Instead of dodging or stepping into him, I threw myself backwards with every ounce of speed and force I could muster. Even my best effort wasn't enough to avoid him completely, but I hadn't expected it to be.

His claws closed on the outside of my arms, tearing into my muscles as my feet came off of the ground and I pulled them up against my chest. His fangs were headed towards my neck, but I managed to get my hands up just high enough to push him back away from my vitals.

We were moving in slow motion now and it seemed as though I could read his mind. He didn't care that I'd stopped him from ripping my throat out because every rule of physics was now working in his favor. We were going to hit the concrete more than hard enough to drive him past my ineffectively scrabbling claws and let him end me.

Our fall stretched out for what felt like hours, but no matter how hard I tried, I couldn't get my claws into anything important. His control of my upper arms was giving him too much leverage, and then there wasn't any time left to continue trying.

We hit with enough force to knock a human being out cold, but hybrid bodies are made out of much sterner stuff and rather than having Nicolas crush me into the ground, my legs had somehow contorted enough to put my feet between the two of us. I converted all of that energy into a throw that launched Nicolas into a row of empty bleachers.

I rolled to my feet at the same time that Nicolas disentangled himself from the wreckage and stumbled down to the circle.

Neither of us was in very good shape by then. My arms were still functioning despite all odds, but I was losing a lot of blood and I was starting to feel the faintest bit lightheaded. Nicolas' wounds from earlier on in the fight had now been joined by two sets of deep punctures in his chest. I'd missed sticking a talon through his heart out of nothing more than sheer dumb luck, but he was obviously approaching the end of his endurance.

"Who the hell are you?"

Despite the pain competing for my attention, I felt my lips pull back in a smile.

"I thought that we'd already established that, Nicolas. What was it that your boss called me? A worthless pawn?"

"No, you're not Isaac Nazir. I fought Isaac Nazir and trounced him soundly."

"What's the matter, worried that Carson showed me stuff that he never trusted you enough to pass on to you?"

The flare of power and rage out of Nicolas was white-hot. It wasn't the kind of demonstration you expected out of a hybrid on his last legs, it was the kind of thing that only the most powerful dominants ever produced. My beast should have responded with a burst of energy of his own, but he didn't. It was more evidence that I didn't have much left to give.

My beast was too far gone to care about posturing, all he cared about was trying to survive.

"There was *nothing* that Carson didn't show me. I was his prize pupil. I was the one he wanted his daughter to marry. The old fool had no idea who he was dealing with until it was too late."

As Nicolas charged in towards me with a roar, I experienced another of those moments when everything slowed down and I became hyper-aware of my surroundings. Celeste looked worried, Jax looked scared, and Onyx looked concerned. None of them had expected for me to last this long, but I couldn't hold that against Celeste. I hadn't expected to last this long either.

My beast was lethargic, as though his attention was directed elsewhere, or maybe he was just making peace with what was coming.

The fight could still go either way, but I was nearly out of tricks, and Nicolas' anger seemed to be giving him the strength he needed to move like he was fresh and uninjured. Time sped back up to normal speed and Nicolas was now less than two steps away from me.

His claws moved towards me impossibly fast, and once again I blocked and stepped forward. It was obvious that my training and reflexes had let me down. It was the same attack that Nicolas had just finished trumping.

It was the end...only it wasn't. Instead of parrying his blow to the outside, I'd parried it to the inside, which meant that his own arm was in the way of any follow-up attack he could launch and his chest and side were completely exposed.

I stabbed him in the chest, puncturing his lung. I would have preferred a straight shot at his heart, but I'd opened up the wrong side of his body for that. It was a vicious, debilitating attack nonetheless, but it wasn't enough to stop him from bringing his arm back around and slamming his elbow into the side of my head.

He knocked me back on my heels and then before I could recover, he wrapped me up in a giant bear hug and lifted me off of my feet. It was the last thing I would have expected out of someone like Nicolas. It was the attack of an enraged bruiser rather than the slick technique of a professional killer, but that didn't stop it from being effective.

Even assuming that I could have matched his strength, I didn't have the leverage that I would have needed to break free of him. My hands were trapped between us, pinned by a combination of our bodies and his vicelike grip around my upper arms.

I tried to get my talons into play. I was cutting him up, but I couldn't get to anything important. He was bleeding so fast that I knew he didn't have much longer, but I could feel one of his hands digging into my back in an attempt to sever my spinal cord.

He was having a hard time getting past all of the ribs and vertebrae, but it was only a matter of time. I was betting that he'd succeed in paralyzing me before he bled to death.

I happened to be looking at Onyx as I struggled in a vain attempt to free myself. I could see the worry and concern disappear, replaced instead by satisfaction as my struggles started to weaken. Just when I was on the point of giving up, I felt Nicolas weaken as the cumulative blood loss finally started to catch up with him. It was a very slight change, but it was all I needed to get one hand just enough free to sink it into his chest.

I'd missed his heart again, too low this time, but I hadn't expected anything different. The important thing was that I could feel his arms relaxing even further.

From where he was standing Onyx shouldn't have been able to see what had happened, but something tipped him off. Maybe it was a change in Nicolas' posture, or maybe it was something in my expression, but he knew as soon as I did when the balance finally shifted irrevocably towards me.

The burning sheet of pain as Onyx used his power on me was all the worse because I hadn't been expecting it. Onyx apparently wasn't willing to stand by and see Nicolas killed, not when he had the ability to save someone that he viewed as being a useful tool.

I yelled again. The agony was too intense for me to hold it inside. Nicolas tightened his grip on me in an attempt to finish me off even faster, but all that did was drive my claws more deeply into his chest.

A tiny, hysterical part of me wanted to tell him not to bother. I'd managed to endure several seconds, maybe even as much as a minute, of Onyx's ability before, but my reserves were already gone this time. I was at the end of my strength, had been for the last quarter of the fight, and I could feel the end approaching.

Just before I felt my heart beat for the last time I started hallucinating. The pain didn't exactly disappear, but it morphed into something else. My core still burned with the same terrible fire, but there was a different, more pleasant, cooling fire burning in my arms and legs.

It started in my claws, which was odd—there aren't any kind of nerve endings there—and spread. About the time my heart stopped beating, I sank my talons into Nicolas' thighs. I couldn't have said why I chose to do that right then.

Maybe it was a simple desire to make sure that I took Nicolas with me. Maybe it was something else, an instinct operating on the subconscious level where my beast preferred to spend most of his time.

Either way, by the time the fire moved up to my knees and elbows I was craving it the way that I normally craved air. I had a fleeting thought that my brain must be approaching the point of running out of oxygen, but I didn't mind, not if that was the price to feel this good.

There was something wrong with that thought, but I was having a hard time reasoning around the drumming in my ears. I wasn't wrong because I was willing to die, although that was wrong too. There was something else. I wasn't supposed to feel good. I should have still been in pain, exquisite pain that exceeded anything else I'd ever felt, but I wasn't.

I opened my eyes back up to check, but Onyx still had the same slightly pinched expression around his eyes. He was still using his ability on me, but it wasn't affecting me anymore.

No, that wasn't quite it. I could still feel the pain out in the very furthest reaches of my body, but it didn't matter anymore. It was so dwarfed by everything else I was feeling that there wasn't any room left over to experience it at the same time.

DEAN MURRAY

The cooling, healing fire had been steadily growing, but now it stopped. It was still washing up my arms and legs, but it had reached a point of stability where the fire in was equal to the fire that was being expended to contain the pain.

I wanted more fire, wanted it more than anything else I'd ever wanted. I...reached...for more fire and felt it just beyond the tips of my claws. I *pulled* and felt it come in faster and faster.

About that time I realized what the drumming was. My heart had started back up. Just as incredibly, I felt strong. I was bursting with strength and vitality. It demanded that I do something with it.

I broke free of Nicolas' hold with ridiculous ease, but dropping to the ground pulled my talons free of him and the amount of fire lapping into my body dropped by half.

I tried to pull even more in through my claws, but a split second after that I felt the source of the healing fire flicker and go out. I didn't realize what had actually happened until Nicolas turned into dead weight in my arms.

He was dead. I'd...sucked him dry like some kind of vampire. It should have been revolting, but I still felt too good for feelings of disgust to stick. Besides, I suddenly had a much more pressing concern.

There wasn't any more good fire entering my body, but the pain was still there, still eating away at my reserves. Based on the rate at which it was being consumed I had a very short period of time before the pain was going to grow back to the point where it would overwhelm me.

I wasn't going to waste that opportunity. I was less than ten feet away from Onyx's dais. I covered that distance in two long bounds and slammed the claws on my right hand into his shoulder before he could process the fact that his ability had failed him for the first time.

He was strong, possibly even strong enough to have pushed up out of his chair despite my best efforts under normal circumstances. These weren't normal circumstances though, not even close. I could have easily held him there pinned in his chair, but I chose to let him up.

My store of healing fire was nearly gone, so I reached through my claws and started new tendrils racing up my arm. It was intoxicating, so much so that I didn't manage to get my arm up in time to block the punch that Onyx threw directly into my chest.

I felt his claws enter my heart, and then felt the muscle contract, tearing itself against the bitter, deadly edges of something that didn't belong there. I should have been panicking, but I merely reached up and pulled his hand out of my chest.

The energy I was siphoning from his body raced into the ruin he'd made and I could feel the flesh knitting back together. I could even feel the blood being replaced. When I looked down there wasn't even a scar there.

Onyx tried to slash me again, but I was ready this time. I blocked his attack with my left hand and then ended him with a single slash across his neck.

I didn't want to kill him that way. Every part of me hungered to drain him dry in the exact same way that I'd drained Nicolas, but the sheer strength of the desire told me that would be a bad idea. I'd never been addicted to anything before, and I didn't want to start now, didn't want to turn into someone that killed solely for the high it gave me.

I turned around to face the rest of the room and saw chaos. Half of Onyx's remaining men had charged the dais and the other half were engaged in a lopsided battle against Celeste, Jax, and the rest of Celeste's people.

The dominants were clearly better fighters, but they were giving way against better than three-to-one odds. The submissives were attacking fearlessly. Some of them had already taken dreadful wounds, but others had latched onto arms and legs and even as I watched, one of the hybrids went down as a wolf latched onto his throat.

The first of Onyx's guys reached me, but I was faster than I'd ever been before. I checked his slash by stabbing him in the arm, and then stepped into him and put my fist into his chest. The second guy reached me while I was still tangled up with the first guy, but I merely stabbed him in the thigh with the talons of my left leg and shoved.

It shouldn't have been possible to stop a full-grown hybrid like that, not when he was charging and I was stationary, not by using only one leg, but I did. More than just stopping him, I threw him nearly thirty feet.

I heard an unfamiliar screech just before the third hybrid reached me, and looked down to find that I'd torn long gouges into the concrete of the dais. I grabbed the third guy and threw him into the obscenely heavy throne with enough force to both knock him unconscious and knock the throne down off of the dais.

The fourth guy arrived too soon after the third guy and managed to stab me in the back. The fire was burning so brightly inside of me that I barely even felt the pain. It wasn't until I turned and backhanded him into the wall that I realized I'd been draining the first guy that entire time.

"Stop!"

My yell practically shook the entire house. It was so loud that everyone actually stopped fighting for the briefest of instants.

"Stop fighting and you will be judged for your crimes. There has been enough killing. You'll all be punished for your crimes, and you may end up being sent out to fight werewolves until you die, but I'll spare anyone I can. No more death."

Chapter 33

Isaac Nazir
Hunt Family Estate
New Orleans, Louisiana

Everyone had decided to separate back to their respective corners rather than continuing to fight. I probably would have gotten more resistance from Celeste's people except for the fact that the pause in the hostilities had given them a chance to see the butcher's bill. Two of them hadn't survived the night and about half of the wolves who were left were going to spend at least a couple of days in bed.

I asked Celeste to send the least injured of her people for cages, but she told me that there was a massive steel and concrete vault on the other end of the house. When I ordered Onyx's guys to follow one of her wolves to the vault I expected them to make a break for it, but none of them did.

LOST

It was about then that I happened to look down and see the sheer amount of light I was giving off. Even Set's queen hadn't glowed that brightly. I didn't look like a mortal being, I looked like some kind of angel.

If I'd been in their shoes I probably would have been in shock too.

After the bad guys were all safely locked up, and I'd helped care for Celeste's people, I found an out-of-the-way bedroom that looked like it hadn't been used in a while and collapsed onto the bed. It took a while, but eventually the energy that I'd stolen from Nicolas, Onyx and the other guy dissipated. Some of it seemed to just soak into the air around me, but it felt like the reservoir inside of me was emptying faster than that could account for. It felt like a lot of that energy was going somewhere else, I just didn't have any idea where.

When the fire was finally all gone, I was exhausted. I wasn't tired physically, but emotionally and mentally I had nothing left to give. Changing back to human form had helped curb the desire to drain someone dry, but it hadn't gone completely away.

I didn't like looking at people as a kind of metaphysical food source, but right now that was all I saw when I looked at any of them. Somewhere along the line I fell asleep and didn't wake until Celeste opened the door.

"Are you okay, Isaac? Do you want to be left alone?"

It was like looking at a new person. She was still Celeste, but her eyes were more guarded and her posture was more submissive.

"No, please come in."

I started to scoot over so that she could sit next to me, but when I looked down at the comforter it was covered in blood, none of it mine.

"I'm sorry, I wasn't thinking. I've ruined the bedspread."

"It's fine. I was talking to Ash when I saw the blood on the carpets. He's graciously offered to replace anything that needs replacing out of his share of our inheritance."

"Sorry, I guess I wasn't really myself after everything that happened."

"Please don't get mad at me, Isaac, but what did happen?"

Even as I answered her I couldn't meet her eyes.

"I fed off of them. First Nicolas, then Onyx, then the first of their guys to attack me. It filled me up with what felt like fire. Their...energy healed me and cushioned me from the pain of having Onyx use his ability on me. I'd never felt anything like it before."

"You must have manifested an ability."

I shook my head. "That's impossible. Mallory looked at a couple of us in Nevada before we split up. It wasn't necessary since she'd known me as a child, but she confirmed just a few weeks ago that I don't have the potential to manifest an ability."

"I don't know who Mallory is, or why you think she'd know whether you were capable of manifesting a power, but she was wrong. You manifested an ability, and it's a huge one. You glowed and I saw Onyx all but rip your heart out of your chest. You're unstoppable."

"No, I wouldn't say that. Hard to kill, yes, but I'm kind of like a variation of Jaclyn Annikov. I'd be useless against a werewolf, and it all only really kicks in once I've stolen quite a bit of energy from someone else."

"You're shortchanging yourself, Isaac. Nobody short of Alec or Puppeteer would have even a hope of beating you."

"You'd be surprised. I can think of a couple of others who could put me down with a little luck or even just the right planning."

"Once you've had a chance to rest we need to start testing the limits of what you can do. It could be the difference between living and dying. You need to know what you're capable of."

"No!"

It wasn't meant for her as much as it was to tell myself that I wasn't going to tap into someone else's life force again, not unless I didn't have any other choice.

Celeste jumped slightly, which surprised me, but before I could ask what was wrong she continued speaking.

"Very well. Ash and Kristin have asked if it would be possible for them to come here."

"What? Of course, why are they even asking?"

She looked at me like she wasn't sure what language I was speaking. "They asked because it's bad form to just stop by and visit a pack without clearing the trip with the pack's alpha. The only exception is if you're planning on challenging for leadership of the pack or you're with the Coun'hij."

"The alpha..."

It all finally clicked. The haze from the fight with Nicolas and Onyx blew away and everything became clear.

"I'm the alpha. That's why you're being so tentative. You're worried that I'm going to turn into another Onyx."

"You and I never established who was dominant to whom, Isaac, but it's obvious now that you're dominant to most of the hybrids in North America. I've never seen anything like what you did today. How would you be acting if our positions were reversed?"

"When you say it like that, I can see why you're worried, but I need you to not change on me, Celeste."

It was hard to get the reason out, but I knew I needed to tell her now or I might not ever tell her. It was important that at least one person know about the craving to kill again and again.

"I left the arena because I was having a hard time being down there in the same place where I'd killed Nicolas and the others."

"I don't understand. You didn't have any other choice. Trust me when I say that everyone you killed today had it coming."

I nodded. "I know, but it wasn't just that I killed them, it was *how* I killed them. Draining someone like that is euphoric, and being full of all that energy made me feel unstoppable. I want to do it again and again, even though I know that it's wrong. Right now I want to find the Coun'hij and kill them and their enforcers until the corpses are piled up taller than this house."

"They all have it coming too, Isaac."

"I know that, but that wouldn't be the reason I'd be doing it. I'd be doing it because their being evil gives me a convenient excuse for doing what I already want to do. But then what? What do I do when all of the bad guys are dead and I'm still craving the high I get now from killing?"

I could see the understanding dawning on her face and I couldn't bring myself to look at her.

"I know I'm asking a lot, Celeste, but I really need someone around who can treat me like a normal person. I need someone to keep me grounded and make sure that I don't forget why I came here in the first place."

"Why did you come here, Isaac? Did you know this was going to happen?"

"No, I had no idea. I thought I was going to die at Onyx's hands."

"Why then? You could have let me come back here by myself, there was no need for you to die."

I still couldn't look at her.

"I couldn't stand the thought of you coming back here and being tortured, Celeste. It wasn't right, you didn't deserve that. I thought maybe if I put on a good show that it might make Onyx think twice about hurting you. Originally I was hoping that Alec could just fly down and kill him for us, but there's something wrong there and by the time we left the enclave I knew he wasn't going to be coming."

"That is what you get for trusting a Graves!"

"No, he would have come if he could have. I shouldn't tell you this, it would cause the rebellion major problems if it got out, but I need one person that I can be completely honest with. There's something wrong with Alec. I don't know what it is, but he's sick or something. He needs to be seen out in the trenches soon or everything will start falling apart."

Celeste reached out and patted me hesitantly on the shoulder. It wasn't how things used to be, but it was a start. Maybe things could never go back to how they'd been, but that simple touch gave me hope that maybe they could.

"Isaac, the rebellion has you now. If Alec needs some time to get his head back in the game, then you can give him that time. You may not be quite as powerful as he is, but you're still a major power in our world now. Knowing that you will be fighting beside them will make wolves and hybrids flock to Alec's banner who otherwise would try to sit this war out."

She was right, and knowing that made me feel less like a monster.

"That's why I need you by my side, Celeste. You know what I need to hear. You see the other side of things—the side that I need to consider if I'm going to stop myself from going back to being the guy I used to be, the one who thinks that I don't have any choices in anything. I need you to stay with me and bring me down a couple pegs from time to time like you used to do back in the enclave."

"I'm not sure I can do that, Isaac."

My world had been balancing on the blade of a knife and now I felt it start to come crashing down. I stood to go, but she grabbed onto me with the same desperate strength that she'd shown right before we'd left the enclave. It was a small thing, but I grabbed onto those memories with both hands and held my breath.

"I can't do that because I'm not that same person, Isaac. To be honest, I stopped being that person from almost the first time I met you. I tried to deny it, tried to tell myself that you were weak, but every time I turned around you proved me wrong.

"You say that you haven't been willing to accept enough responsibility, that you haven't always been willing to do what needed to be done, but I had the other problem. I was willing to accept any evil in the name of expediency. I was willing to do *anything* to save my people and only sheer dumb luck saved me from doing something even worse than the things that I did end up doing.

"I've been in love with you for weeks now. I'm sorry that I was willing to sacrifice your friends and the future of the rebellion to try and save my family, but until I met you I didn't realize that there was any kind of higher cause than protecting what was *mine*.

"I understand if you can't bring yourself to forgive me. I can't ask for your forgiveness, not after all you've done for me and my people out of nothing more than your inherent goodness, but I hope that someday I'll be able to earn it regardless."

I was so stunned that I couldn't find the right words to respond, and Celeste took my silence to mean the worst.

"I'm sorry that I burdened you with my feelings after everything you've been through today, but I wouldn't have been able to live with myself if I'd left this room without telling you how I really feel. It seemed like we came so close there at the enclave, but there was still always some kind of wall between us."

She let go of my arm and turned to go, but I reached out and stopped her before she could take a second step.

"The wall was the fact that you'd said you were going to ask the queen for a way to save your people instead of a way to save Kristin and end this war. I couldn't bring myself to fully trust someone who would use me like that when I was putting my life on the line to get us the chance to ask that question."

I could hear the tears in her voice as she responded.

"I'm sorry about that, Isaac. I wish I could have done things differently, but I didn't."

"That's just the point though, Celeste. You did do things differently. When we finally got a chance to talk to the queen you asked *our* question rather than how to save your people. Regardless of what you said, your actions were all that I could have hoped for.

"I've been in love with you for weeks too. I'm sorry that I couldn't just come right out and tell you what was making me hold back, but I felt like if I did that then you'd only be doing the right thing because it was what I wanted."

She turned to look at me and there were tears in her eyes, but they'd transformed into tears of happiness. I stepped closer and raised her chin up as I bent down to meet her.

The feeling as our lips met was incredible in ways that I'd never before experienced. It was more than just the feeling of her taut waist under my hands or how soft her lips were as they brushed against mine. It was more than just gorgeous blond hair or perfect skin. It wasn't because we'd survived a close brush with death, although that added a certain euphoria to the experience.

It was a double measure of gratification that had been delayed until the timing was perfect. It was shared trials and being part of a relationship where we'd already helped each other become more and better than we'd been before we'd met.

It was about being with someone who had been through terrible things and used them to grow stronger, who'd made those terrible things part of her strength rather than just papering over the hole inside of herself.

As much as I'd loved Jess, I knew that what I'd had with her was a pale shadow of what I already had with Celeste.

Author's Note

Writing the author's note to any given book is generally one of the last things I do before loading the book up for preorder. In a way that's good because it means that by the time I sit down to write the author's note I've had a few months to distance myself from the writing process. It means I can look back on the book with a little more clarity than I'd be able to otherwise.

Lost was an incredibly challenging book. For the first time ever I was juggling three separate timelines. I had to make sure that what was happening to Isaac matched up with the story from Driven and the nebulous events from the Reflections book that would be following Lost.

Not only that, the introduction of the lamias required I defined a lot more of the history of the world I've been writing about. To be honest there are times in most books where I am really tempted to throw in the towel and go back to an accounting job, but that urge was at least ten times worse with Lost than it had ever been with any previous book.

It's fortunate that when I have those kinds of decision points that I have an amazing support system to rely on. When everything hung in the balance I knew that there were lots of readers out there eagerly awaiting the next installment in the Sanctuary Pack's story.

If you're reading this then you're part of my most dedicated readers. You're one of the amazing fans that have followed me through an epic story that has spanned more than 1.1 million words so far. You are part of the select group that I write for. Your reviews and your efforts to spread the word about my writing mean more than you can ever know. I hope you'll continue to tell your friends and family about the Reflections and Dark Reflections books so that I can continue to write them.

Thank you all!
Dean

Acknowledgements

As always, I'd like to thank the group that helps make all of this possible. My editors, RJ Locksley and Amy Jirsa-Smith continue to work very hard to catch all of the typos and occasional plot holes. Likewise, my advance readers continue to serve as valuable sources of feedback and a very important safety net that I couldn't do without. In no particular order they are: Mom, Dad, Shalese, Matthew, Lachele, Mark, Mimi, Britney, Kim, Heather, Janelle, Jenine, and Mei. Thank you all for all of your help and support.

Even with all of the help from all of those other people, these books still couldn't become a reality without the help of my wife, Katie. She edits, provides feedback, and creates beautiful covers while still being an excellent mother to our two beautiful daughters. Thank you, Katie!

About the Author

Dean Murray is a prolific author with dozens of titles across multiple pen names and more than half a million copies of his work currently in circulation.

Dean started reading seriously in the second grade due to a competition and has spent most of the subsequent three decades lost in other people's worlds.

Things worsened, or improved depending on your point of view, when he first started experimenting with writing while finishing up his accounting degree.

These days Dean has a wonderful wife and two lovely daughters to keep him rather more grounded, but the idea of bringing others along with him as he meets interesting new people in universes nobody else has ever seen tends to drag him back to his computer on a fairly regular basis.

Keep up to speed on Dean's latest projects at www.DeanWrites.com.

Frozen Prospects

The invitation to join the secretive Guadel should have been the fulfillment of dreams Va'del didn't even realize he had. When his sponsors are killed in an ambush a short time later, he instead finds his probationary status revoked, and becomes a pawn between various factions inside the Guadel ruling body.

Jain's never known any life but that of a Guadel in training. She'd thought herself reconciled to the idea of a loveless marriage for the good of her people, but meeting Va'del changes everything. Their growing attraction flies against hundreds of years of precedent, but as wide-spread attacks threaten their world, the Guadel have no choice but to use even Jain and Va'del in their fight for survival.

CHET:
Whispers From The Past
By Larry Murray

30 years ago Charles Tucker lost everything that made life worth living. A brutal car accident killed his son. A short time later painful cancer took his wife.

The arrival of the Saunders family casts Charles' life into turmoil, tearing open unhealed wounds. Without his help the Saunders' financial troubles threaten to destroy them, but helping them risks destroying everything Charles spent a lifetime building.

Over all the turmoil looms Chet, the battered old '64 Chevy pickup that carried Charles' son to his death. For 29 years Charles blamed the old pickup for his devastating losses, locking Chet away in an old barn.

The most intriguing mysteries refuse to stay locked up. Solving this one promises an enchanting adventure for the whole family.

www.ingramcontent.com/pod-product-compliance
Lightning Source LLC
Chambersburg PA
CBHW020824030726
47496CB00001B/82